KNUCKLES ™
THE ECHIDNA
ARCHIVES VOLUME 4

featuring the talents of

IAN FLYNN, PATRICK "SPAZ" SPAZIANTE, KEN PENDERS, JOSH RAY, MANNY GALAN, ANDREW PEPOY, BARRY GROSSMAN, & VICKIE WILLIAMS

cover by
PATRICK "SPAZ" SPAZIANTE

SPECIAL THANKS TO ANTHONY GACCIONE & CINDY CHAU @ SEGA LICENSING

ARCHIE COMIC PUBLICATIONS, INC.
JONATHAN GOLDWATER, publisher/co-ceo
NANCY SILBERKLEIT, co-ceo
MIKE PELLERITO, president
VICTOR GORELICK, co-president/editor-in-chief

KNUCKLES ARCHIVES, Volume 4. Printed in USA. Published by Archie Comic Publications, Inc., 325 Fayette Mamaroneck, NY 10543-2318. Sega is registered in the U.S. Patent and Trademark Office. SEGA, S Hedgehog, and all related characters and indicia are either registered trademarks or trademarks of CORPORATION © 1991-2013. SEGA CORPORATION and SONICTEAM, LTD./SEGA CORPORA 2001-2013. All Rights Reserved. The product is manufactured under license from Sega of America, Rhode Island St., Ste. 400, San Francisco, CA 94103 www.sega.com. Any similarities between cha names, persons, and/or institutions in this book and any living, dead or fictional characters, names, and/or institutions are not intended and if they exist, are purely coincidental. Nothing may be reprinte or part without written permission from Archie Comic Publications, Inc.
ISBN: 978-1-936975-43-3

TABLE OF CONTENTS

KTE #16 "REUNIONS"...Page 5
There are big changes coming up in Knuckles' life,
and that brings the attention of the Brotherhood of
Guardians! Why is this secret cabal gathering in Haven?
And what do they have planned for Rad Red?

**KTE #17 "DEEP COVER Part I -
THE GUARDIAN WHO FAILED!!!"...Page 31**
The long-lost Guardian Tobor has returned to
Angel Island! But with him comes a terrible and tragic
secret. To fill the gaps, Knuckles goes to face his
fiercest foe: Grandmaster Kragok!

**KTE #18 "DEEP COVER Part II -
DEBT OF HONOR"...Page 57**
It's Knuckles vs. Kragok -- in this world and beyond!
Knuckles' strange powers begin to manifest, and it might
mean the end of him and his foe! It falls upon Tobor to
save the day, but at what cost?

KTE #19 "THE FORBIDDEN ZONE Part I - WHATEVER HAPPENED TO QUEEN ALICIA?"...Page 84
Geoffrey St. John and the Secret Service arrive
on Angel Island in search of Queen Alicia.
Knuckles would help -- if he weren't busy saving
the citizens from a freak blizzard!

KTE #20 "THE FORBIDDEN ZONE Part II - ONCE UPON A TIME IN MOBOTROPOLIS"...Page 110
Knuckles searches for his missing mother in
the blinding snow storm with the help of the
E.S.T. -- but finds far more than he bargained for!
The same goes for the Secret Service as they
discover the long-lost Prince of Acorns!

KTE #21 "THE FORBIDDEN ZONE Part III - THE MANY FACETS OF THE TRUTH"...Page 136
Knuckles has discovered Haven -- and the traitor
within! As Knuckles fights for his life against the
ancient double-agent, Locke must rescue the
Secret Service and Prince Elias from the elements.

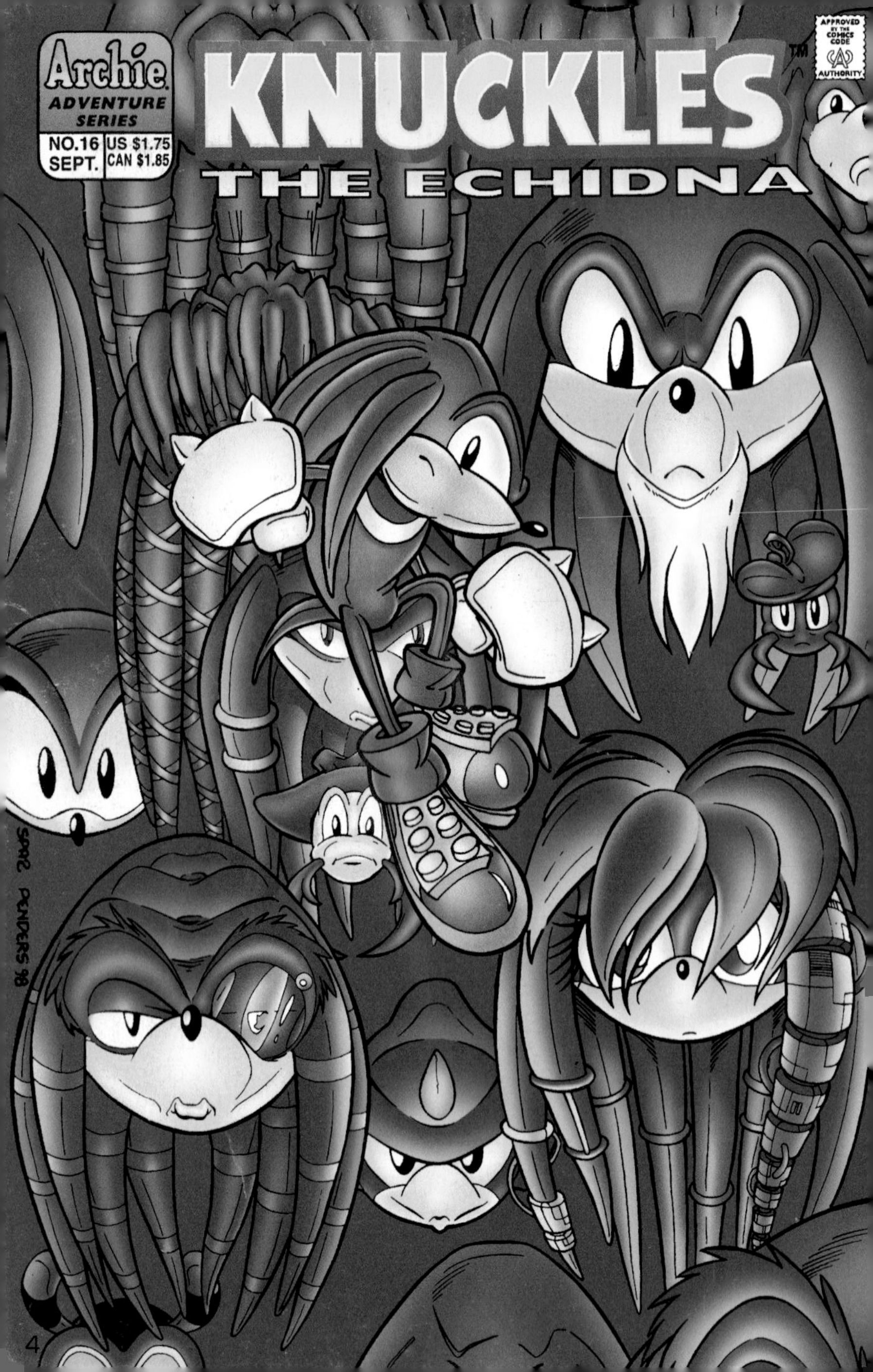
Archie
ADVENTURE SERIES
NO.16 SEPT.
US $1.75 CAN $1.85
KNUCKLES™
THE ECHIDNA
APPROVED BY THE COMICS CODE AUTHORITY
SPAZ PENDERS 98

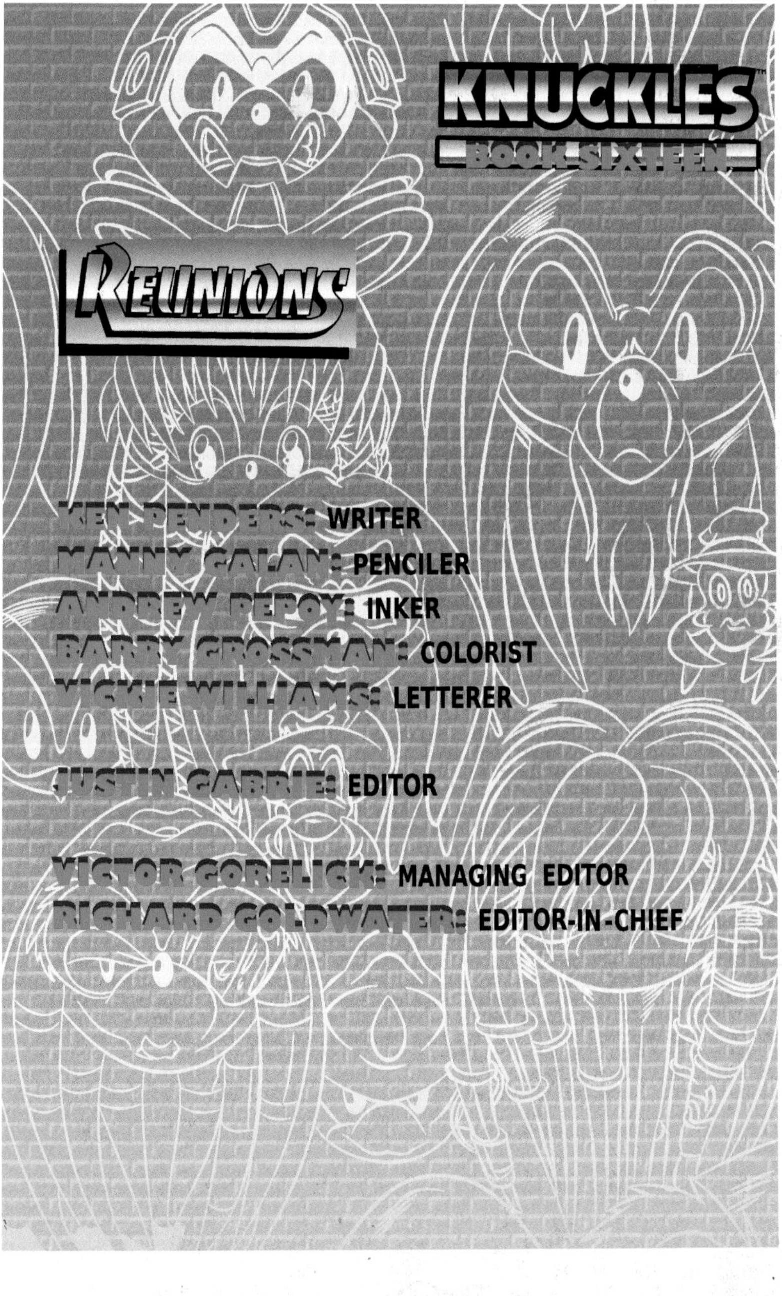
KNUCKLES™
BOOK SIXTEEN
REUNIONS
KEN PENDERS: WRITER
MANNY GALAN: PENCILER
ANDREW PEPOY: INKER
BARRY GROSSMAN: COLORIST
VICKIE WILLIAMS: LETTERER
JUSTIN GABRIE: EDITOR
VICTOR GORELICK: MANAGING EDITOR
RICHARD GOLDWATER: EDITOR-IN-CHIEF

BORN TO THE MOST NOBLE OF ECHIDNA HOUSES, THE LATEST TO CONTINUE THE FAMILY HERITAGE AND RESPONSIBILITY AS GUARDIAN OF THE FLOATING ISLAND, DEFENDER OF ALL FROM THE FORCES OF EVIL FROM THE WORLD BEYOND AS WELL AS THOSE WHO WOULD THREATEN IT FROM WITHIN, HE IS NONE OTHER THAN KNUCKLES THE ECHIDNA!

WHEN WE LAST SAW OUR HEROES, THE CHAOTIX HAD WITNESSED THE ACKNOWLEDGMENT CEREMONY OF THEIR FRIEND CHARMY, WHO REMAINED BEHIND AS PRINCE OF HIS OWN PEOPLE WHILE ESPIO, MIGHTY, VECTOR AND JULIE-SU RETURNED TO THEIR HOMES ON THE FLOATING ISLAND.

MEANWHILE, DEEP WITHIN HAVEN, LOCKE AND SABRE WITNESSED KNUCKLES' HARNESSING POWER BEYOND BELIEF BEFORE VANISHING FROM SIGHT, PRESUMABLY RETURNING TO THE FLOATING ISLAND AFTER HIS DISCOVERY OF ALBION.

NOW, AS A NEW DAY DAWNS, THOUGHTS TURN NOT TO THOSE OF EXCITEMENT AND ADVENTURE, BUT OF FEELINGS OF LONGING AND SPENDING TIME WITH THOSE ONE CHERISHES, AS WE FIND LARA-LE THIS MORNING IN THE SANCTITY OF THE AURORIUM...

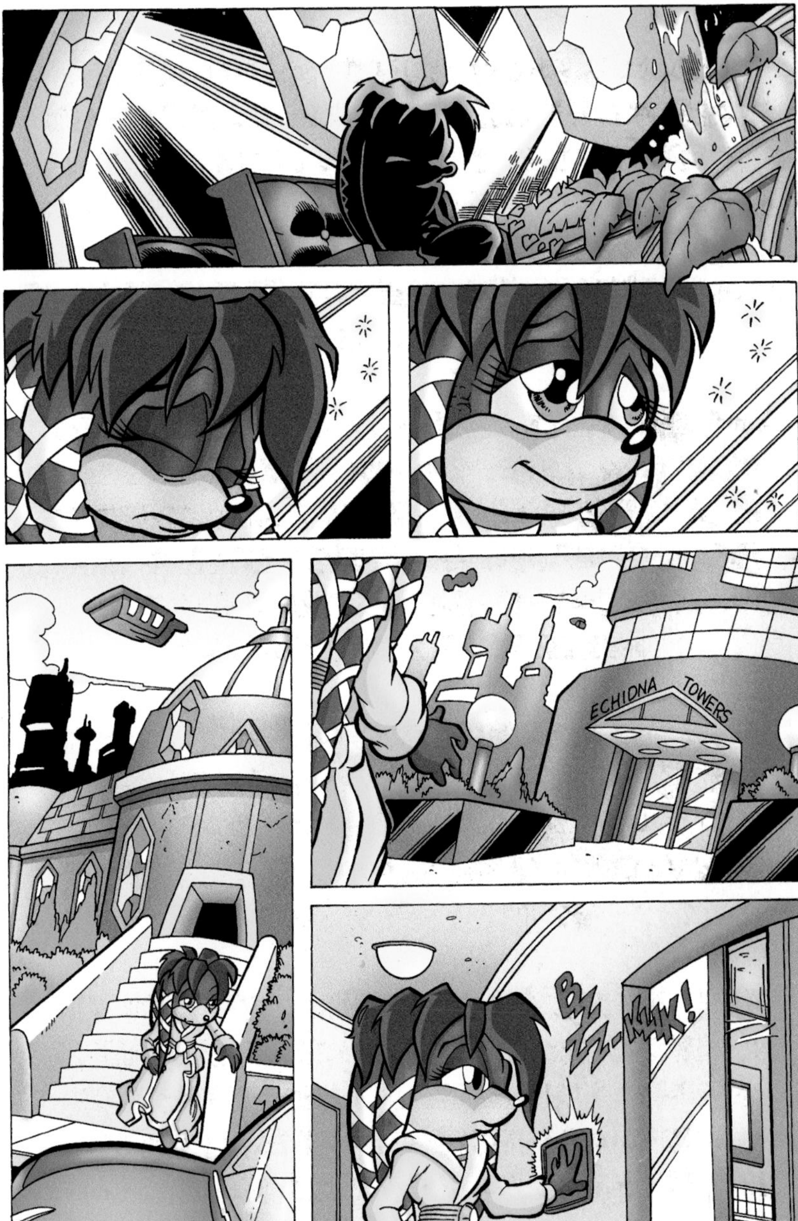
ECHIDNA TOWERS
BZZZ-KLAK!

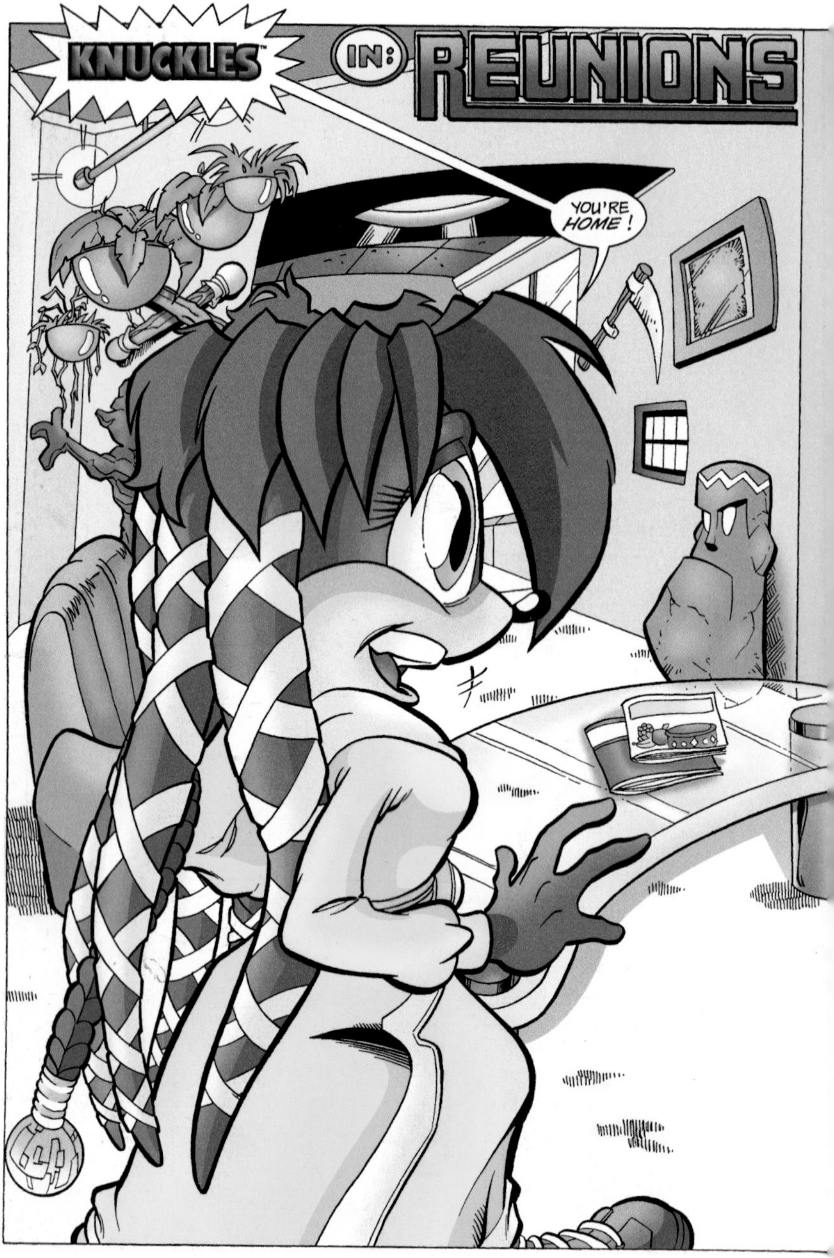
KNUCKLES™
IN:
REUNIONS
YOU'RE HOME!

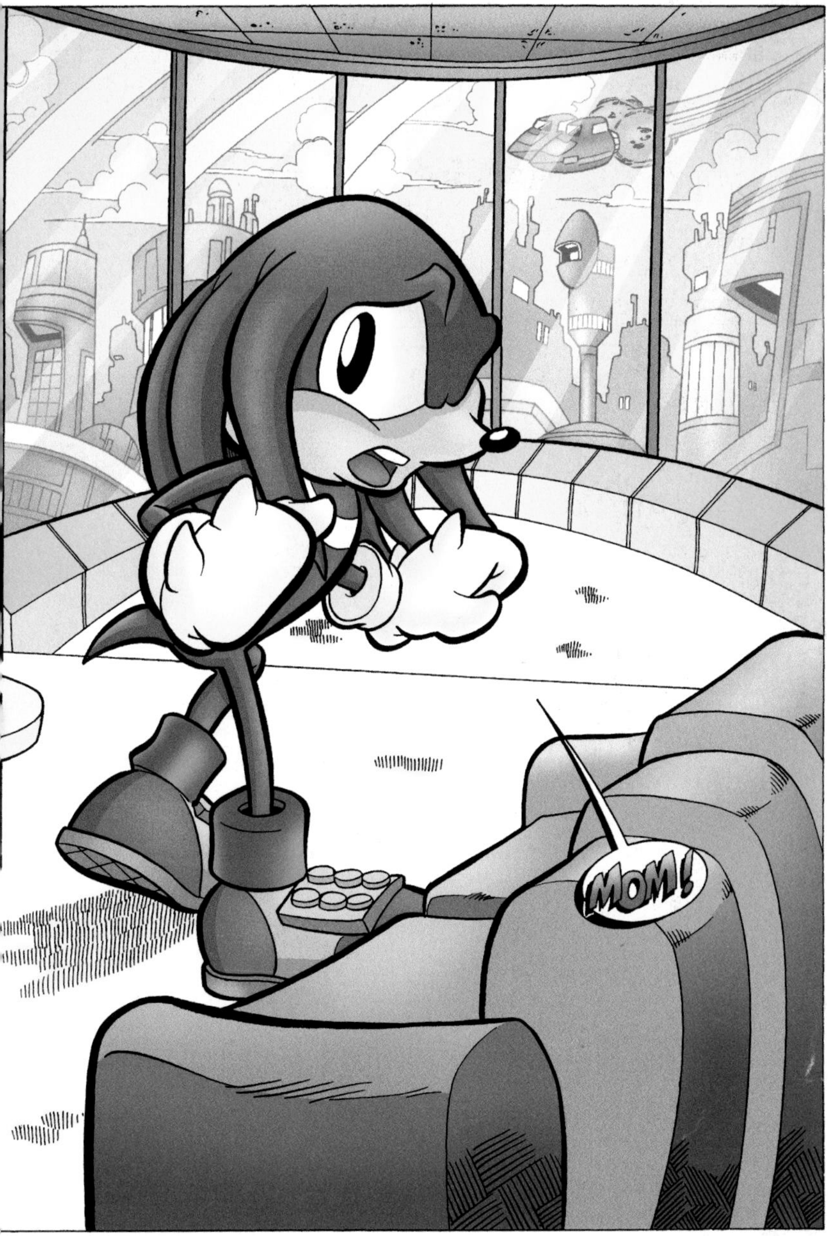
MOM!

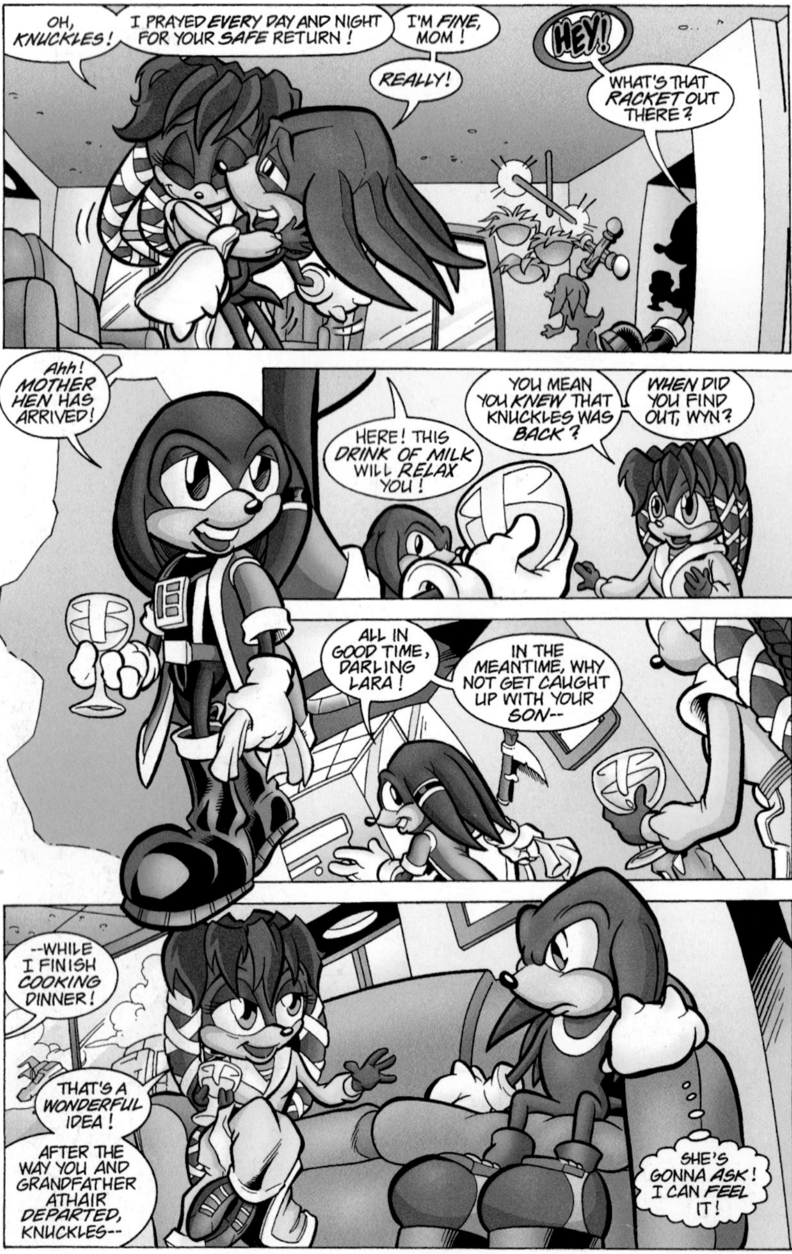
OH, KNUCKLES!
I PRAYED EVERY DAY AND NIGHT FOR YOUR SAFE RETURN!
I'M FINE, MOM!
REALLY!
HEY!
WHAT'S THAT RACKET OUT THERE?
Ahh! MOTHER HEN HAS ARRIVED!
HERE! THIS DRINK OF MILK WILL RELAX YOU!
YOU MEAN YOU KNEW THAT KNUCKLES WAS BACK?
WHEN DID YOU FIND OUT, WYN?
ALL IN GOOD TIME, DARLING LARA!
IN THE MEANTIME, WHY NOT GET CAUGHT UP WITH YOUR SON--
--WHILE I FINISH COOKING DINNER!
THAT'S A WONDERFUL IDEA!
AFTER THE WAY YOU AND GRANDFATHER ATHAIR DEPARTED, KNUCKLES--
SHE'S GONNA ASK! I CAN FEEL IT!

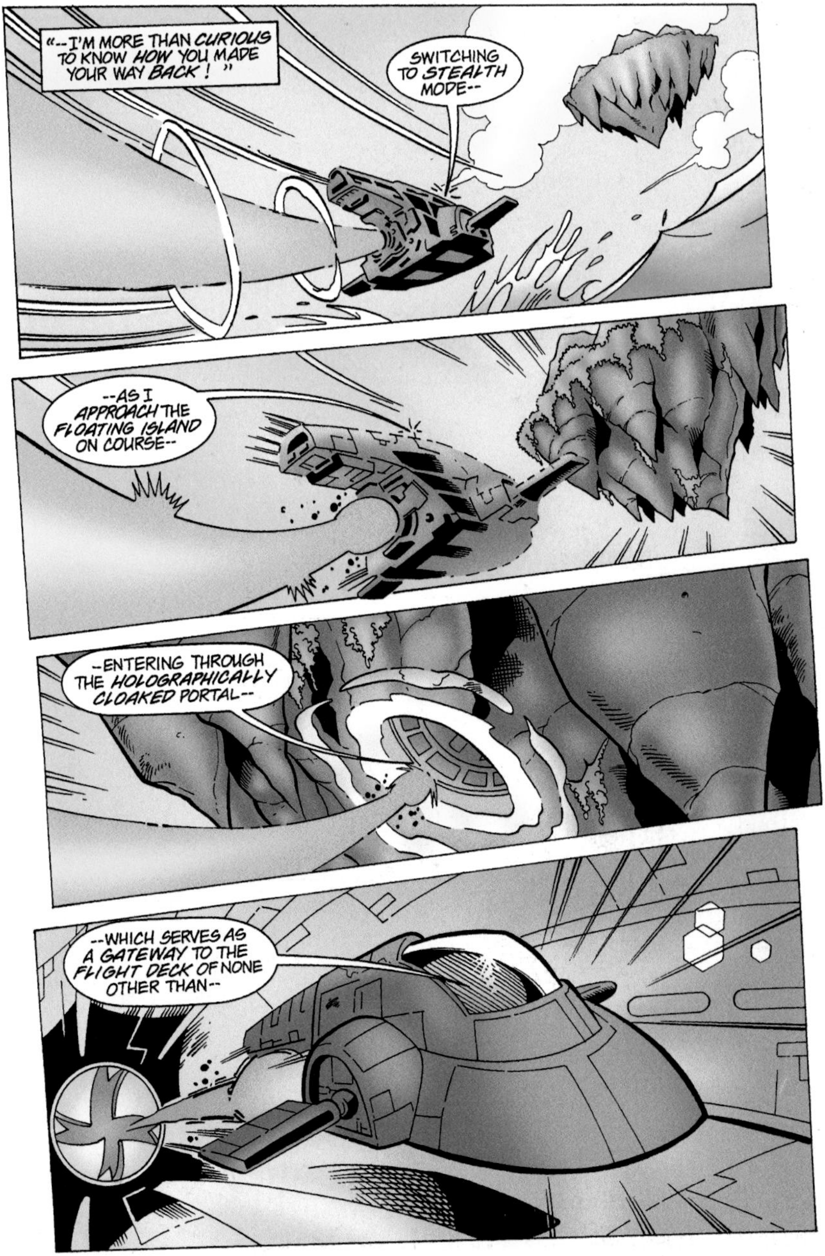
"--I'M MORE THAN CURIOUS TO KNOW HOW YOU MADE YOUR WAY BACK!"
SWITCHING TO STEALTH MODE--
--AS I APPROACH THE FLOATING ISLAND ON COURSE--
--ENTERING THROUGH THE HOLOGRAPHICALLY CLOAKED PORTAL--
--WHICH SERVES AS A GATEWAY TO THE FLIGHT DECK OF NONE OTHER THAN--

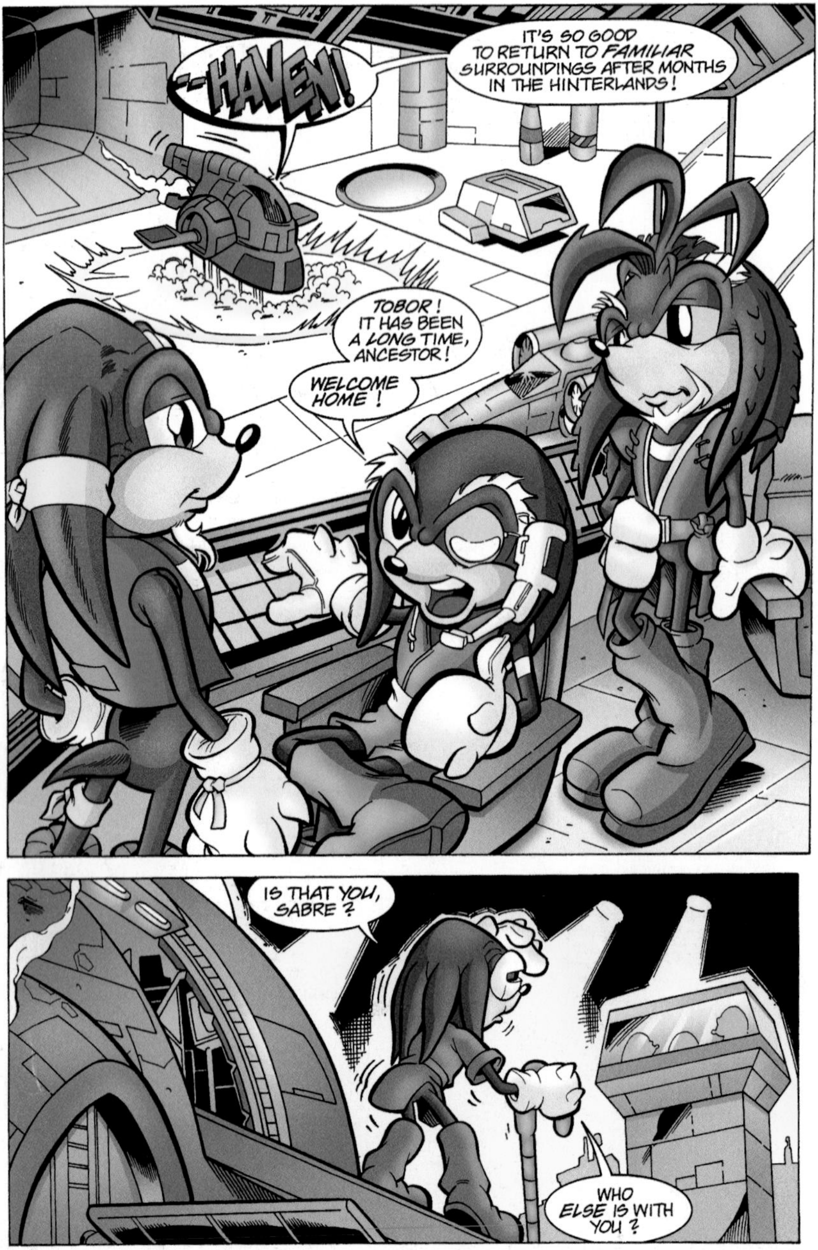
--HAVEN!
IT'S SO GOOD TO RETURN TO FAMILIAR SURROUNDINGS AFTER MONTHS IN THE HINTERLANDS!
TOBOR! IT HAS BEEN A LONG TIME, ANCESTOR!
WELCOME HOME!
IS THAT YOU, SABRE?
WHO ELSE IS WITH YOU?

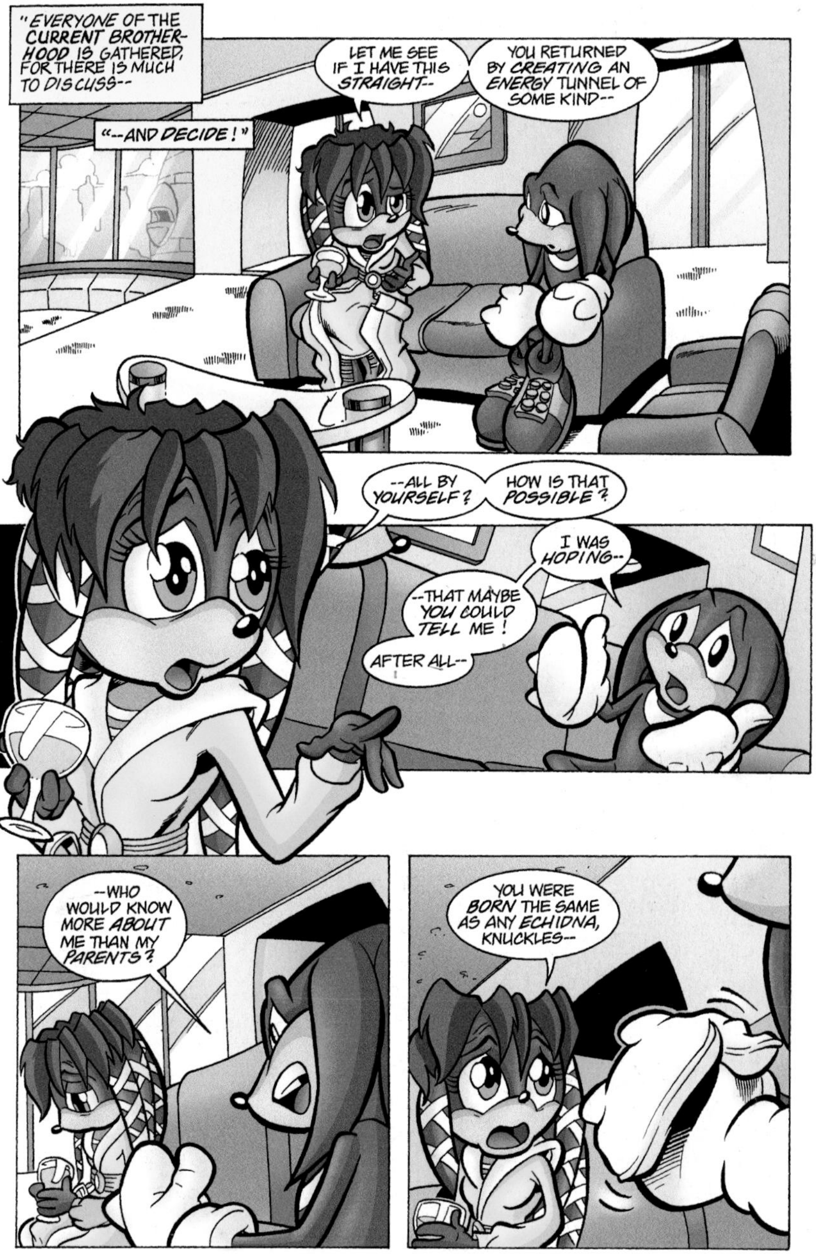
"EVERYONE OF THE CURRENT BROTHERHOOD IS GATHERED, FOR THERE IS MUCH TO DISCUSS--
"--AND DECIDE!"
LET ME SEE IF I HAVE THIS STRAIGHT--
YOU RETURNED BY CREATING AN ENERGY TUNNEL OF SOME KIND--
--ALL BY YOURSELF?
HOW IS THAT POSSIBLE?
I WAS HOPING--
--THAT MAYBE YOU COULD TELL ME!
AFTER ALL--
--WHO WOULD KNOW MORE ABOUT ME THAN MY PARENTS?
YOU WERE BORN THE SAME AS ANY ECHIDNA, KNUCKLES--

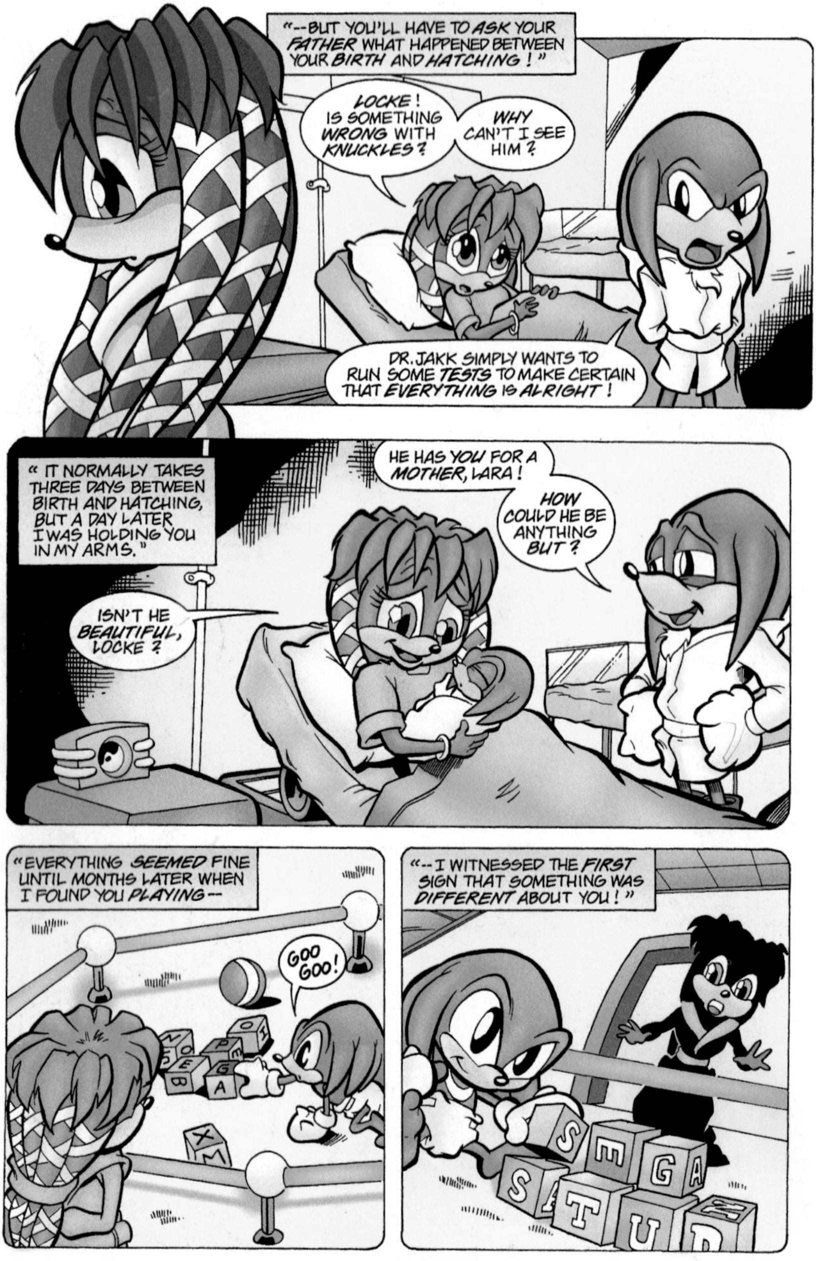
"--BUT YOU'LL HAVE TO ASK YOUR FATHER WHAT HAPPENED BETWEEN YOUR BIRTH AND HATCHING!"
LOCKE! IS SOMETHING WRONG WITH KNUCKLES?
WHY CAN'T I SEE HIM?
DR. JAKK SIMPLY WANTS TO RUN SOME TESTS TO MAKE CERTAIN THAT EVERYTHING IS ALRIGHT!
"IT NORMALLY TAKES THREE DAYS BETWEEN BIRTH AND HATCHING, BUT A DAY LATER I WAS HOLDING YOU IN MY ARMS."
HE HAS YOU FOR A MOTHER, LARA!
HOW COULD HE BE ANYTHING BUT?
ISN'T HE BEAUTIFUL, LOCKE?
"EVERYTHING SEEMED FINE UNTIL MONTHS LATER WHEN I FOUND YOU PLAYING--
GOO GOO!
"--I WITNESSED THE FIRST SIGN THAT SOMETHING WAS DIFFERENT ABOUT YOU!"
SEGA
STUD

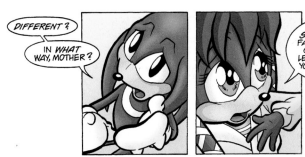

DIFFERENT?

IN *WHAT* WAY, MOTHER?

YOU WERE *SPELLING* WORDS FAR IN *ADVANCE* OF YOUR AGE LEVEL! *BEFORE* YOU COULD EVEN *SPEAK!*

WORDS EVEN I HAD TROUBLE WITH SOMETIMES!

" WHEN YOU WERE BUT THREE YEARS OF AGE, IT WAS YOUR *FATHER* WHO SUPERVISED YOUR TRAINING, AND *DETERMINED* WHAT WAS IN YOUR *BEST* INTERESTS! "

DON'T YOU THINK *I* SHOULD HAVE *SOME* SAY, LOCKE? HE'S *MY* SON AS WELL!

$$E = MC^2$$
$$x^2 + y^2$$

THIS IS HOW *I* WAS BROUGHT UP, LARA--

--AS WERE MY *ANCESTORS* BEFORE ME!

" FEELING OUT OF MY DEPTH, I SOUGHT *COUNCEL* FROM YOUR GRANDMOTHER *JENNA-LU!* "

I JUST WISH I *KNEW* WHAT TO *DO!*

YOU KNOW WHAT THE *PROBLEM* IS, LARA-LE?

15

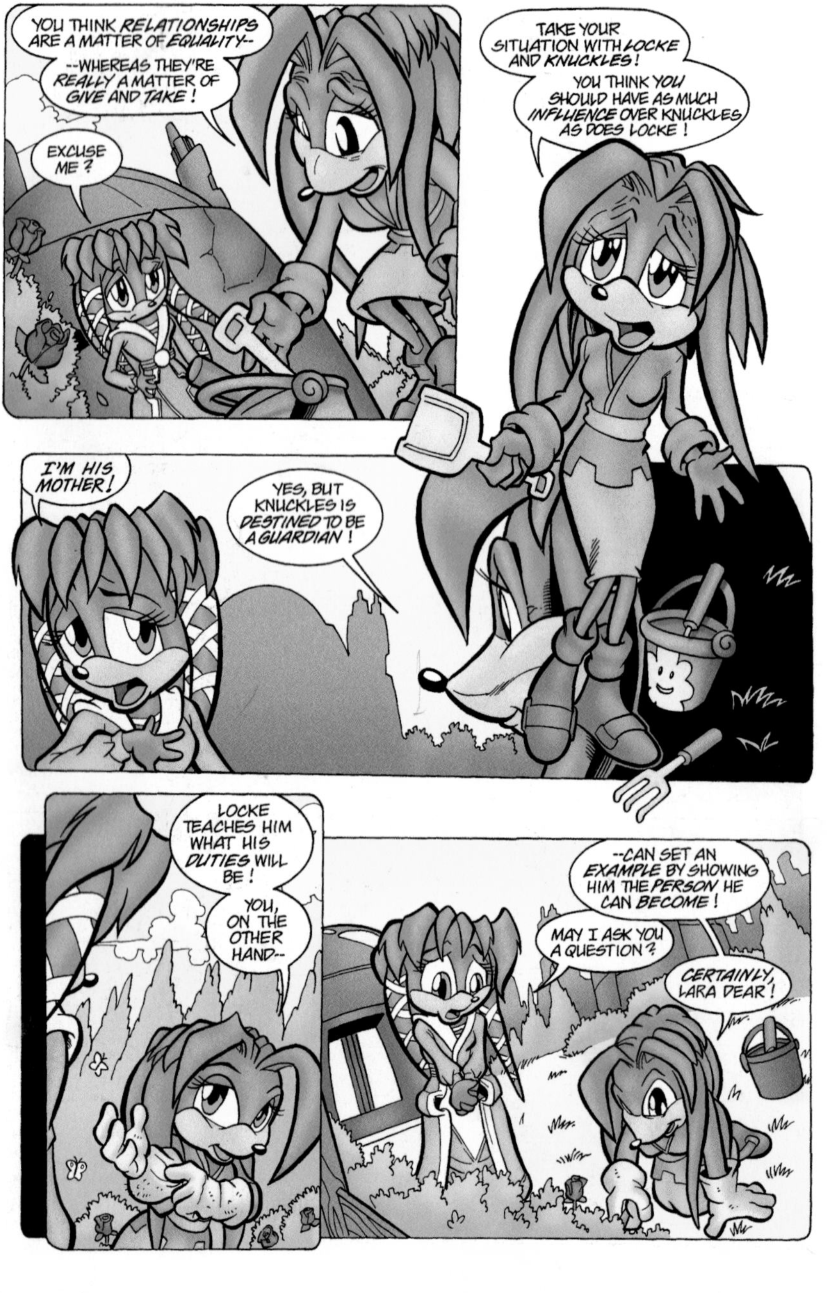
YOU THINK RELATIONSHIPS ARE A MATTER OF EQUALITY--
--WHEREAS THEY'RE REALLY A MATTER OF GIVE AND TAKE!
EXCUSE ME?
TAKE YOUR SITUATION WITH LOCKE AND KNUCKLES!
YOU THINK YOU SHOULD HAVE AS MUCH INFLUENCE OVER KNUCKLES AS DOES LOCKE!
I'M HIS MOTHER!
YES, BUT KNUCKLES IS DESTINED TO BE A GUARDIAN!
LOCKE TEACHES HIM WHAT HIS DUTIES WILL BE!
YOU, ON THE OTHER HAND--
--CAN SET AN EXAMPLE BY SHOWING HIM THE PERSON HE CAN BECOME!
MAY I ASK YOU A QUESTION?
CERTAINLY, LARA DEAR!

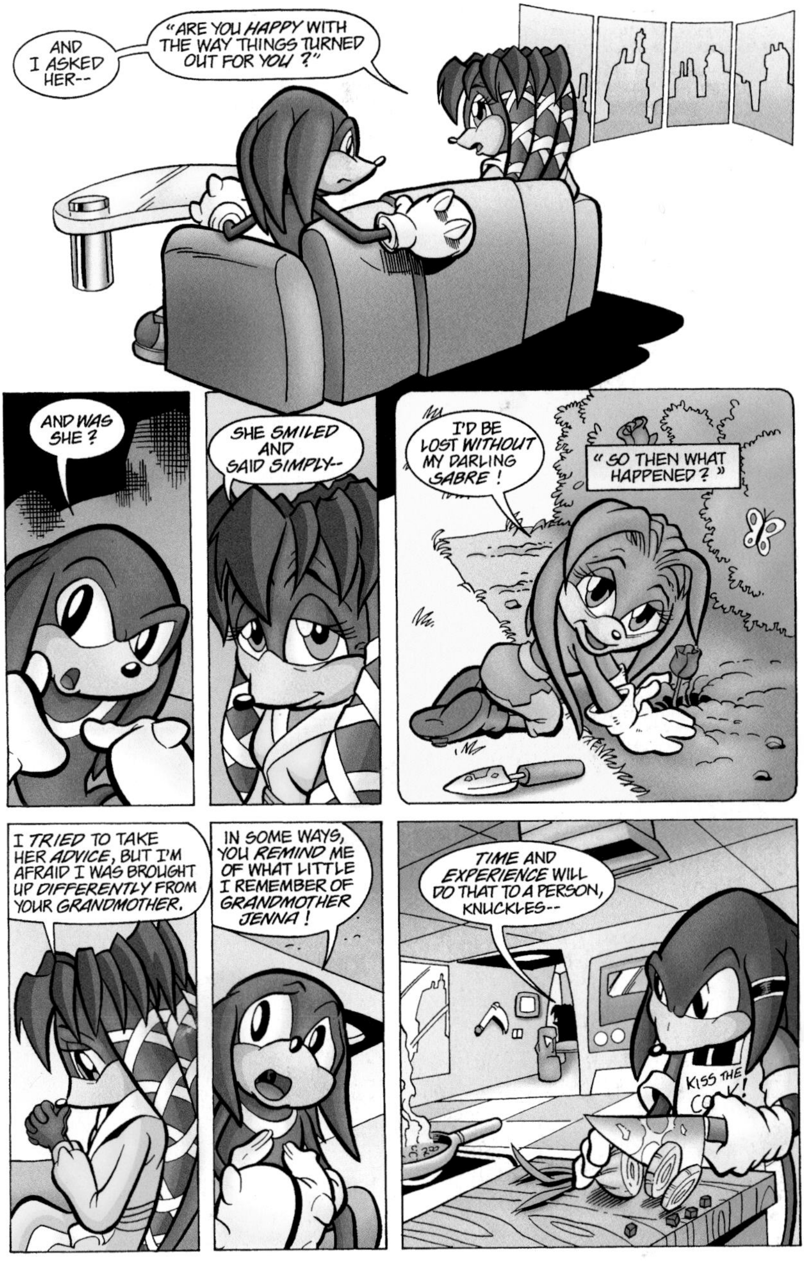
AND I ASKED HER--
"ARE YOU *HAPPY* WITH THE WAY THINGS TURNED OUT FOR *YOU* ?"
AND *WAS* SHE ?
SHE *SMILED* AND SAID *SIMPLY*--
I'D BE LOST *WITHOUT* MY DARLING SABRE !
" SO THEN WHAT HAPPENED ? "
I *TRIED* TO TAKE HER *ADVICE*, BUT I'M AFRAID I WAS BROUGHT UP *DIFFERENTLY* FROM YOUR *GRANDMOTHER*.
IN SOME WAYS, YOU *REMIND* ME OF WHAT LITTLE I REMEMBER OF *GRANDMOTHER JENNA* !
TIME AND *EXPERIENCE* WILL DO THAT TO A PERSON, KNUCKLES--
KISS THE COOK!

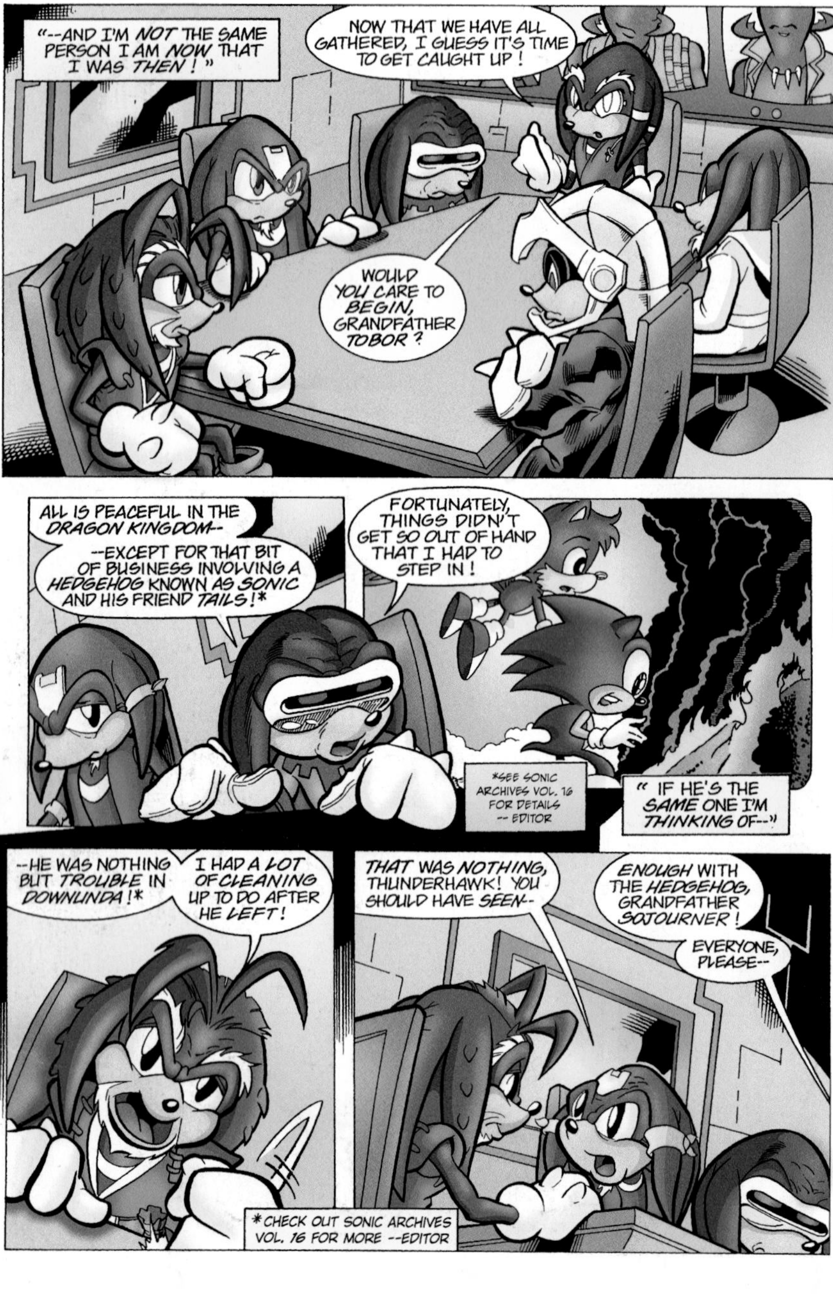
"--AND I'M NOT THE SAME PERSON I AM NOW THAT I WAS THEN!"
NOW THAT WE HAVE ALL GATHERED, I GUESS IT'S TIME TO GET CAUGHT UP!
WOULD YOU CARE TO BEGIN, GRANDFATHER TOBOR?
ALL IS PEACEFUL IN THE DRAGON KINGDOM--
--EXCEPT FOR THAT BIT OF BUSINESS INVOLVING A HEDGEHOG KNOWN AS SONIC AND HIS FRIEND TAILS!*
FORTUNATELY, THINGS DIDN'T GET SO OUT OF HAND THAT I HAD TO STEP IN!
*SEE SONIC ARCHIVES VOL. 16 FOR DETAILS --EDITOR
" IF HE'S THE SAME ONE I'M THINKING OF--"
--HE WAS NOTHING BUT TROUBLE IN DOWNUNDA!*
I HAD A LOT OF CLEANING UP TO DO AFTER HE LEFT!
*CHECK OUT SONIC ARCHIVES VOL. 16 FOR MORE --EDITOR
THAT WAS NOTHING, THUNDERHAWK! YOU SHOULD HAVE SEEN--
ENOUGH WITH THE HEDGEHOG, GRANDFATHER SOJOURNER!
EVERYONE, PLEASE--

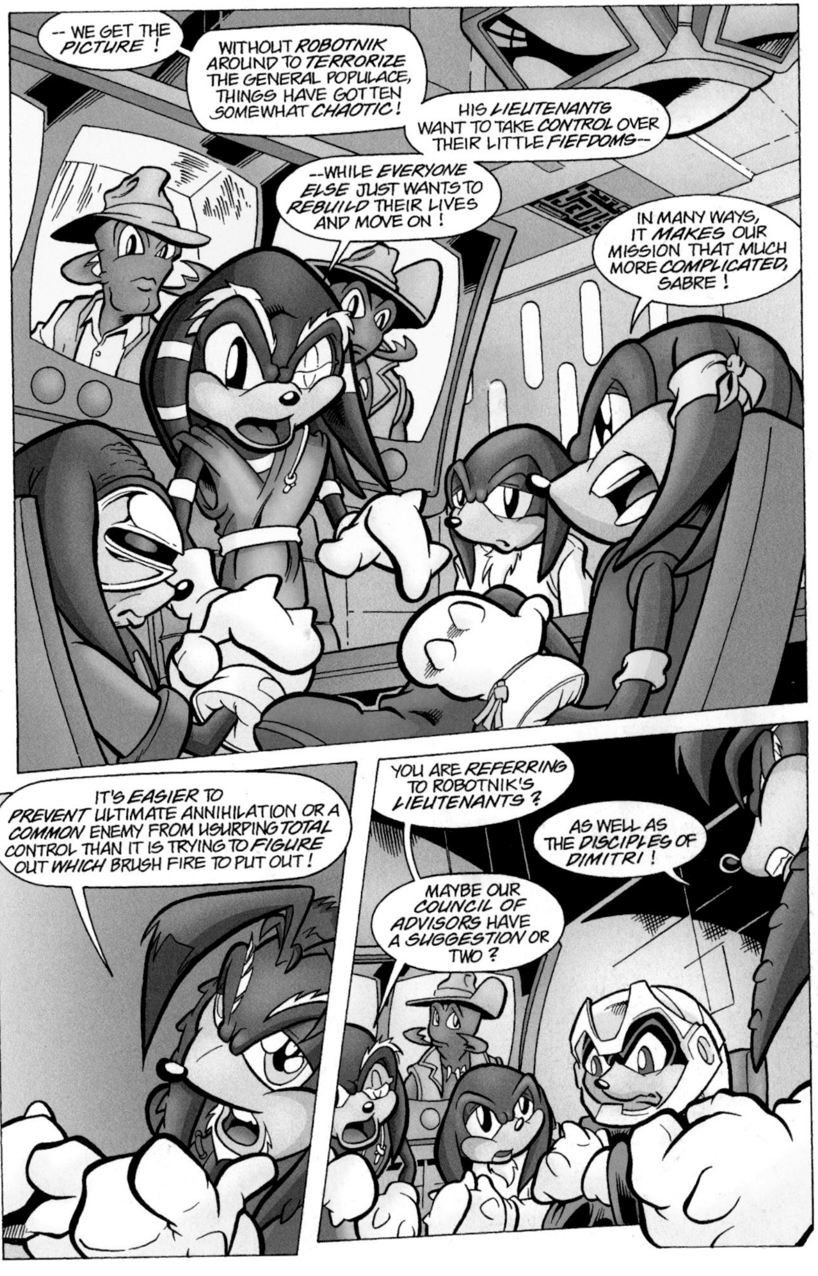
-- WE GET THE PICTURE !
WITHOUT ROBOTNIK AROUND TO TERRORIZE THE GENERAL POPULACE, THINGS HAVE GOTTEN SOMEWHAT CHAOTIC !
HIS LIEUTENANTS WANT TO TAKE CONTROL OVER THEIR LITTLE FIEFDOMS--
--WHILE EVERYONE ELSE JUST WANTS TO REBUILD THEIR LIVES AND MOVE ON !
IN MANY WAYS, IT MAKES OUR MISSION THAT MUCH MORE COMPLICATED, SABRE !
IT'S EASIER TO PREVENT ULTIMATE ANNIHILATION OR A COMMON ENEMY FROM USURPING TOTAL CONTROL THAN IT IS TRYING TO FIGURE OUT WHICH BRUSH FIRE TO PUT OUT !
YOU ARE REFERRING TO ROBOTNIK'S LIEUTENANTS ?
AS WELL AS THE DISCIPLES OF DIMITRI !
MAYBE OUR COUNCIL OF ADVISORS HAVE A SUGGESTION OR TWO ?

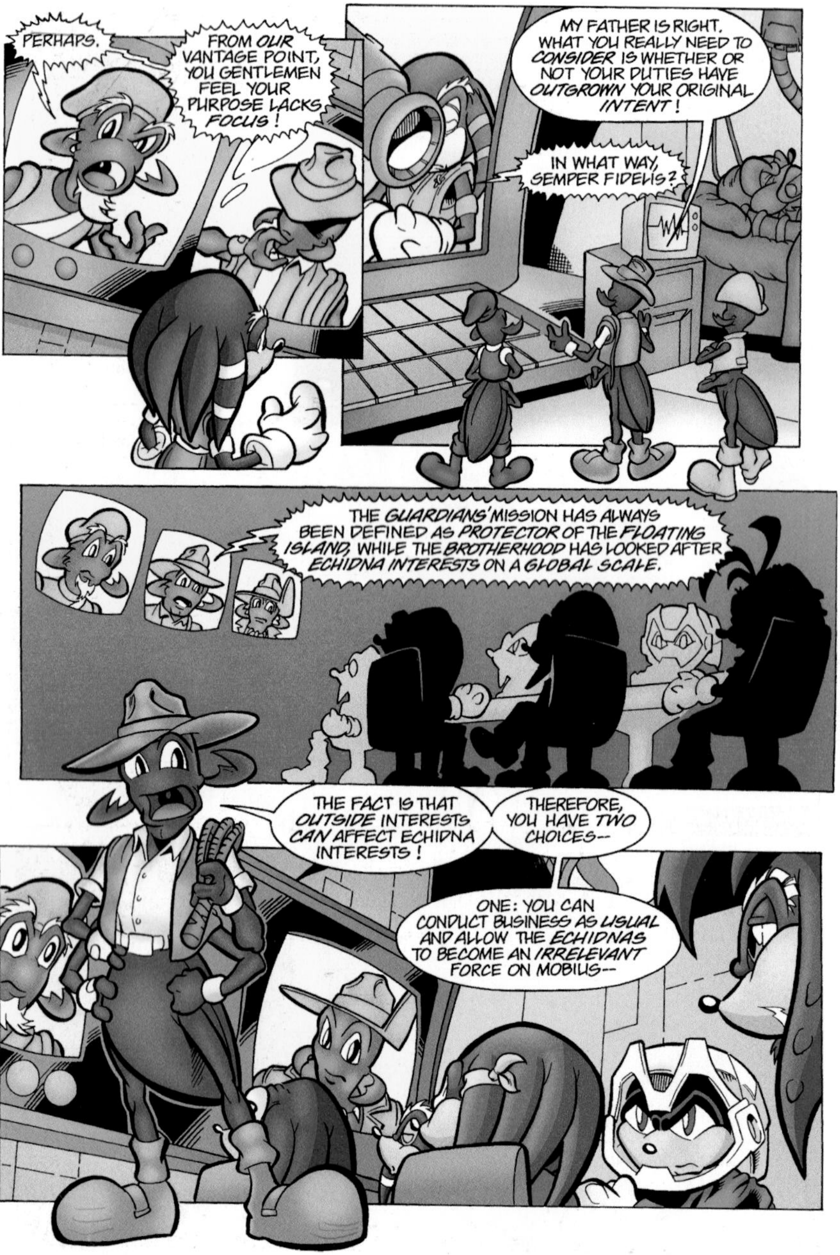
PERHAPS.
FROM OUR VANTAGE POINT, YOU GENTLEMEN FEEL YOUR PURPOSE LACKS FOCUS!
MY FATHER IS RIGHT. WHAT YOU REALLY NEED TO CONSIDER IS WHETHER OR NOT YOUR DUTIES HAVE OUTGROWN YOUR ORIGINAL INTENT!
IN WHAT WAY, SEMPER FIDELIS?
THE GUARDIANS' MISSION HAS ALWAYS BEEN DEFINED AS PROTECTOR OF THE FLOATING ISLAND, WHILE THE BROTHERHOOD HAS LOOKED AFTER ECHIDNA INTERESTS ON A GLOBAL SCALE.
THE FACT IS THAT OUTSIDE INTERESTS CAN AFFECT ECHIDNA INTERESTS!
THEREFORE, YOU HAVE TWO CHOICES--
ONE: YOU CAN CONDUCT BUSINESS AS USUAL AND ALLOW THE ECHIDNAS TO BECOME AN IRRELEVANT FORCE ON MOBIUS--

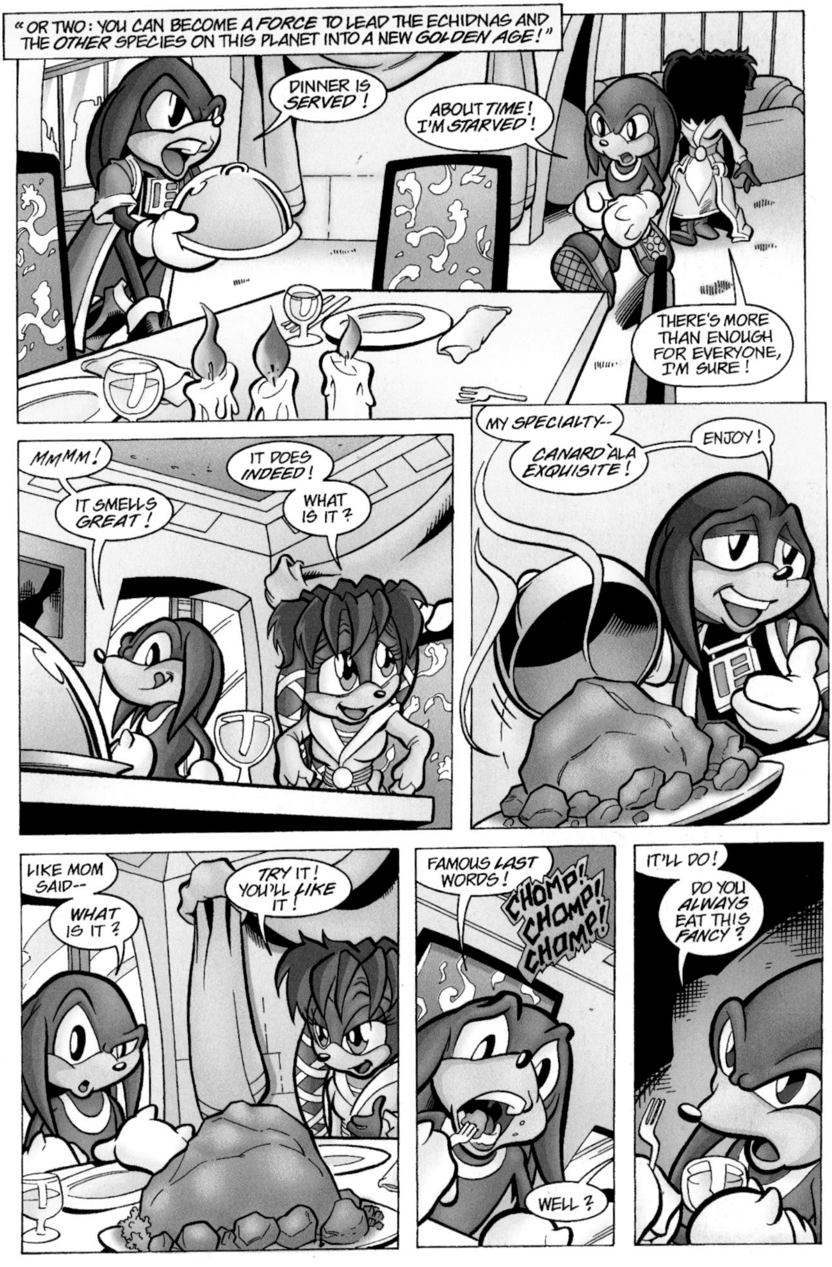
"OR TWO: YOU CAN BECOME A FORCE TO LEAD THE ECHIDNAS AND THE OTHER SPECIES ON THIS PLANET INTO A NEW GOLDEN AGE!"
DINNER IS SERVED!
ABOUT TIME! I'M STARVED!
THERE'S MORE THAN ENOUGH FOR EVERYONE, I'M SURE!
MMMM!
IT SMELLS GREAT!
IT DOES INDEED!
WHAT IS IT?
MY SPECIALTY--
CANARD`ALA EXQUISITE!
ENJOY!
LIKE MOM SAID--
WHAT IS IT?
TRY IT! YOU'LL LIKE IT!
FAMOUS LAST WORDS!
CHOMP! CHOMP! CHOMP!
WELL?
IT'LL DO!
DO YOU ALWAYS EAT THIS FANCY?

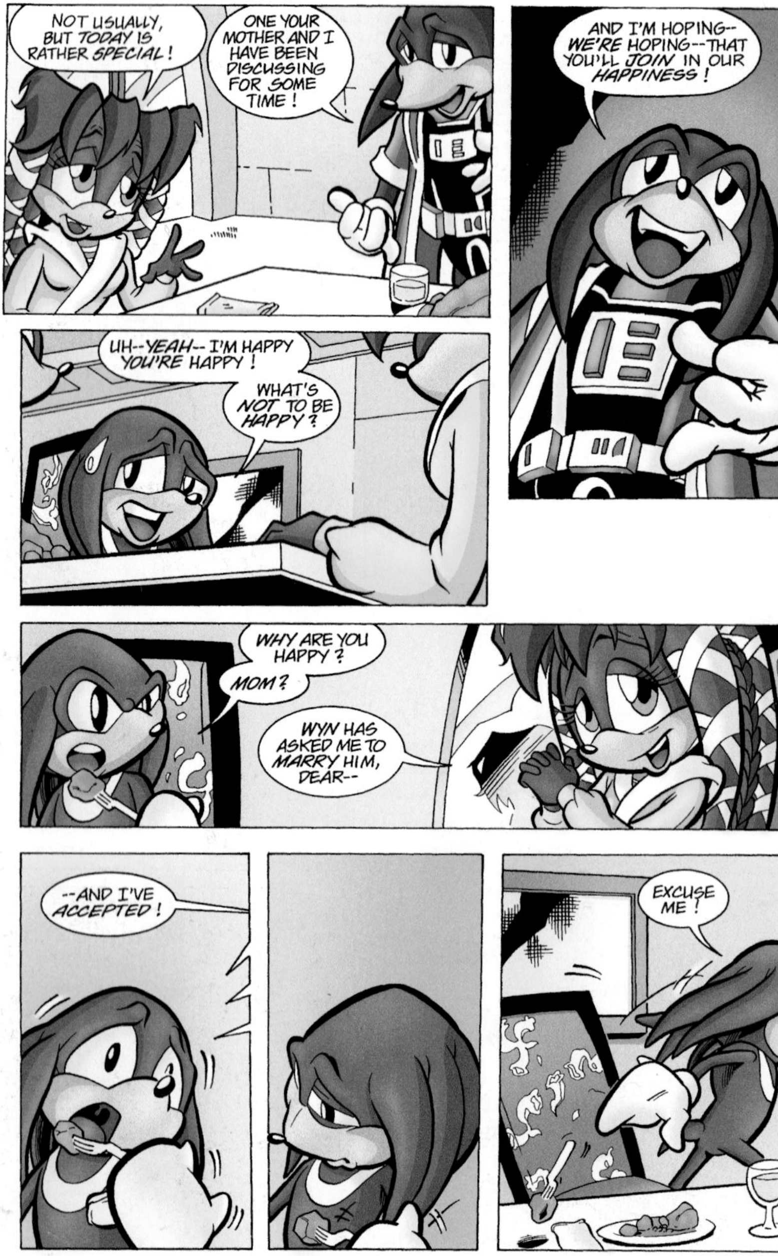
NOT USUALLY, BUT TODAY IS RATHER SPECIAL!
ONE YOUR MOTHER AND I HAVE BEEN DISCUSSING FOR SOME TIME!
AND I'M HOPING-- WE'RE HOPING--THAT YOU'LL JOIN IN OUR HAPPINESS!
UH--YEAH-- I'M HAPPY YOU'RE HAPPY!
WHAT'S NOT TO BE HAPPY?
WHY ARE YOU HAPPY?
MOM?
WYN HAS ASKED ME TO MARRY HIM, DEAR--
--AND I'VE ACCEPTED!
EXCUSE ME!

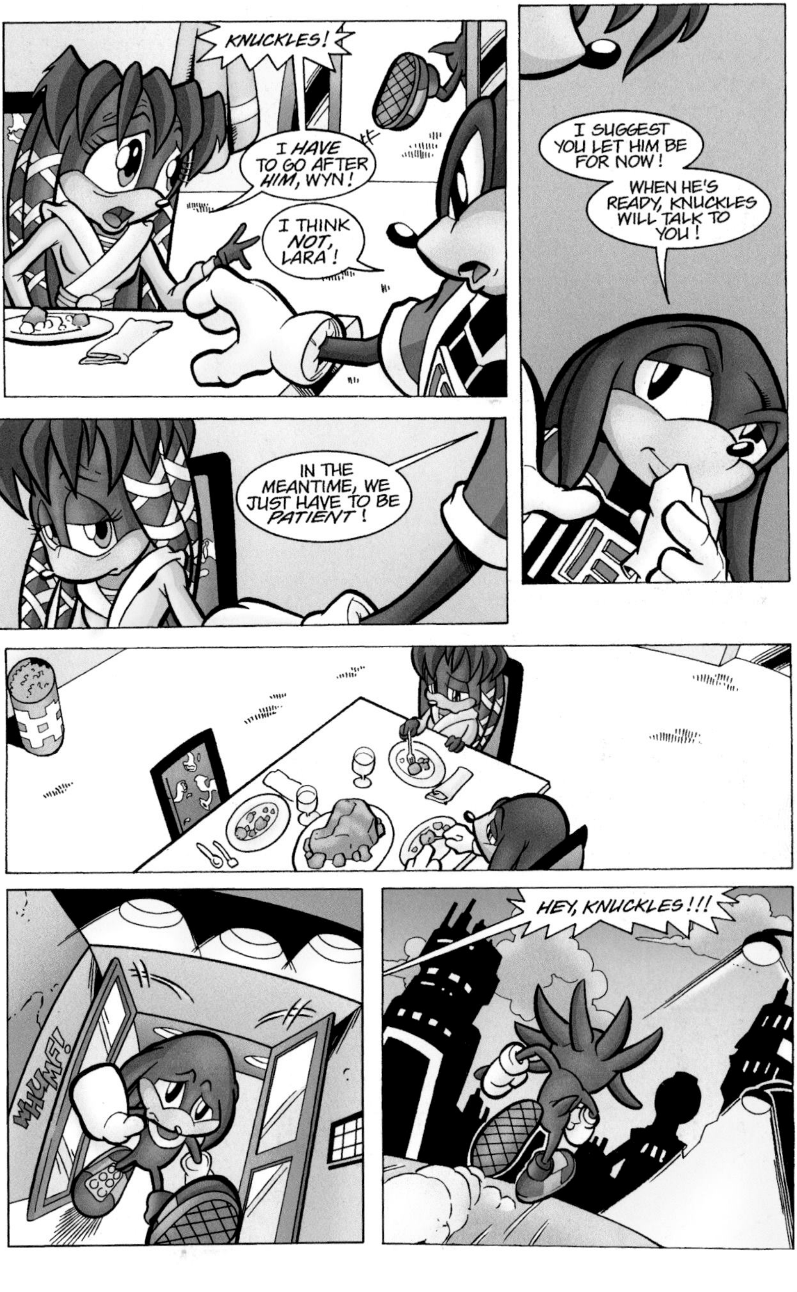
KNUCKLES!
I *HAVE* TO GO AFTER *HIM*, WYN!
I THINK *NOT*, LARA!
I SUGGEST YOU LET HIM BE FOR NOW!
WHEN HE'S READY, KNUCKLES WILL TALK TO YOU!
IN THE MEANTIME, WE JUST HAVE TO BE *PATIENT*!
WHUMF!
HEY, KNUCKLES!!!

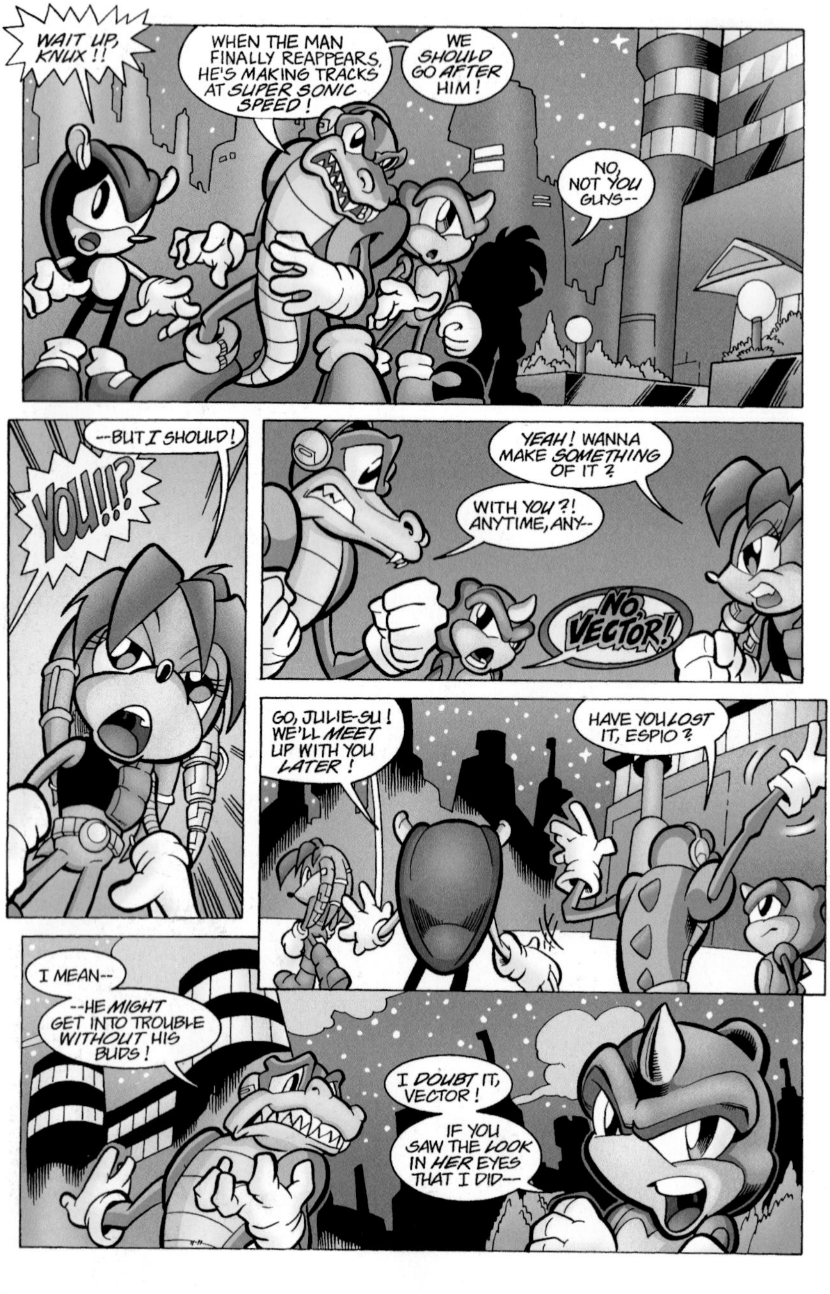
WAIT UP, KNUX!!
WHEN THE MAN FINALLY REAPPEARS, HE'S MAKING TRACKS AT SUPER SONIC SPEED!
WE SHOULD GO AFTER HIM!
NO, NOT YOU GUYS--
--BUT I SHOULD!
YOU!!?
YEAH! WANNA MAKE SOMETHING OF IT?
WITH YOU?! ANYTIME, ANY--
NO, VECTOR!
GO, JULIE-SU! WE'LL MEET UP WITH YOU LATER!
HAVE YOU LOST IT, ESPIO?
I MEAN--
--HE MIGHT GET INTO TROUBLE WITHOUT HIS BUDS!
I DOUBT IT, VECTOR!
IF YOU SAW THE LOOK IN HER EYES THAT I DID--

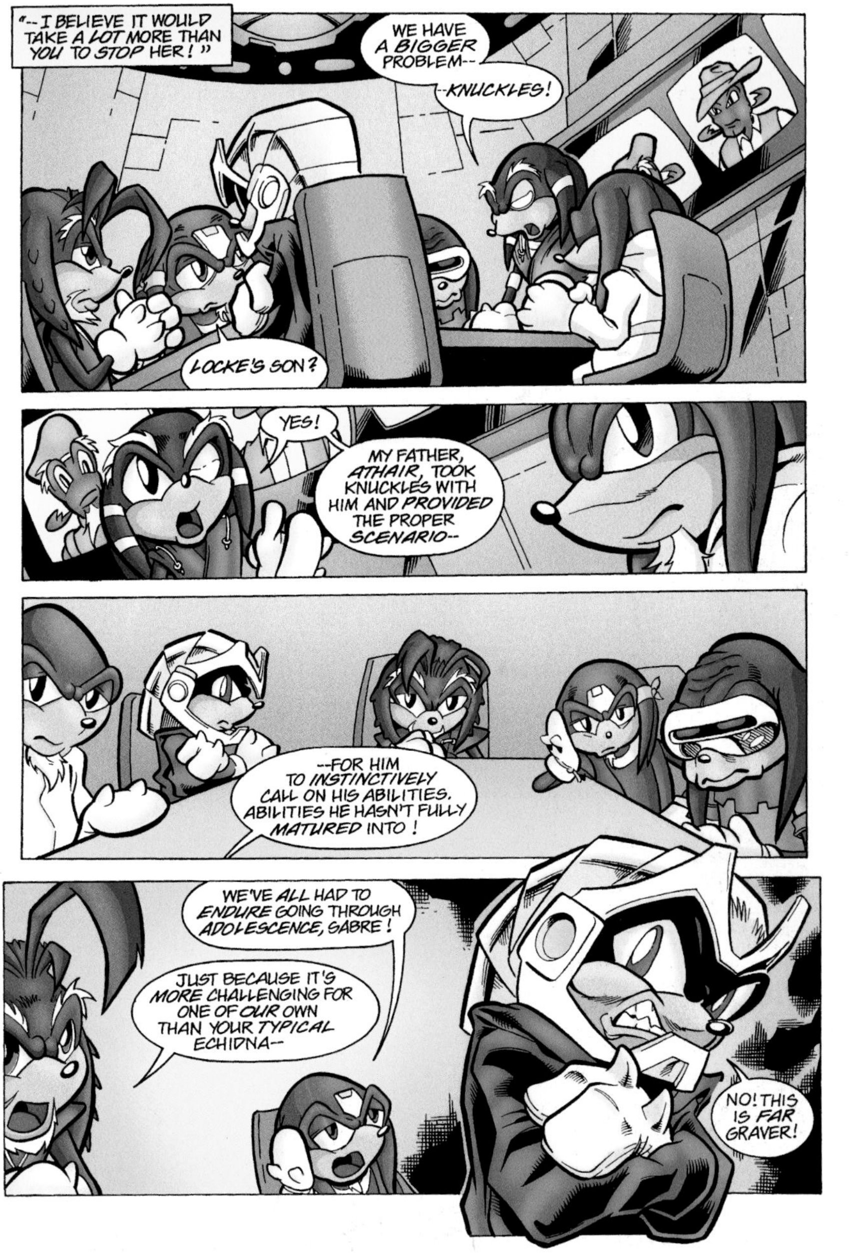
"--I BELIEVE IT WOULD TAKE A LOT MORE THAN YOU TO STOP HER!"
WE HAVE A BIGGER PROBLEM--
--KNUCKLES!
LOCKE'S SON?
YES!
MY FATHER, ATHAIR, TOOK KNUCKLES WITH HIM AND PROVIDED THE PROPER SCENARIO--
--FOR HIM TO INSTINCTIVELY CALL ON HIS ABILITIES. ABILITIES HE HASN'T FULLY MATURED INTO!
WE'VE ALL HAD TO ENDURE GOING THROUGH ADOLESCENCE, SABRE!
JUST BECAUSE IT'S MORE CHALLENGING FOR ONE OF OUR OWN THAN YOUR TYPICAL ECHIDNA--
NO! THIS IS FAR GRAVER!

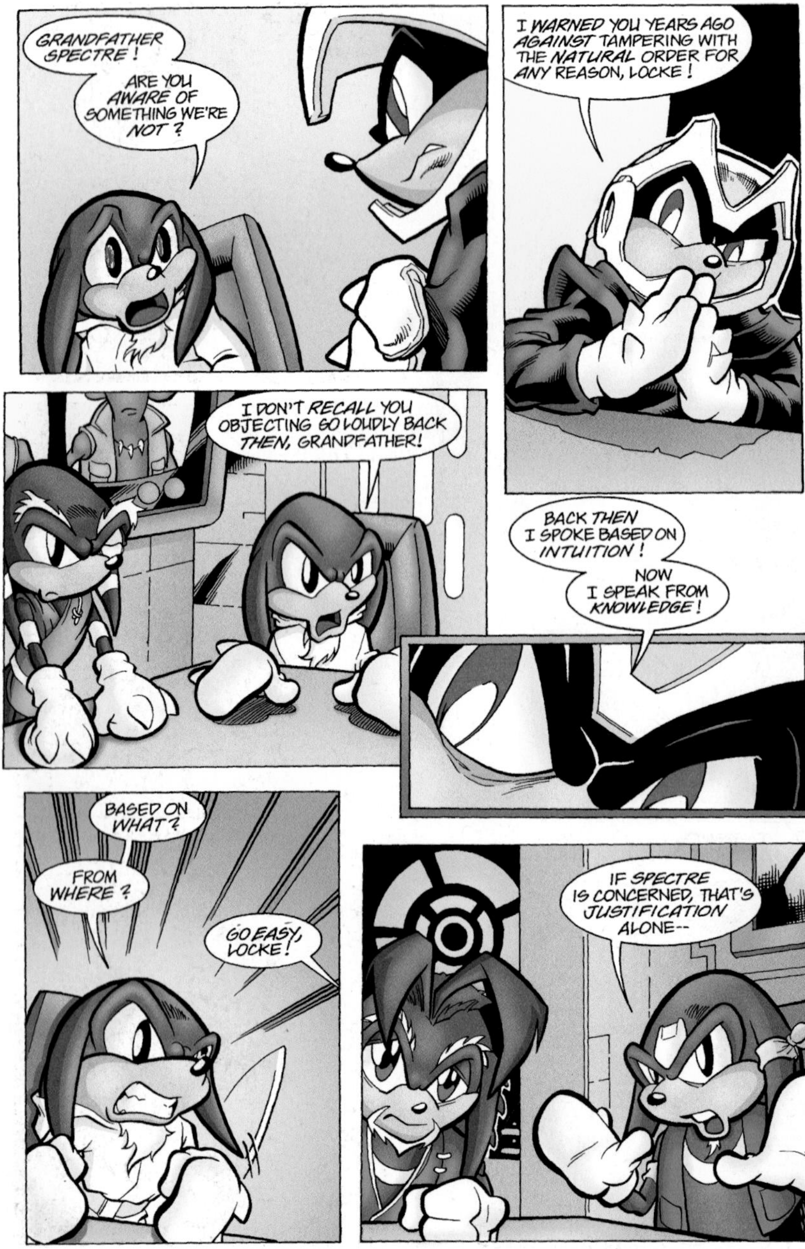
GRANDFATHER SPECTRE!
ARE YOU AWARE OF SOMETHING WE'RE NOT?
I WARNED YOU YEARS AGO AGAINST TAMPERING WITH THE NATURAL ORDER FOR ANY REASON, LOCKE!
I DON'T RECALL YOU OBJECTING SO LOUDLY BACK THEN, GRANDFATHER!
BACK THEN I SPOKE BASED ON INTUITION!
NOW I SPEAK FROM KNOWLEDGE!
BASED ON WHAT?
FROM WHERE?
GO EASY, LOCKE!
IF SPECTRE IS CONCERNED, THAT'S JUSTIFICATION ALONE--

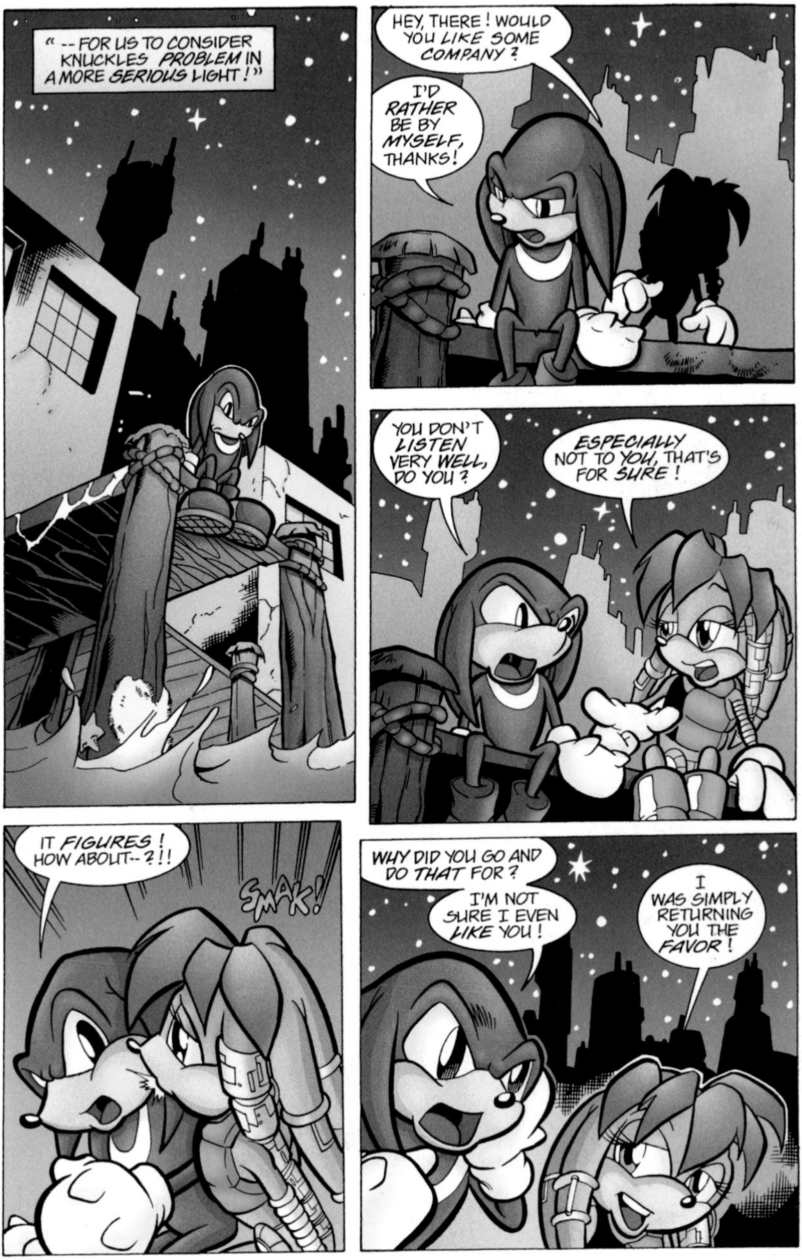
" -- FOR US TO CONSIDER KNUCKLES PROBLEM IN A MORE SERIOUS LIGHT!"
HEY, THERE! WOULD YOU LIKE SOME COMPANY?
I'D RATHER BE BY MYSELF, THANKS!
YOU DON'T LISTEN VERY WELL, DO YOU?
ESPECIALLY NOT TO YOU, THAT'S FOR SURE!
IT FIGURES! HOW ABOUT-- ?!!
SMAK!
WHY DID YOU GO AND DO THAT FOR?
I'M NOT SURE I EVEN LIKE YOU!
I WAS SIMPLY RETURNING YOU THE FAVOR!

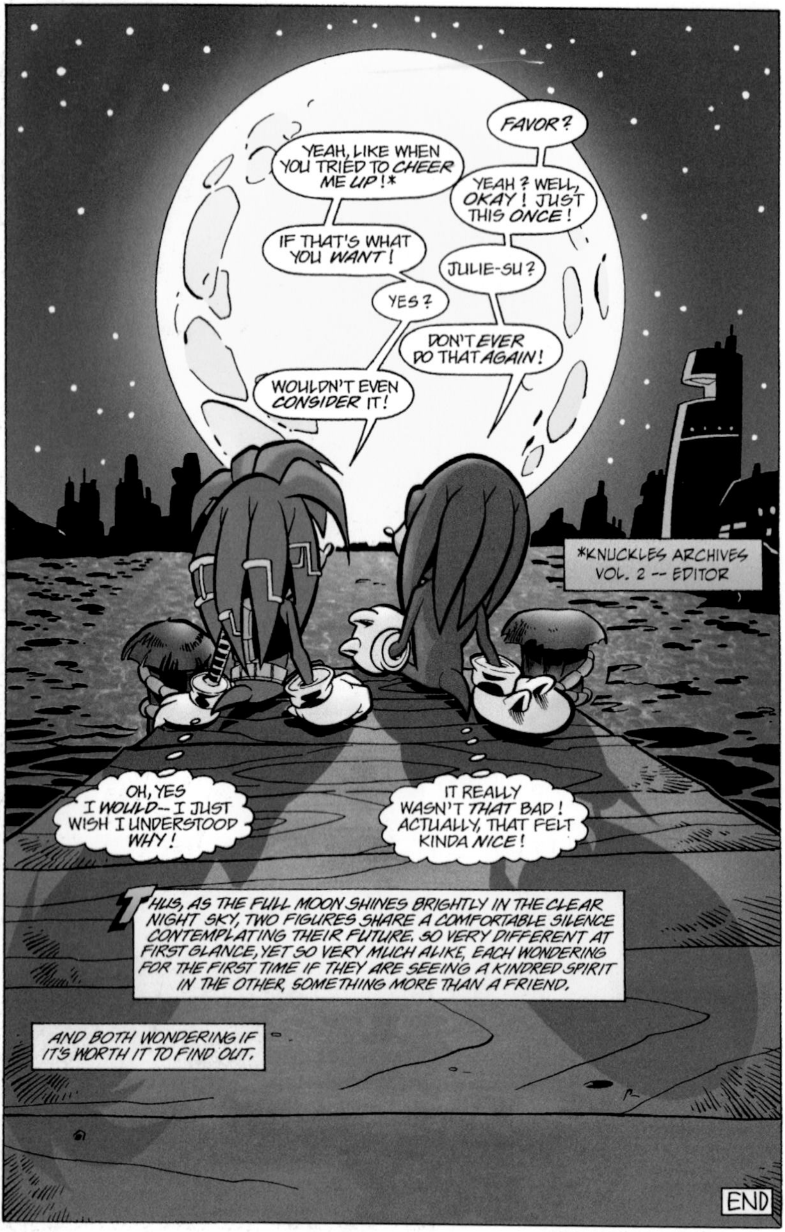
YEAH, LIKE WHEN YOU TRIED TO CHEER ME UP!*
FAVOR?
YEAH? WELL, OKAY! JUST THIS ONCE!
IF THAT'S WHAT YOU WANT!
JULIE-SU?
YES?
DON'T EVER DO THAT AGAIN!
WOULDN'T EVEN CONSIDER IT!
*KNUCKLES ARCHIVES VOL. 2 -- EDITOR
OH, YES I WOULD-- I JUST WISH I UNDERSTOOD WHY!
IT REALLY WASN'T THAT BAD! ACTUALLY, THAT FELT KINDA NICE!
THUS, AS THE FULL MOON SHINES BRIGHTLY IN THE CLEAR NIGHT SKY, TWO FIGURES SHARE A COMFORTABLE SILENCE CONTEMPLATING THEIR FUTURE. SO VERY DIFFERENT AT FIRST GLANCE, YET SO VERY MUCH ALIKE, EACH WONDERING FOR THE FIRST TIME IF THEY ARE SEEING A KINDRED SPIRIT IN THE OTHER, SOMETHING MORE THAN A FRIEND.
AND BOTH WONDERING IF IT'S WORTH IT TO FIND OUT.
END

TAKE AN EXCLUSIVE LOOK BEHIND THE SCENES OF *KNUCKLES THE ECHIDNA*, AS WE REVEAL...

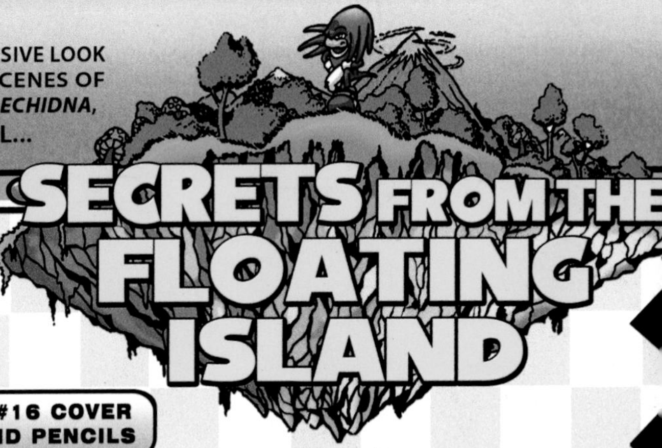

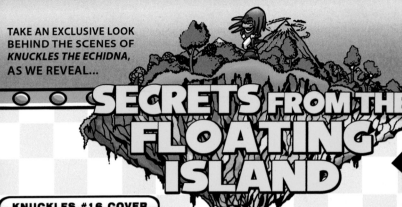

SECRETS FROM THE FLOATING ISLAND

KNUCKLES #16 COVER BACKGROUND PENCILS

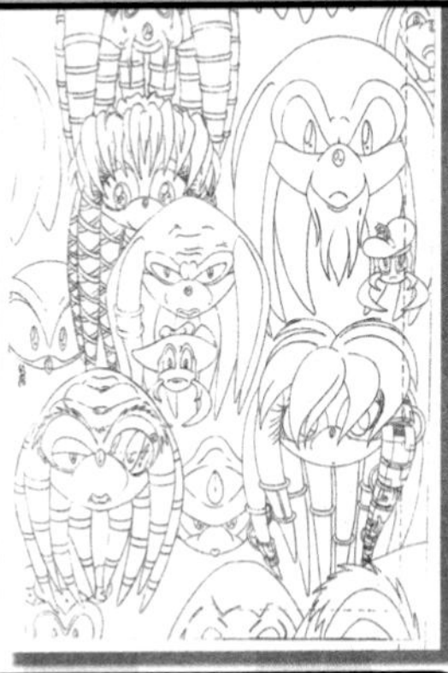

KNUCKLES #16 COVER KNUCKLES PENCILS

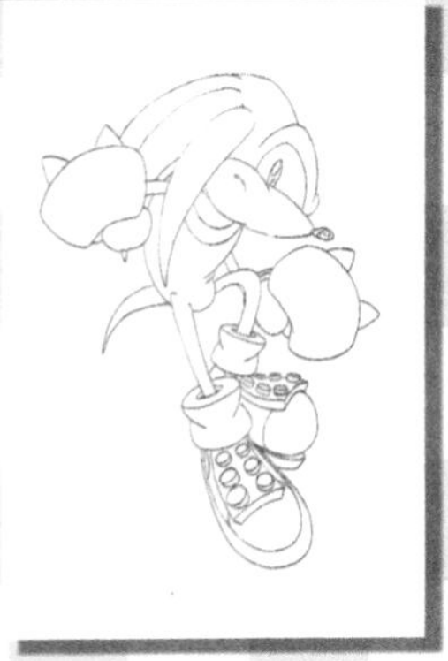

KNUCKLES #16 COVER FINAL LINEWORK

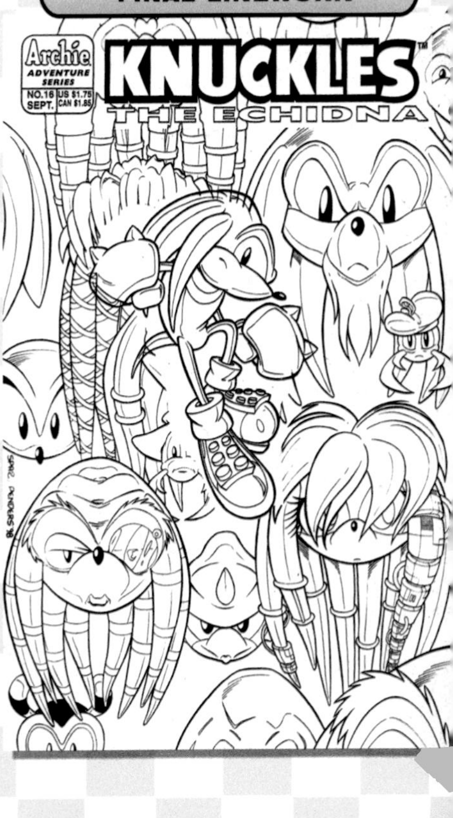
Archie
ADVENTURE SERIES
NO.16 SEPT.
US $1.75
CAN $1.85
KNUCKLES™
THE ECHIDNA

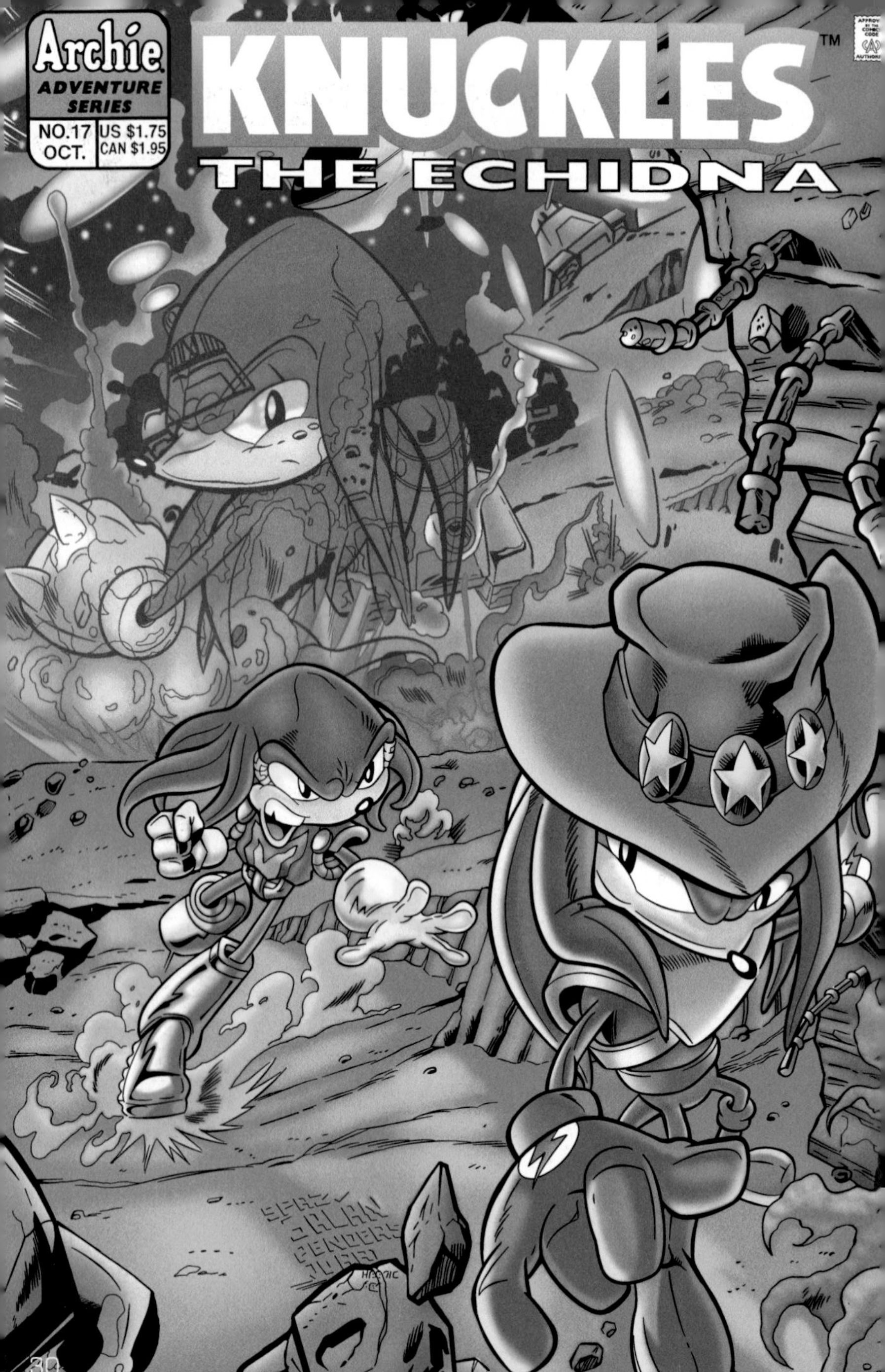
Archie
ADVENTURE SERIES
NO.17 OCT.
US $1.75
CAN $1.95
KNUCKLES™
THE ECHIDNA

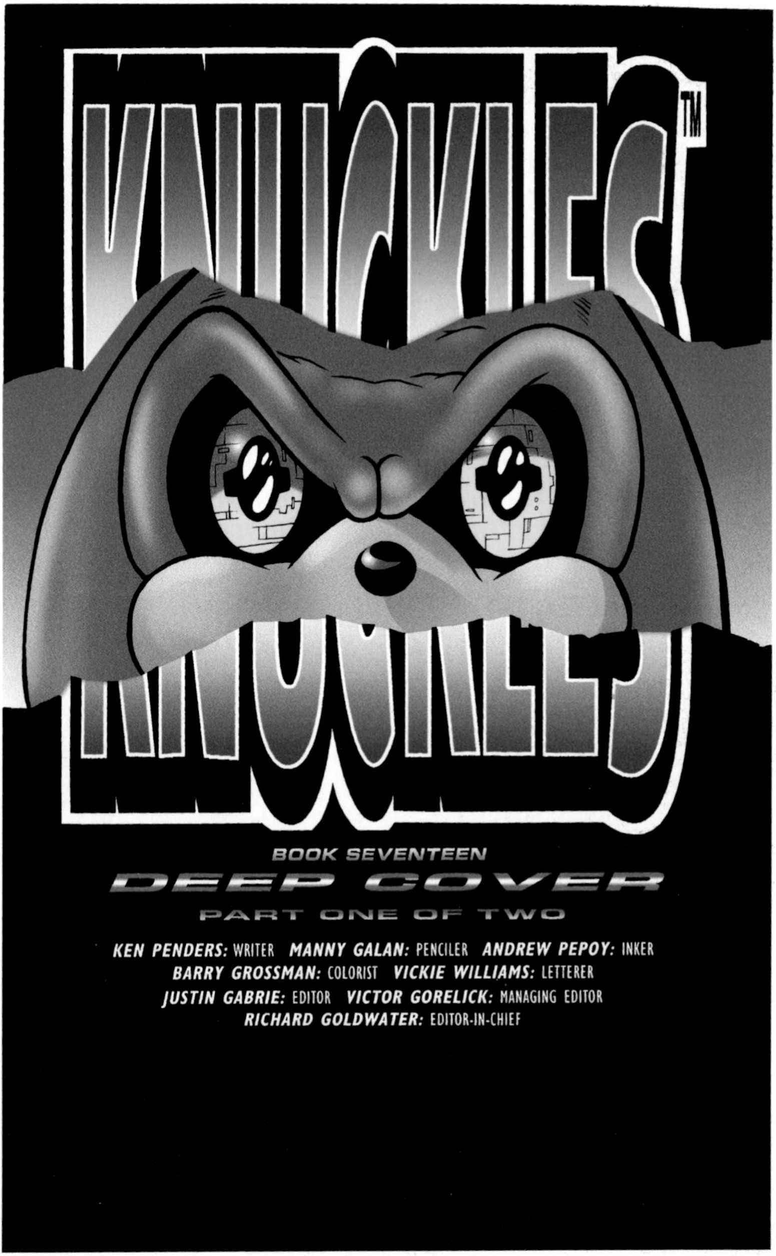
KNUCKLES™

BOOK SEVENTEEN

DEEP COVER

PART ONE OF TWO

KEN PENDERS: WRITER ***MANNY GALAN:*** PENCILER ***ANDREW PEPOY:*** INKER
BARRY GROSSMAN: COLORIST ***VICKIE WILLIAMS:*** LETTERER
JUSTIN GABRIE: EDITOR ***VICTOR GORELICK:*** MANAGING EDITOR
RICHARD GOLDWATER: EDITOR-IN-CHIEF

BORN TO THE MOST NOBLE OF ECHIDNA HOUSES, THE LATEST TO
CONTINUE THE FAMILY HERITAGE AND RESPONSIBILITY AS GUARDIAN
OF THE FLOATING ISLAND, DEFENDER OF ALL FROM THE FORCES OF
EVIL FROM THE WORLD BEYOND AS WELL AS THOSE WHO WOULD
THREATEN WITHIN, HE IS NONE OTHER THAN
KNUCKLES THE ECHIDNA!

LAST ISSUE, WE LEFT KNUCKLES CONTEMPLATING MANY
QUESTIONS ALONGSIDE JULIE-SU, WHO HAD MORE THAN A FEW
THOUGHTS OF HER OWN. WHILE THEY MAY HAVE BEEN LOST IN
THEIR OWN REFLECTIONS, THERE WERE OTHERS WHO WERE
THINKING ABOUT THEM, AND WONDERING WHETHER OR NOT
ANY ACTION SHOULD BE TAKEN.

BECAUSE, YOU SEE, THESE OTHERS KNOW SOMETHING ABOUT
KNUCKLES THAT NOT EVEN HE KNOWS...
YET.

A SECRET SO MONUMENTAL, THAT IT COULD HAVE IMPORTANT
CONSEQUENCES FOR MANY... ESPECIALLY FOR KNUCKLES.

UNFORTUNATELY FOR KNUCKLES, THERE ARE MANY OTHER
SECRETS ABOUT HIS FAMILY HE DOES NOT YET KNOW, WHICH
NOT ONLY COULD PORTEND DIRE CONSEQUENCES FOR HIM, BUT
FOR ALL OF HIS FELLOW ECHIDNAS AS WELL.

IT IS ON THE SURFACE OF MOBIUS THAT ONE OF THE KEYS TO
UNLOCKING THESE SECRETS MAKES ITSELF KNOWN...

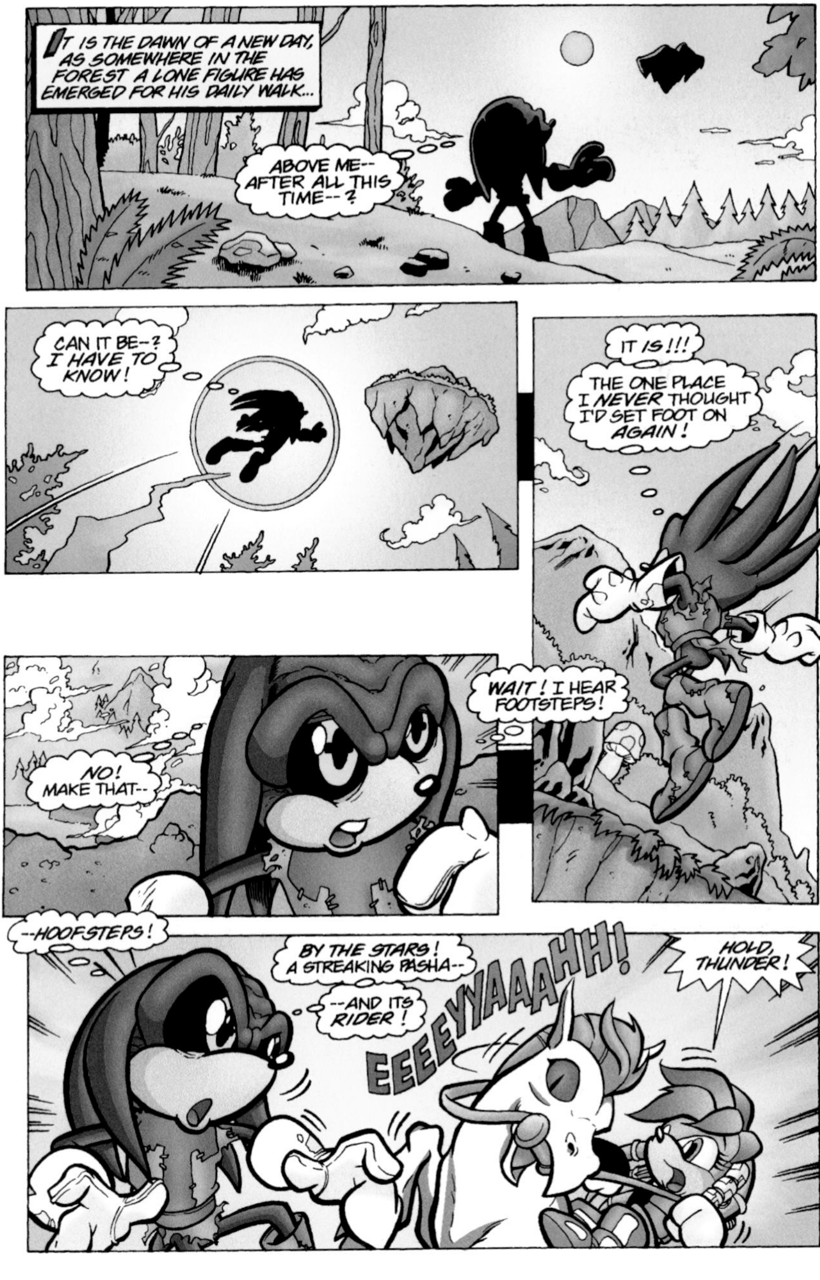
IT IS THE DAWN OF A NEW DAY, AS SOMEWHERE IN THE FOREST A LONE FIGURE HAS EMERGED FOR HIS DAILY WALK...
ABOVE ME-- AFTER ALL THIS TIME--?
CAN IT BE--? I HAVE TO KNOW!
IT IS!!!
THE ONE PLACE I NEVER THOUGHT I'D SET FOOT ON AGAIN!
WAIT! I HEAR FOOTSTEPS!
NO! MAKE THAT--
--HOOFSTEPS!
BY THE STARS! A STREAKING PASHA--
--AND ITS RIDER!
EEEEYYAAAAHH!
HOLD, THUNDER!

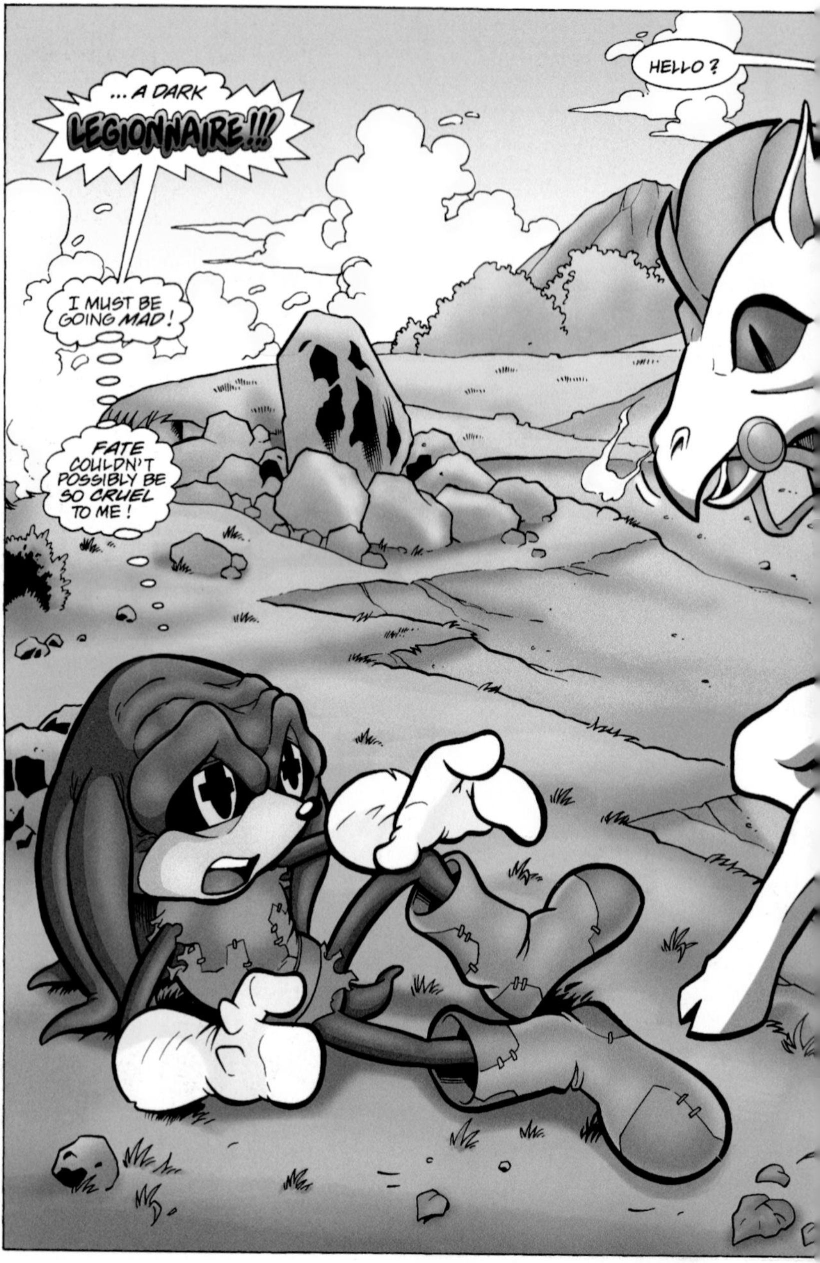
HELLO?
... A DARK LEGIONNAIRE!!!
I MUST BE GOING MAD!
FATE COULDN'T POSSIBLY BE SO CRUEL TO ME!

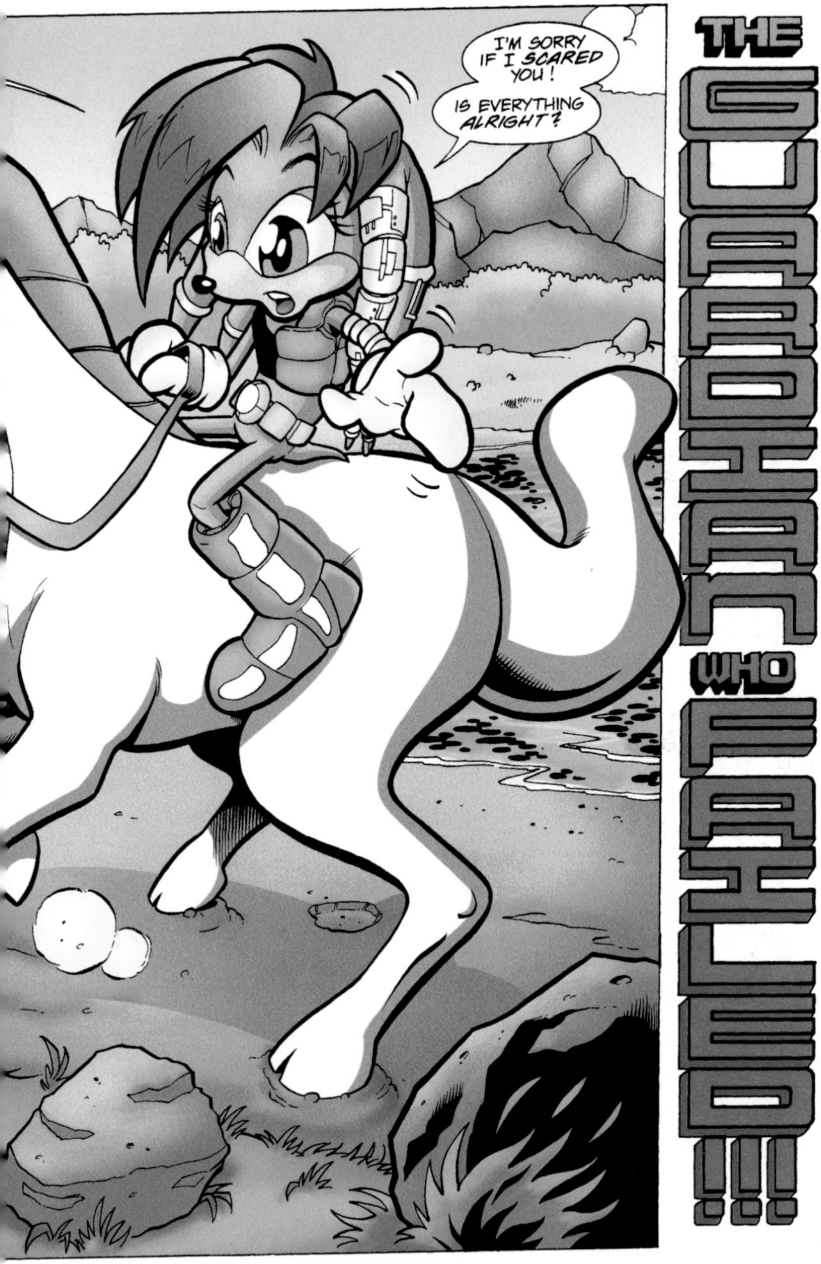
I'M SORRY IF I SCARED YOU!
IS EVERYTHING ALRIGHT?
THE GUARDIAN WHO FAILED!!!!

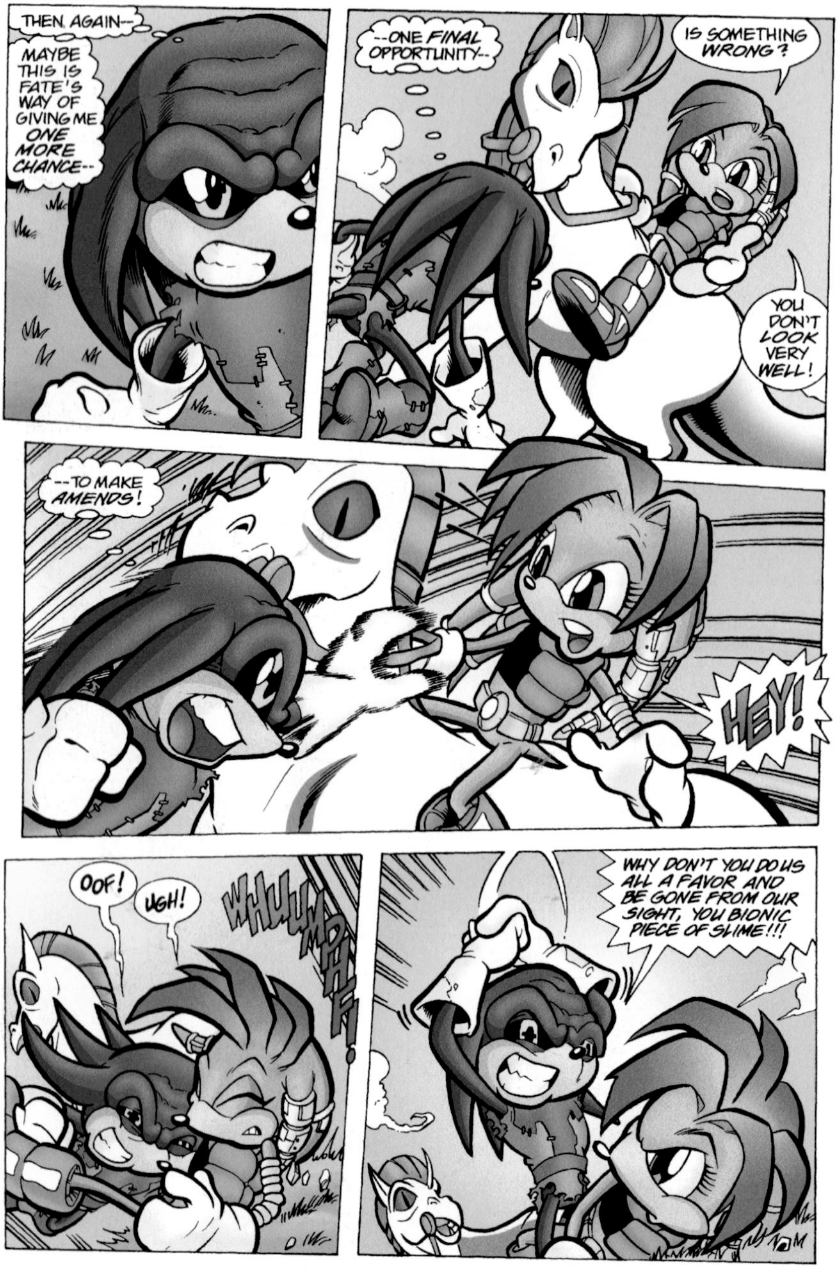
THEN, AGAIN--
MAYBE THIS IS FATE'S WAY OF GIVING ME ONE MORE CHANCE--
--ONE FINAL OPPORTUNITY--
IS SOMETHING WRONG?
YOU DON'T LOOK VERY WELL!
--TO MAKE AMENDS!
HEY!
OOF!
UGH!
WHUUMPHH!
WHY DON'T YOU DO US ALL A FAVOR AND BE GONE FROM OUR SIGHT, YOU BIONIC PIECE OF SLIME!!!

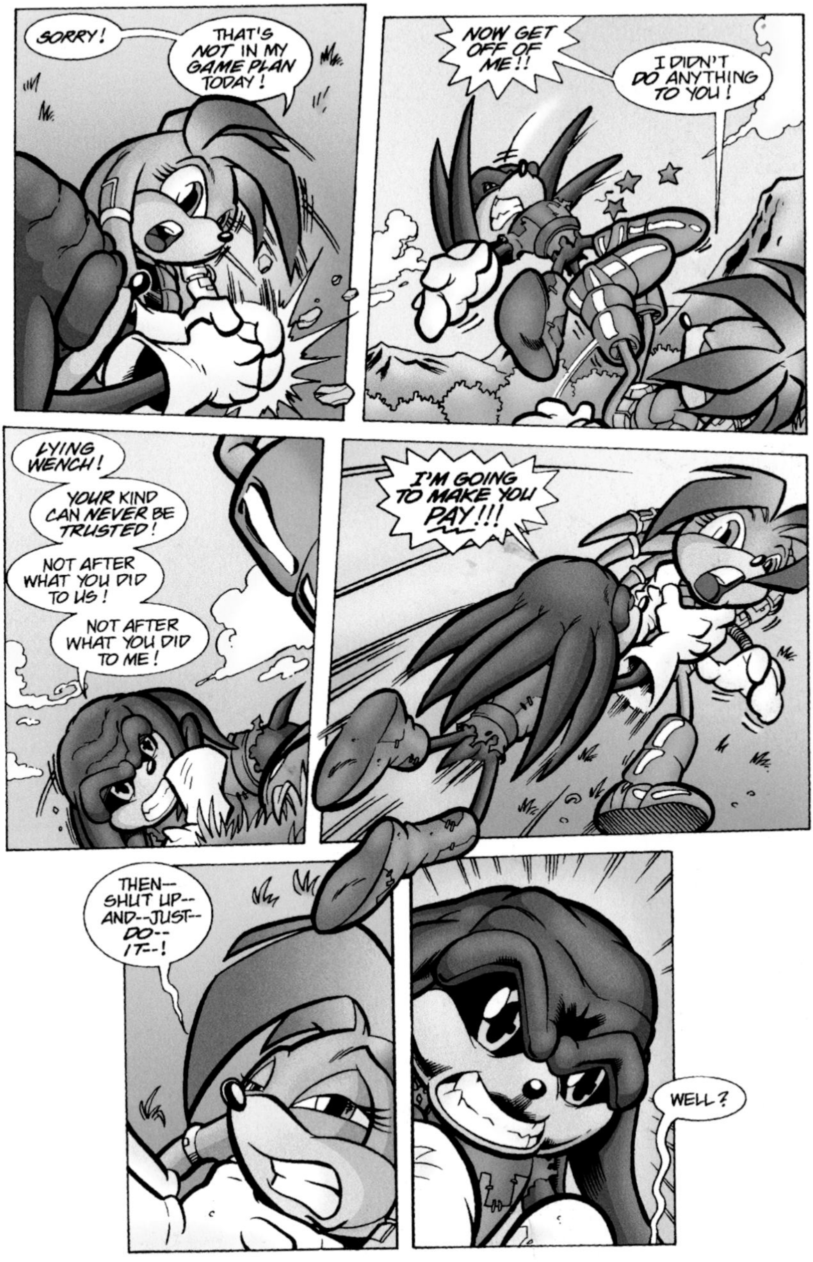
SORRY!
THAT'S NOT IN MY GAME PLAN TODAY!
NOW GET OFF OF ME!!
I DIDN'T DO ANYTHING TO YOU!
LYING WENCH!
YOUR KIND CAN NEVER BE TRUSTED!
NOT AFTER WHAT YOU DID TO US!
NOT AFTER WHAT YOU DID TO ME!
I'M GOING TO MAKE YOU PAY!!!
THEN-- SHUT UP-- AND--JUST-- DO-- IT--!
WELL?

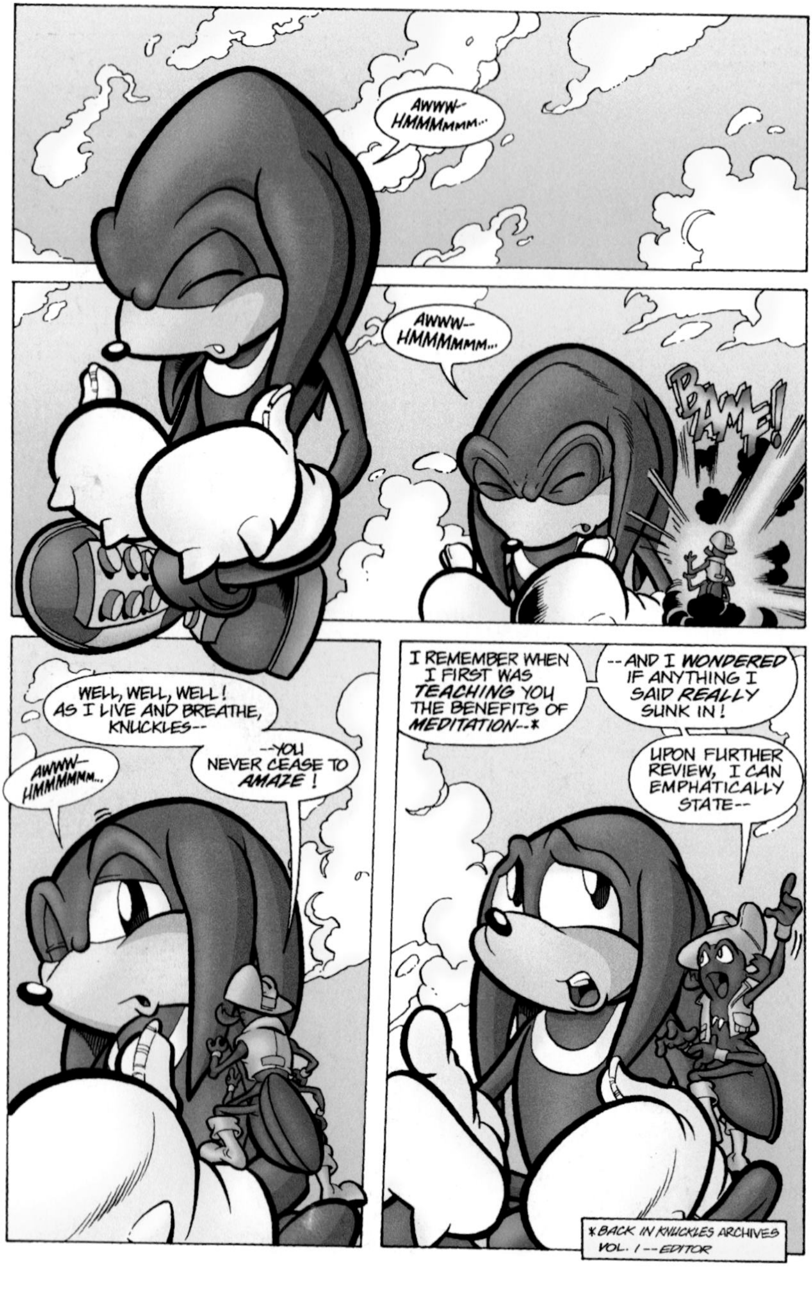
AWWW-
HMMMmmm...
AWWW--
HMMMMMM...
BAMF!
WELL, WELL, WELL!
AS I LIVE AND BREATHE, KNUCKLES--
--YOU NEVER CEASE TO AMAZE!
AWWW-
HMMMMM...
I REMEMBER WHEN I FIRST WAS TEACHING YOU THE BENEFITS OF MEDITATION--*
--AND I WONDERED IF ANYTHING I SAID REALLY SUNK IN!
UPON FURTHER REVIEW, I CAN EMPHATICALLY STATE--
*BACK IN KNUCKLES ARCHIVES VOL. 1 --EDITOR

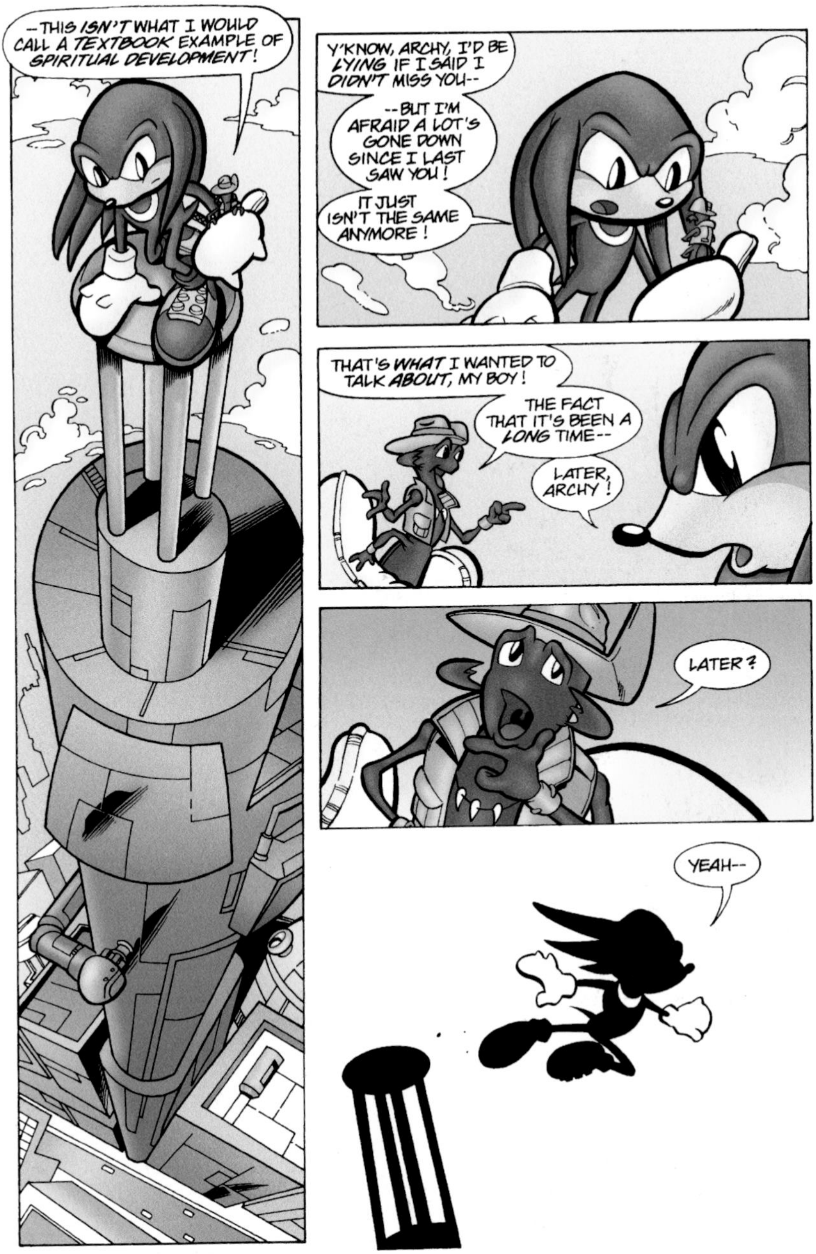
--THIS ISN'T WHAT I WOULD CALL A TEXTBOOK EXAMPLE OF SPIRITUAL DEVELOPMENT!
Y'KNOW, ARCHY, I'D BE LYING IF I SAID I DIDN'T MISS YOU--
--BUT I'M AFRAID A LOT'S GONE DOWN SINCE I LAST SAW YOU!
IT JUST ISN'T THE SAME ANYMORE!
THAT'S WHAT I WANTED TO TALK ABOUT, MY BOY!
THE FACT THAT IT'S BEEN A LONG TIME--
LATER, ARCHY!
LATER?
YEAH--

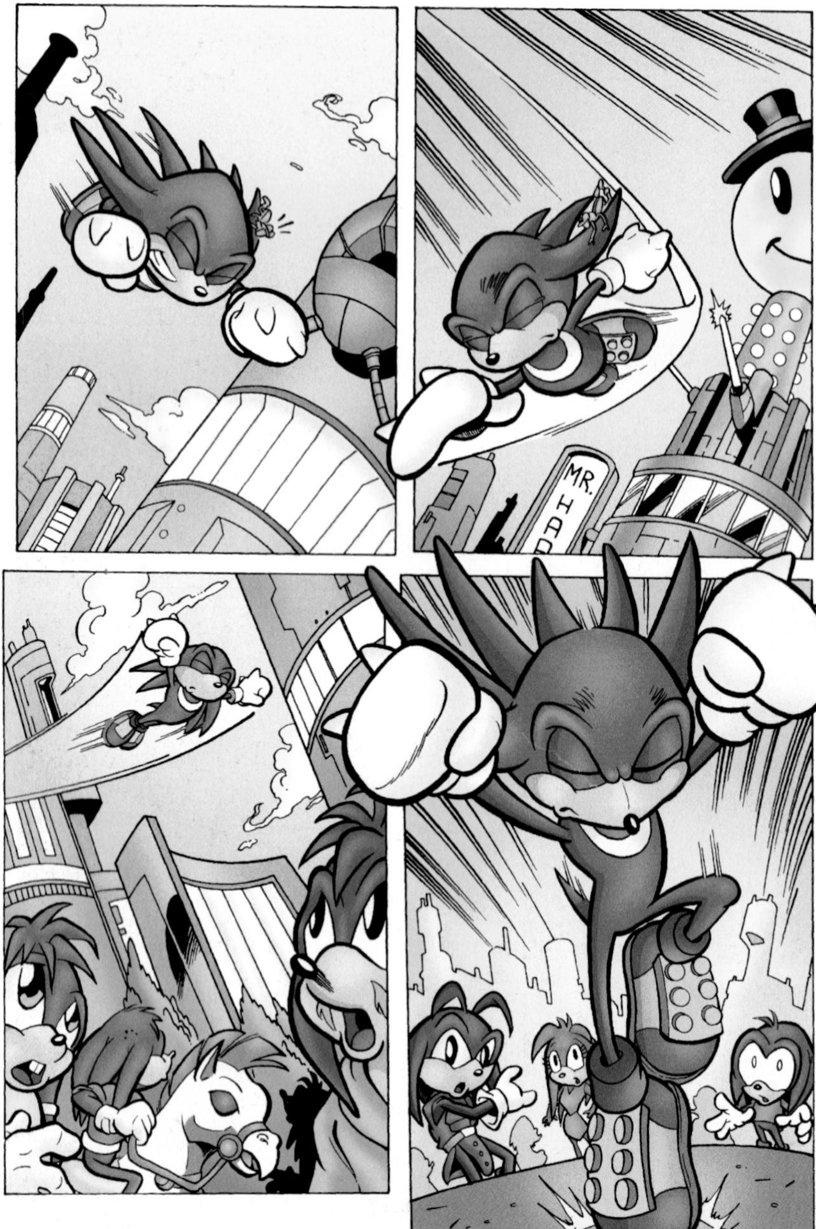
MR.

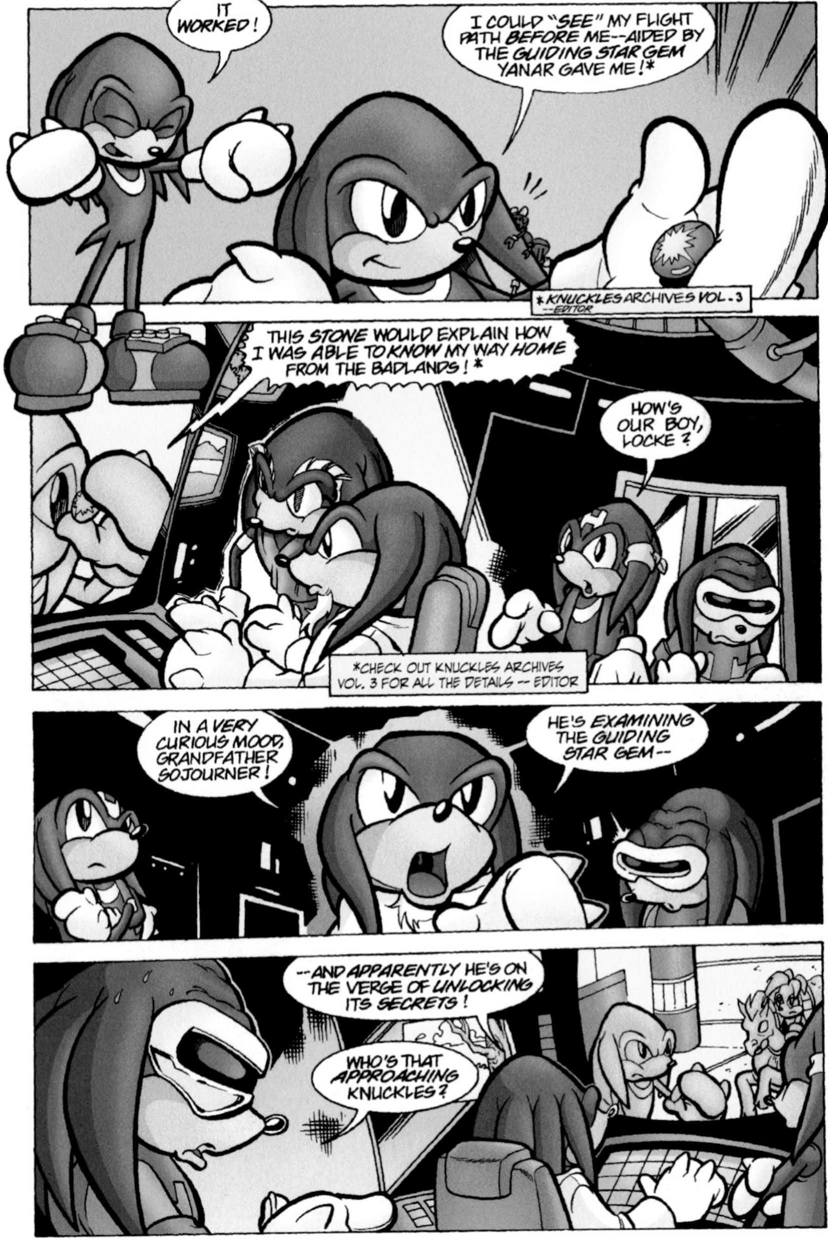
IT WORKED!
I COULD "SEE" MY FLIGHT PATH BEFORE ME--AIDED BY THE GUIDING STAR GEM YANAR GAVE ME!*
*KNUCKLES ARCHIVES VOL. 3 --EDITOR
THIS STONE WOULD EXPLAIN HOW I WAS ABLE TO KNOW MY WAY HOME FROM THE BADLANDS!*
HOW'S OUR BOY, LOCKE?
*CHECK OUT KNUCKLES ARCHIVES VOL. 3 FOR ALL THE DETAILS -- EDITOR
IN A VERY CURIOUS MOOD, GRANDFATHER SOJOURNER!
HE'S EXAMINING THE GUIDING STAR GEM--
--AND APPARENTLY HE'S ON THE VERGE OF UNLOCKING ITS SECRETS!
WHO'S THAT APPROACHING KNUCKLES?

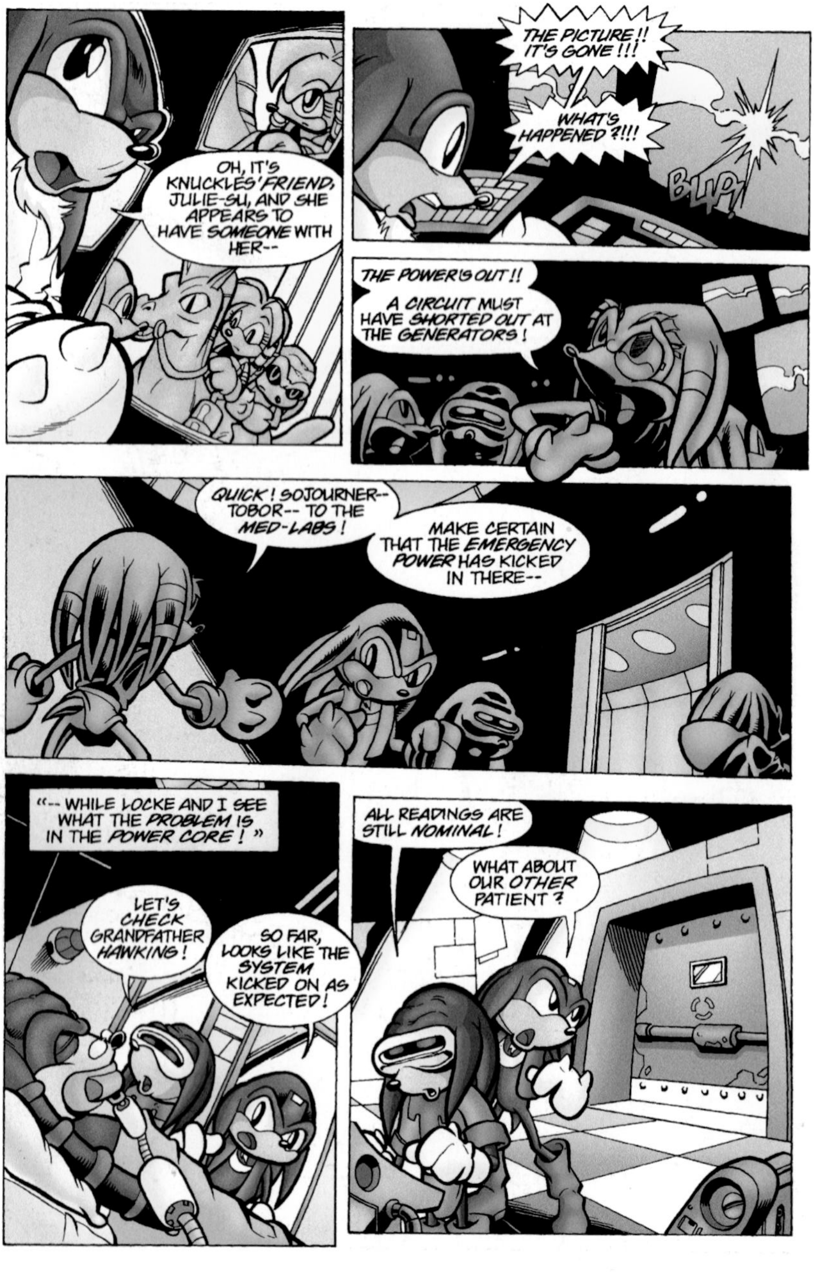
OH, IT'S KNUCKLES' FRIEND, JULIE-SU, AND SHE APPEARS TO HAVE SOMEONE WITH HER--
THE PICTURE!! IT'S GONE!!!
WHAT'S HAPPENED?!!!
BLIP!
THE POWER'S OUT!!
A CIRCUIT MUST HAVE SHORTED OUT AT THE GENERATORS!
QUICK! SOJOURNER-- TOBOR-- TO THE MED-LABS!
MAKE CERTAIN THAT THE EMERGENCY POWER HAS KICKED IN THERE--
"-- WHILE LOCKE AND I SEE WHAT THE PROBLEM IS IN THE POWER CORE!"
LET'S CHECK GRANDFATHER HAWKING!
SO FAR, LOOKS LIKE THE SYSTEM KICKED ON AS EXPECTED!
ALL READINGS ARE STILL NOMINAL!
WHAT ABOUT OUR OTHER PATIENT?

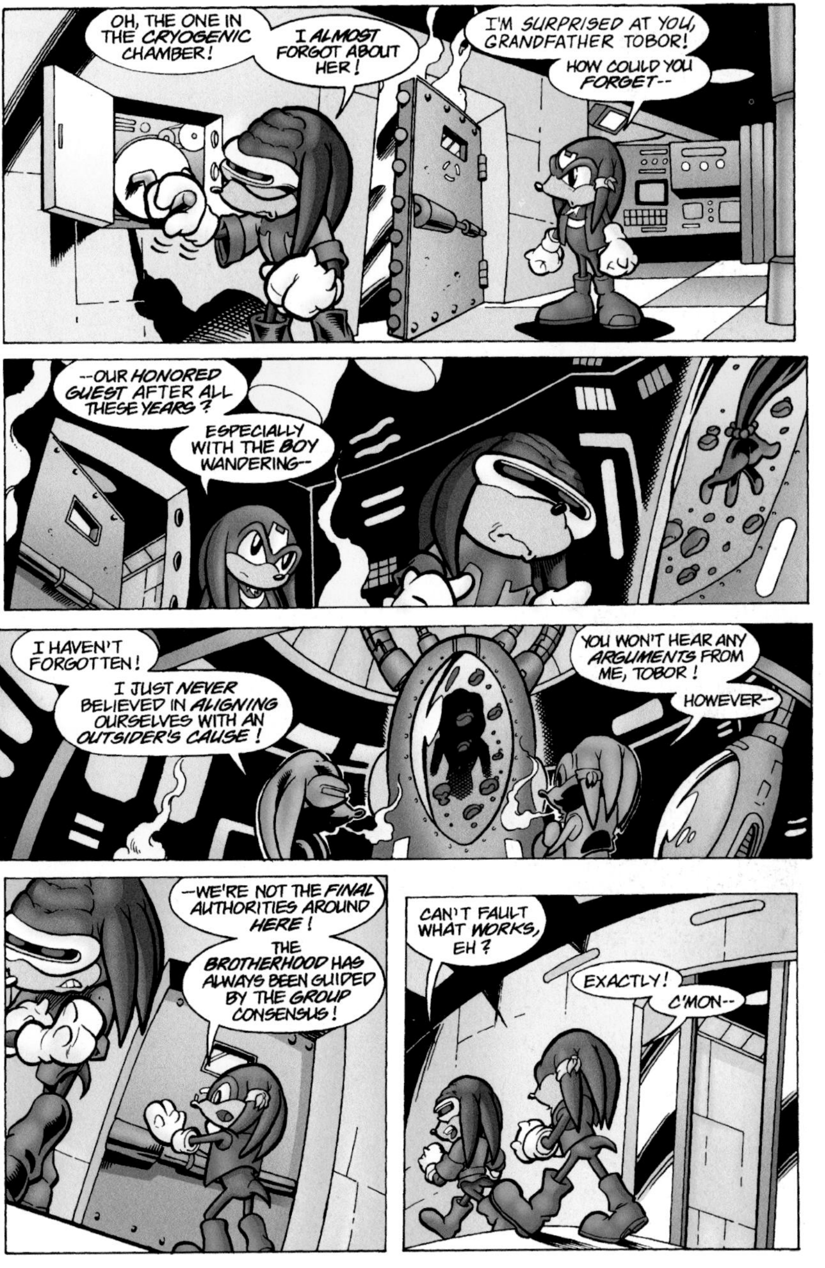
OH, THE ONE IN THE CRYOGENIC CHAMBER!
I ALMOST FORGOT ABOUT HER!
I'M SURPRISED AT YOU, GRANDFATHER TOBOR!
HOW COULD YOU FORGET--
--OUR HONORED GUEST AFTER ALL THESE YEARS?
ESPECIALLY WITH THE BOY WANDERING--
I HAVEN'T FORGOTTEN!
I JUST NEVER BELIEVED IN ALIGNING OURSELVES WITH AN OUTSIDER'S CAUSE!
YOU WON'T HEAR ANY ARGUMENTS FROM ME, TOBOR!
HOWEVER--
--WE'RE NOT THE FINAL AUTHORITIES AROUND HERE!
THE BROTHERHOOD HAS ALWAYS BEEN GUIDED BY THE GROUP CONSENSUS!
CAN'T FAULT WHAT WORKS, EH?
EXACTLY!
C'MON--

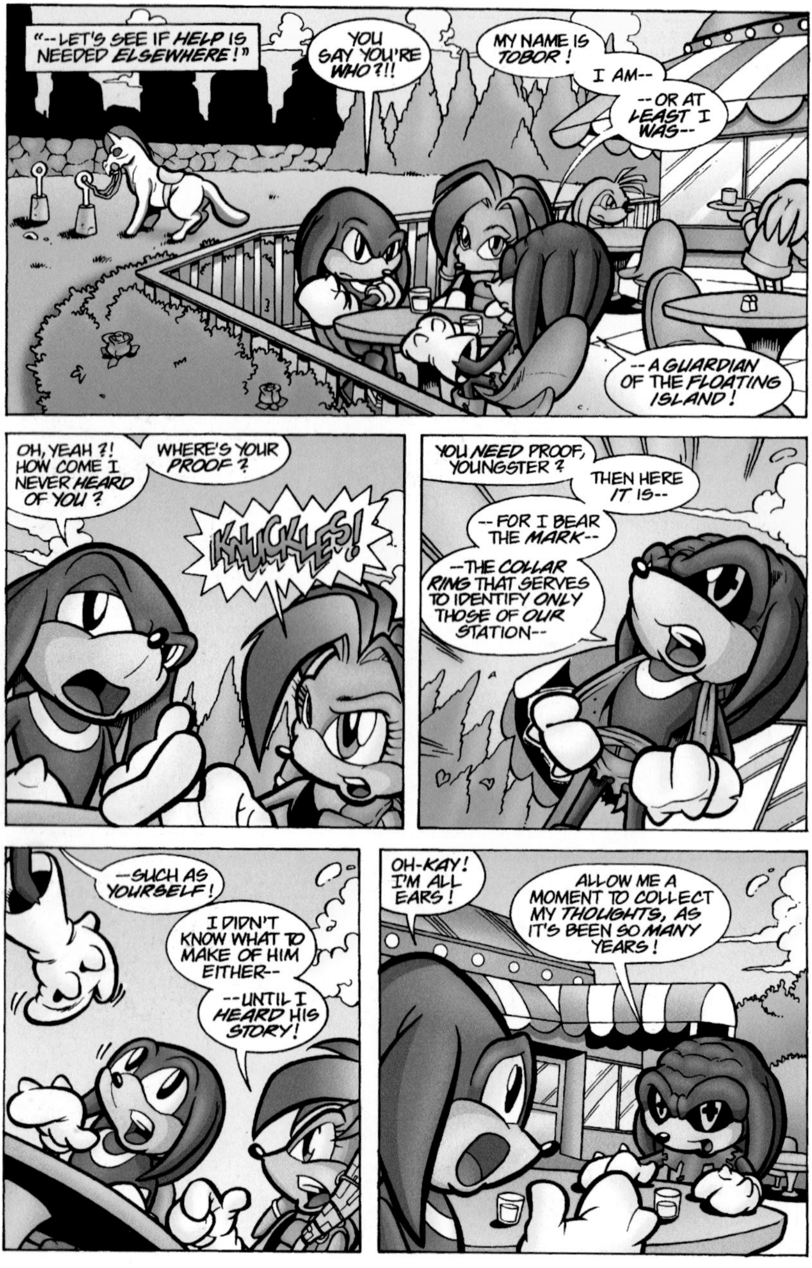
"--LET'S SEE IF HELP IS NEEDED ELSEWHERE!"
YOU SAY YOU'RE WHO?!!
MY NAME IS TOBOR!
I AM--
--OR AT LEAST I WAS--
--A GUARDIAN OF THE FLOATING ISLAND!
OH, YEAH?! HOW COME I NEVER HEARD OF YOU?
WHERE'S YOUR PROOF?
KNUCKLES!
YOU NEED PROOF, YOUNGSTER?
THEN HERE IT IS--
--FOR I BEAR THE MARK--
--THE COLLAR RING THAT SERVES TO IDENTIFY ONLY THOSE OF OUR STATION--
--SUCH AS YOURSELF!
I DIDN'T KNOW WHAT TO MAKE OF HIM EITHER--
--UNTIL I HEARD HIS STORY!
OH-KAY! I'M ALL EARS!
ALLOW ME A MOMENT TO COLLECT MY THOUGHTS, AS IT'S BEEN SO MANY YEARS!

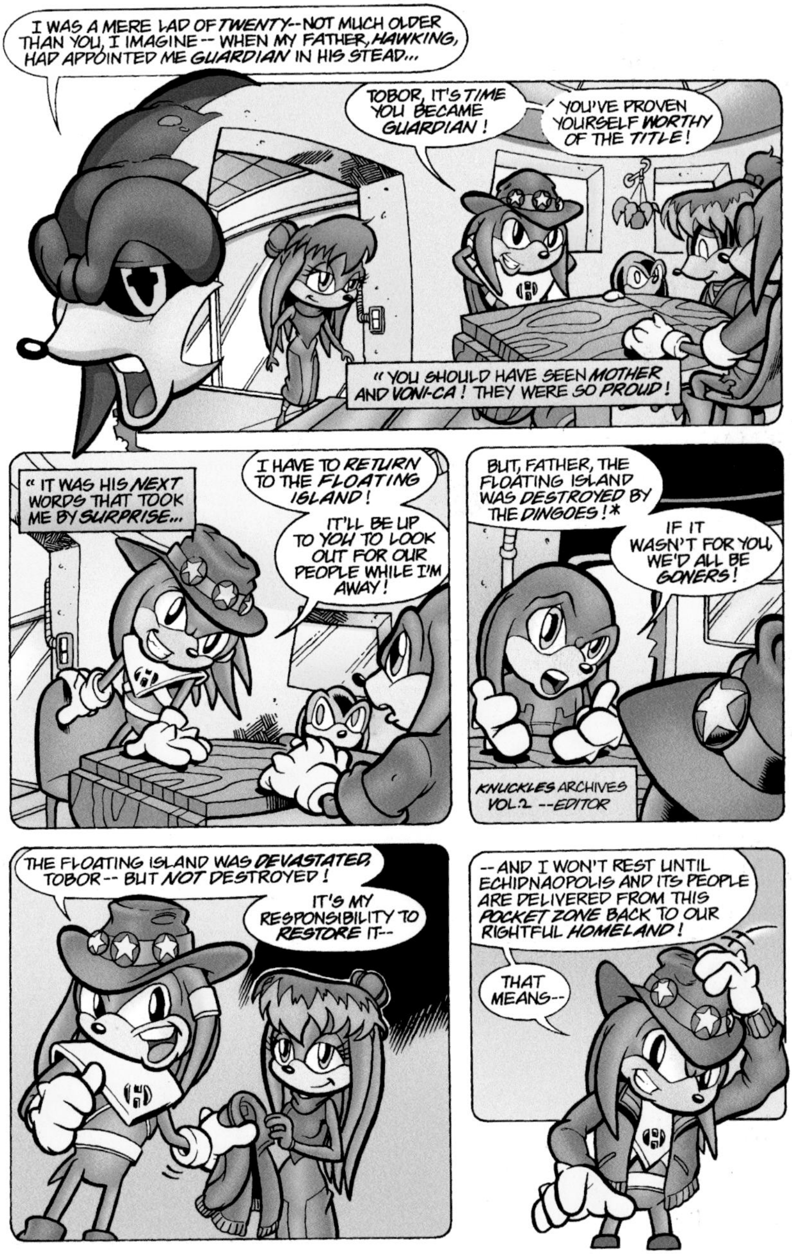

I WAS A MERE LAD OF TWENTY--NOT MUCH OLDER THAN YOU, I IMAGINE -- WHEN MY FATHER, HAWKING, HAD APPOINTED ME GUARDIAN IN HIS STEAD...
TOBOR, IT'S TIME YOU BECAME GUARDIAN!
YOU'VE PROVEN YOURSELF WORTHY OF THE TITLE!
"YOU SHOULD HAVE SEEN MOTHER AND VONI-CA! THEY WERE SO PROUD!
" IT WAS HIS NEXT WORDS THAT TOOK ME BY SURPRISE...
I HAVE TO RETURN TO THE FLOATING ISLAND!
IT'LL BE UP TO YOU TO LOOK OUT FOR OUR PEOPLE WHILE I'M AWAY!
BUT, FATHER, THE FLOATING ISLAND WAS DESTROYED BY THE DINGOES!*
IF IT WASN'T FOR YOU, WE'D ALL BE GONERS!
KNUCKLES ARCHIVES VOL.2 --EDITOR
THE FLOATING ISLAND WAS DEVASTATED, TOBOR -- BUT NOT DESTROYED!
IT'S MY RESPONSIBILITY TO RESTORE IT--
--AND I WON'T REST UNTIL ECHIDNAOPOLIS AND ITS PEOPLE ARE DELIVERED FROM THIS POCKET ZONE BACK TO OUR RIGHTFUL HOMELAND!
THAT MEANS--

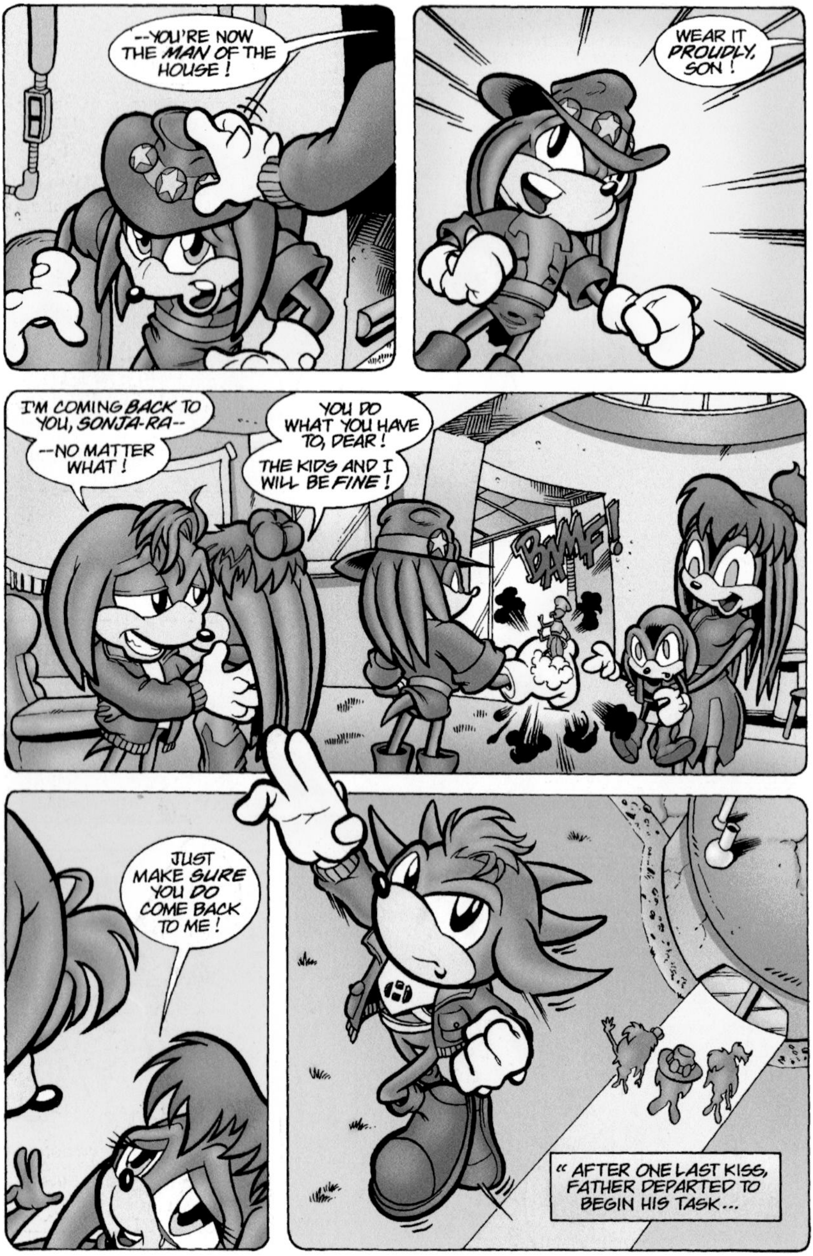

--YOU'RE NOW THE MAN OF THE HOUSE!
WEAR IT PROUDLY, SON!
I'M COMING BACK TO YOU, SONJA-RA--
--NO MATTER WHAT!
YOU DO WHAT YOU HAVE TO, DEAR!
THE KIDS AND I WILL BE FINE!
BAMF!
JUST MAKE SURE YOU DO COME BACK TO ME!
" AFTER ONE LAST KISS, FATHER DEPARTED TO BEGIN HIS TASK...

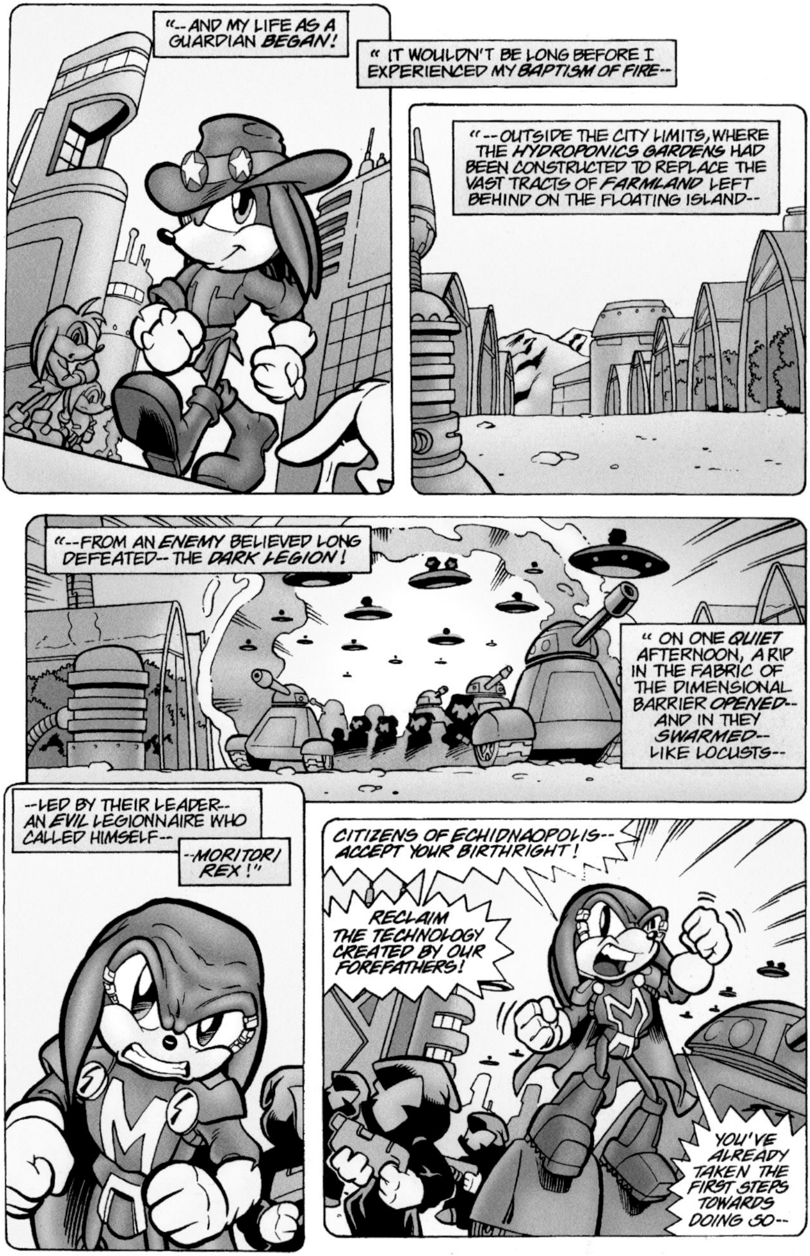
"--AND MY LIFE AS A GUARDIAN BEGAN!
" IT WOULDN'T BE LONG BEFORE I EXPERIENCED MY BAPTISM OF FIRE--
"--OUTSIDE THE CITY LIMITS, WHERE THE HYDROPONICS GARDENS HAD BEEN CONSTRUCTED TO REPLACE THE VAST TRACTS OF FARMLAND LEFT BEHIND ON THE FLOATING ISLAND--
"--FROM AN ENEMY BELIEVED LONG DEFEATED-- THE DARK LEGION!
" ON ONE QUIET AFTERNOON, A RIP IN THE FABRIC OF THE DIMENSIONAL BARRIER OPENED-- AND IN THEY SWARMED-- LIKE LOCUSTS--
--LED BY THEIR LEADER-- AN EVIL LEGIONNAIRE WHO CALLED HIMSELF--
--MORITORI REX!"
CITIZENS OF ECHIDNAOPOLIS-- ACCEPT YOUR BIRTHRIGHT!
RECLAIM THE TECHNOLOGY CREATED BY OUR FOREFATHERS!
YOU'VE ALREADY TAKEN THE FIRST STEPS TOWARDS DOING SO--

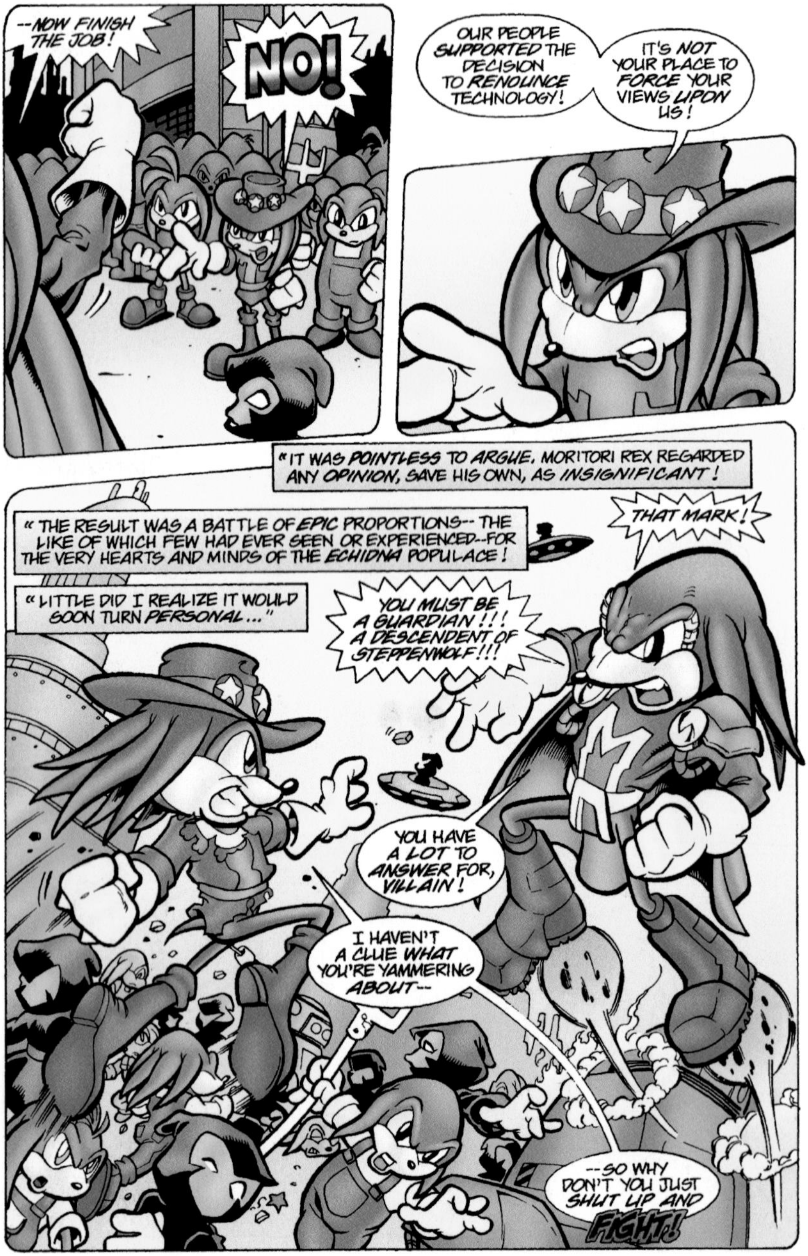
--NOW FINISH THE JOB!
NO!
OUR PEOPLE SUPPORTED THE DECISION TO RENOUNCE TECHNOLOGY!
IT'S NOT YOUR PLACE TO FORCE YOUR VIEWS UPON US!
"IT WAS POINTLESS TO ARGUE. MORITORI REX REGARDED ANY OPINION, SAVE HIS OWN, AS INSIGNIFICANT!
"THE RESULT WAS A BATTLE OF EPIC PROPORTIONS-- THE LIKE OF WHICH FEW HAD EVER SEEN OR EXPERIENCED--FOR THE VERY HEARTS AND MINDS OF THE ECHIDNA POPULACE!
"LITTLE DID I REALIZE IT WOULD SOON TURN PERSONAL..."
THAT MARK!
YOU MUST BE A GUARDIAN!!! A DESCENDENT OF STEPPENWOLF!!!
YOU HAVE A LOT TO ANSWER FOR, VILLAIN!
I HAVEN'T A CLUE WHAT YOU'RE YAMMERING ABOUT--
--SO WHY DON'T YOU JUST SHUT UP AND FIGHT!

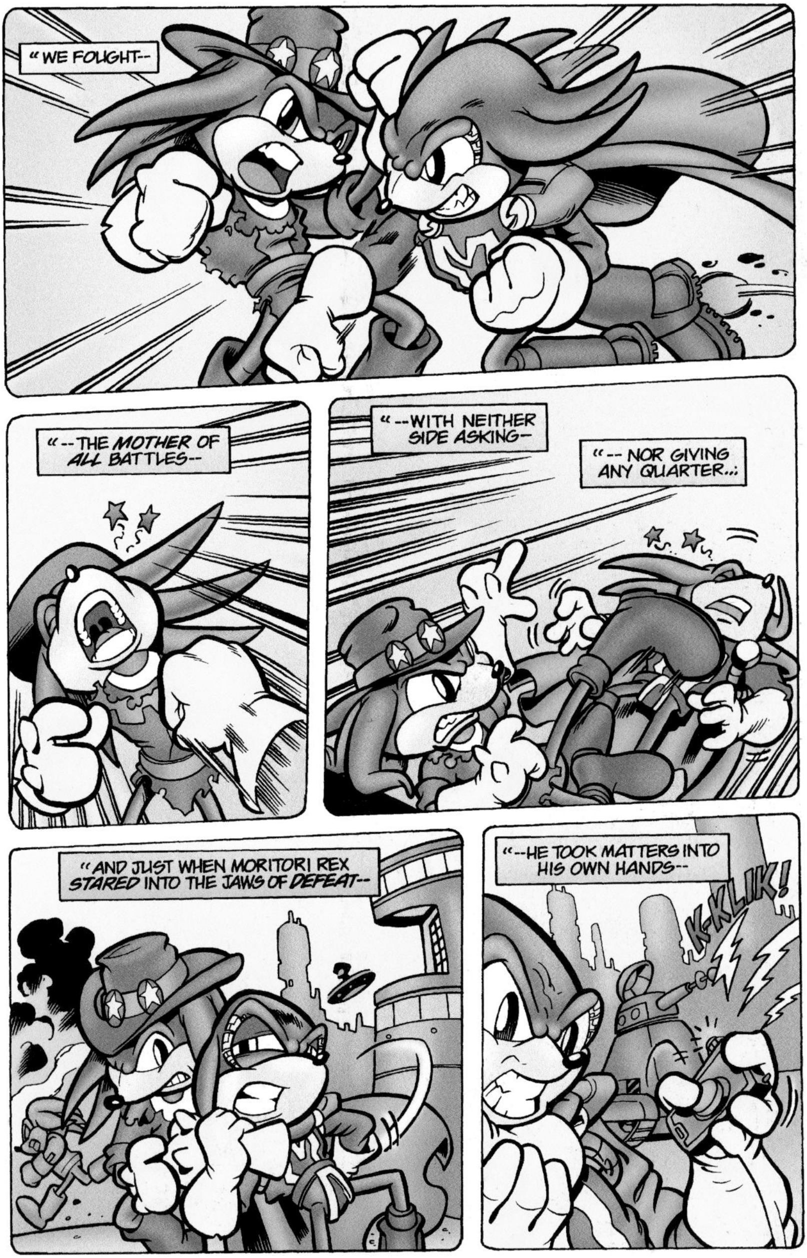
"WE FOUGHT--
"--THE MOTHER OF ALL BATTLES--
"--WITH NEITHER SIDE ASKING--
"--NOR GIVING ANY QUARTER...;
"AND JUST WHEN MORITORI REX STARED INTO THE JAWS OF DEFEAT--
"--HE TOOK MATTERS INTO HIS OWN HANDS--
K-KLIK!

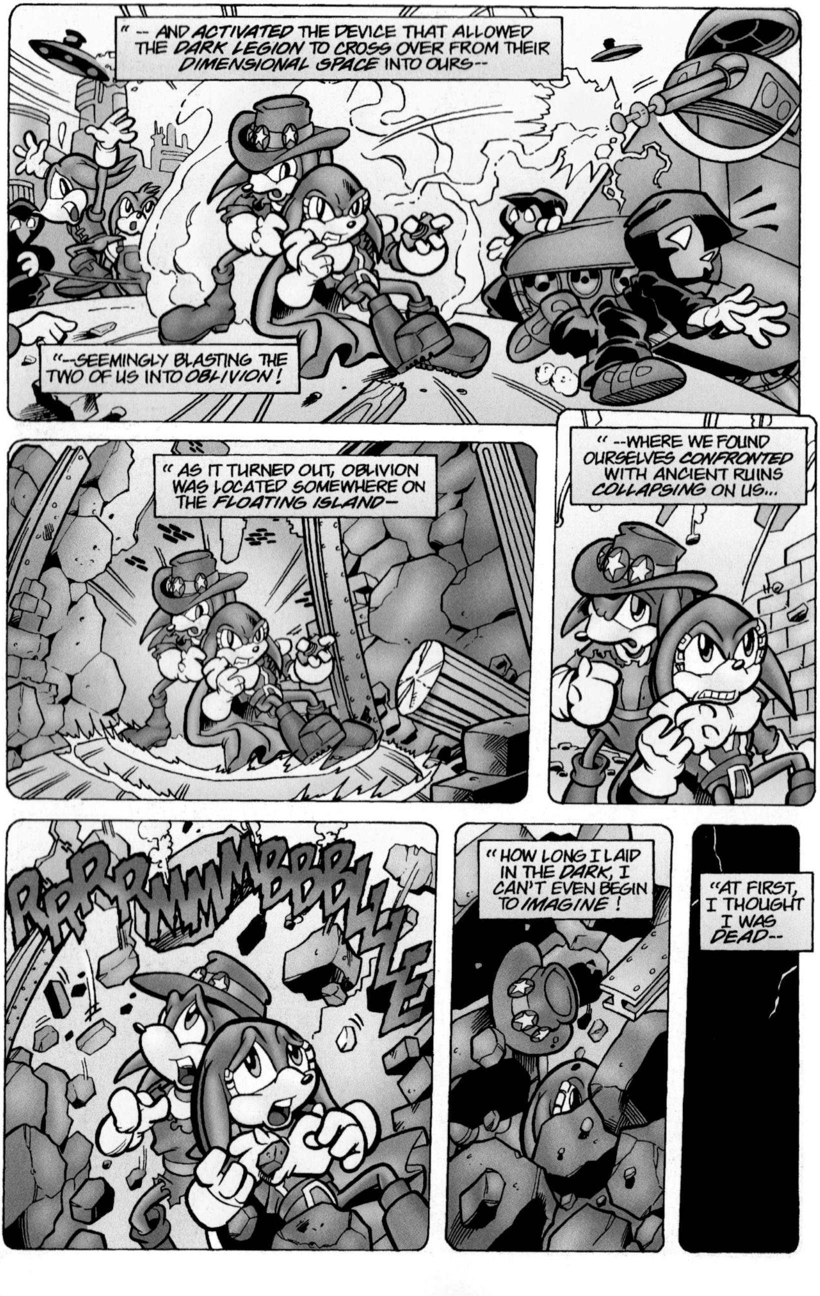
"-- AND ACTIVATED THE DEVICE THAT ALLOWED THE DARK LEGION TO CROSS OVER FROM THEIR DIMENSIONAL SPACE INTO OURS--
"--SEEMINGLY BLASTING THE TWO OF US INTO OBLIVION!
" AS IT TURNED OUT, OBLIVION WAS LOCATED SOMEWHERE ON THE FLOATING ISLAND--
" --WHERE WE FOUND OURSELVES CONFRONTED WITH ANCIENT RUINS COLLAPSING ON US...
RRRRUMMMBBBBLLLE
" HOW LONG I LAID IN THE DARK, I CAN'T EVEN BEGIN TO IMAGINE!
"AT FIRST, I THOUGHT I WAS DEAD--

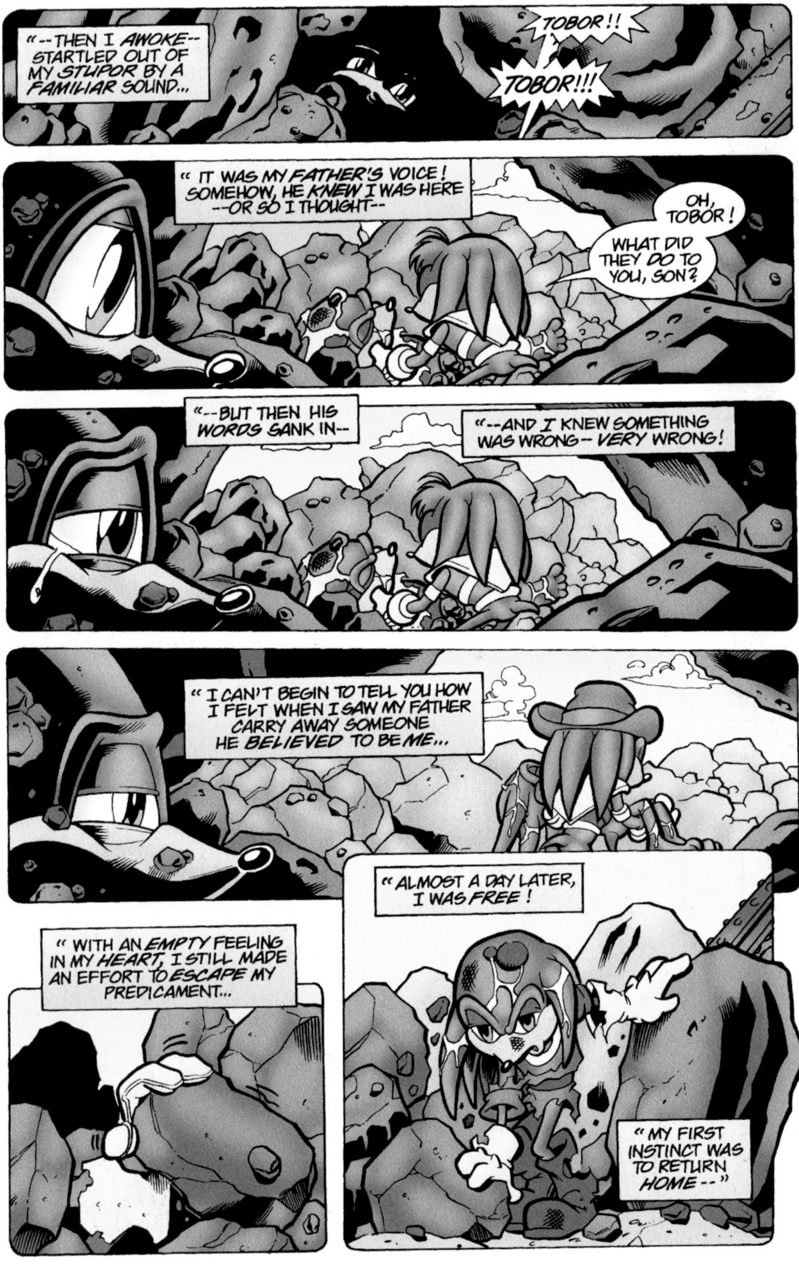
"--THEN I AWOKE-- STARTLED OUT OF MY STUPOR BY A FAMILIAR SOUND...
TOBOR!!
TOBOR!!!
" IT WAS MY FATHER'S VOICE! SOMEHOW, HE KNEW I WAS HERE --OR SO I THOUGHT--
OH, TOBOR!
WHAT DID THEY DO TO YOU, SON?
"--BUT THEN HIS WORDS SANK IN--
"--AND I KNEW SOMETHING WAS WRONG-- VERY WRONG!
" I CAN'T BEGIN TO TELL YOU HOW I FELT WHEN I SAW MY FATHER CARRY AWAY SOMEONE HE BELIEVED TO BE ME...
" WITH AN EMPTY FEELING IN MY HEART, I STILL MADE AN EFFORT TO ESCAPE MY PREDICAMENT...
" ALMOST A DAY LATER, I WAS FREE!
" MY FIRST INSTINCT WAS TO RETURN HOME--"

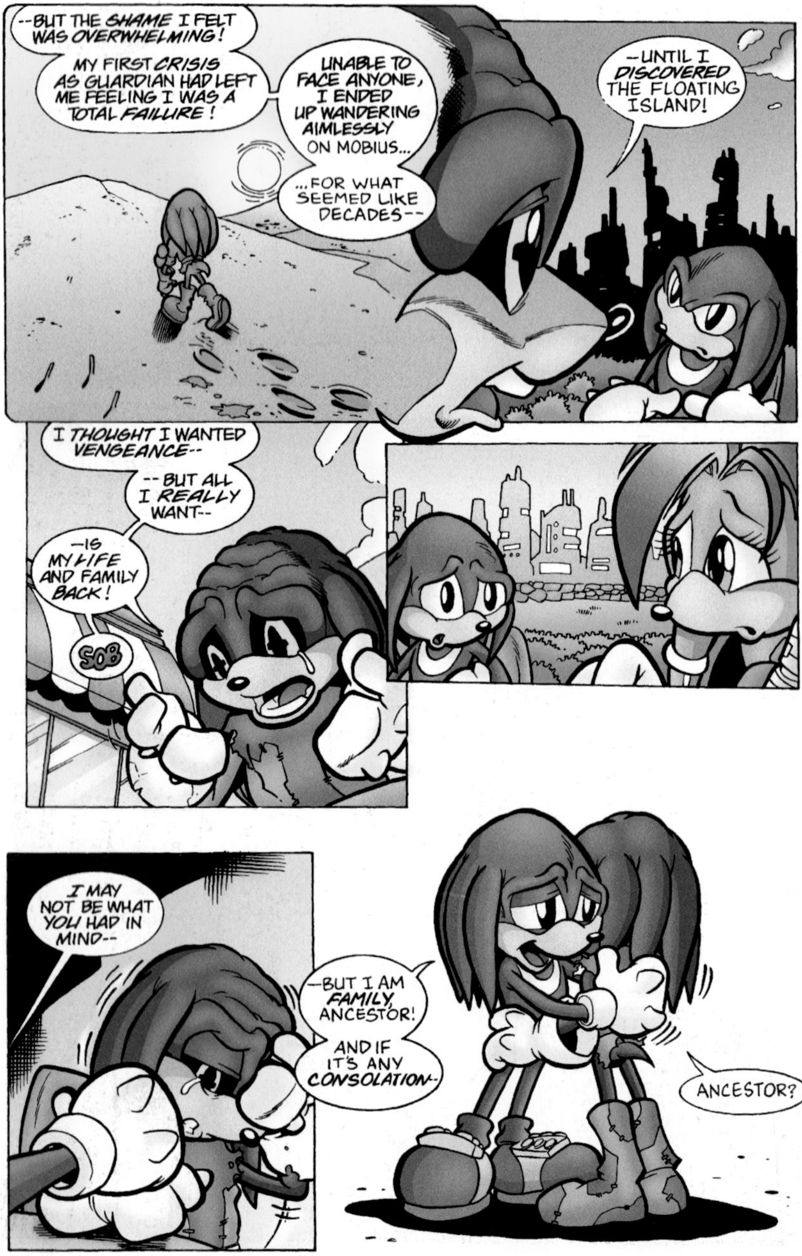
--BUT THE SHAME I FELT WAS OVERWHELMING!
MY FIRST CRISIS AS GUARDIAN HAD LEFT ME FEELING I WAS A TOTAL FAILURE!
UNABLE TO FACE ANYONE, I ENDED UP WANDERING AIMLESSLY ON MOBIUS...
...FOR WHAT SEEMED LIKE DECADES--
--UNTIL I DISCOVERED THE FLOATING ISLAND!
I THOUGHT I WANTED VENGEANCE--
--BUT ALL I REALLY WANT--
--IS MY LIFE AND FAMILY BACK!
SOB
I MAY NOT BE WHAT YOU HAD IN MIND--
--BUT I AM FAMILY, ANCESTOR!
AND IF IT'S ANY CONSOLATION--
ANCESTOR?

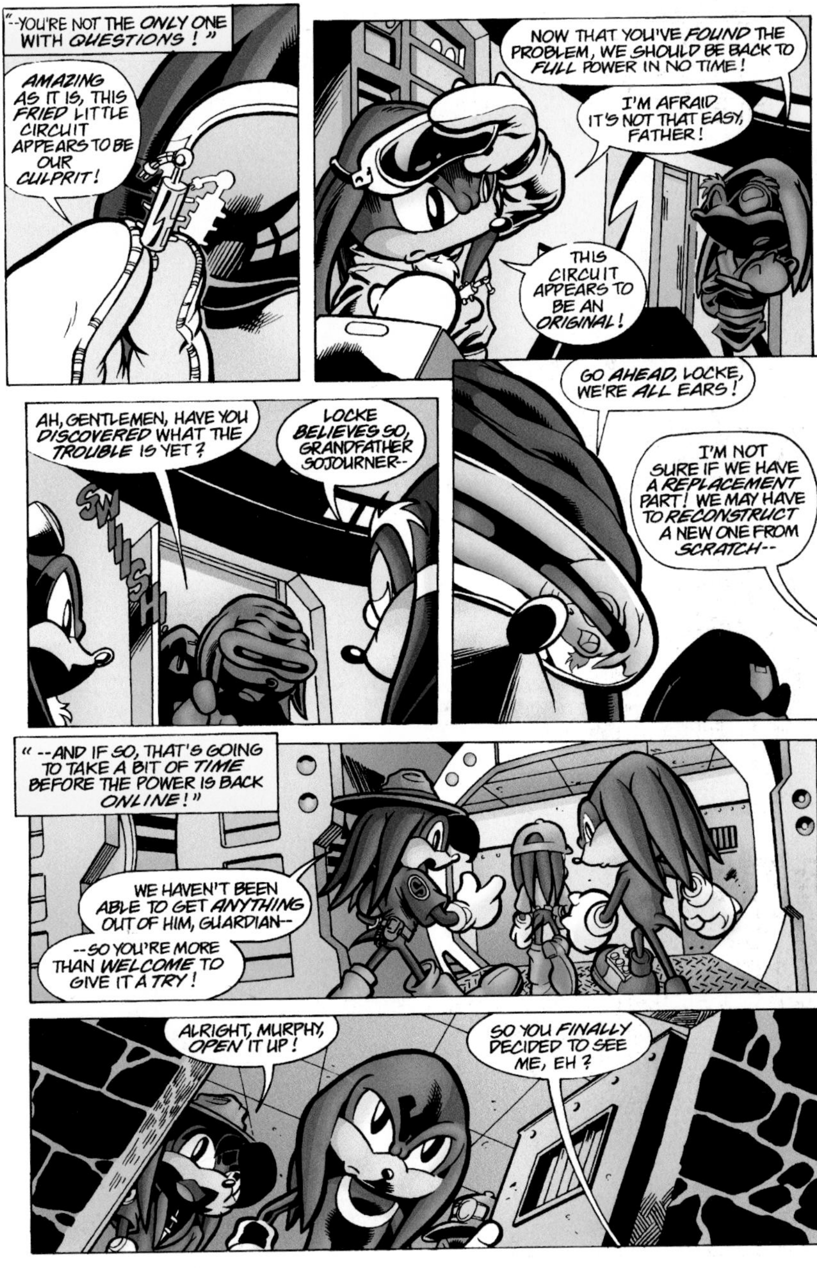
"--YOU'RE NOT THE ONLY ONE WITH QUESTIONS!"
AMAZING AS IT IS, THIS FRIED LITTLE CIRCUIT APPEARS TO BE OUR CULPRIT!
NOW THAT YOU'VE FOUND THE PROBLEM, WE SHOULD BE BACK TO FULL POWER IN NO TIME!
I'M AFRAID IT'S NOT THAT EASY, FATHER!
THIS CIRCUIT APPEARS TO BE AN ORIGINAL!
AH, GENTLEMEN, HAVE YOU DISCOVERED WHAT THE TROUBLE IS YET?
SWIISH!
LOCKE BELIEVES SO, GRANDFATHER SOJOURNER--
GO AHEAD, LOCKE, WE'RE ALL EARS!
I'M NOT SURE IF WE HAVE A REPLACEMENT PART! WE MAY HAVE TO RECONSTRUCT A NEW ONE FROM SCRATCH--
"--AND IF SO, THAT'S GOING TO TAKE A BIT OF TIME BEFORE THE POWER IS BACK ONLINE!"
WE HAVEN'T BEEN ABLE TO GET ANYTHING OUT OF HIM, GUARDIAN--
--SO YOU'RE MORE THAN WELCOME TO GIVE IT A TRY!
ALRIGHT, MURPHY, OPEN IT UP!
SO YOU FINALLY DECIDED TO SEE ME, EH?

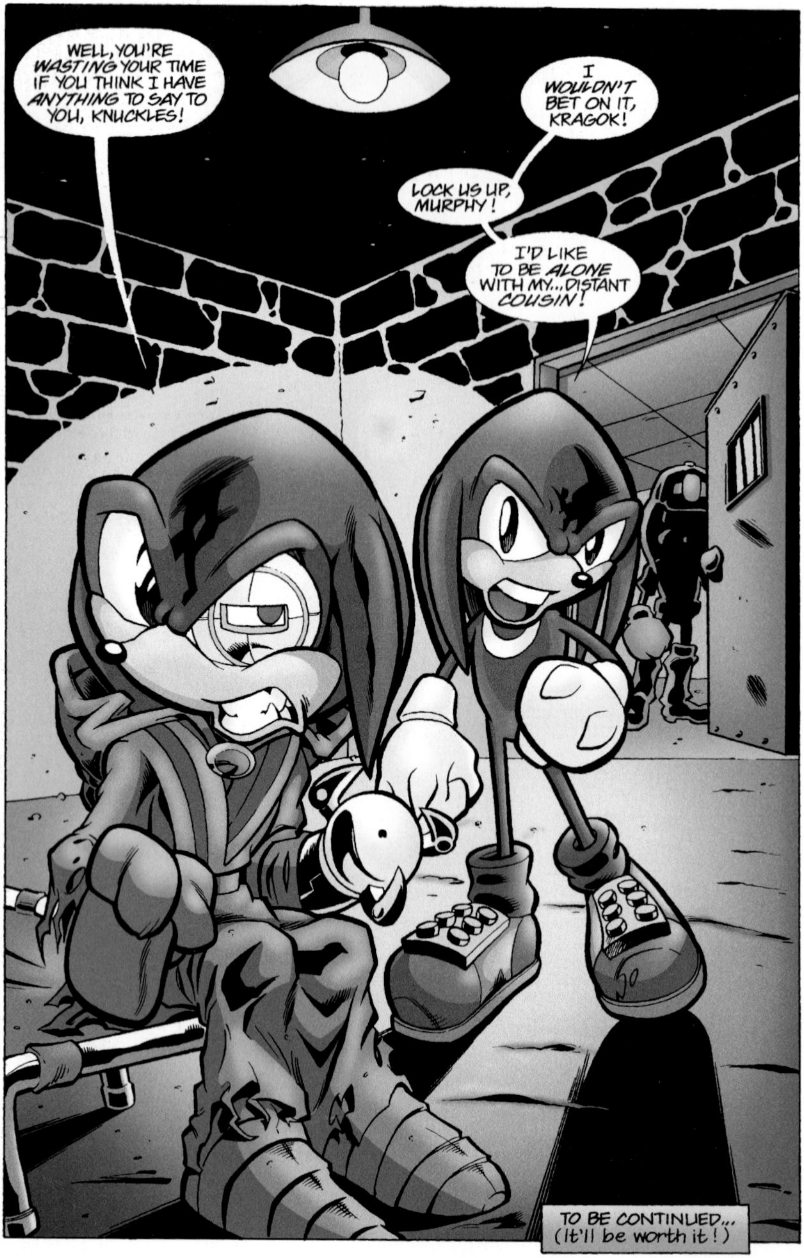
WELL, YOU'RE WASTING YOUR TIME IF YOU THINK I HAVE ANYTHING TO SAY TO YOU, KNUCKLES!
I WOULDN'T BET ON IT, KRAGOK!
LOCK US UP, MURPHY!
I'D LIKE TO BE ALONE WITH MY... DISTANT COUSIN!
TO BE CONTINUED... (It'll be worth it!)

TAKE AN EXCLUSIVE LOOK BEHIND THE SCENES OF *KNUCKLES THE ECHIDNA*, AS WE REVEAL...

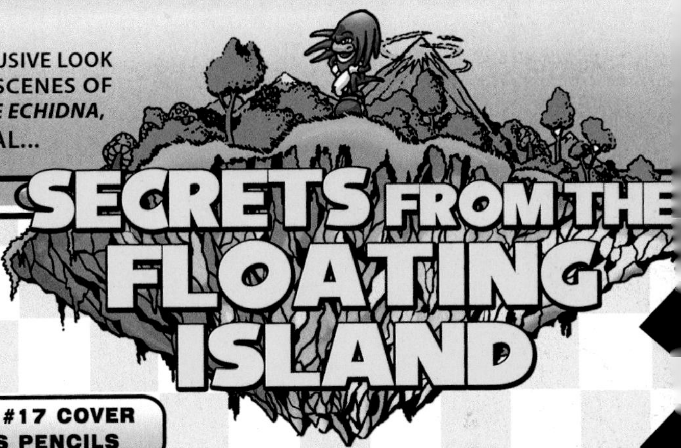

SECRETS FROM THE FLOATING ISLAND

KNUCKLES #17 COVER KNUCKLES PENCILS

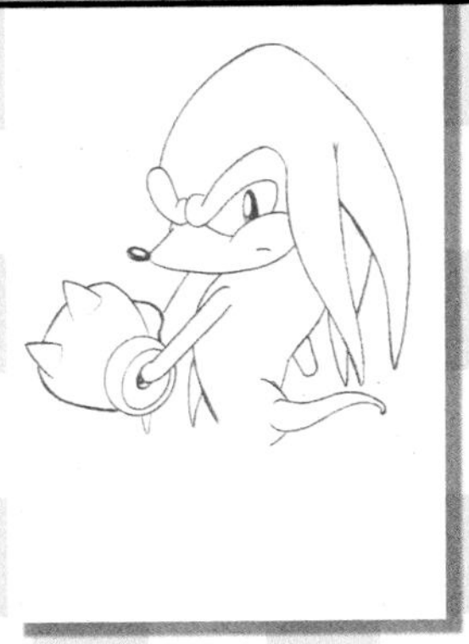

KNUCKLES #17 COVER PENCILS BY PATRICK "SPAZ" SPAZIANT

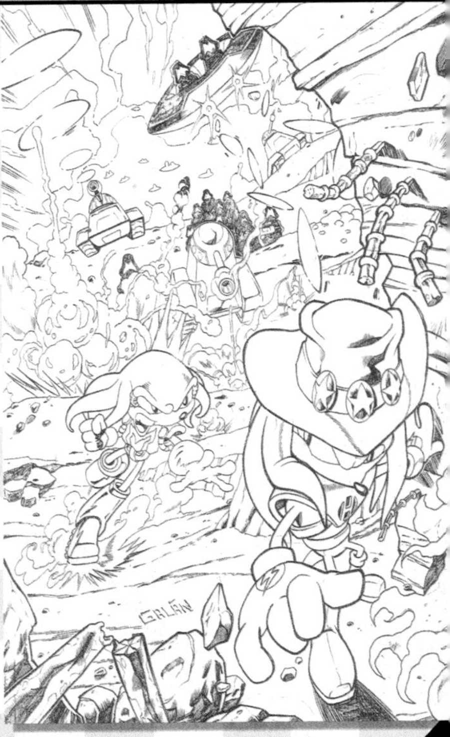
GALÁN

KNUCKLES #18 COVER PENCILS

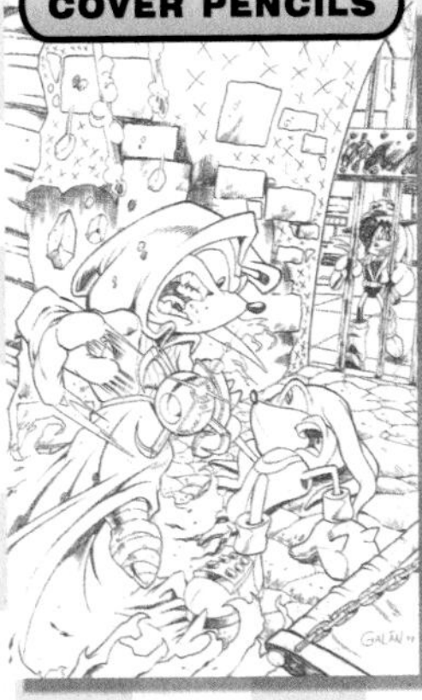

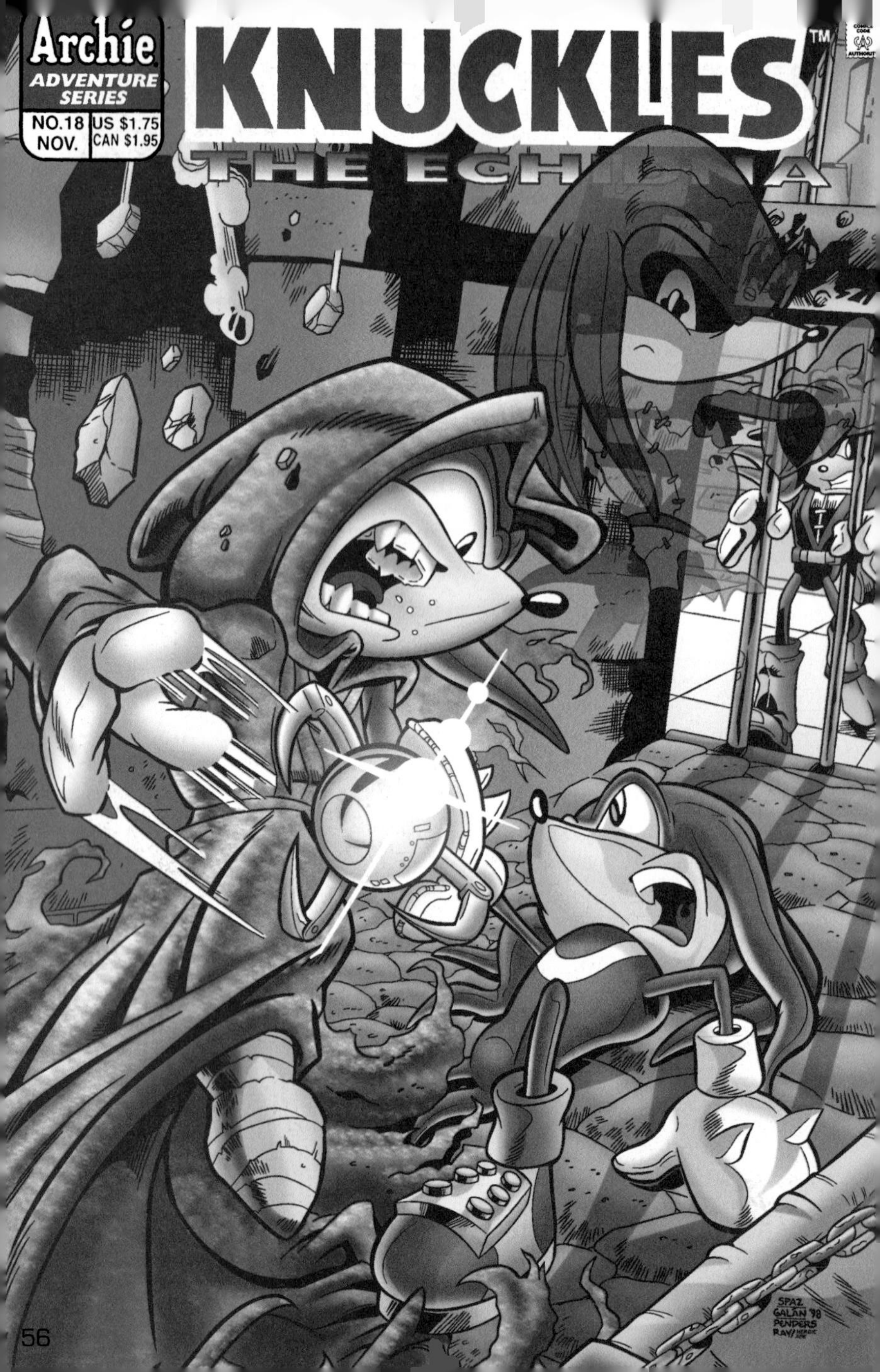
Archie
ADVENTURE SERIES
NO.18
NOV.
US $1.75
CAN $1.95
KNUCKLES™
THE ECH
A
SPAZ
GALAN '98
PENDERS
RAY/

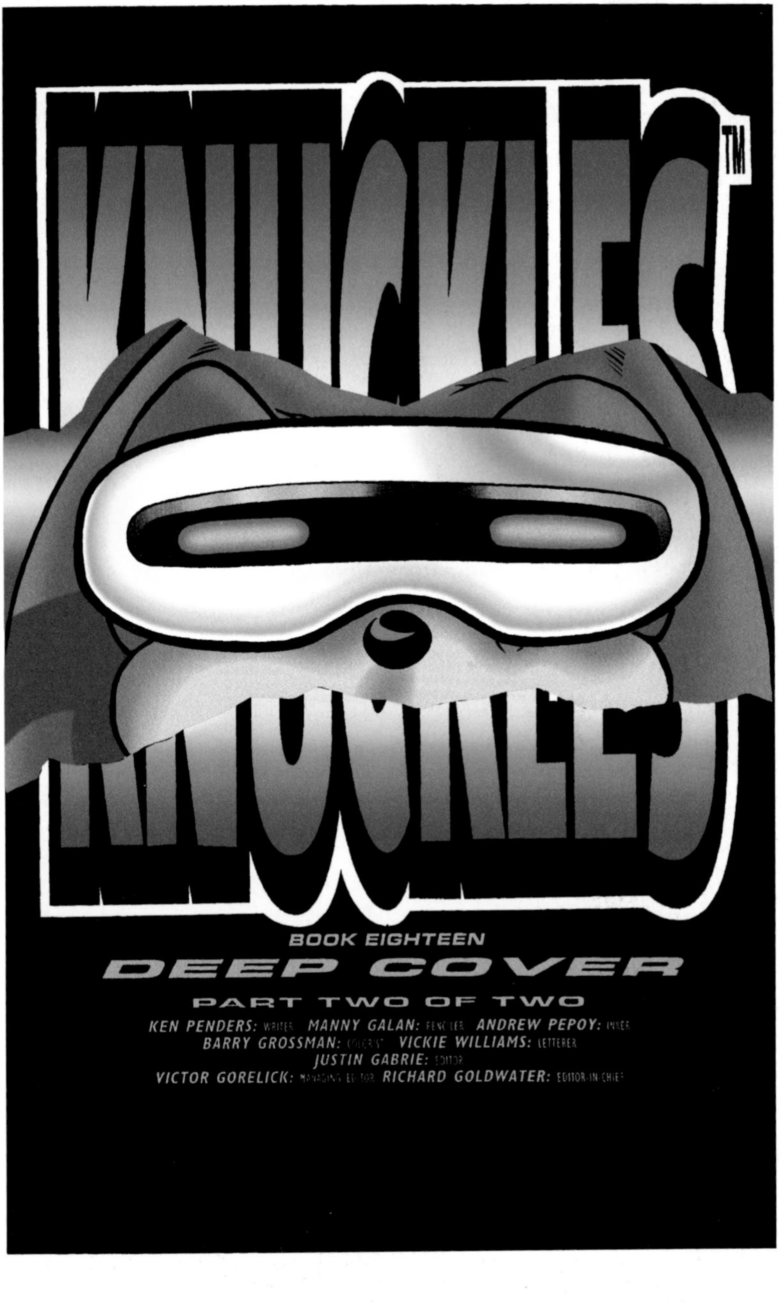
KNUCKLES™
BOOK EIGHTEEN
DEEP COVER
PART TWO OF TWO
KEN PENDERS: WRITER MANNY GALAN: PENCILER ANDREW PEPOY: INKER
BARRY GROSSMAN: COLORIST VICKIE WILLIAMS: LETTERER
JUSTIN GABRIE: EDITOR
VICTOR GORELICK: MANAGING EDITOR RICHARD GOLDWATER: EDITOR-IN-CHIEF

BORN TO THE MOST NOBLE OF ECHIDNA HOUSES, THE LATEST TO CONTINUE THE FAMILY HERITAGE AND RESPONSIBILITY AS **GUARDIAN OF THE FLOATING ISLAND,** DEFENDER OF ALL FROM THE FORCES OF EVIL FROM THE WORLD BEYOND AS WELL AS THOSE WHO WOULD THREATEN WITHIN, HE IS NONE OTHER THAN **KNUCKLES THE ECHIDNA!**

LAST ISSUE, KNUCKLES DISCOVERED THAT A WANDERING STRANGER JULIE-SU HAD ENCOUNTERED WAS IN FACT HIS **GRANDFATHER TOBOR,** WHO HAD BEEN THE VICTIM OF A CASE OF MISTAKEN IDENTITY. SO GREAT WAS HIS SHAME, HAVING LOST TO THE **DARK LEGION** IN THE FIRST CRISIS HE HAD EVER FACED, THAT TOBOR FOUND HIMSELF UNABLE TO RETURN HOME AND FACE HIS FAMILY.

SENSING AN INSIDIOUS DARK LEGION PLOT BEHIND THIS, KNUCKLES HAS VENTURED FORTH TO THE JAIL CELLS OF THE **ECHIDNA SECURITY AGENCY,** WHERE THE ONE ECHIDNA WHO MAY HAVE THE ANSWERS IS CURRENTLY INCARCERATED, WHILE HIS GRANDFATHER TOBOR IS LEFT IN THE CARE OF **LARA-LE** AND **JULIE-SU...**

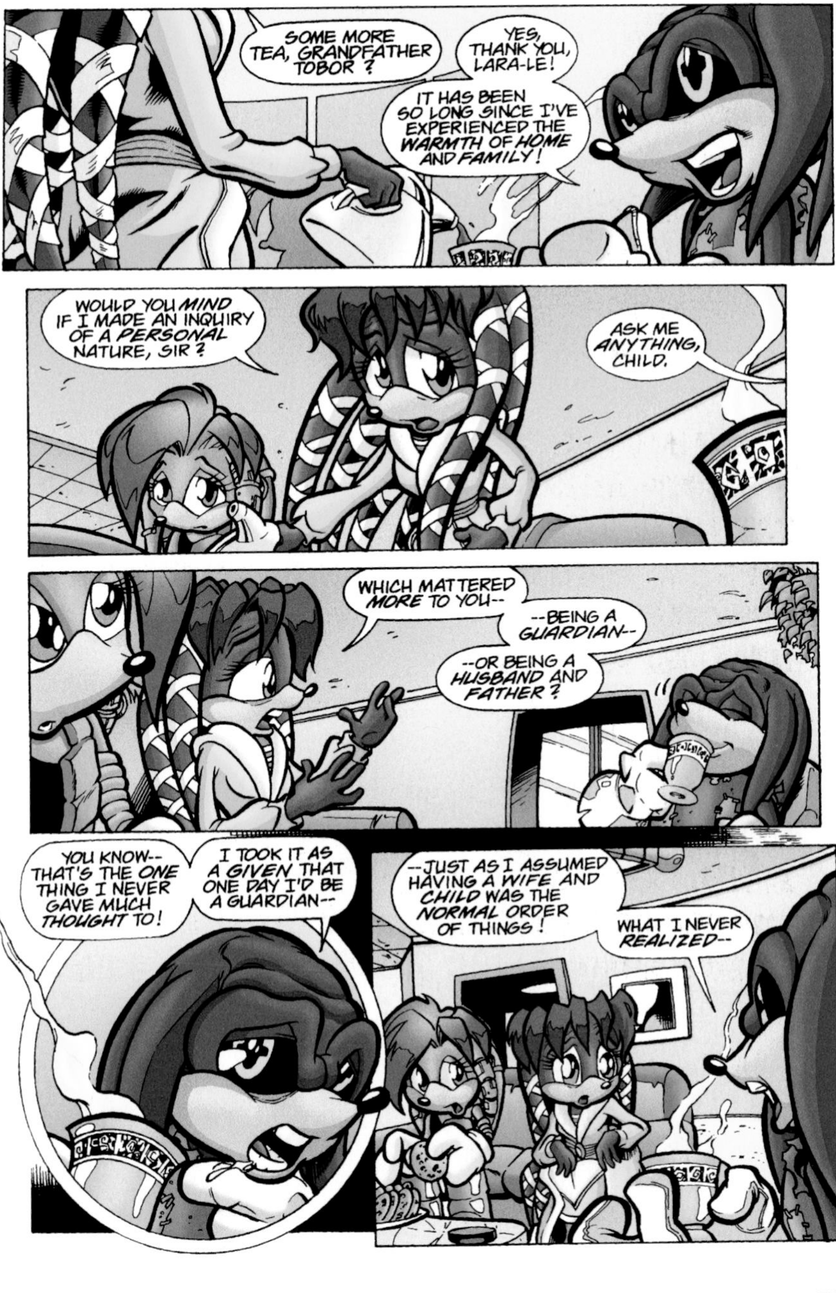
SOME MORE TEA, GRANDFATHER TOBOR ?
YES, THANK YOU, LARA-LE!
IT HAS BEEN SO LONG SINCE I'VE EXPERIENCED THE WARMTH OF HOME AND FAMILY!
WOULD YOU MIND IF I MADE AN INQUIRY OF A PERSONAL NATURE, SIR ?
ASK ME ANYTHING, CHILD.
WHICH MATTERED MORE TO YOU--
--BEING A GUARDIAN--
--OR BEING A HUSBAND AND FATHER ?
YOU KNOW-- THAT'S THE ONE THING I NEVER GAVE MUCH THOUGHT TO!
I TOOK IT AS A GIVEN THAT ONE DAY I'D BE A GUARDIAN--
--JUST AS I ASSUMED HAVING A WIFE AND CHILD WAS THE NORMAL ORDER OF THINGS !
WHAT I NEVER REALIZED--

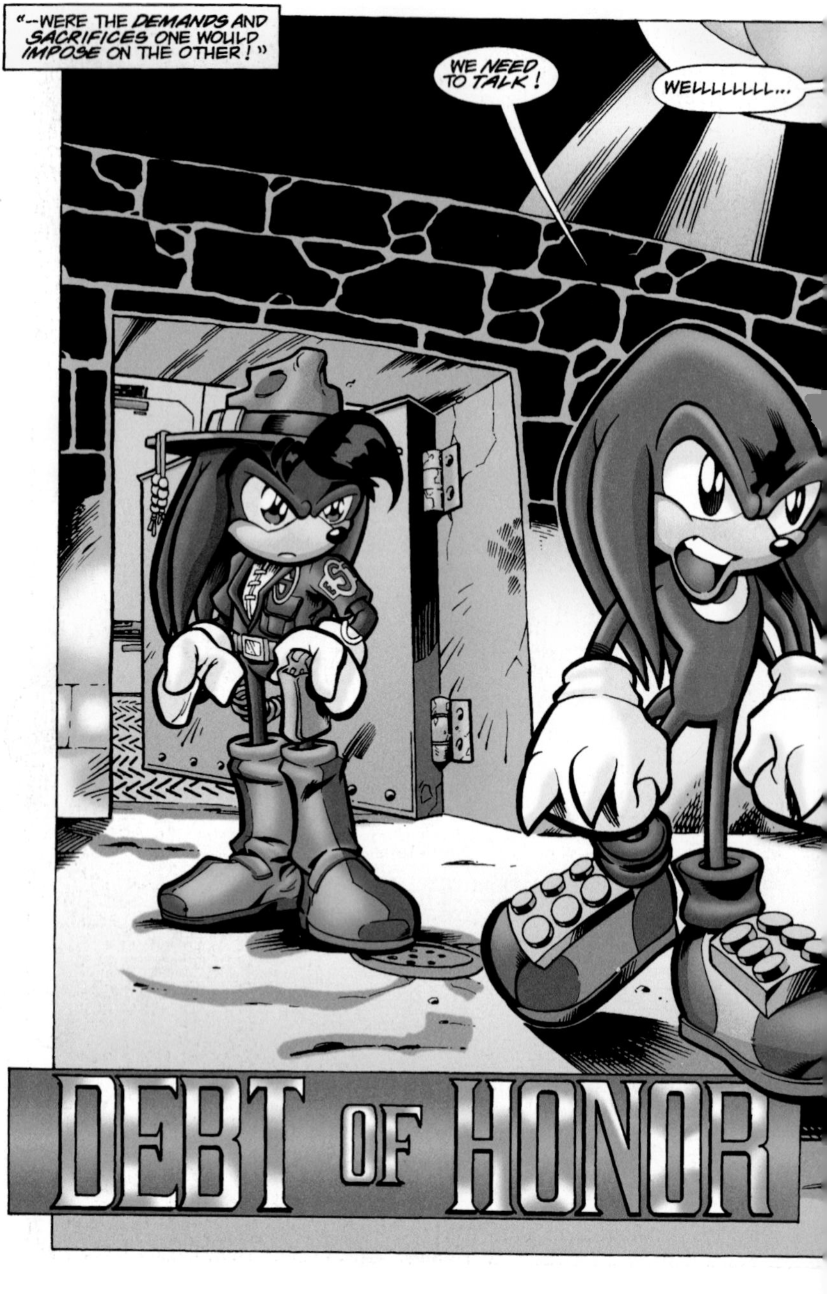
"--WERE THE DEMANDS AND SACRIFICES ONE WOULD IMPOSE ON THE OTHER!"
WE NEED TO TALK!
WELLLLLLLLL...
DEBT OF HONOR

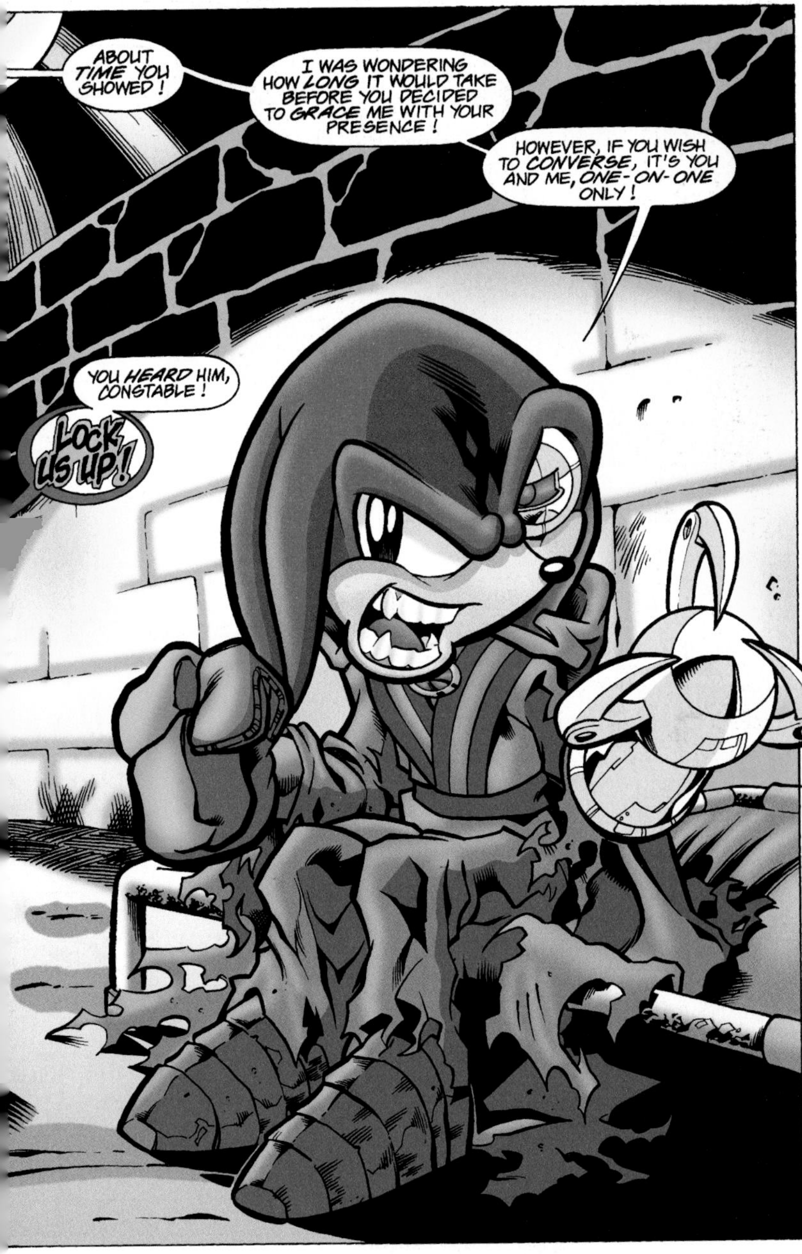
ABOUT TIME YOU SHOWED!
I WAS WONDERING HOW LONG IT WOULD TAKE BEFORE YOU DECIDED TO GRACE ME WITH YOUR PRESENCE!
HOWEVER, IF YOU WISH TO CONVERSE, IT'S YOU AND ME, ONE-ON-ONE ONLY!
YOU HEARD HIM, CONSTABLE!
LOCK US UP!

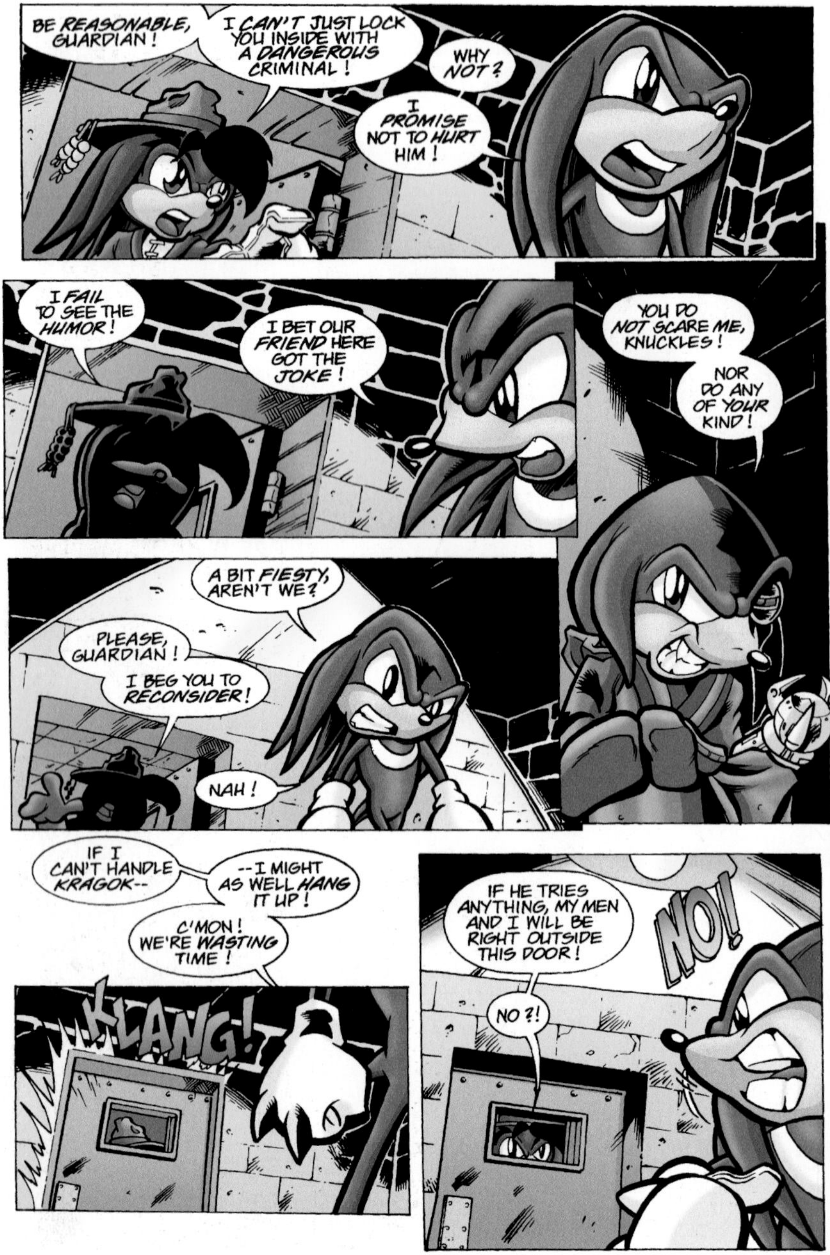
BE REASONABLE, GUARDIAN!
I CAN'T JUST LOCK YOU INSIDE WITH A DANGEROUS CRIMINAL!
WHY NOT?
I PROMISE NOT TO HURT HIM!
I FAIL TO SEE THE HUMOR!
I BET OUR FRIEND HERE GOT THE JOKE!
YOU DO NOT SCARE ME, KNUCKLES!
NOR DO ANY OF YOUR KIND!
A BIT FIESTY, AREN'T WE?
PLEASE, GUARDIAN!
I BEG YOU TO RECONSIDER!
NAH!
IF I CAN'T HANDLE KRAGOK--
--I MIGHT AS WELL HANG IT UP!
C'MON! WE'RE WASTING TIME!
KLANG!
IF HE TRIES ANYTHING, MY MEN AND I WILL BE RIGHT OUTSIDE THIS DOOR!
NO?!
NO!

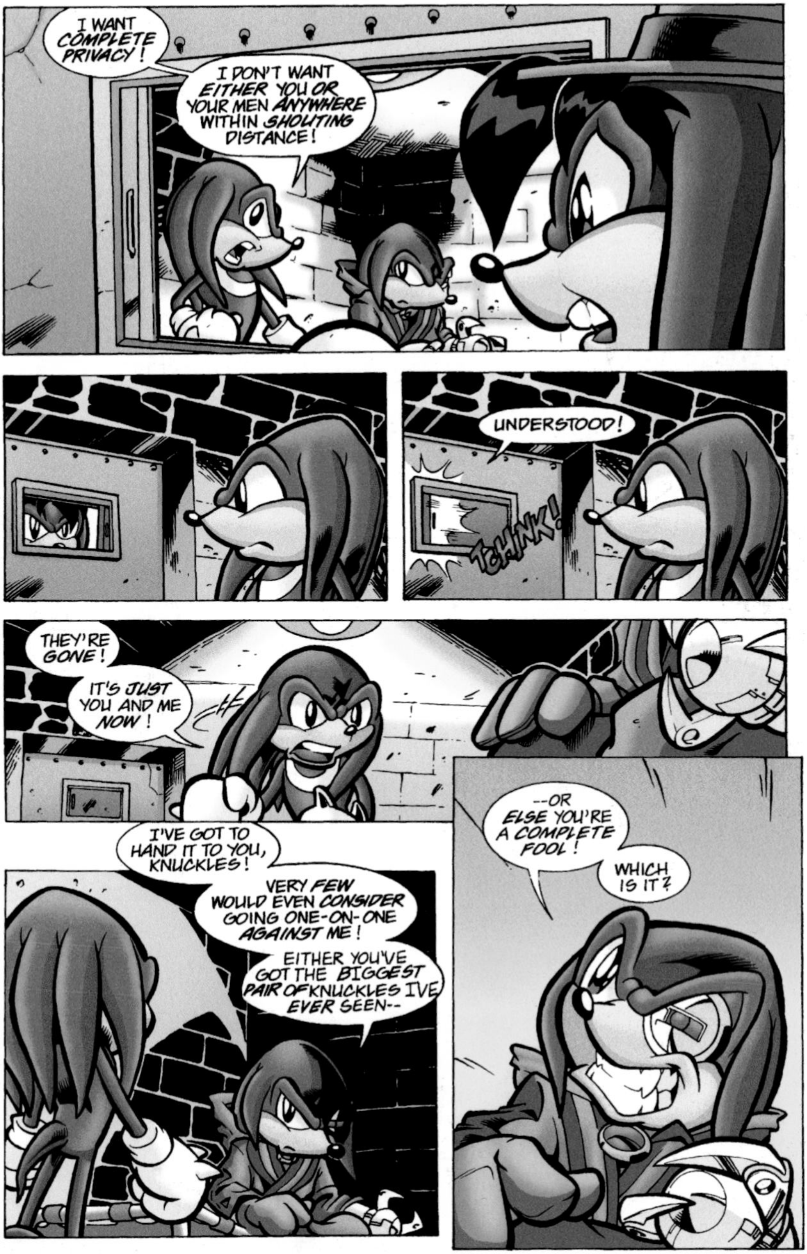
I WANT COMPLETE PRIVACY!
I DON'T WANT EITHER YOU OR YOUR MEN ANYWHERE WITHIN SHOUTING DISTANCE!
UNDERSTOOD!
TCHINK!
THEY'RE GONE!
IT'S JUST YOU AND ME NOW!
I'VE GOT TO HAND IT TO YOU, KNUCKLES!
VERY FEW WOULD EVEN CONSIDER GOING ONE-ON-ONE AGAINST ME!
EITHER YOU'VE GOT THE BIGGEST PAIR OF KNUCKLES I'VE EVER SEEN--
--OR ELSE YOU'RE A COMPLETE FOOL!
WHICH IS IT?

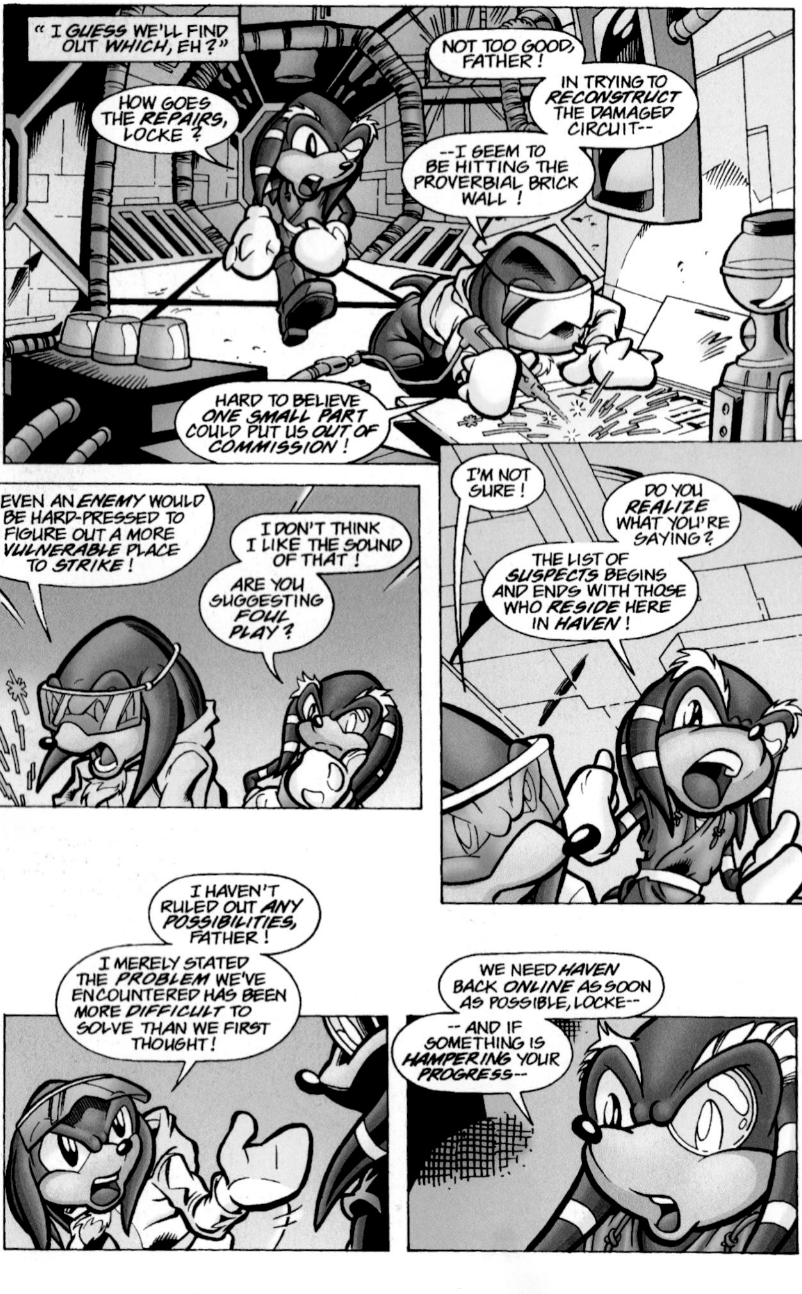
"I GUESS WE'LL FIND OUT WHICH, EH?"
HOW GOES THE REPAIRS, LOCKE?
NOT TOO GOOD, FATHER!
IN TRYING TO RECONSTRUCT THE DAMAGED CIRCUIT--
--I SEEM TO BE HITTING THE PROVERBIAL BRICK WALL!
HARD TO BELIEVE ONE SMALL PART COULD PUT US OUT OF COMMISSION!
EVEN AN ENEMY WOULD BE HARD-PRESSED TO FIGURE OUT A MORE VULNERABLE PLACE TO STRIKE!
I DON'T THINK I LIKE THE SOUND OF THAT!
ARE YOU SUGGESTING FOUL PLAY?
I'M NOT SURE!
DO YOU REALIZE WHAT YOU'RE SAYING?
THE LIST OF SUSPECTS BEGINS AND ENDS WITH THOSE WHO RESIDE HERE IN HAVEN!
I HAVEN'T RULED OUT ANY POSSIBILITIES, FATHER!
I MERELY STATED THE PROBLEM WE'VE ENCOUNTERED HAS BEEN MORE DIFFICULT TO SOLVE THAN WE FIRST THOUGHT!
WE NEED HAVEN BACK ONLINE AS SOON AS POSSIBLE, LOCKE--
-- AND IF SOMETHING IS HAMPERING YOUR PROGRESS--

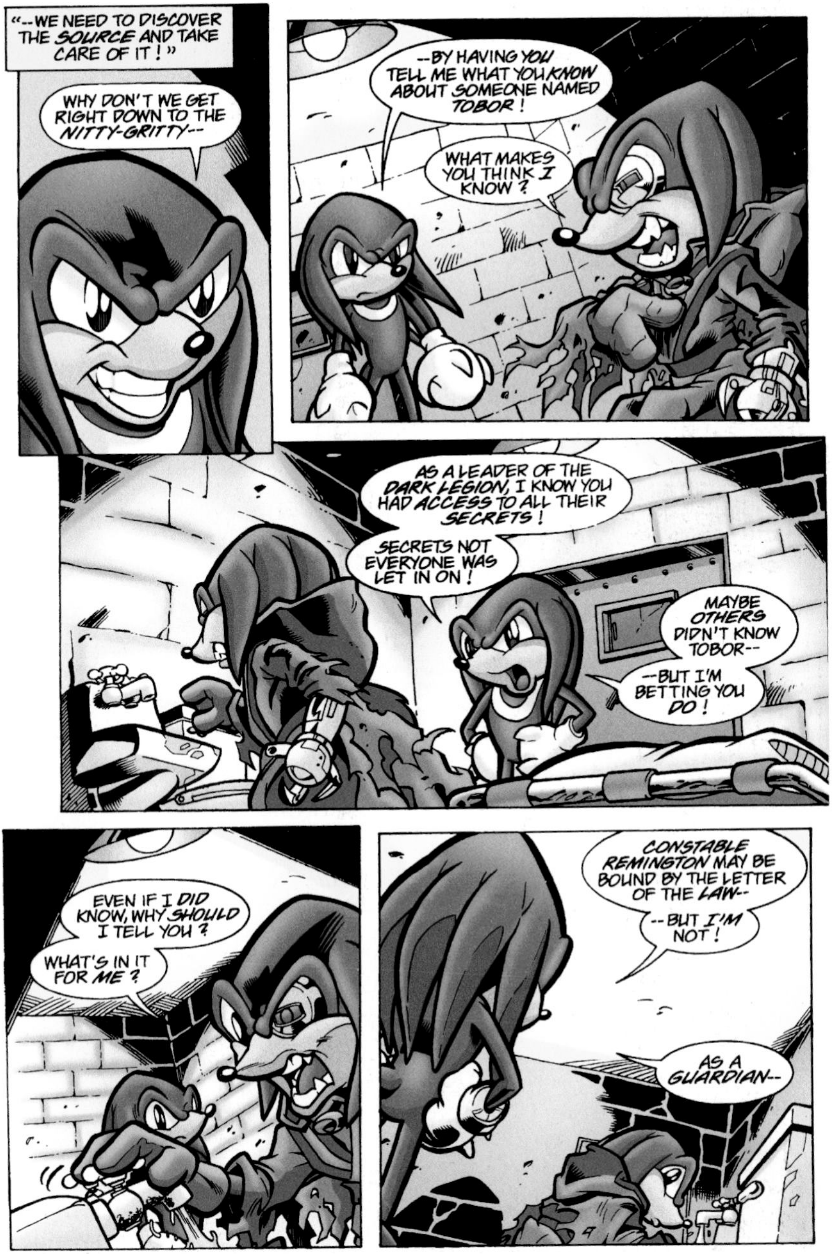
"--WE NEED TO DISCOVER THE SOURCE AND TAKE CARE OF IT!"
WHY DON'T WE GET RIGHT DOWN TO THE NITTY-GRITTY--
--BY HAVING YOU TELL ME WHAT YOU KNOW ABOUT SOMEONE NAMED TOBOR!
WHAT MAKES YOU THINK I KNOW?
AS A LEADER OF THE DARK LEGION, I KNOW YOU HAD ACCESS TO ALL THEIR SECRETS!
SECRETS NOT EVERYONE WAS LET IN ON!
MAYBE OTHERS DIDN'T KNOW TOBOR--
--BUT I'M BETTING YOU DO!
EVEN IF I DID KNOW, WHY SHOULD I TELL YOU?
WHAT'S IN IT FOR ME?
CONSTABLE REMINGTON MAY BE BOUND BY THE LETTER OF THE LAW--
--BUT I'M NOT!
AS A GUARDIAN--

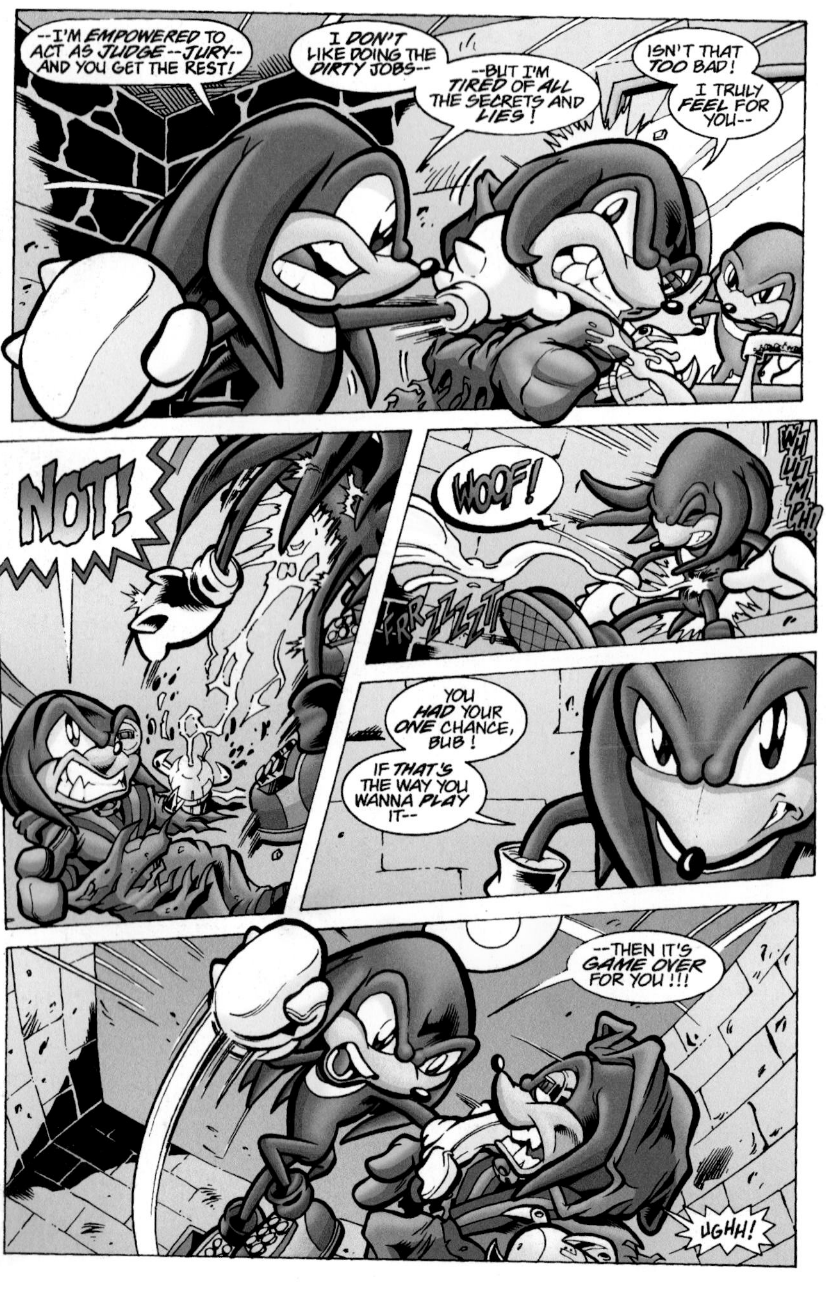
--I'M EMPOWERED TO ACT AS JUDGE--JURY--AND YOU GET THE REST!
I DON'T LIKE DOING THE DIRTY JOBS--
--BUT I'M TIRED OF ALL THE SECRETS AND LIES!
ISN'T THAT TOO BAD!
I TRULY FEEL FOR YOU--
NOT!
WOOF!
WHUUMPH!
F-RRZZZZT!
YOU HAD YOUR ONE CHANCE, BUB!
IF THAT'S THE WAY YOU WANNA PLAY IT--
--THEN IT'S GAME OVER FOR YOU!!!
UGHH!

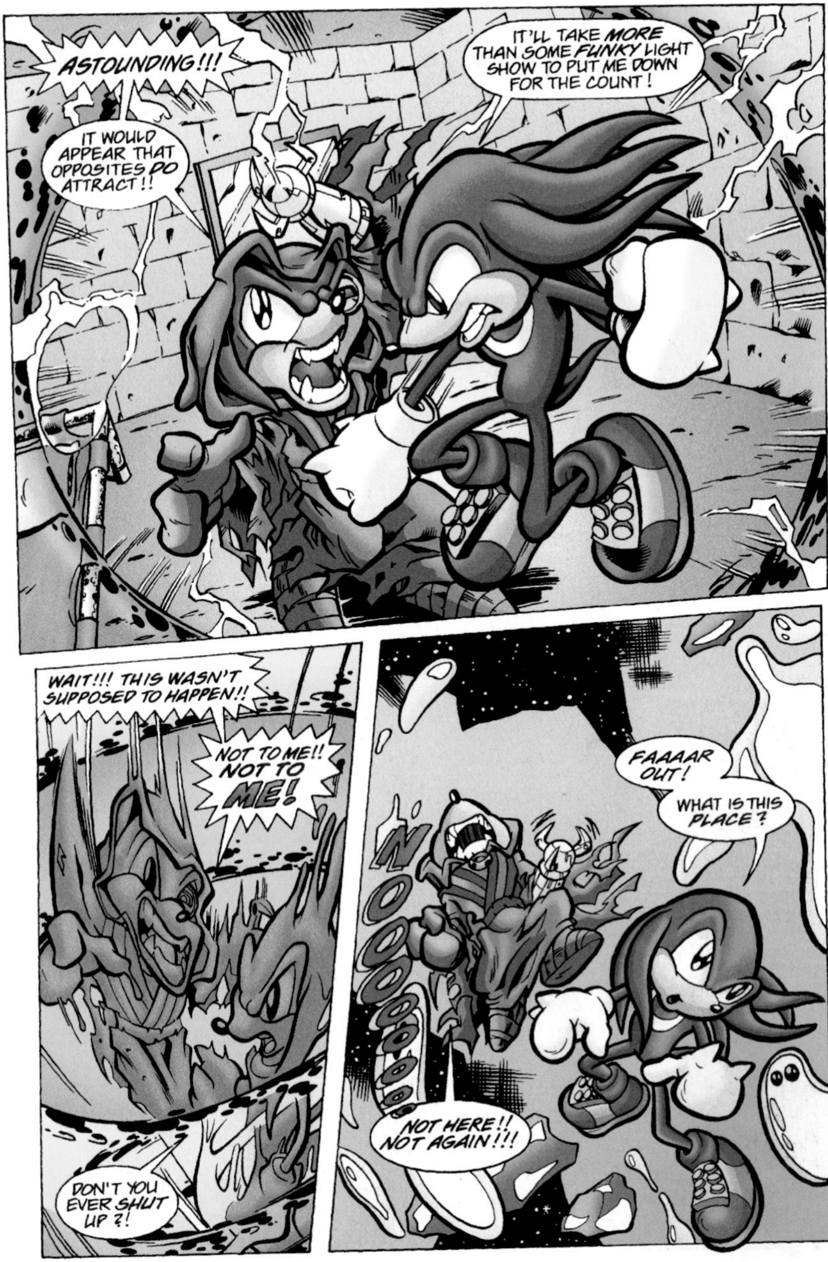
ASTOUNDING!!!
IT WOULD APPEAR THAT OPPOSITES DO ATTRACT!!
IT'LL TAKE MORE THAN SOME FUNKY LIGHT SHOW TO PUT ME DOWN FOR THE COUNT!
WAIT!!! THIS WASN'T SUPPOSED TO HAPPEN!!
NOT TO ME!! NOT TO ME!
DON'T YOU EVER SHUT UP?!
FAAAAR OUT!
WHAT IS THIS PLACE?
NOT HERE!! NOT AGAIN!!!

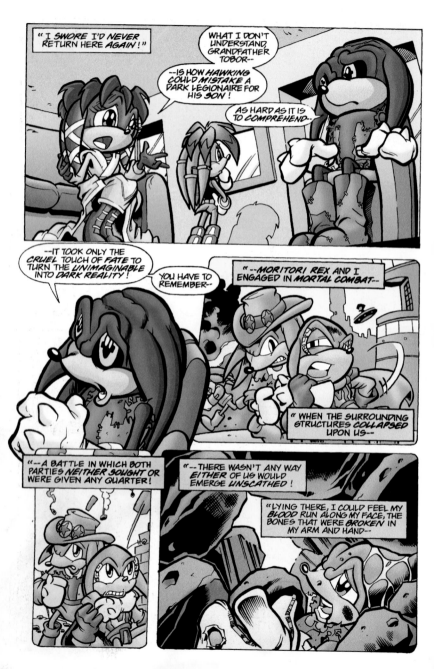

"I SWORE I'D NEVER RETURN HERE *AGAIN*!"

WHAT I DON'T UNDERSTAND, GRANDFATHER TOBOR--

--IS HOW *HAWKING* COULD MISTAKE A DARK LEGIONAIRE FOR HIS *SON*!

AS HARD AS IT IS TO *COMPREHEND*--

--IT TOOK ONLY THE *CRUEL* TOUCH OF *FATE* TO TURN THE *UNIMAGINABLE* INTO *DARK REALITY*!

YOU HAVE TO REMEMBER--

"--*MORITORI REX* AND I ENGAGED IN *MORTAL COMBAT*--

" WHEN THE SURROUNDING STRUCTURES *COLLAPSED* UPON US--

"--A BATTLE IN WHICH BOTH PARTIES *NEITHER SOUGHT OR* WERE GIVEN ANY QUARTER!

"--THERE WASN'T ANY WAY *EITHER* OF US WOULD EMERGE *UNSCATHED*!

"LYING THERE, I COULD FEEL MY *BLOOD* RUN ALONG MY FACE, THE BONES THAT WERE *BROKEN* IN MY ARM AND HAND--

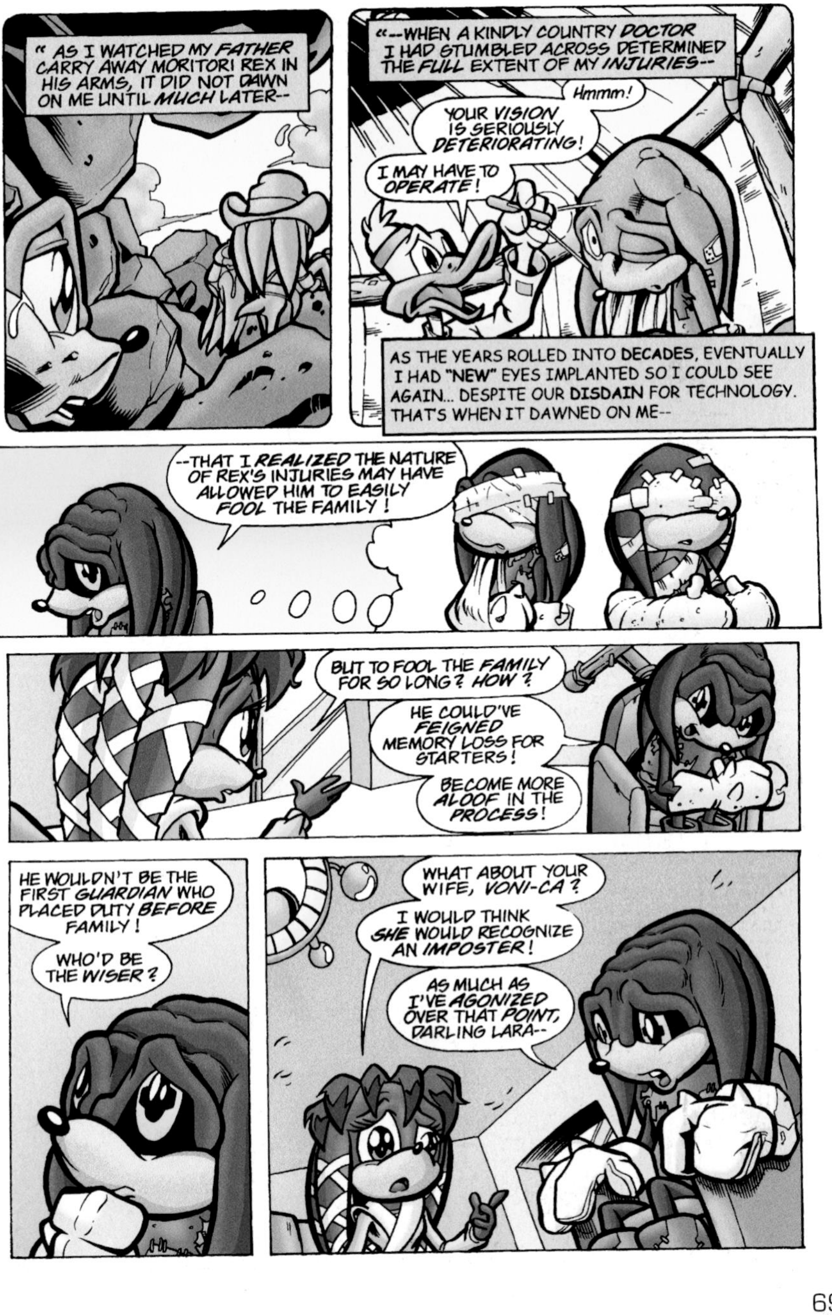
"AS I WATCHED MY FATHER CARRY AWAY MORITORI REX IN HIS ARMS, IT DID NOT DAWN ON ME UNTIL MUCH LATER--
"--WHEN A KINDLY COUNTRY DOCTOR I HAD STUMBLED ACROSS DETERMINED THE FULL EXTENT OF MY INJURIES--
Hmmm!
YOUR VISION IS SERIOUSLY DETERIORATING!
I MAY HAVE TO OPERATE!
AS THE YEARS ROLLED INTO DECADES, EVENTUALLY I HAD "NEW" EYES IMPLANTED SO I COULD SEE AGAIN... DESPITE OUR DISDAIN FOR TECHNOLOGY. THAT'S WHEN IT DAWNED ON ME--
--THAT I REALIZED THE NATURE OF REX'S INJURIES MAY HAVE ALLOWED HIM TO EASILY FOOL THE FAMILY!
BUT TO FOOL THE FAMILY FOR SO LONG? HOW?
HE COULD'VE FEIGNED MEMORY LOSS FOR STARTERS!
BECOME MORE ALOOF IN THE PROCESS!
HE WOULDN'T BE THE FIRST GUARDIAN WHO PLACED DUTY BEFORE FAMILY!
WHO'D BE THE WISER?
WHAT ABOUT YOUR WIFE, VONI-CA?
I WOULD THINK SHE WOULD RECOGNIZE AN IMPOSTER!
AS MUCH AS I'VE AGONIZED OVER THAT POINT, DARLING LARA--

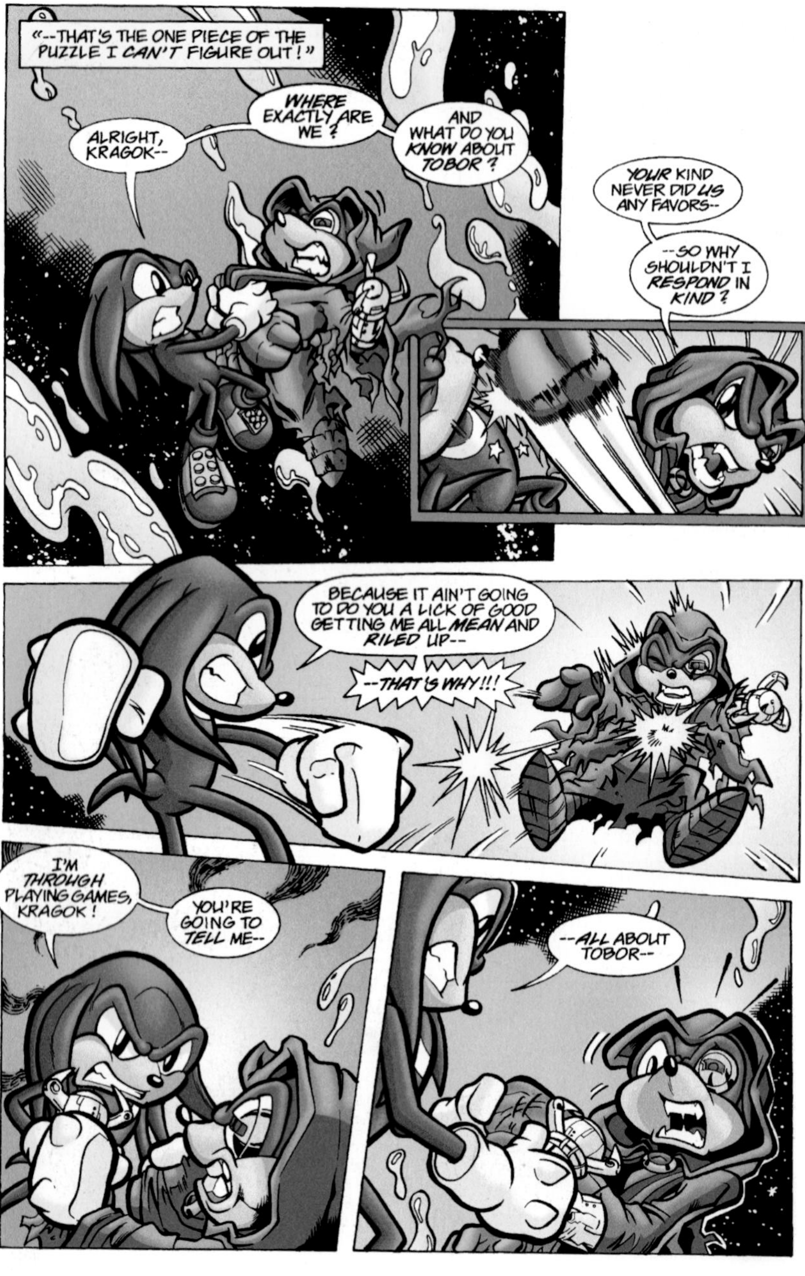
"--THAT'S THE ONE PIECE OF THE PUZZLE I CAN'T FIGURE OUT!"
ALRIGHT, KRAGOK--
WHERE EXACTLY ARE WE?
AND WHAT DO YOU KNOW ABOUT TOBOR?
YOUR KIND NEVER DID US ANY FAVORS--
--SO WHY SHOULDN'T I RESPOND IN KIND?
BECAUSE IT AIN'T GOING TO DO YOU A LICK OF GOOD GETTING ME ALL MEAN AND RILED UP--
--THAT'S WHY!!!
I'M THROUGH PLAYING GAMES, KRAGOK!
YOU'RE GOING TO TELL ME--
--ALL ABOUT TOBOR--

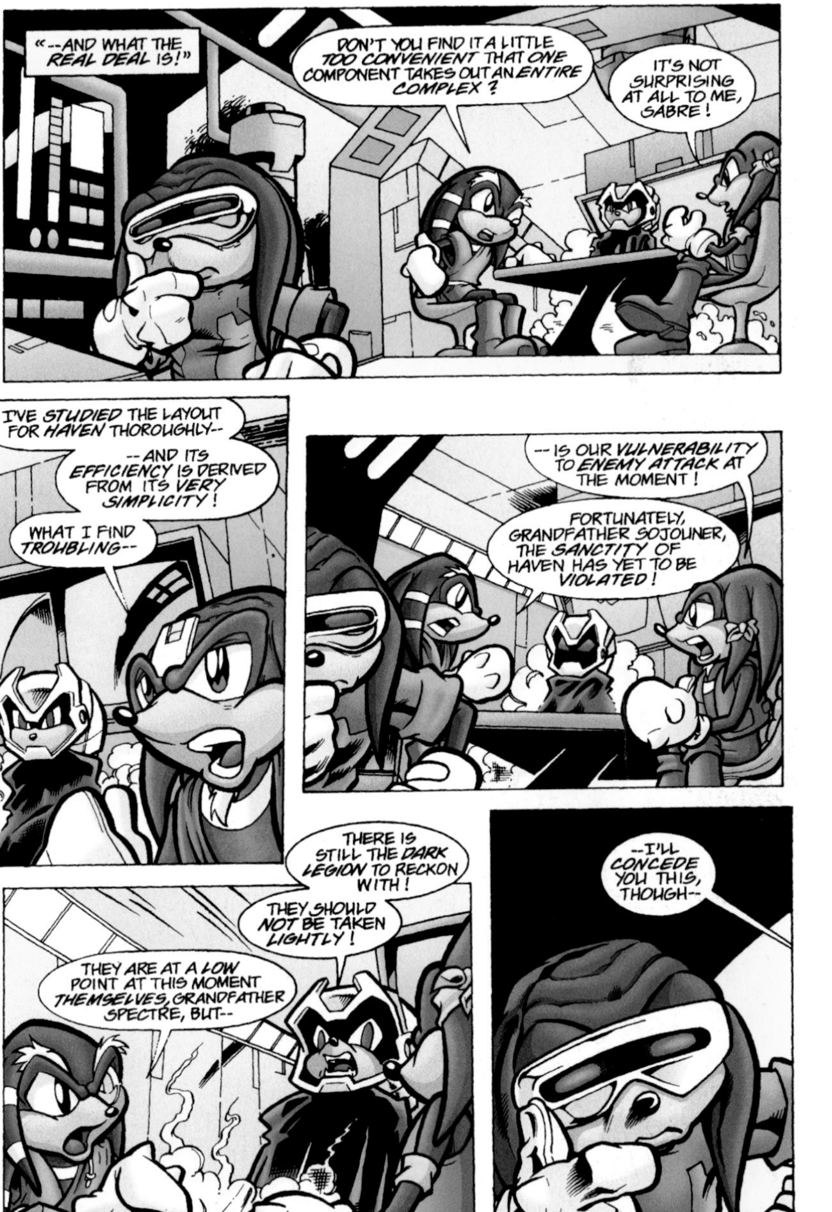
"--AND WHAT THE REAL DEAL IS!"
DON'T YOU FIND IT A LITTLE TOO CONVENIENT THAT ONE COMPONENT TAKES OUT AN ENTIRE COMPLEX?
IT'S NOT SURPRISING AT ALL TO ME, SABRE!
I'VE STUDIED THE LAYOUT FOR HAVEN THOROUGHLY--
--AND ITS EFFICIENCY IS DERIVED FROM ITS VERY SIMPLICITY!
WHAT I FIND TROUBLING--
--IS OUR VULNERABILITY TO ENEMY ATTACK AT THE MOMENT!
FORTUNATELY, GRANDFATHER SOJOUNER, THE SANCTITY OF HAVEN HAS YET TO BE VIOLATED!
THERE IS STILL THE DARK LEGION TO RECKON WITH!
THEY SHOULD NOT BE TAKEN LIGHTLY!
THEY ARE AT A LOW POINT AT THIS MOMENT THEMSELVES, GRANDFATHER SPECTRE, BUT--
--I'LL CONCEDE YOU THIS, THOUGH--

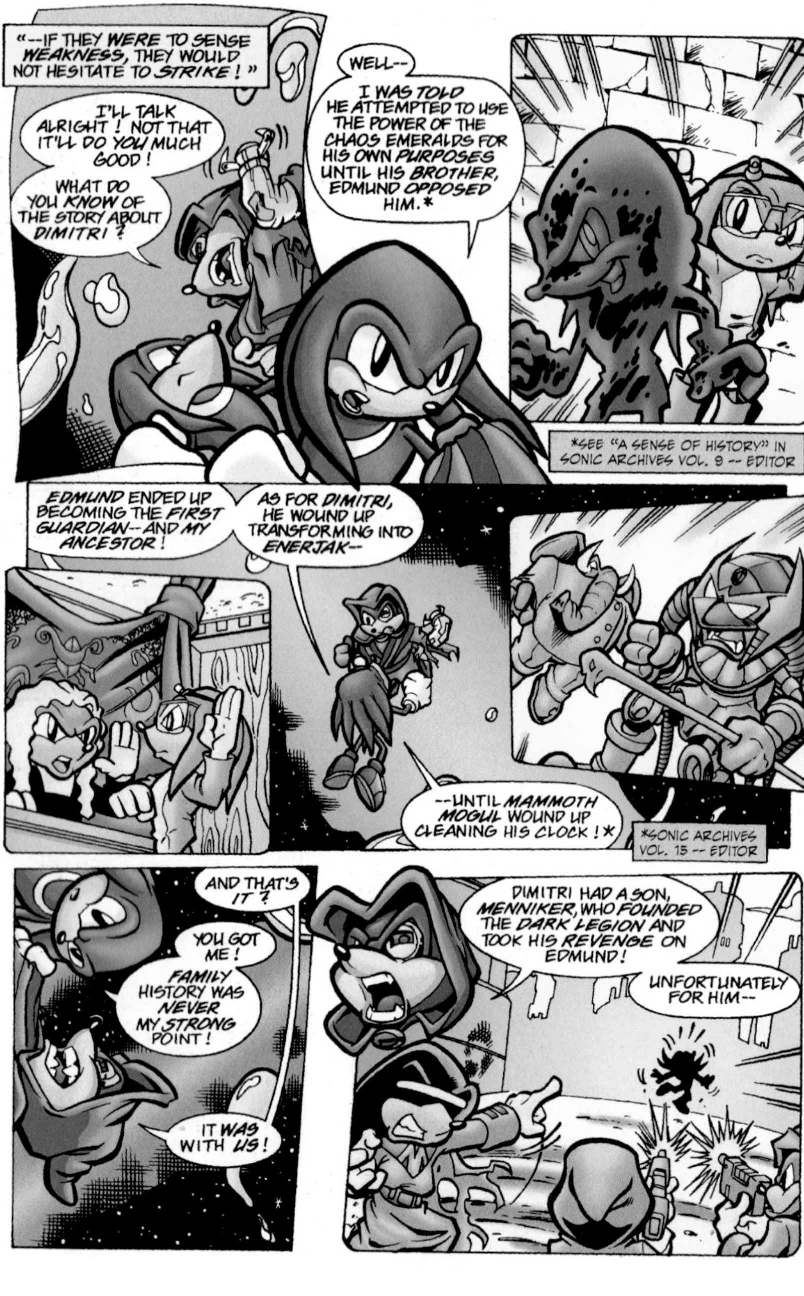
"--IF THEY WERE TO SENSE WEAKNESS, THEY WOULD NOT HESITATE TO STRIKE!"
I'LL TALK ALRIGHT! NOT THAT IT'LL DO YOU MUCH GOOD!
WHAT DO YOU KNOW OF THE STORY ABOUT DIMITRI?
WELL--
I WAS TOLD HE ATTEMPTED TO USE THE POWER OF THE CHAOS EMERALDS FOR HIS OWN PURPOSES UNTIL HIS BROTHER, EDMUND OPPOSED HIM.*
*SEE "A SENSE OF HISTORY" IN SONIC ARCHIVES VOL. 9 -- EDITOR
EDMUND ENDED UP BECOMING THE FIRST GUARDIAN--AND MY ANCESTOR!
AS FOR DIMITRI, HE WOUND UP TRANSFORMING INTO ENERJAK--
--UNTIL MAMMOTH MOGUL WOUND UP CLEANING HIS CLOCK!*
*SONIC ARCHIVES VOL. 15 -- EDITOR
AND THAT'S IT?
YOU GOT ME!
FAMILY HISTORY WAS NEVER MY STRONG POINT!
IT WAS WITH US!
DIMITRI HAD A SON, MENNIKER, WHO FOUNDED THE DARK LEGION AND TOOK HIS REVENGE ON EDMUND!
UNFORTUNATELY FOR HIM--

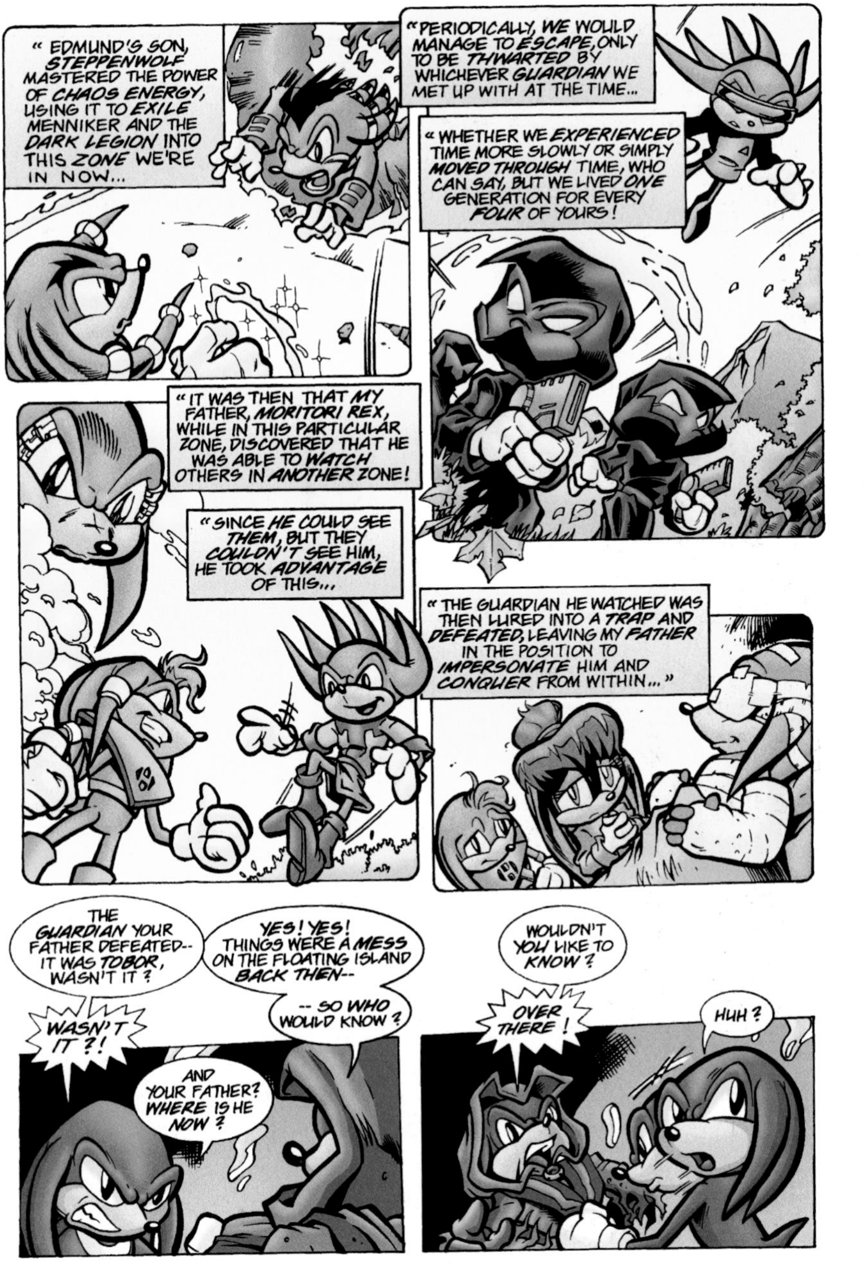
"EDMUND'S SON, STEPPENWOLF MASTERED THE POWER OF CHAOS ENERGY, USING IT TO EXILE MENNIKER AND THE DARK LEGION INTO THIS ZONE WE'RE IN NOW...
"PERIODICALLY, WE WOULD MANAGE TO ESCAPE, ONLY TO BE THWARTED BY WHICHEVER GUARDIAN WE MET UP WITH AT THE TIME...
"WHETHER WE EXPERIENCED TIME MORE SLOWLY OR SIMPLY MOVED THROUGH TIME, WHO CAN SAY, BUT WE LIVED ONE GENERATION FOR EVERY FOUR OF YOURS!
"IT WAS THEN THAT MY FATHER, MORITORI REX, WHILE IN THIS PARTICULAR ZONE, DISCOVERED THAT HE WAS ABLE TO WATCH OTHERS IN ANOTHER ZONE!
"SINCE HE COULD SEE THEM, BUT THEY COULDN'T SEE HIM, HE TOOK ADVANTAGE OF THIS...
"THE GUARDIAN HE WATCHED WAS THEN LURED INTO A TRAP AND DEFEATED, LEAVING MY FATHER IN THE POSITION TO IMPERSONATE HIM AND CONQUER FROM WITHIN..."
THE GUARDIAN YOUR FATHER DEFEATED-- IT WAS TOBOR, WASN'T IT?
WASN'T IT?!
YES! YES! THINGS WERE A MESS ON THE FLOATING ISLAND BACK THEN--
-- SO WHO WOULD KNOW?
AND YOUR FATHER? WHERE IS HE NOW?
WOULDN'T YOU LIKE TO KNOW?
OVER THERE!
HUH?

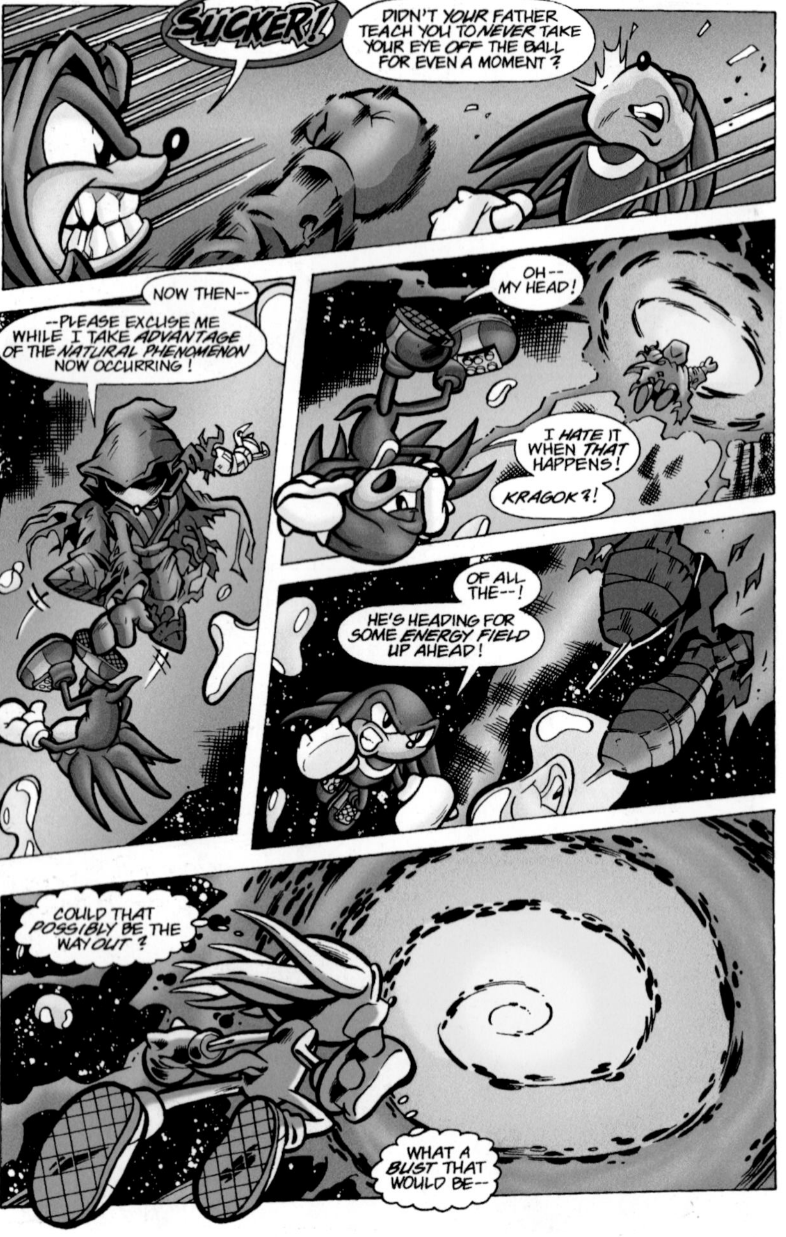
SUCKER!!
DIDN'T YOUR FATHER TEACH YOU TO NEVER TAKE YOUR EYE OFF THE BALL FOR EVEN A MOMENT?
NOW THEN--
--PLEASE EXCUSE ME WHILE I TAKE ADVANTAGE OF THE NATURAL PHENOMENON NOW OCCURRING!
OH-- MY HEAD!
I HATE IT WHEN THAT HAPPENS!
KRAGOK?!
OF ALL THE--!
HE'S HEADING FOR SOME ENERGY FIELD UP AHEAD!
COULD THAT POSSIBLY BE THE WAY OUT?
WHAT A BUST THAT WOULD BE--

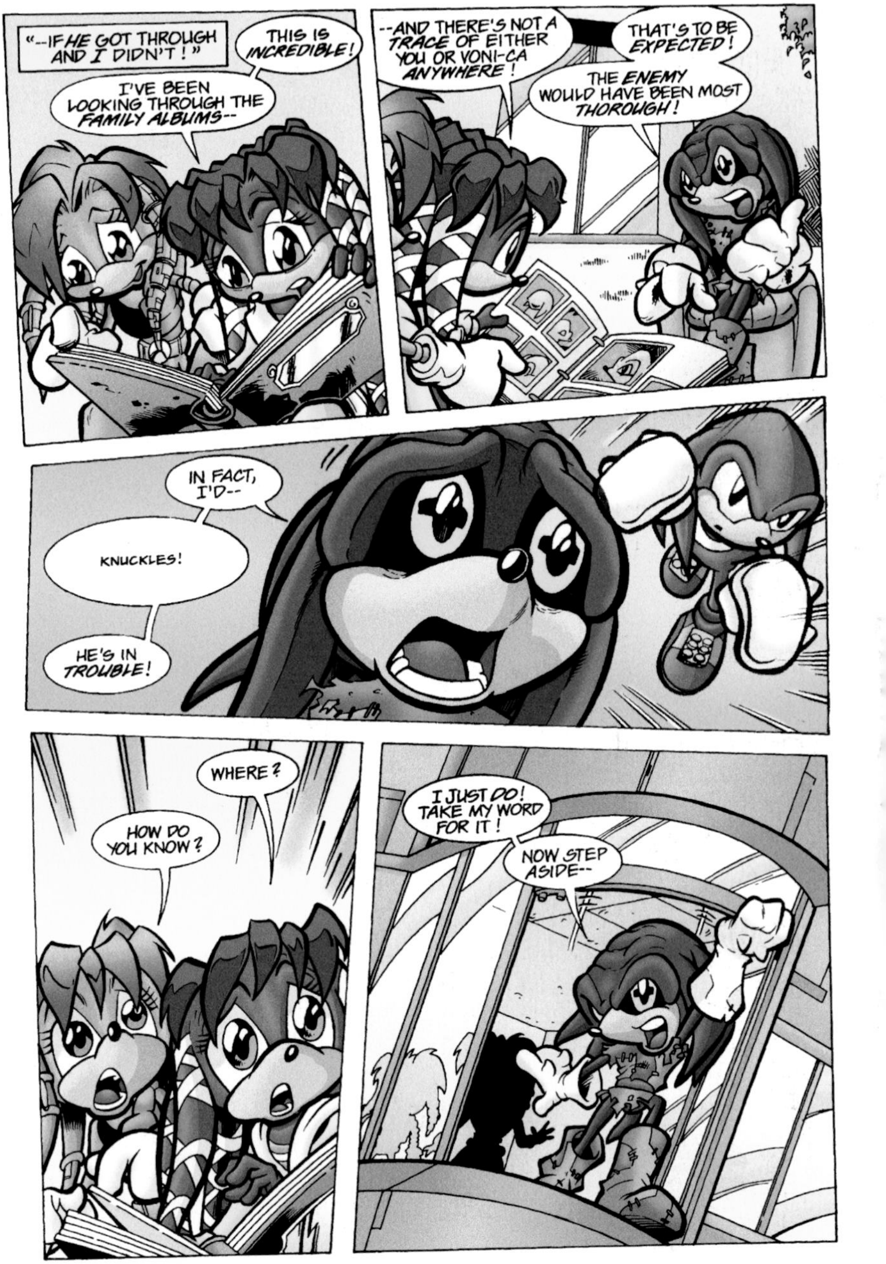
"--IF HE GOT THROUGH AND I DIDN'T!"
THIS IS INCREDIBLE!
I'VE BEEN LOOKING THROUGH THE FAMILY ALBUMS--
--AND THERE'S NOT A TRACE OF EITHER YOU OR VONI-CA ANYWHERE!
THAT'S TO BE EXPECTED!
THE ENEMY WOULD HAVE BEEN MOST THOROUGH!
IN FACT, I'D--
KNUCKLES!
HE'S IN TROUBLE!
WHERE?
HOW DO YOU KNOW?
I JUST DO! TAKE MY WORD FOR IT!
NOW STEP ASIDE--

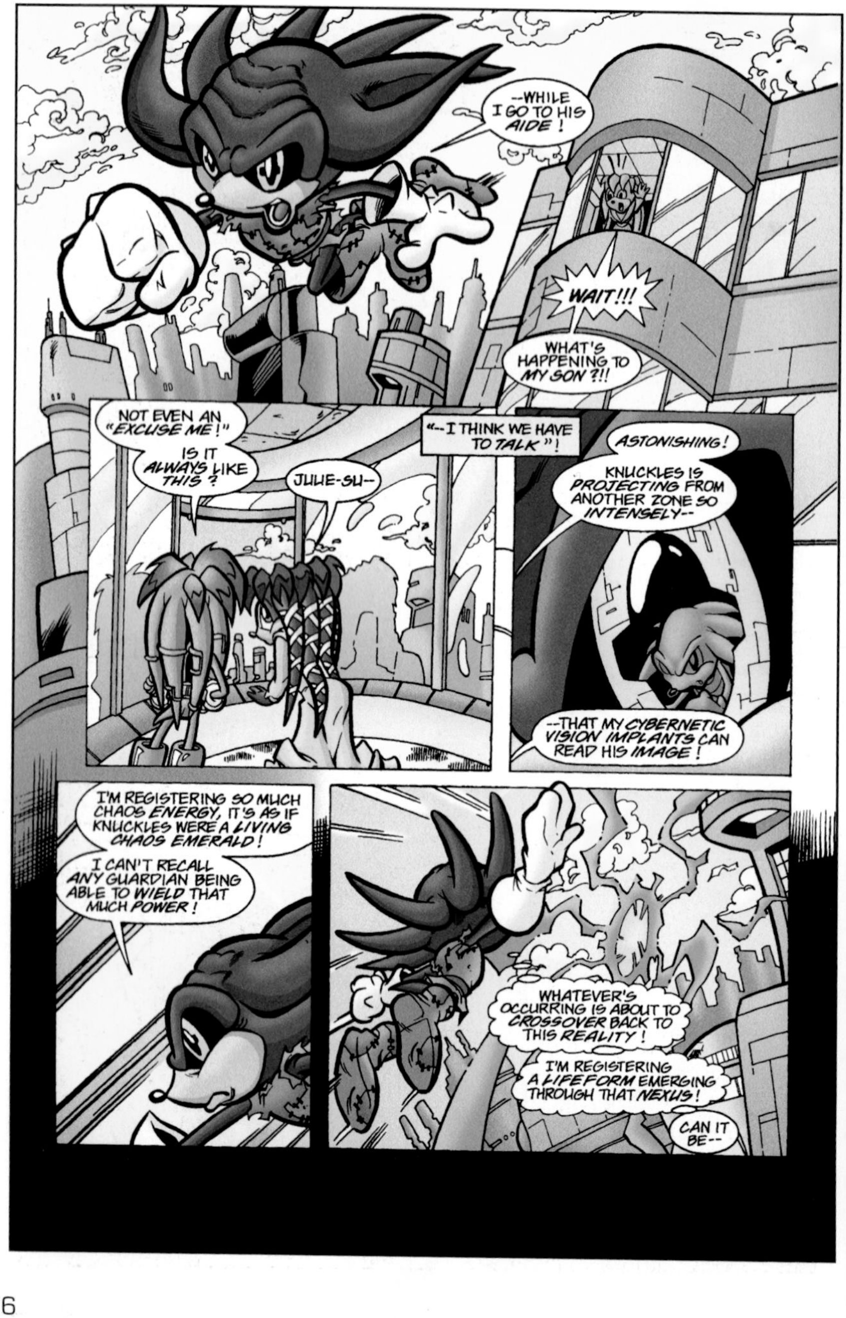
--WHILE I GO TO HIS AIDE!
WAIT!!!
WHAT'S HAPPENING TO MY SON?!!
NOT EVEN AN "EXCUSE ME!"
IS IT ALWAYS LIKE THIS?
JULIE-SU--
"--I THINK WE HAVE TO TALK"!
ASTONISHING!
KNUCKLES IS PROJECTING FROM ANOTHER ZONE SO INTENSELY--
--THAT MY CYBERNETIC VISION IMPLANTS CAN READ HIS IMAGE!
I'M REGISTERING SO MUCH CHAOS ENERGY, IT'S AS IF KNUCKLES WERE A LIVING CHAOS EMERALD!
I CAN'T RECALL ANY GUARDIAN BEING ABLE TO WIELD THAT MUCH POWER!
WHATEVER'S OCCURRING IS ABOUT TO CROSSOVER BACK TO THIS REALITY!
I'M REGISTERING A LIFEFORM EMERGING THROUGH THAT NEXUS!
CAN IT BE--

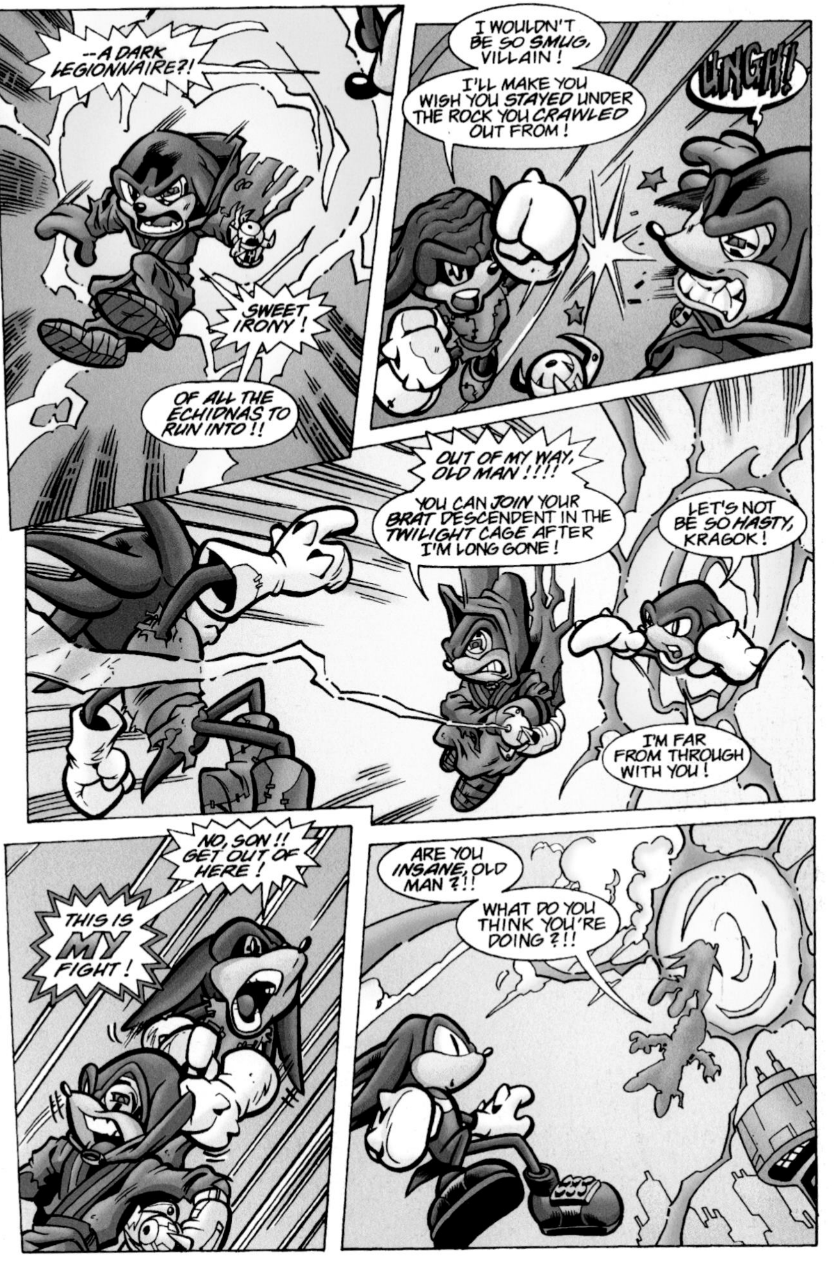
--A DARK LEGIONNAIRE?!
SWEET IRONY!
OF ALL THE ECHIDNAS TO RUN INTO!!
I WOULDN'T BE SO SMUG, VILLAIN!
I'LL MAKE YOU WISH YOU STAYED UNDER THE ROCK YOU CRAWLED OUT FROM!
UNGH!
OUT OF MY WAY, OLD MAN!!!!
YOU CAN JOIN YOUR BRAT DESCENDENT IN THE TWILIGHT CAGE AFTER I'M LONG GONE!
LET'S NOT BE SO HASTY, KRAGOK!
I'M FAR FROM THROUGH WITH YOU!
NO, SON!! GET OUT OF HERE!
THIS IS MY FIGHT!
ARE YOU INSANE, OLD MAN?!!
WHAT DO YOU THINK YOU'RE DOING?!!

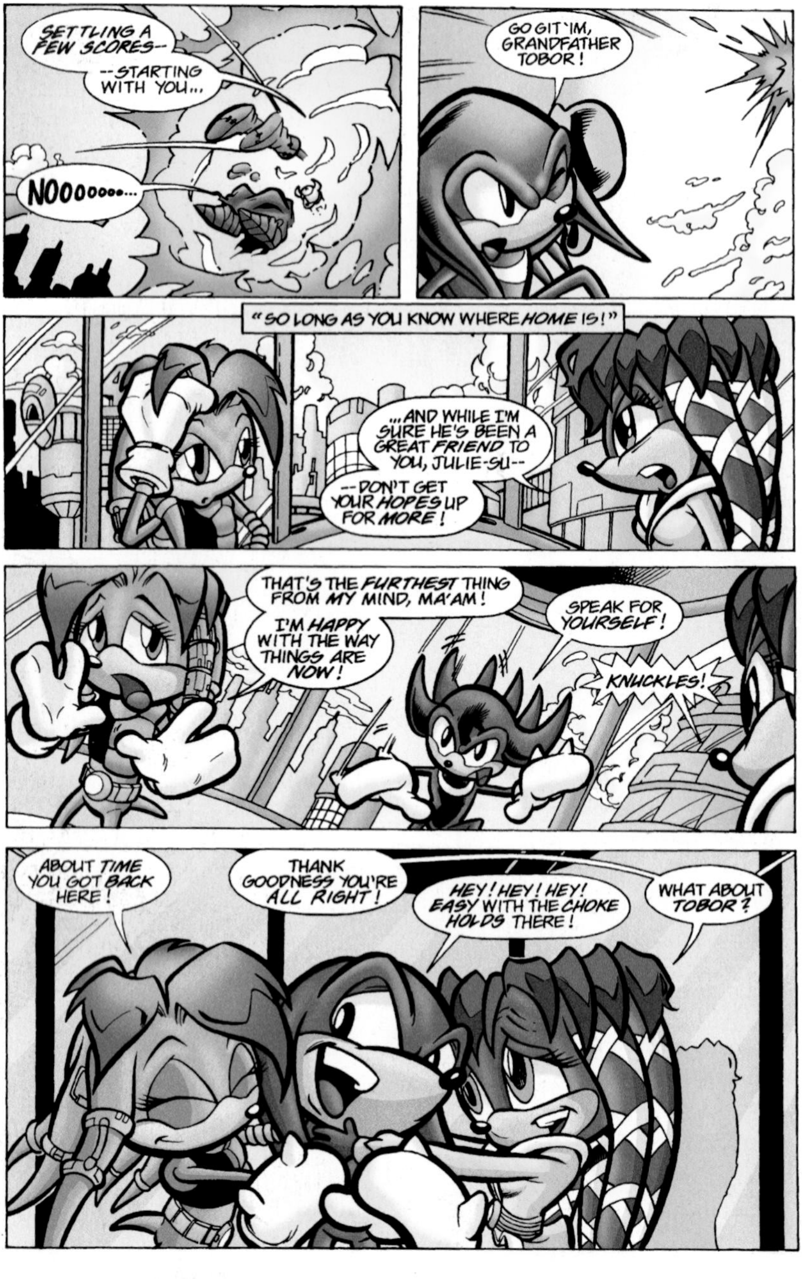
SETTLING A FEW SCORES--
--STARTING WITH YOU...
NOOOoooo...
GO GIT 'IM, GRANDFATHER TOBOR!
"SO LONG AS YOU KNOW WHERE HOME IS!"
...AND WHILE I'M SURE HE'S BEEN A GREAT FRIEND TO YOU, JULIE-SU--
--DON'T GET YOUR HOPES UP FOR MORE!
THAT'S THE FURTHEST THING FROM MY MIND, MA'AM!
I'M HAPPY WITH THE WAY THINGS ARE NOW!
SPEAK FOR YOURSELF!
KNUCKLES!
ABOUT TIME YOU GOT BACK HERE!
THANK GOODNESS YOU'RE ALL RIGHT!
HEY! HEY! HEY! EASY WITH THE CHOKE HOLDS THERE!
WHAT ABOUT TOBOR?

"HE'S TAKING CARE OF *BUSINESS* AT THE MOMENT!"

AT LAST! *ALL* SYSTEMS ARE A GO!

BRING UP THE *MONITORS* ONLINE!

I'D LIKE TO SEE IF THE SITUATION HAS *REMAINED* STATUS QUO--

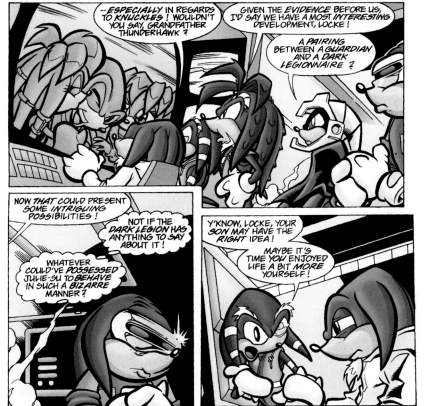

--*ESPECIALLY* IN REGARDS TO *KNUCKLES!* WOULDN'T YOU SAY, GRANDFATHER THUNDERHAWK?

GIVEN THE *EVIDENCE* BEFORE US, I'D SAY WE HAVE A MOST *INTERESTING* DEVELOPMENT, LOCKE!

A *PAIRING* BETWEEN A *GUARDIAN* AND A *DARK LEGIONNAIRE?*

NOW *THAT* COULD PRESENT SOME *INTRIGUING* POSSIBILITIES!

NOT IF THE *DARK LEGION* HAS ANYTHING TO SAY ABOUT IT!

WHATEVER COULD'VE *POSSESSED* JULIE-SU TO *BEHAVE* IN SUCH A *BIZARRE* MANNER?

Y'KNOW, LOCKE, YOUR *SON* MAY HAVE THE *RIGHT* IDEA!

MAYBE IT'S TIME *YOU* ENJOYED LIFE A BIT *MORE* YOURSELF!

79

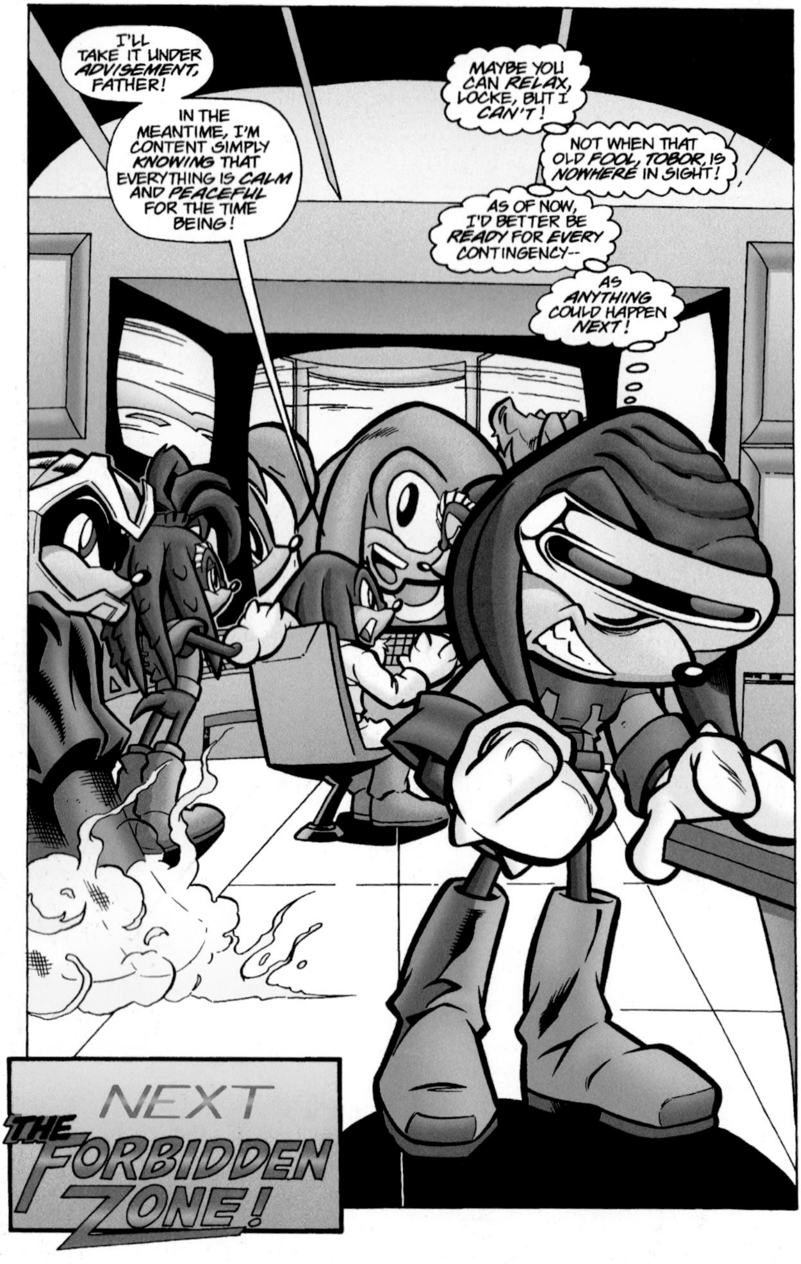

I'LL TAKE IT UNDER ADVISEMENT, FATHER!
IN THE MEANTIME, I'M CONTENT SIMPLY KNOWING THAT EVERYTHING IS CALM AND PEACEFUL FOR THE TIME BEING!
MAYBE YOU CAN RELAX, LOCKE, BUT I CAN'T!
NOT WHEN THAT OLD FOOL, TOBOR, IS NOWHERE IN SIGHT!
AS OF NOW, I'D BETTER BE READY FOR EVERY CONTINGENCY--
AS ANYTHING COULD HAPPEN NEXT!
NEXT
THE FORBIDDEN ZONE!

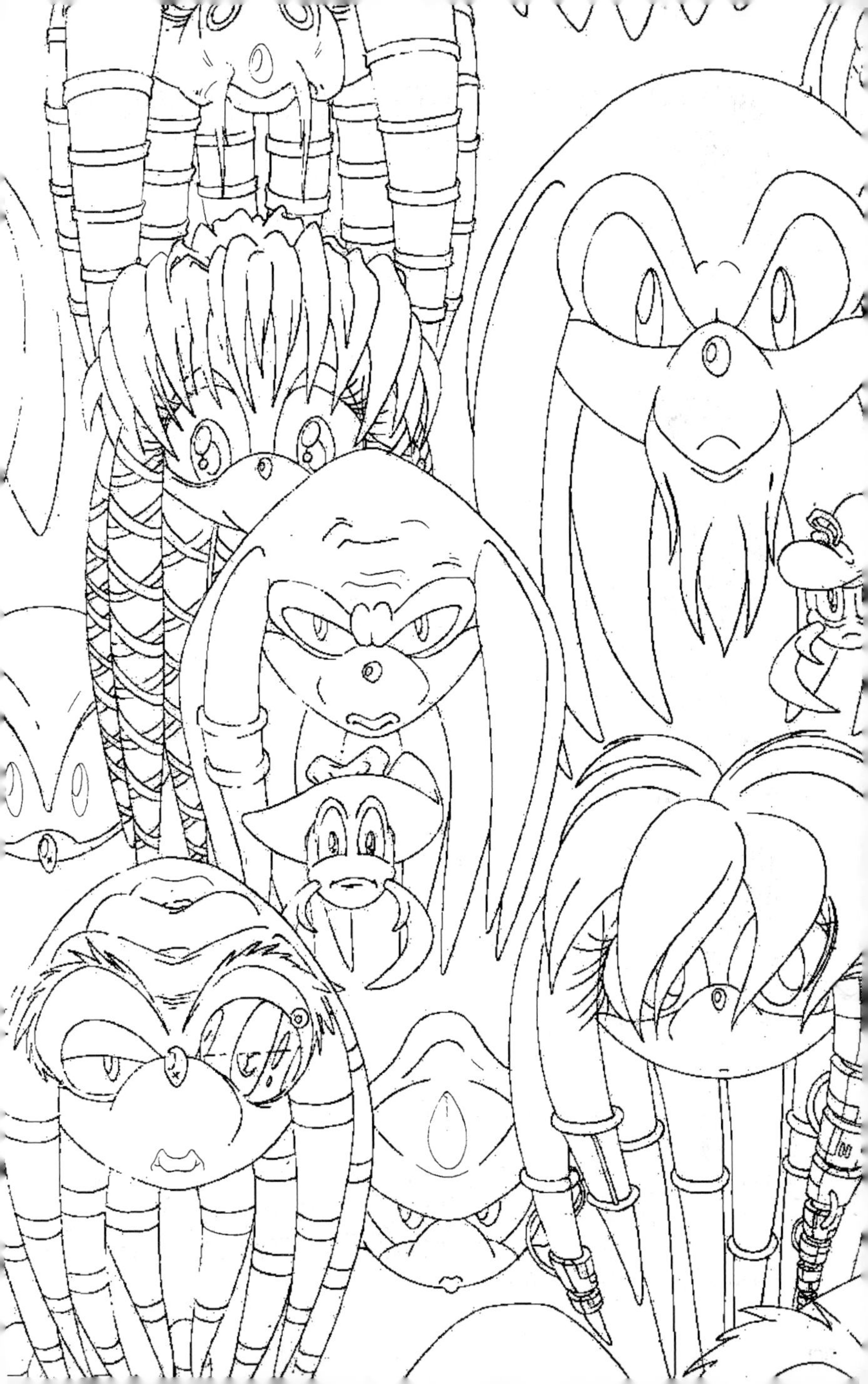

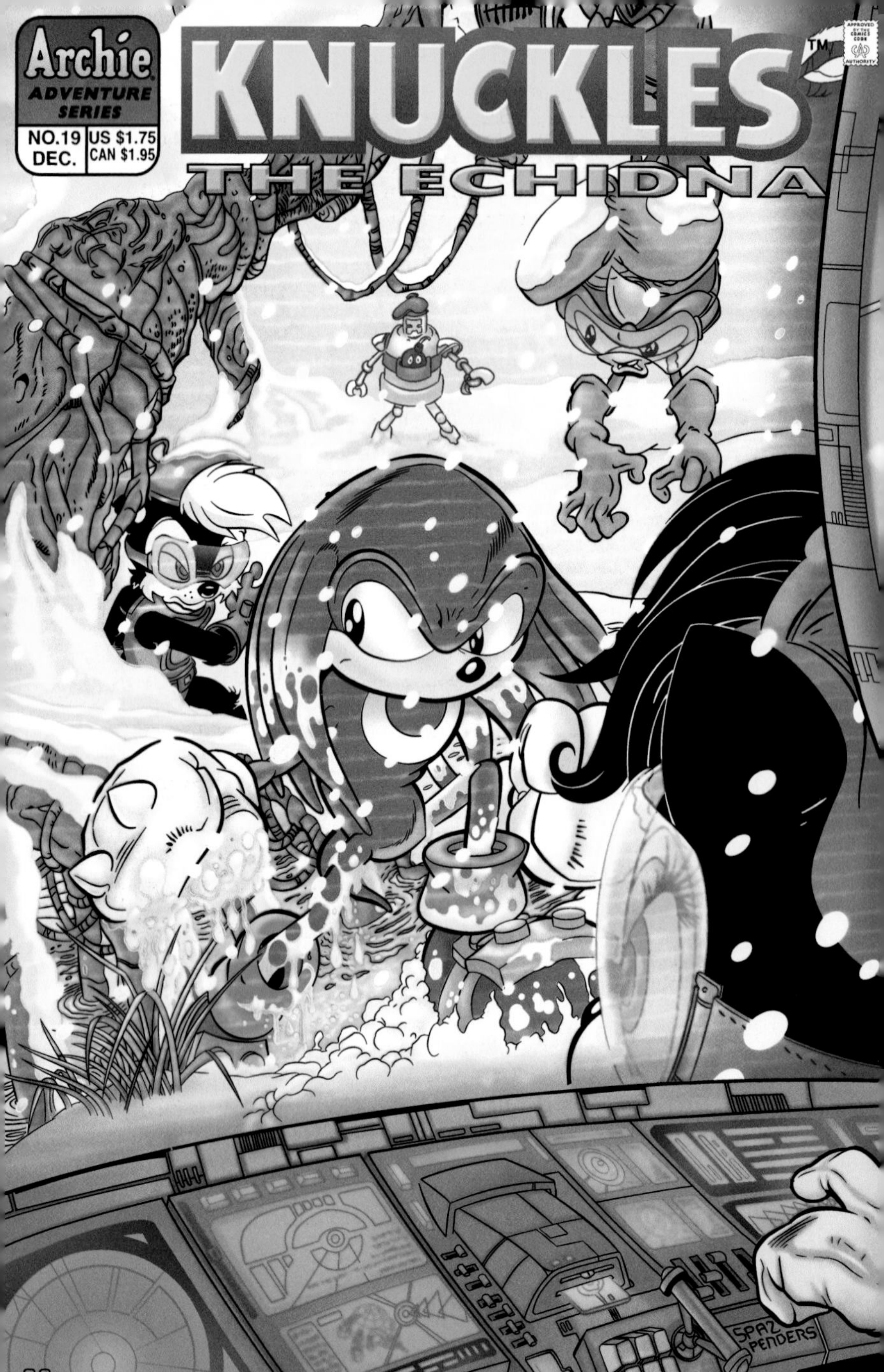
Archie
ADVENTURE SERIES
NO.19
DEC.
US $1.75
CAN $1.95
KNUCKLES™
THE ECHIDNA
SPAZ
PENDERS

BOOK NINETEEN

The
Forbidden
Zone
Part One of Three

Ken Penders
Writer
Manny Galan
Penciler
Andrew Pepoy
Inker
Barry Grossman
Colorist
Vickie Williams
Letterer

Justin Gabrie
Editor

Victor Gorelick
Managing Editor

Richard Goldwater
Editor-in-Chief

Born to the most noble of Echidna houses, the latest to continue the family heritage and responsibility as **GUARDIAN OF THE FLOATING ISLAND,** defender of all the forces of evil from the world beyond as well as those who would threaten within, he is none other than... **KNUCKLES THE ECHIDNA!**

SPAZ
PENDERS

Many years ago, during the **Great War,** when **Princess Sally** was but an infant, **King Acorn** sent his wife **Queen Alicia** to The Floating Island in order to insure the safety of his Queen and **the future of Mobotropolis**. It resulted in failure.

Recently, the newly-returned, now-healthy King assigned a squad of his elite commandos to return to The Floating Island and ascertain the true fate of his loved ones.

It is here our tale begins...

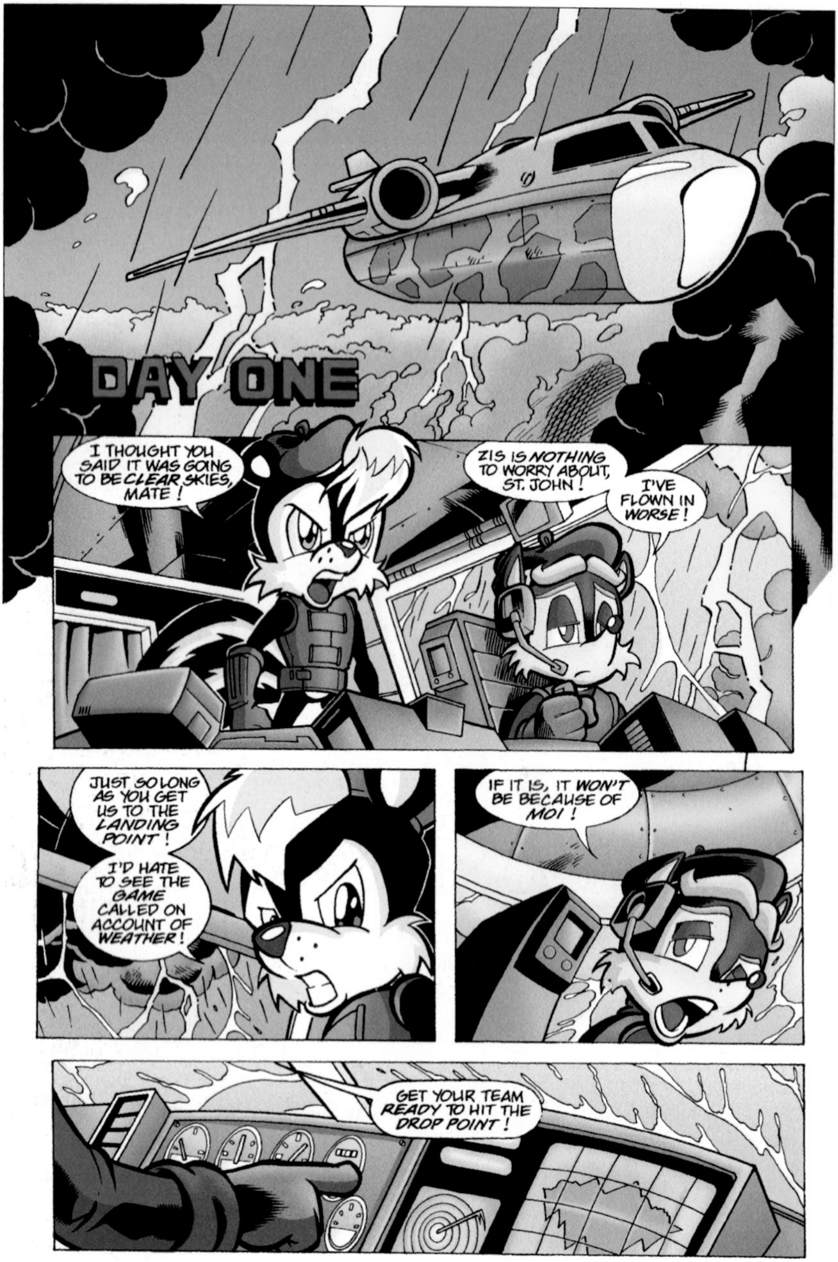
DAY ONE
I THOUGHT YOU SAID IT WAS GOING TO BE CLEAR SKIES, MATE!
ZIS IS NOTHING TO WORRY ABOUT, ST. JOHN!
I'VE FLOWN IN WORSE!
JUST SO LONG AS YOU GET US TO THE LANDING POINT!
I'D HATE TO SEE THE GAME CALLED ON ACCOUNT OF WEATHER!
IF IT IS, IT WON'T BE BECAUSE OF MOI!
GET YOUR TEAM READY TO HIT THE DROP POINT!

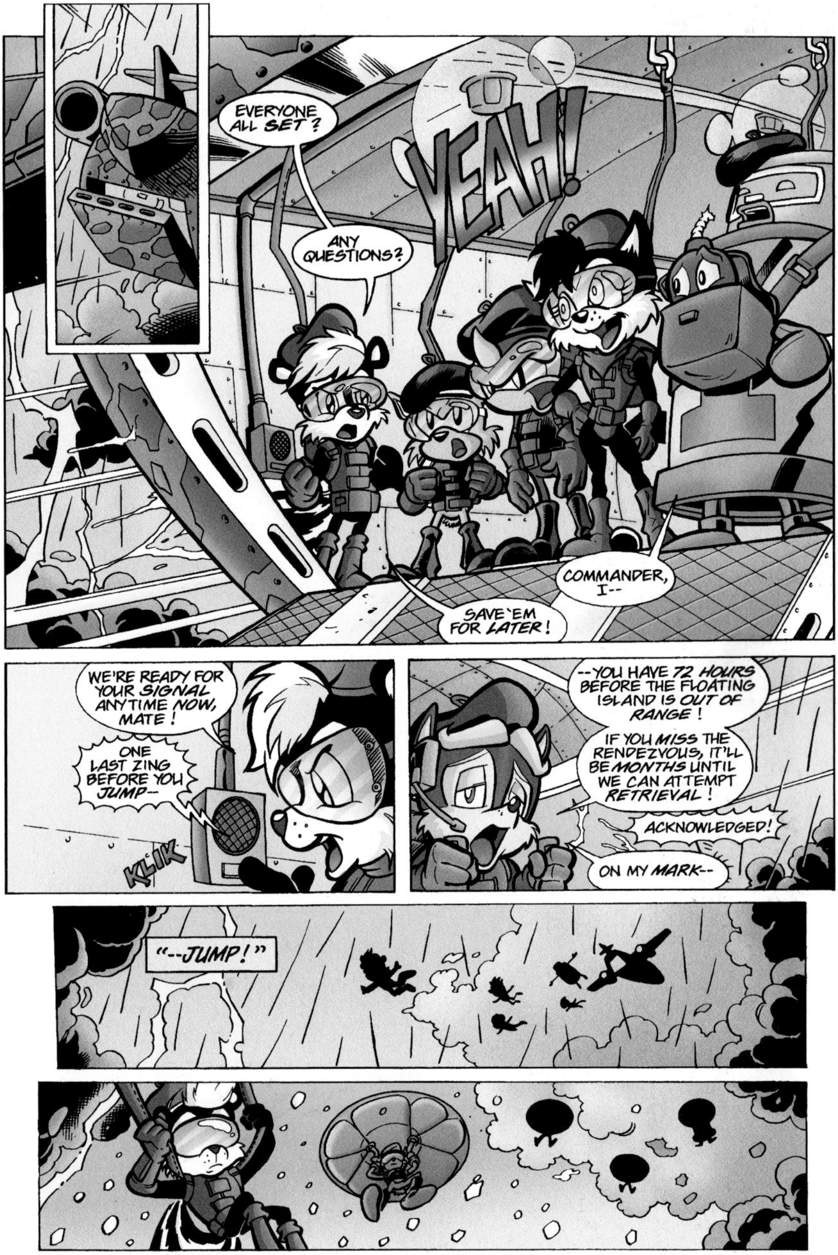
EVERYONE ALL SET?
YEAH!
ANY QUESTIONS?
COMMANDER, I--
SAVE 'EM FOR LATER!
WE'RE READY FOR YOUR SIGNAL ANYTIME NOW, MATE!
ONE LAST ZING BEFORE YOU JUMP--
KLIK
--YOU HAVE 72 HOURS BEFORE THE FLOATING ISLAND IS OUT OF RANGE!
IF YOU MISS THE RENDEZVOUS, IT'LL BE MONTHS UNTIL WE CAN ATTEMPT RETRIEVAL!
ACKNOWLEDGED!
ON MY MARK--
"--JUMP!"

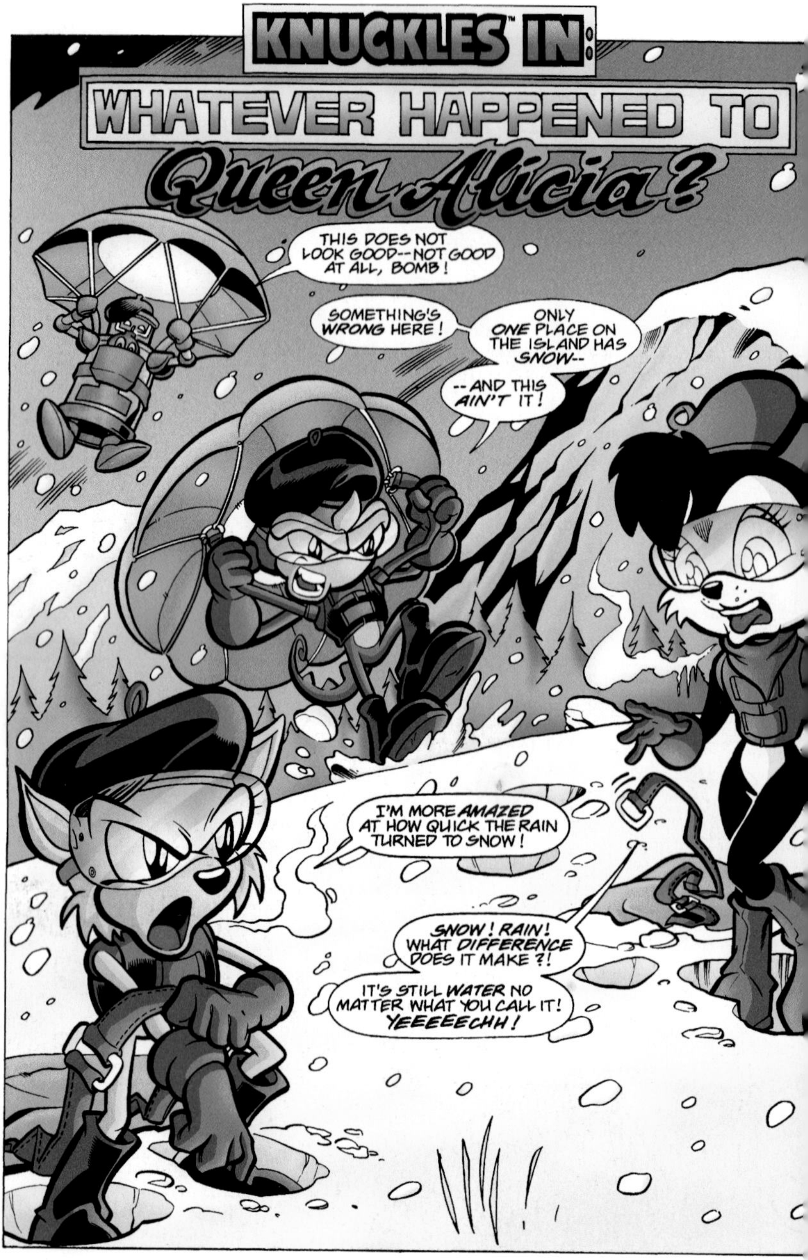
KNUCKLES™ IN:
WHATEVER HAPPENED TO
Queen Alicia?
THIS DOES NOT LOOK GOOD--NOT GOOD AT ALL, BOMB!
SOMETHING'S WRONG HERE!
ONLY ONE PLACE ON THE ISLAND HAS SNOW--
--AND THIS AIN'T IT!
I'M MORE AMAZED AT HOW QUICK THE RAIN TURNED TO SNOW!
SNOW! RAIN! WHAT DIFFERENCE DOES IT MAKE?!
IT'S STILL WATER NO MATTER WHAT YOU CALL IT! YEEEEECHH!

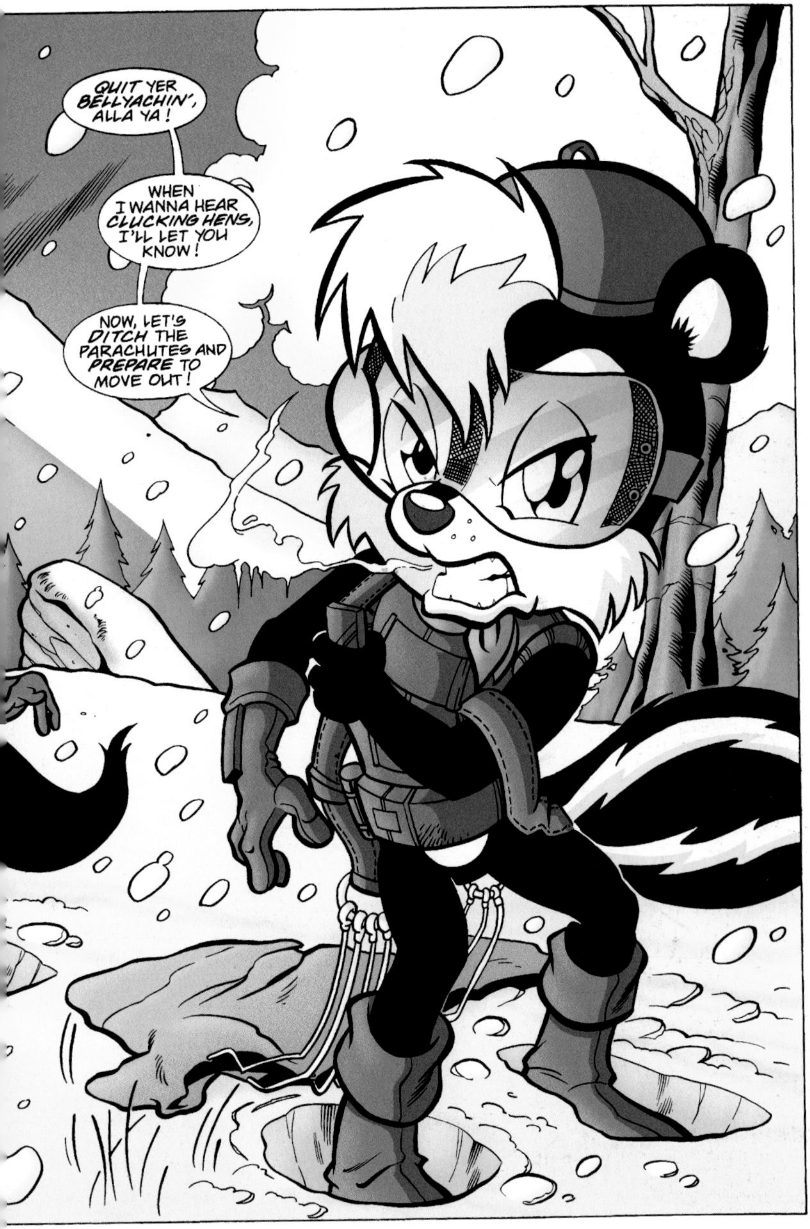
QUIT YER BELLYACHIN', ALLA YA!
WHEN I WANNA HEAR CLUCKING HENS, I'LL LET YOU KNOW!
NOW, LET'S DITCH THE PARACHUTES AND PREPARE TO MOVE OUT!

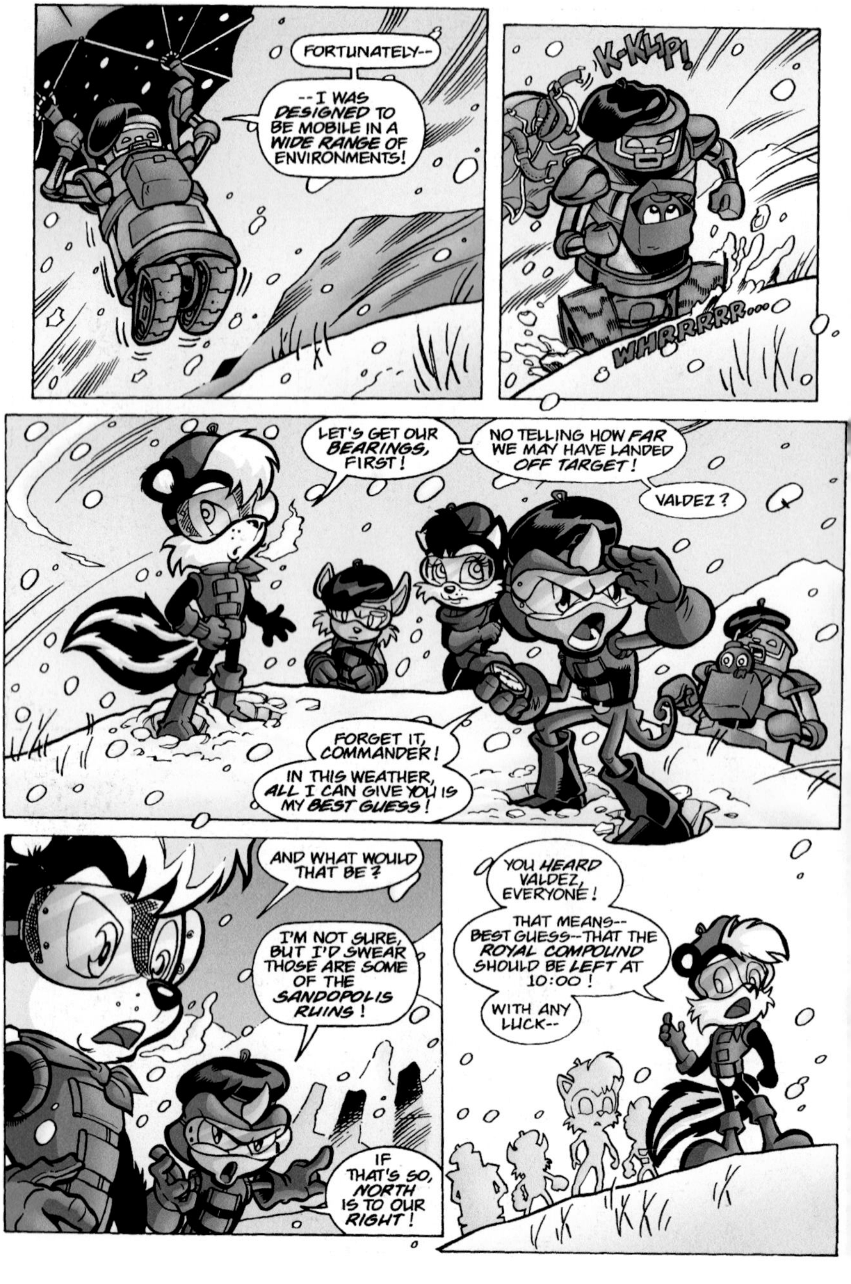
FORTUNATELY--
--I WAS DESIGNED TO BE MOBILE IN A WIDE RANGE OF ENVIRONMENTS!
K-KLIP!
WHRRRRR...
LET'S GET OUR BEARINGS, FIRST!
NO TELLING HOW FAR WE MAY HAVE LANDED OFF TARGET!
VALDEZ?
FORGET IT, COMMANDER!
IN THIS WEATHER, ALL I CAN GIVE YOU IS MY BEST GUESS!
AND WHAT WOULD THAT BE?
I'M NOT SURE, BUT I'D SWEAR THOSE ARE SOME OF THE SANDOPOLIS RUINS!
IF THAT'S SO, NORTH IS TO OUR RIGHT!
YOU HEARD VALDEZ, EVERYONE!
THAT MEANS-- BEST GUESS--THAT THE ROYAL COMPOUND SHOULD BE LEFT AT 10:00!
WITH ANY LUCK--

"--WE SHOULD REACH THE COMPOUND BEFORE *NIGHTFALL*!"

FATHER!

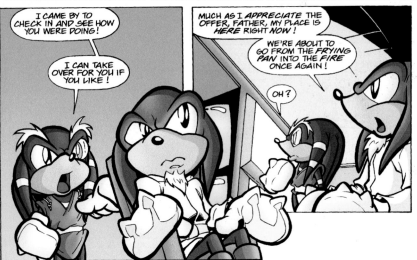

I CAME BY TO CHECK IN AND *SEE* HOW YOU WERE DOING!

I CAN *TAKE OVER* FOR YOU IF YOU LIKE!

MUCH AS I *APPRECIATE* THE OFFER, FATHER, MY PLACE IS *HERE* RIGHT *NOW*!

WE'RE ABOUT TO *GO* FROM THE *FRYING PAN* INTO THE *FIRE* ONCE AGAIN!

OH?

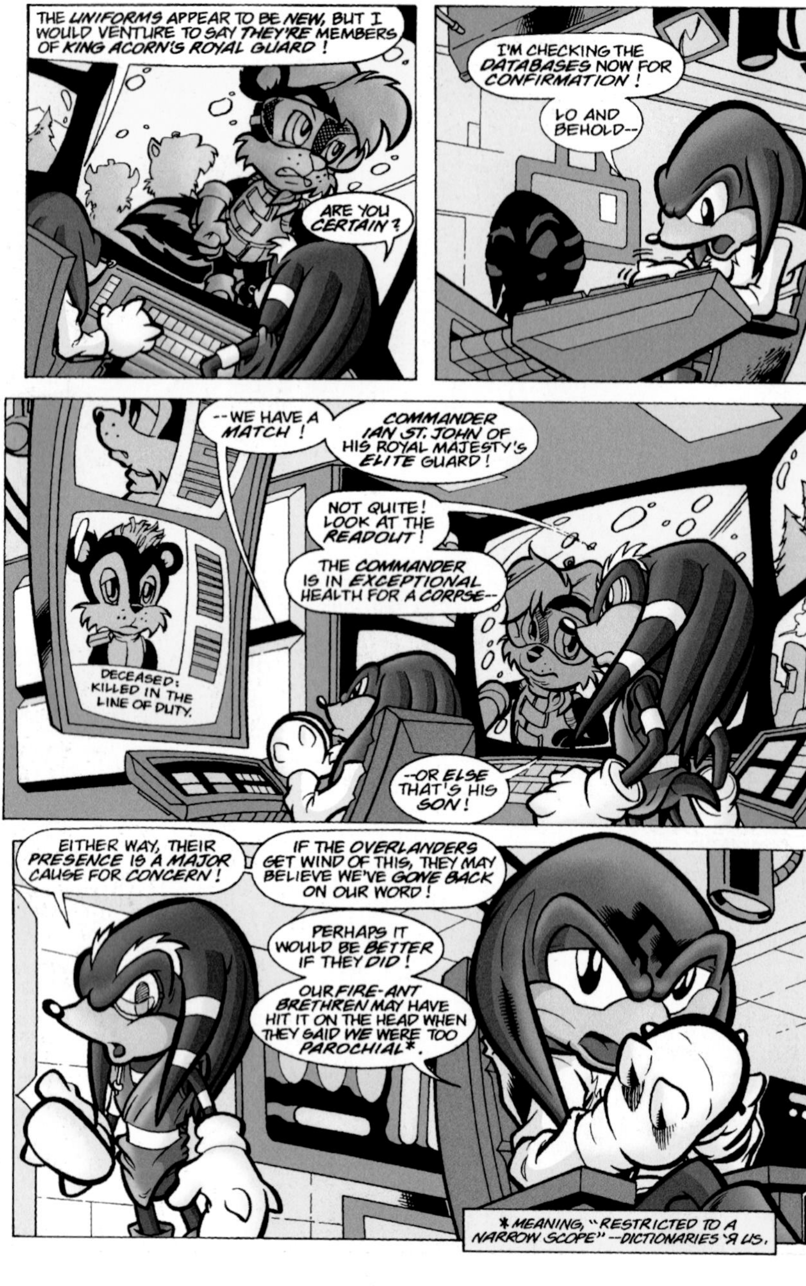
THE UNIFORMS APPEAR TO BE NEW, BUT I WOULD VENTURE TO SAY THEY'RE MEMBERS OF KING ACORN'S ROYAL GUARD!
ARE YOU CERTAIN?
I'M CHECKING THE DATABASES NOW FOR CONFIRMATION!
LO AND BEHOLD--
--WE HAVE A MATCH!
COMMANDER IAN ST. JOHN OF HIS ROYAL MAJESTY'S ELITE GUARD!
DECEASED: KILLED IN THE LINE OF DUTY.
NOT QUITE! LOOK AT THE READOUT!
THE COMMANDER IS IN EXCEPTIONAL HEALTH FOR A CORPSE--
--OR ELSE THAT'S HIS SON!
EITHER WAY, THEIR PRESENCE IS A MAJOR CAUSE FOR CONCERN!
IF THE OVERLANDERS GET WIND OF THIS, THEY MAY BELIEVE WE'VE GONE BACK ON OUR WORD!
PERHAPS IT WOULD BE BETTER IF THEY DID!
OUR FIRE-ANT BRETHREN MAY HAVE HIT IT ON THE HEAD WHEN THEY SAID WE WERE TOO PAROCHIAL*.
* MEANING, "RESTRICTED TO A NARROW SCOPE" --DICTIONARIES 'Я US.

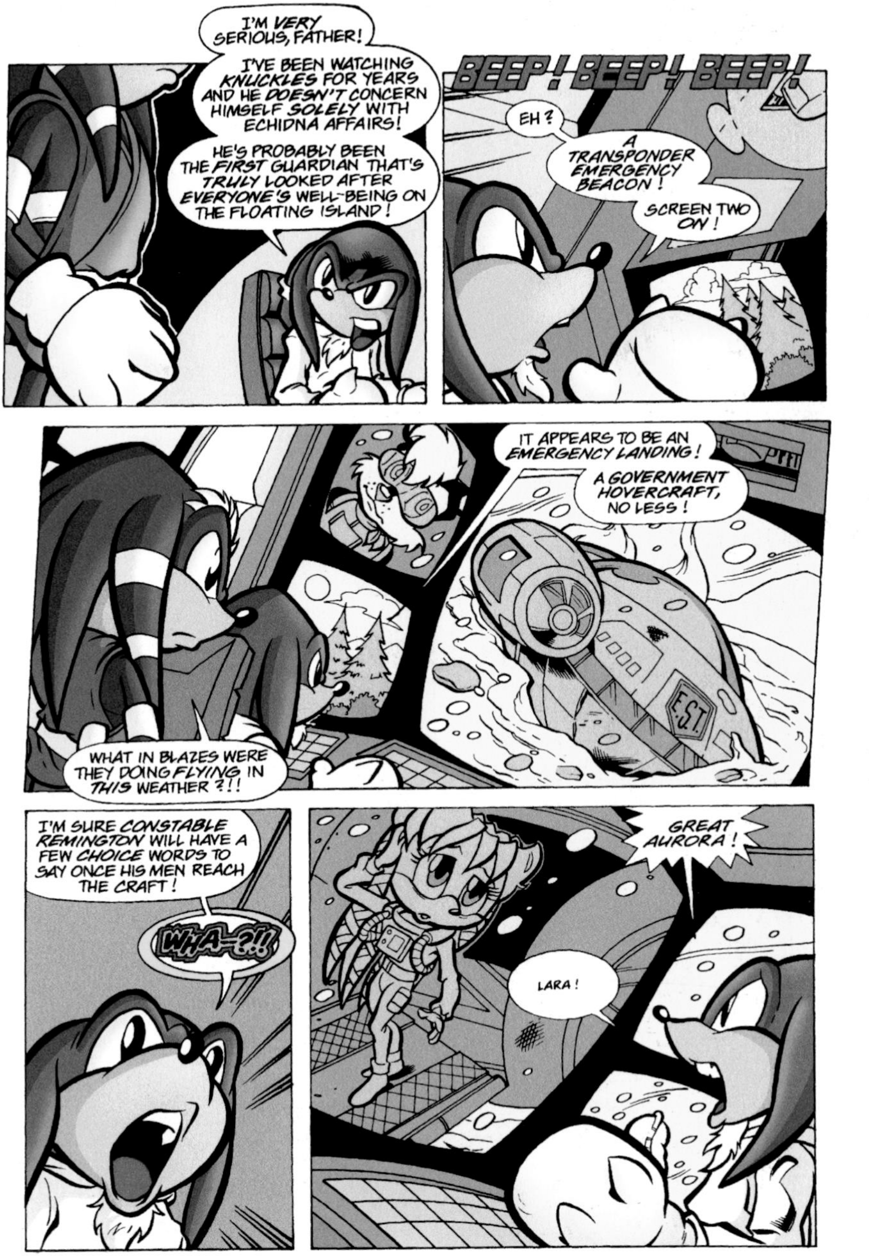
I'M VERY SERIOUS, FATHER!
I'VE BEEN WATCHING KNUCKLES FOR YEARS AND HE DOESN'T CONCERN HIMSELF SOLELY WITH ECHIDNA AFFAIRS!
HE'S PROBABLY BEEN THE FIRST GUARDIAN THAT'S TRULY LOOKED AFTER EVERYONE'S WELL-BEING ON THE FLOATING ISLAND!
BEEP! BEEP! BEEP!
EH?
A TRANSPONDER EMERGENCY BEACON!
SCREEN TWO ON!
IT APPEARS TO BE AN EMERGENCY LANDING!
A GOVERNMENT HOVERCRAFT, NO LESS!
E.S.T.
WHAT IN BLAZES WERE THEY DOING FLYING IN THIS WEATHER?!!
I'M SURE CONSTABLE REMINGTON WILL HAVE A FEW CHOICE WORDS TO SAY ONCE HIS MEN REACH THE CRAFT!
WHA-?!!
GREAT AURORA!
LARA!

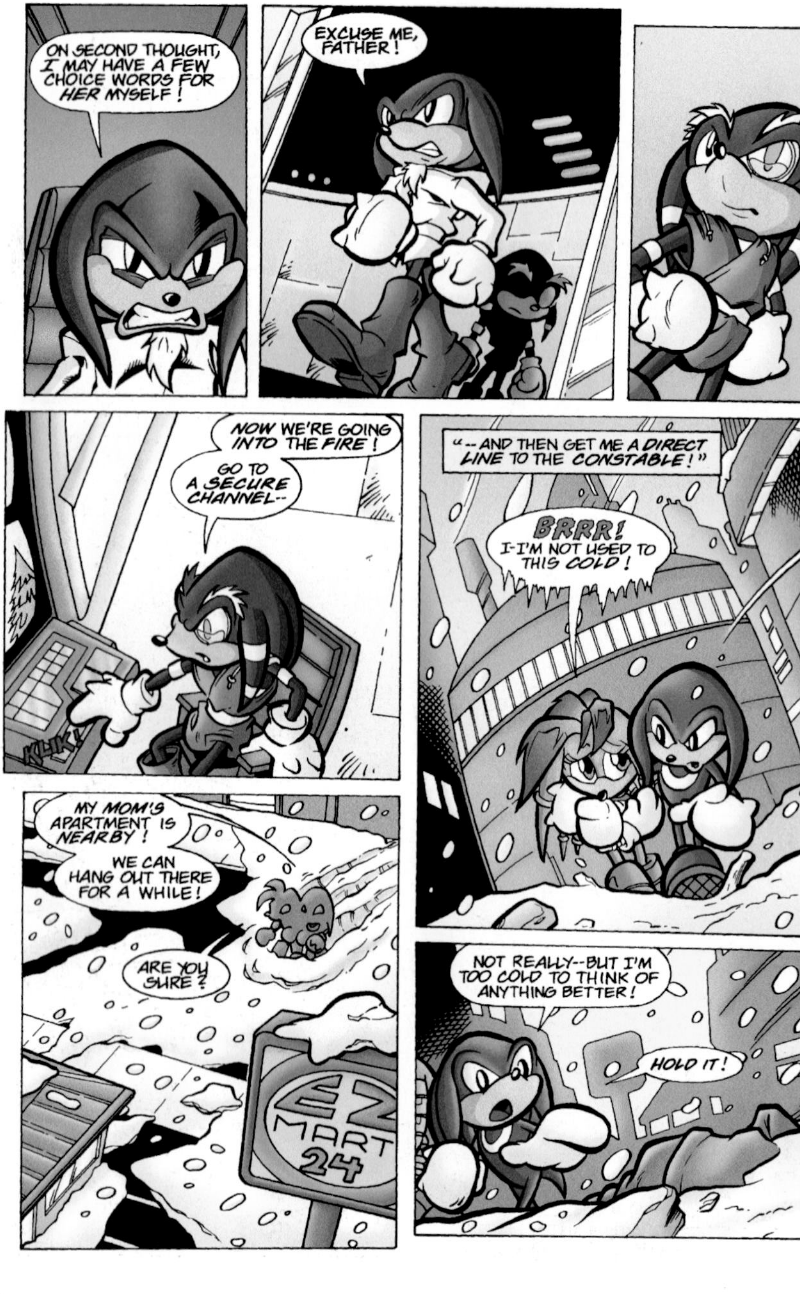
ON SECOND THOUGHT, I MAY HAVE A FEW CHOICE WORDS FOR HER MYSELF!
EXCUSE ME, FATHER!
NOW WE'RE GOING INTO THE FIRE!
GO TO A SECURE CHANNEL--
KLIK!
"--AND THEN GET ME A DIRECT LINE TO THE CONSTABLE!"
BRRRR! I-I'M NOT USED TO THIS COLD!
MY MOM'S APARTMENT IS NEARBY!
WE CAN HANG OUT THERE FOR A WHILE!
ARE YOU SURE?
EZ MART 24
NOT REALLY--BUT I'M TOO COLD TO THINK OF ANYTHING BETTER!
HOLD IT!

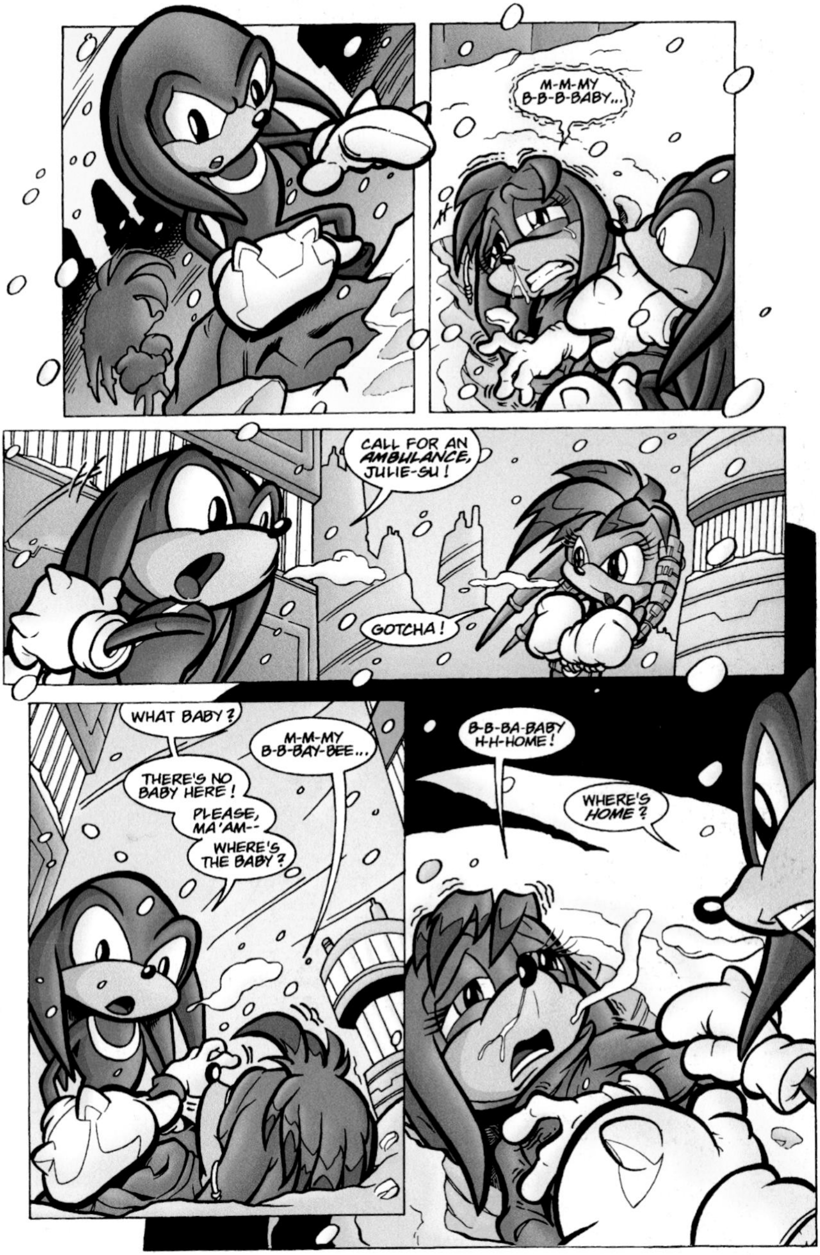
M-M-MY B-B-B-BABY...
CALL FOR AN AMBULANCE, JULIE-SU!
GOTCHA!
WHAT BABY?
THERE'S NO BABY HERE!
PLEASE, MA'AM--
WHERE'S THE BABY?
M-M-MY B-B-BAY-BEE...
B-B-BA-BABY H-H-HOME!
WHERE'S HOME?

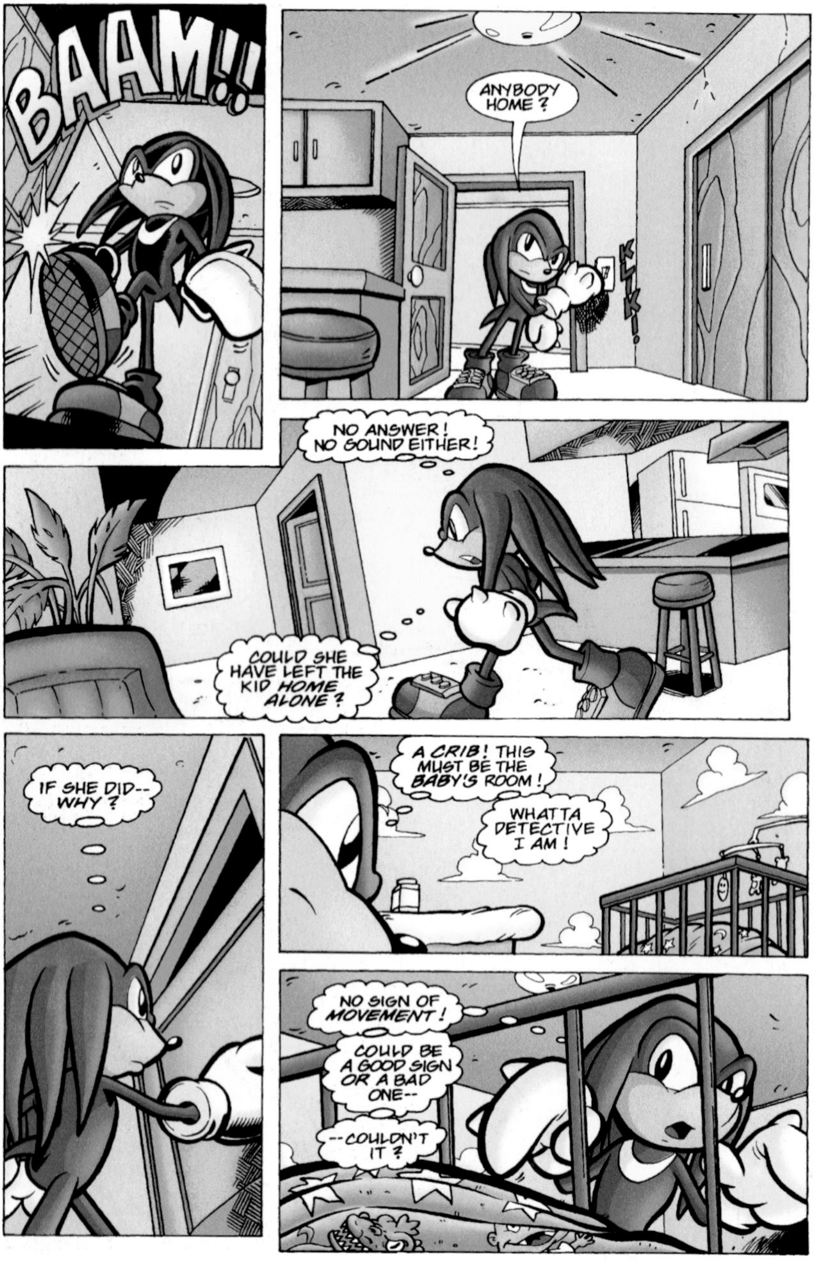
BAAM!!
ANYBODY HOME?
KLIK!
NO ANSWER! NO SOUND EITHER!
COULD SHE HAVE LEFT THE KID HOME ALONE?
IF SHE DID-- WHY?
A CRIB! THIS MUST BE THE BABY'S ROOM!
WHATTA DETECTIVE I AM!
NO SIGN OF MOVEMENT!
COULD BE A GOOD SIGN OR A BAD ONE--
--COULDN'T IT?

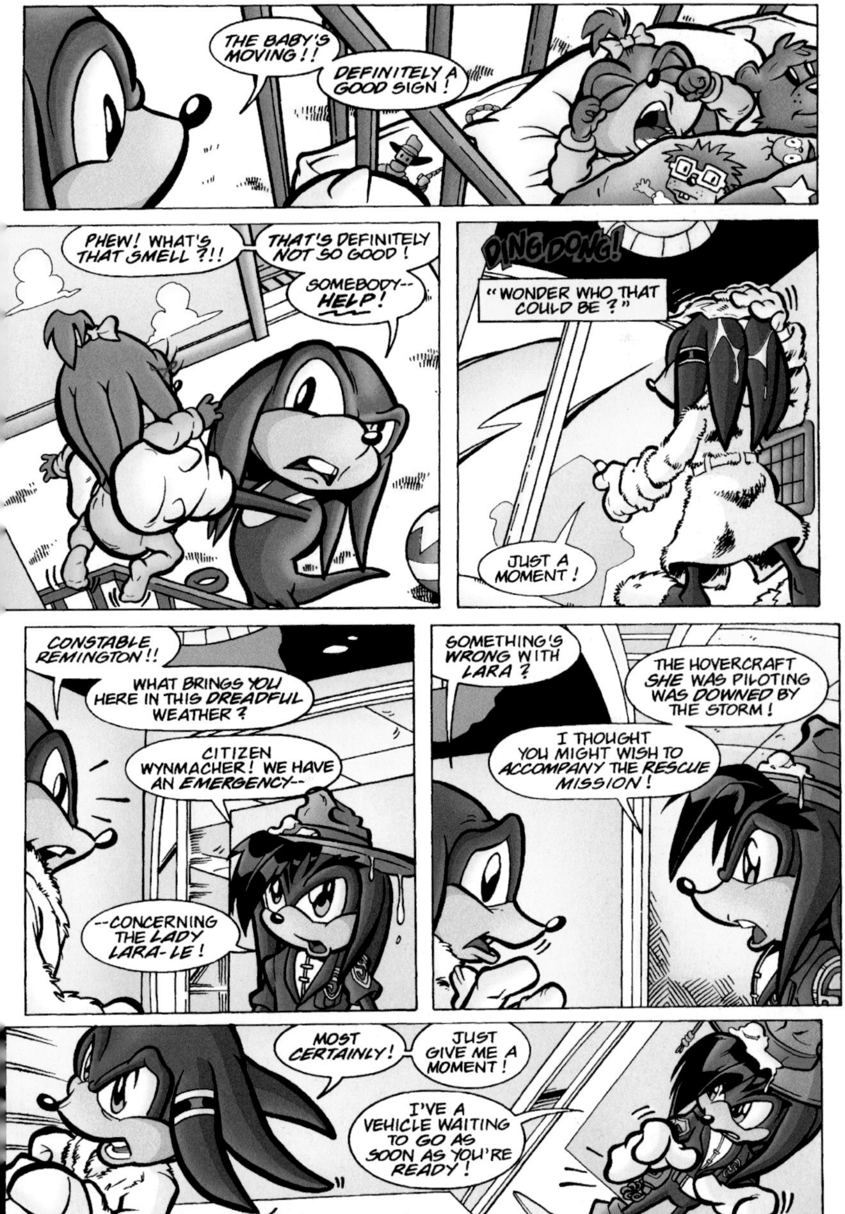
THE BABY'S MOVING!!
DEFINITELY A GOOD SIGN!
PHEW! WHAT'S THAT SMELL?!!
THAT'S DEFINITELY NOT SO GOOD!
SOMEBODY-- HELP!
DING DONG!
"WONDER WHO THAT COULD BE?"
JUST A MOMENT!
CONSTABLE REMINGTON!!
WHAT BRINGS YOU HERE IN THIS DREADFUL WEATHER?
CITIZEN WYNMACHER! WE HAVE AN EMERGENCY--
--CONCERNING THE LADY LARA-LE!
SOMETHING'S WRONG WITH LARA?
THE HOVERCRAFT SHE WAS PILOTING WAS DOWNED BY THE STORM!
I THOUGHT YOU MIGHT WISH TO ACCOMPANY THE RESCUE MISSION!
MOST CERTAINLY!
JUST GIVE ME A MOMENT!
I'VE A VEHICLE WAITING TO GO AS SOON AS YOU'RE READY!

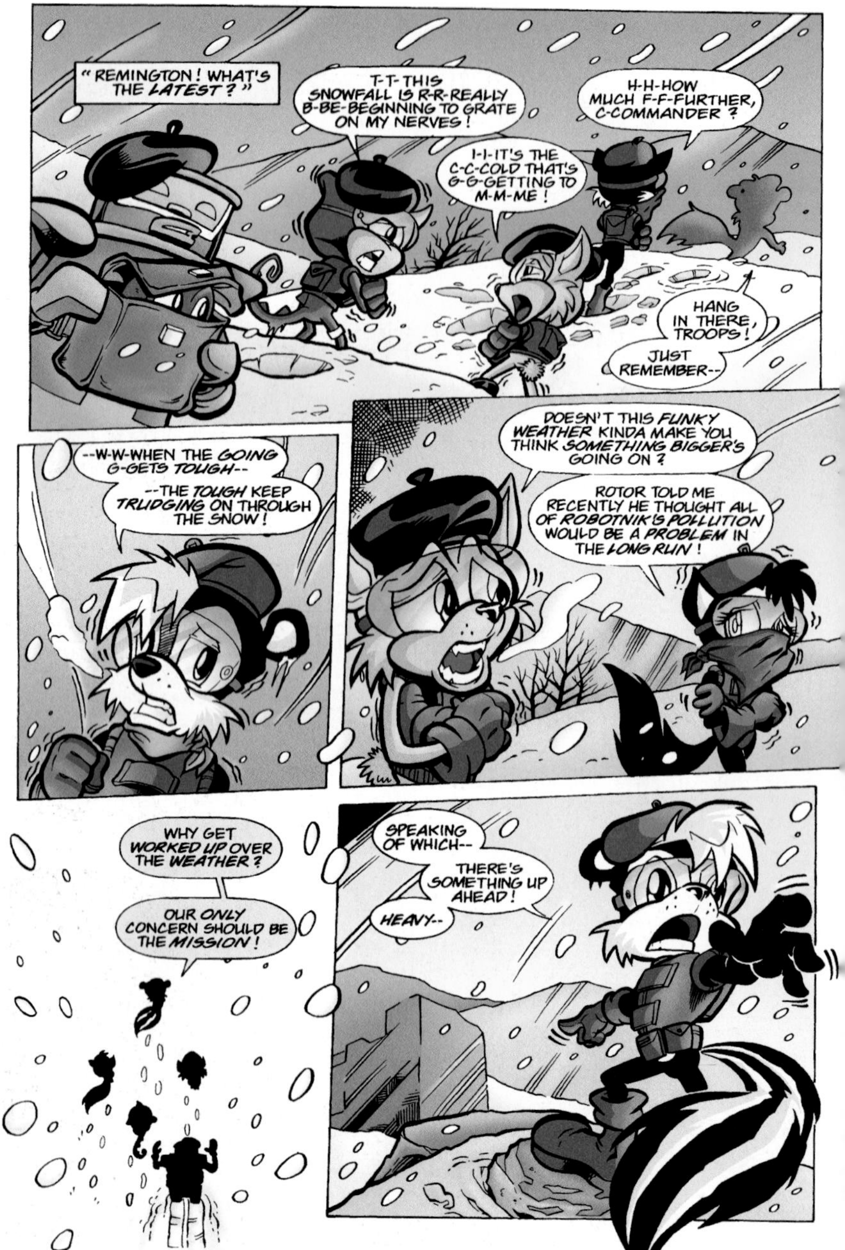
"REMINGTON! WHAT'S THE *LATEST?*"
T-T-THIS SNOWFALL IS R-R-REALLY B-BE-BEGINNING TO GRATE ON MY NERVES!
I-I-IT'S THE C-C-COLD THAT'S G-G-GETTING TO M-M-ME!
H-H-HOW MUCH F-F-FURTHER, C-COMMANDER?
HANG IN THERE, TROOPS!
JUST REMEMBER--
--W-W-WHEN THE *GOING* G-GETS *TOUGH*--
--THE *TOUGH* KEEP *TRUDGING* ON THROUGH THE SNOW!
DOESN'T THIS *FUNKY WEATHER* KINDA MAKE YOU THINK *SOMETHING BIGGER'S* GOING ON?
ROTOR TOLD ME RECENTLY HE THOUGHT *ALL* OF *ROBOTNIK'S POLLUTION* WOULD BE A *PROBLEM* IN THE *LONG RUN*!
WHY GET *WORKED UP* OVER THE *WEATHER?*
OUR *ONLY* CONCERN SHOULD BE THE *MISSION*!
SPEAKING OF WHICH--
THERE'S SOMETHING UP AHEAD!
HEAVY--

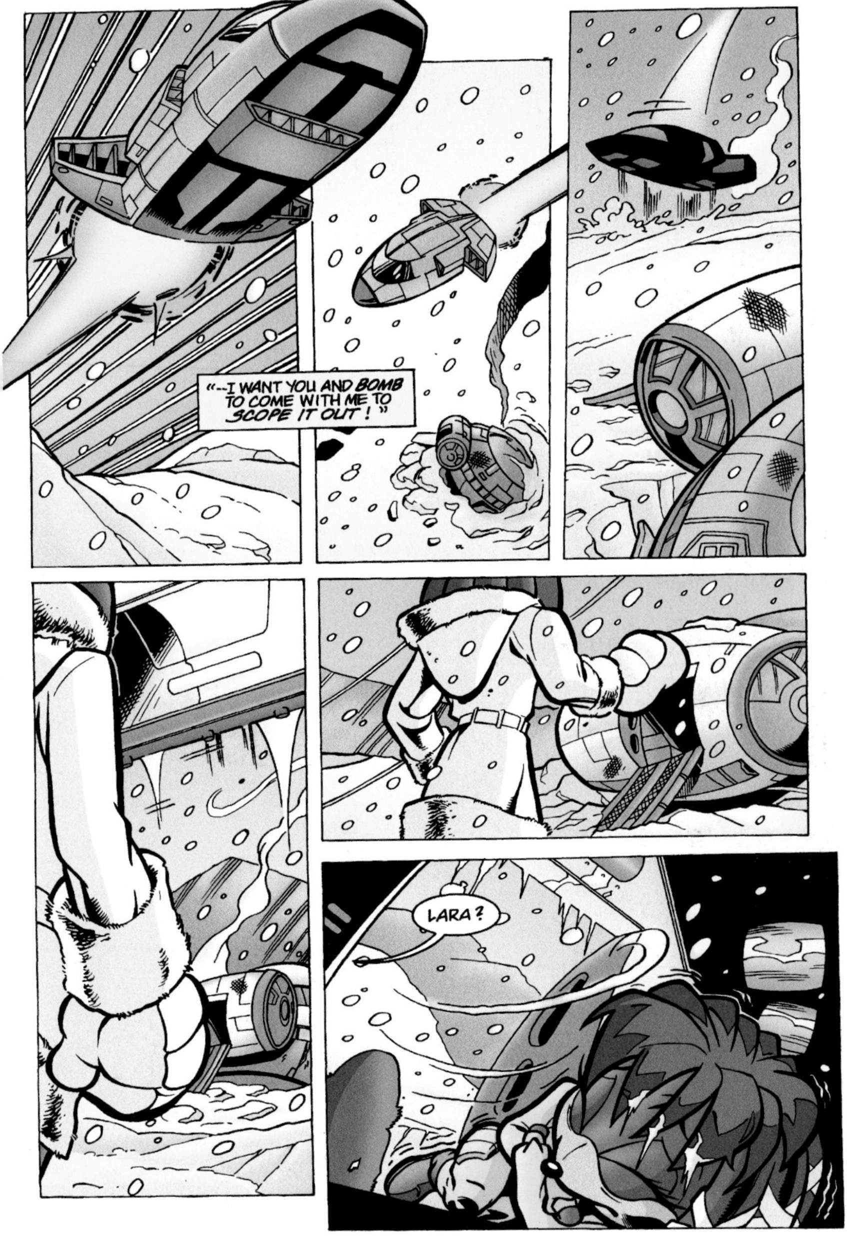
"--I WANT YOU AND BOMB TO COME WITH ME TO SCOPE IT OUT!"
LARA?

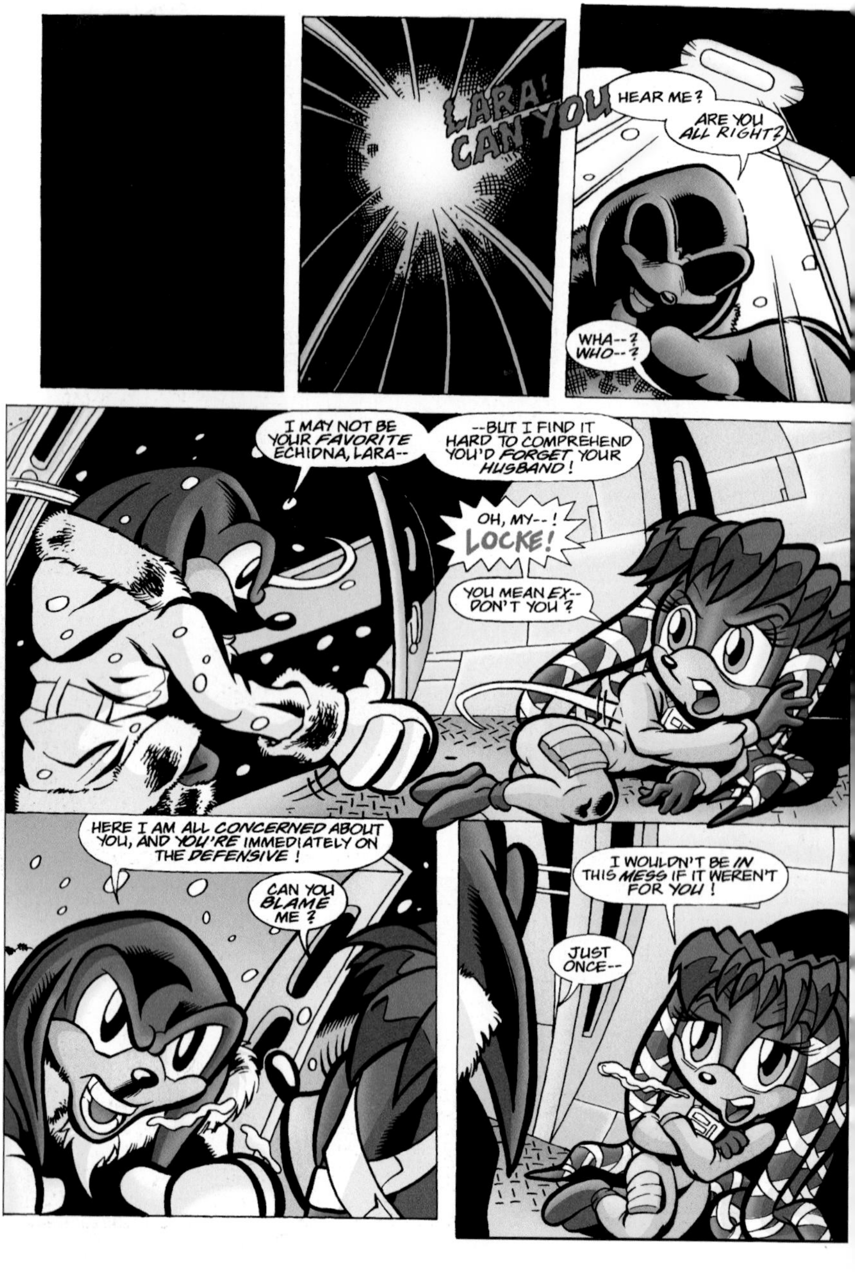
LARA! CAN YOU
HEAR ME?
ARE YOU ALL RIGHT?
WHA--? WHO--?
I MAY NOT BE YOUR FAVORITE ECHIDNA, LARA--
--BUT I FIND IT HARD TO COMPREHEND YOU'D FORGET YOUR HUSBAND!
OH, MY--! LOCKE!
YOU MEAN EX-- DON'T YOU?
HERE I AM ALL CONCERNED ABOUT YOU, AND YOU'RE IMMEDIATELY ON THE DEFENSIVE!
CAN YOU BLAME ME?
I WOULDN'T BE IN THIS MESS IF IT WEREN'T FOR YOU!
JUST ONCE--

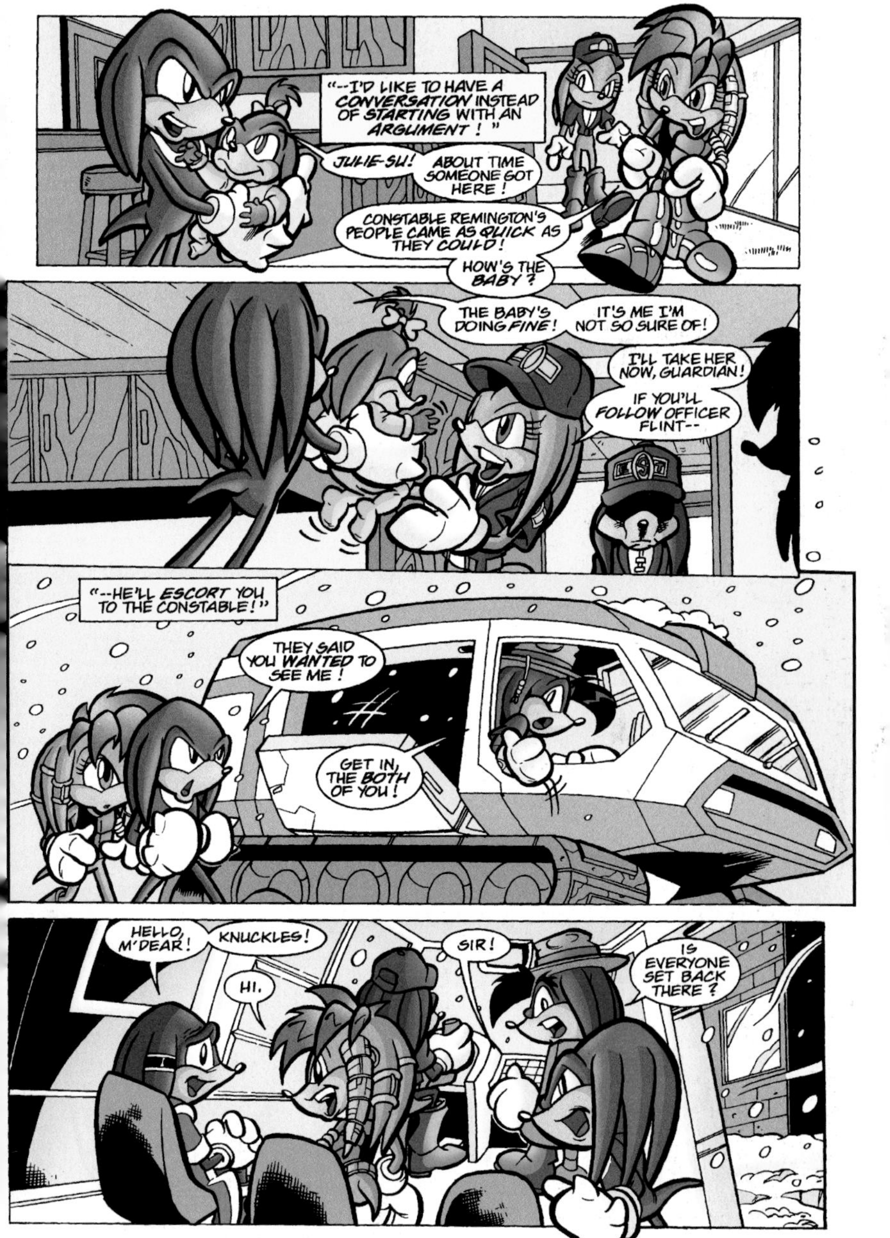
"--I'D LIKE TO HAVE A CONVERSATION INSTEAD OF STARTING WITH AN ARGUMENT!"
JULIE-SU!
ABOUT TIME SOMEONE GOT HERE!
CONSTABLE REMINGTON'S PEOPLE CAME AS QUICK AS THEY COULD!
HOW'S THE BABY?
THE BABY'S DOING FINE!
IT'S ME I'M NOT SO SURE OF!
I'LL TAKE HER NOW, GUARDIAN!
IF YOU'LL FOLLOW OFFICER FLINT--
"--HE'LL ESCORT YOU TO THE CONSTABLE!"
THEY SAID YOU WANTED TO SEE ME!
GET IN, THE BOTH OF YOU!
HELLO, M'DEAR!
KNUCKLES!
HI.
SIR!
IS EVERYONE SET BACK THERE?

TAKE US TO THE HOVER-PORT, DRIVER!

OUR SHUTTLE IS WAITING!

WHAT'S THE RUSH, CONSTABLE?

WHAT COULD POSSIBLY BE WORTH RISKING OUR NECKS FLYING UNDER THESE CONDITIONS?

I'D SAY YOUR MOTHER IS WORTH IT, WOULDN'T YOU?

MOM?!!

WHAT HAPPENED? WHERE IS SHE?

THAT'S WHAT WE'RE GOING TO FIND OUT!

ARE YOU SAYING NOBODY KNOWS NOTHING?!

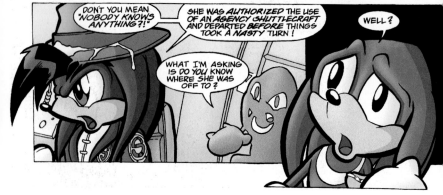

DON'T YOU MEAN "NOBODY KNOWS ANYTHING?!"

SHE WAS AUTHORIZED THE USE OF AN AGENCY SHUTTLECRAFT AND DEPARTED BEFORE THINGS TOOK A NASTY TURN!

WHAT I'M ASKING IS DO YOU KNOW WHERE SHE WAS OFF TO?

WELL?

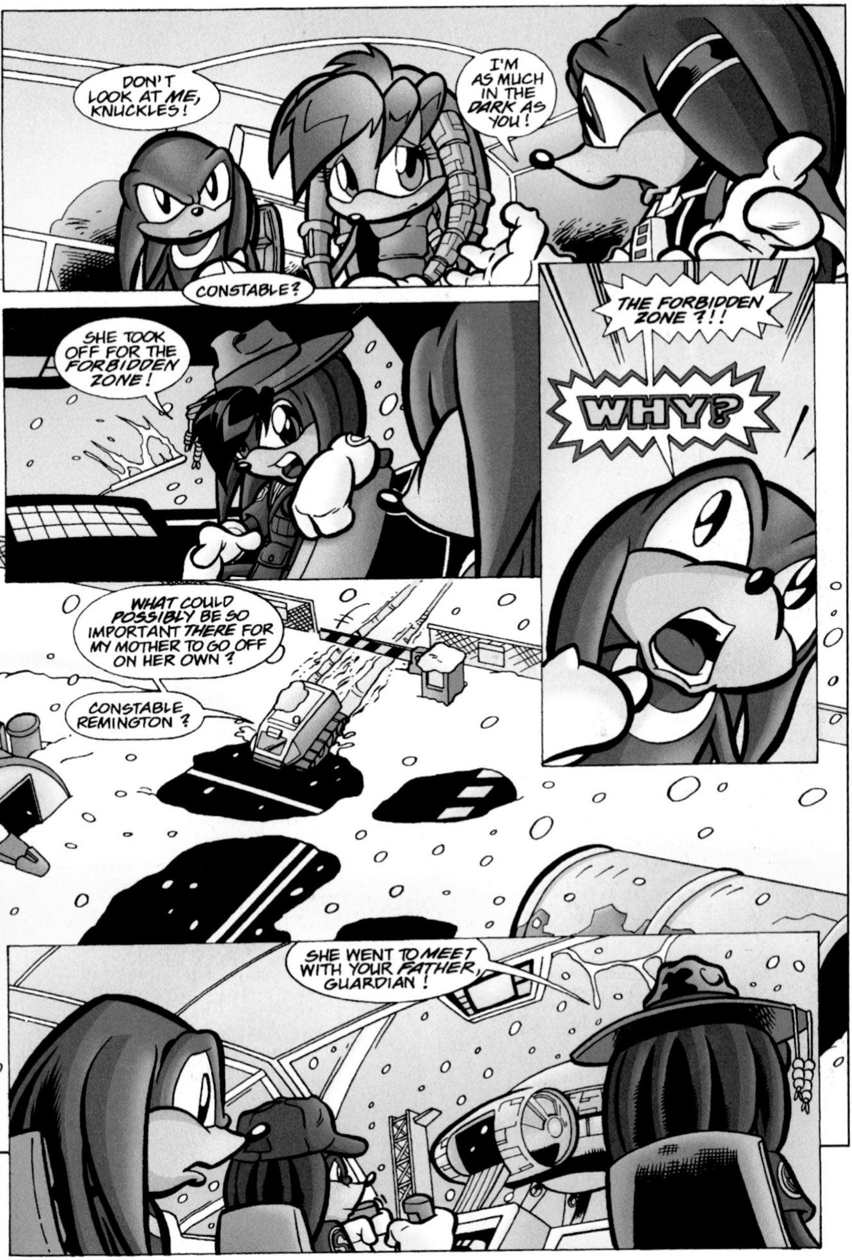
DON'T LOOK AT ME, KNUCKLES!
I'M AS MUCH IN THE DARK AS YOU!
CONSTABLE?
SHE TOOK OFF FOR THE FORBIDDEN ZONE!
THE FORBIDDEN ZONE?!!
WHY?
WHAT COULD POSSIBLY BE SO IMPORTANT THERE FOR MY MOTHER TO GO OFF ON HER OWN?
CONSTABLE REMINGTON?
SHE WENT TO MEET WITH YOUR FATHER, GUARDIAN!

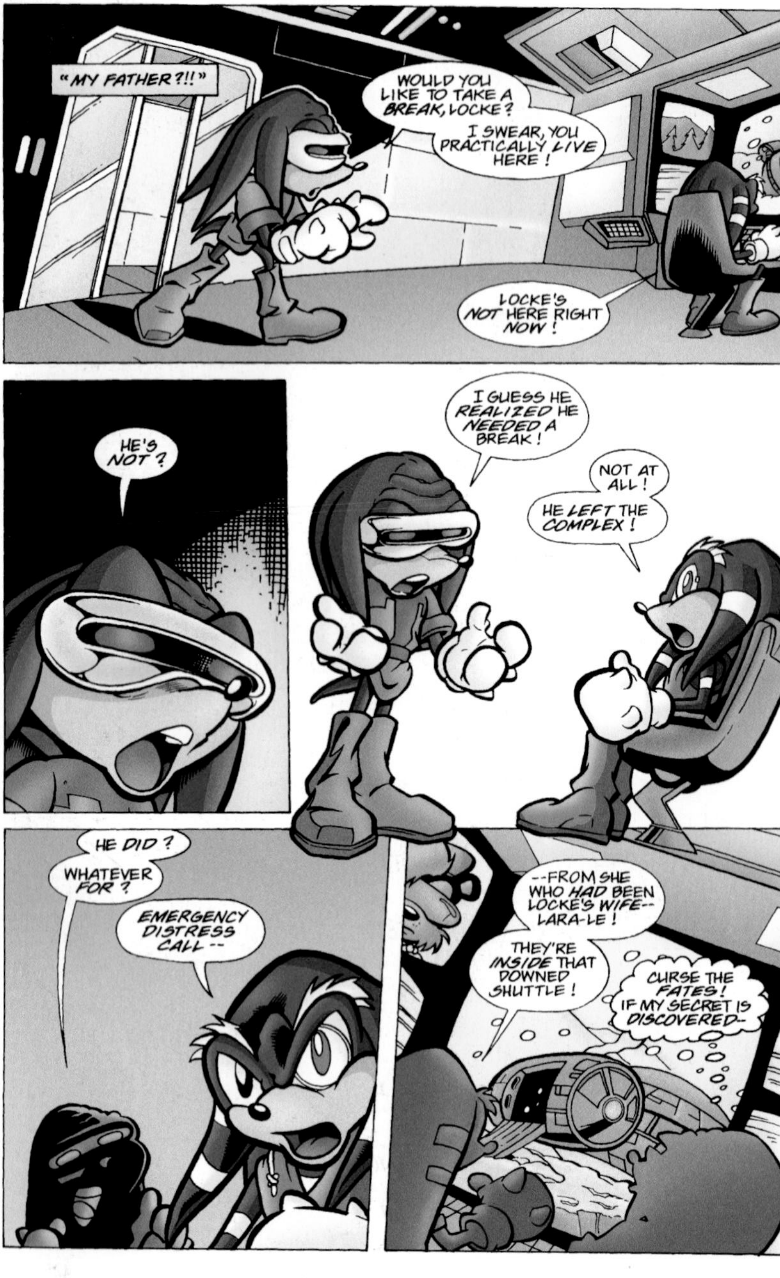
"MY FATHER?!!"
WOULD YOU LIKE TO TAKE A BREAK, LOCKE?
I SWEAR, YOU PRACTICALLY LIVE HERE!
LOCKE'S NOT HERE RIGHT NOW!
HE'S NOT?
I GUESS HE REALIZED HE NEEDED A BREAK!
NOT AT ALL!
HE LEFT THE COMPLEX!
HE DID?
WHATEVER FOR?
EMERGENCY DISTRESS CALL --
--FROM SHE WHO HAD BEEN LOCKE'S WIFE-- LARA-LE!
THEY'RE INSIDE THAT DOWNED SHUTTLE!
CURSE THE FATES! IF MY SECRET IS DISCOVERED--

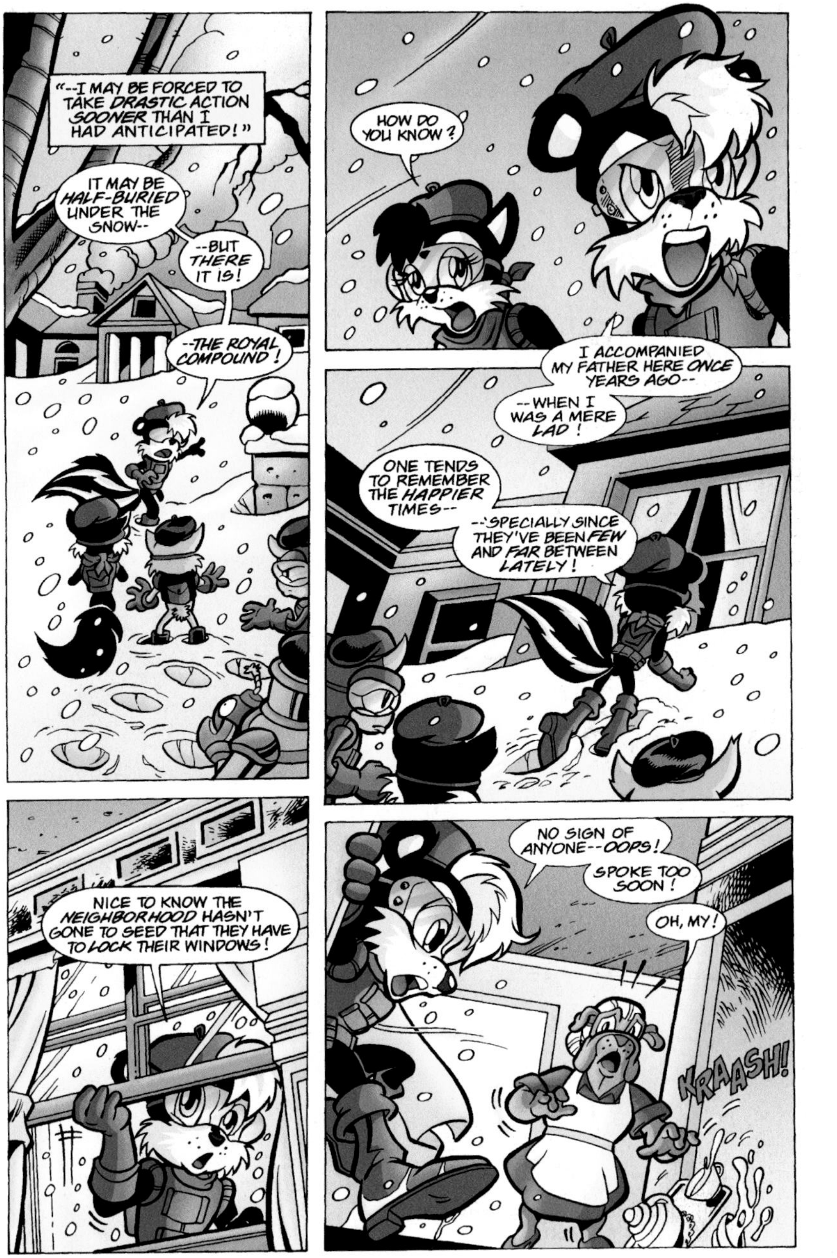
"--I MAY BE FORCED TO TAKE DRASTIC ACTION SOONER THAN I HAD ANTICIPATED!"
IT MAY BE HALF-BURIED UNDER THE SNOW--
--BUT THERE IT IS!
--THE ROYAL COMPOUND!
HOW DO YOU KNOW?
I ACCOMPANIED MY FATHER HERE ONCE YEARS AGO--
--WHEN I WAS A MERE LAD!
ONE TENDS TO REMEMBER THE HAPPIER TIMES--
--'SPECIALLY SINCE THEY'VE BEEN FEW AND FAR BETWEEN LATELY!
NICE TO KNOW THE NEIGHBORHOOD HASN'T GONE TO SEED THAT THEY HAVE TO LOCK THEIR WINDOWS!
NO SIGN OF ANYONE--OOPS!
SPOKE TOO SOON!
OH, MY!
KRAASH!

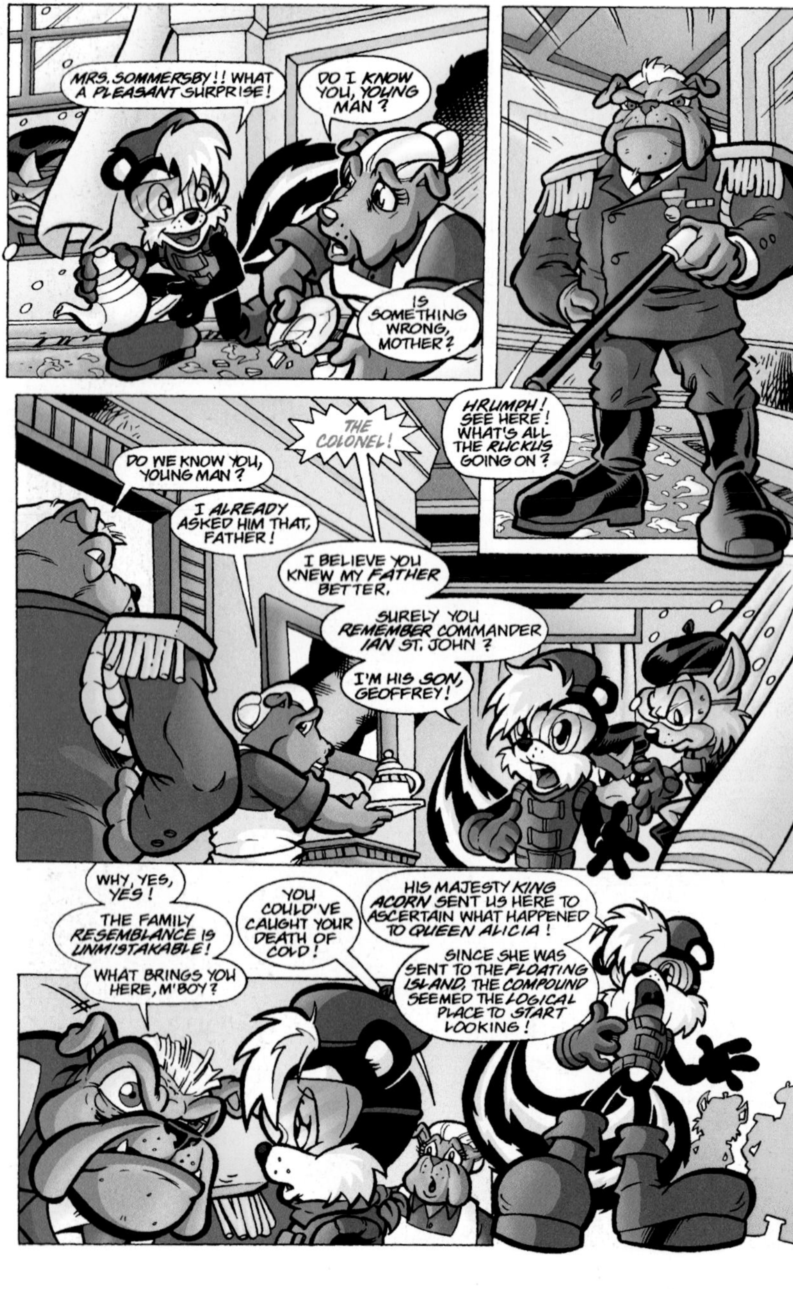
MRS. SOMMERSBY!! WHAT A PLEASANT SURPRISE!
DO I KNOW YOU, YOUNG MAN?
IS SOMETHING WRONG, MOTHER?
HRUMPH! SEE HERE! WHAT'S ALL THE RUCKUS GOING ON?
THE COLONEL!
DO WE KNOW YOU, YOUNG MAN?
I ALREADY ASKED HIM THAT, FATHER!
I BELIEVE YOU KNEW MY FATHER BETTER.
SURELY YOU REMEMBER COMMANDER IAN ST. JOHN?
I'M HIS SON, GEOFFREY!
WHY, YES, YES!
THE FAMILY RESEMBLANCE IS UNMISTAKABLE!
WHAT BRINGS YOU HERE, M'BOY?
YOU COULD'VE CAUGHT YOUR DEATH OF COLD!
HIS MAJESTY KING ACORN SENT US HERE TO ASCERTAIN WHAT HAPPENED TO QUEEN ALICIA!
SINCE SHE WAS SENT TO THE FLOATING ISLAND, THE COMPOUND SEEMED THE LOGICAL PLACE TO START LOOKING!

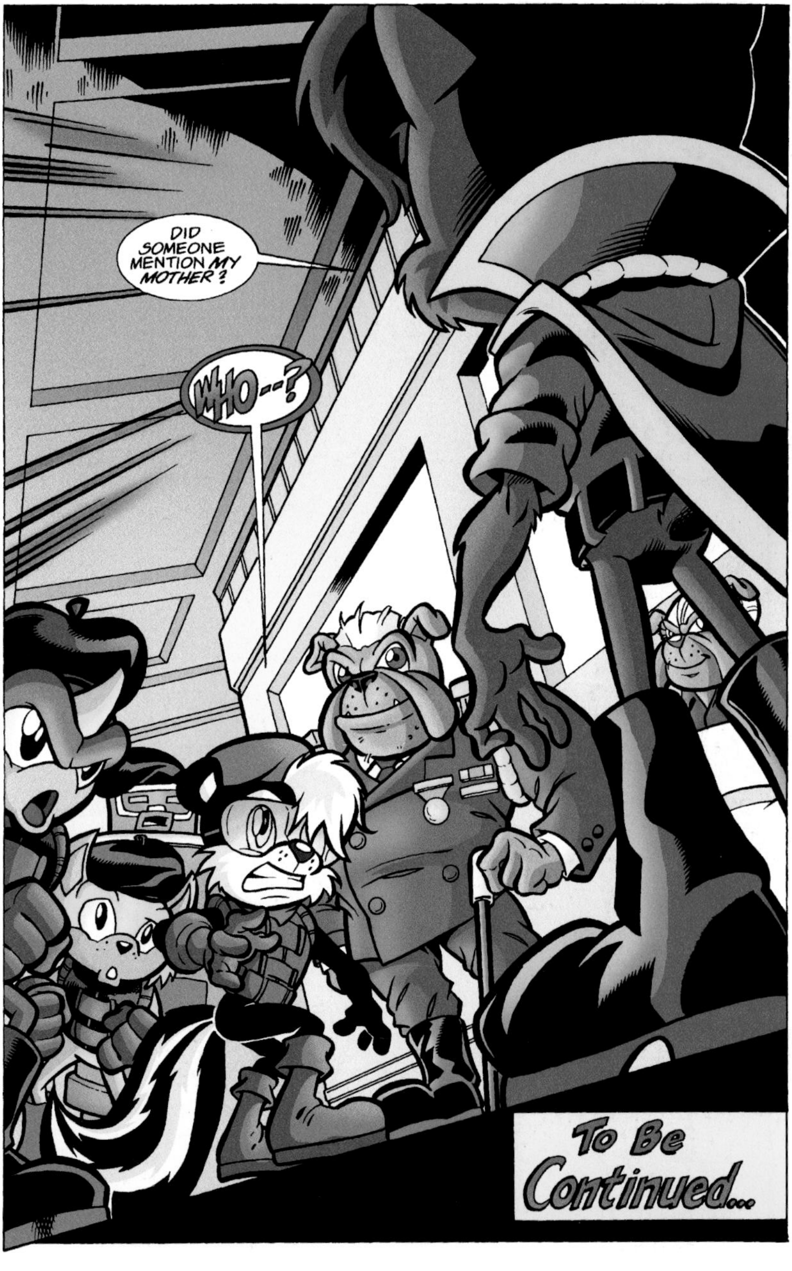
DID SOMEONE MENTION MY MOTHER?
WHO--?
To Be Continued...

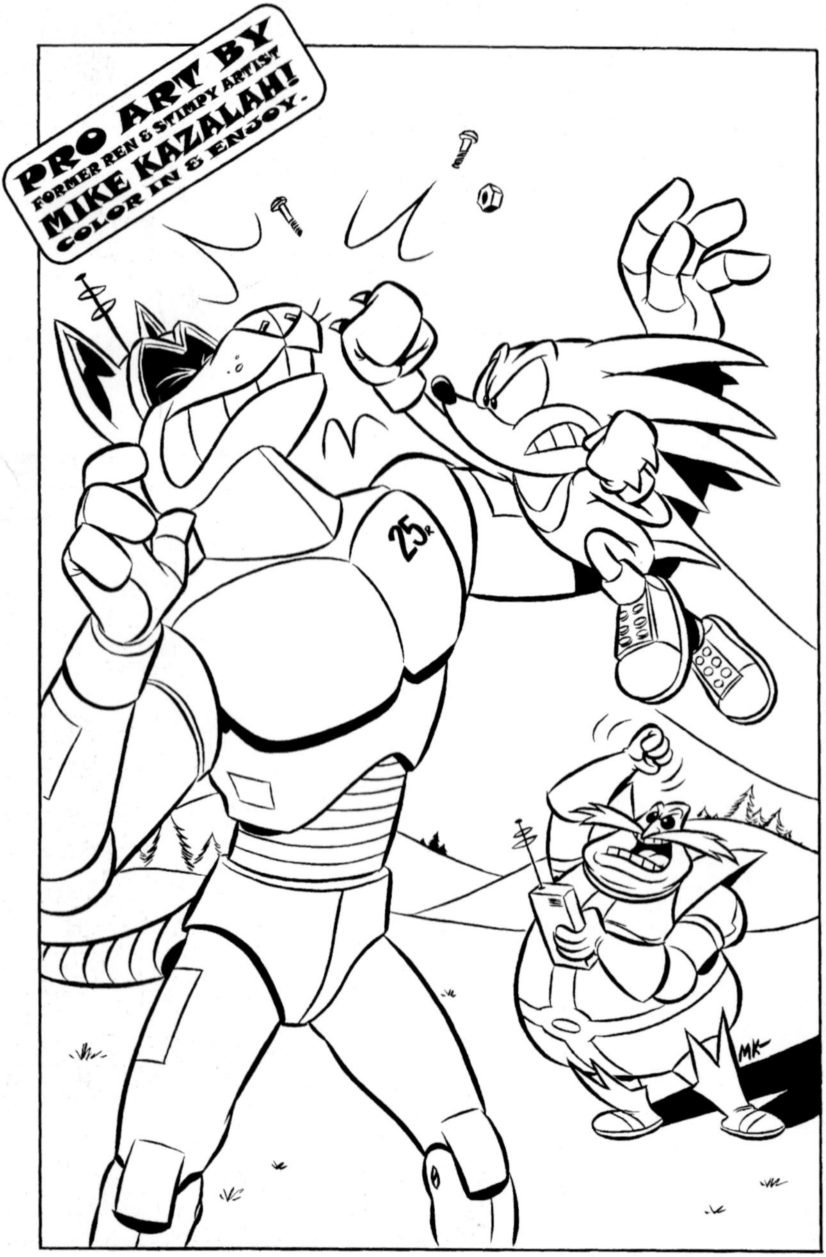
PRO ART BY
FORMER REN & STIMPY ARTIST
MIKE KAZALAH!
COLOR IN & ENJOY.
25R
MK

KE AN EXCLUSIVE LOOK
HIND THE SCENES OF
UCKLES THE ECHIDNA,
WE REVEAL...

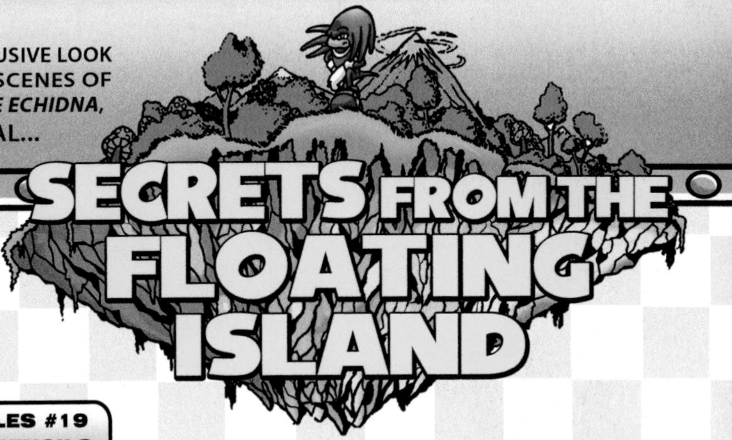

SECRETS FROM THE FLOATING ISLAND

KNUCKLES #19 COVER PENCILS

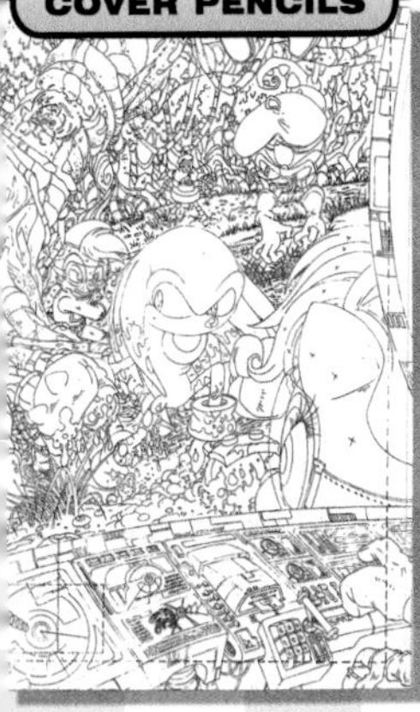

KNUCKLES #19 COVER FINAL INKS

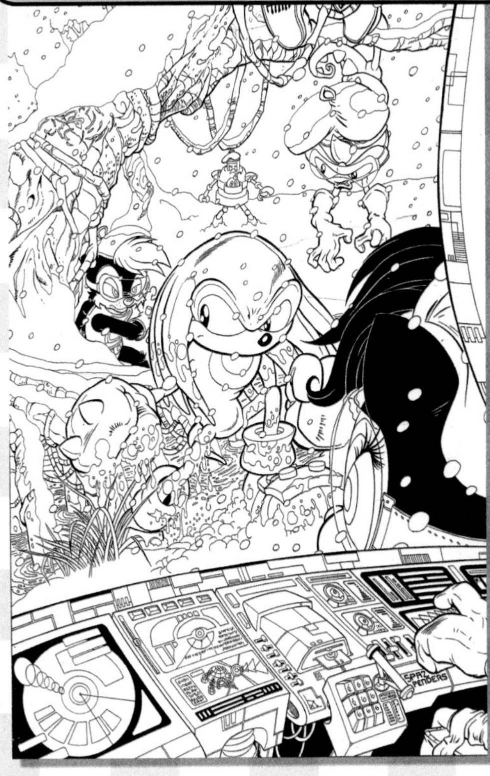
SPAZ PENDERS

NUCKLES #18 COVER TOBOR PENCILS

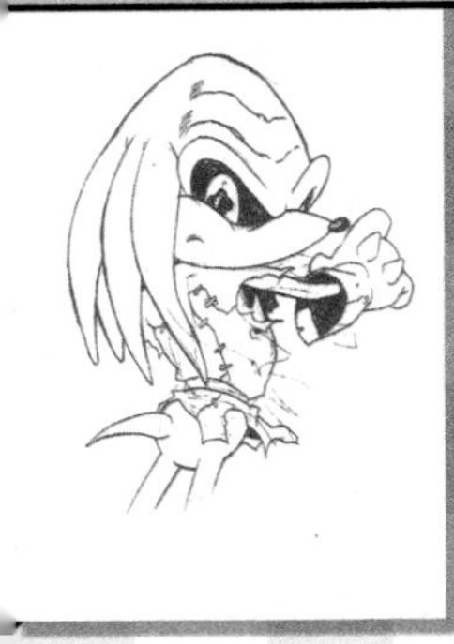

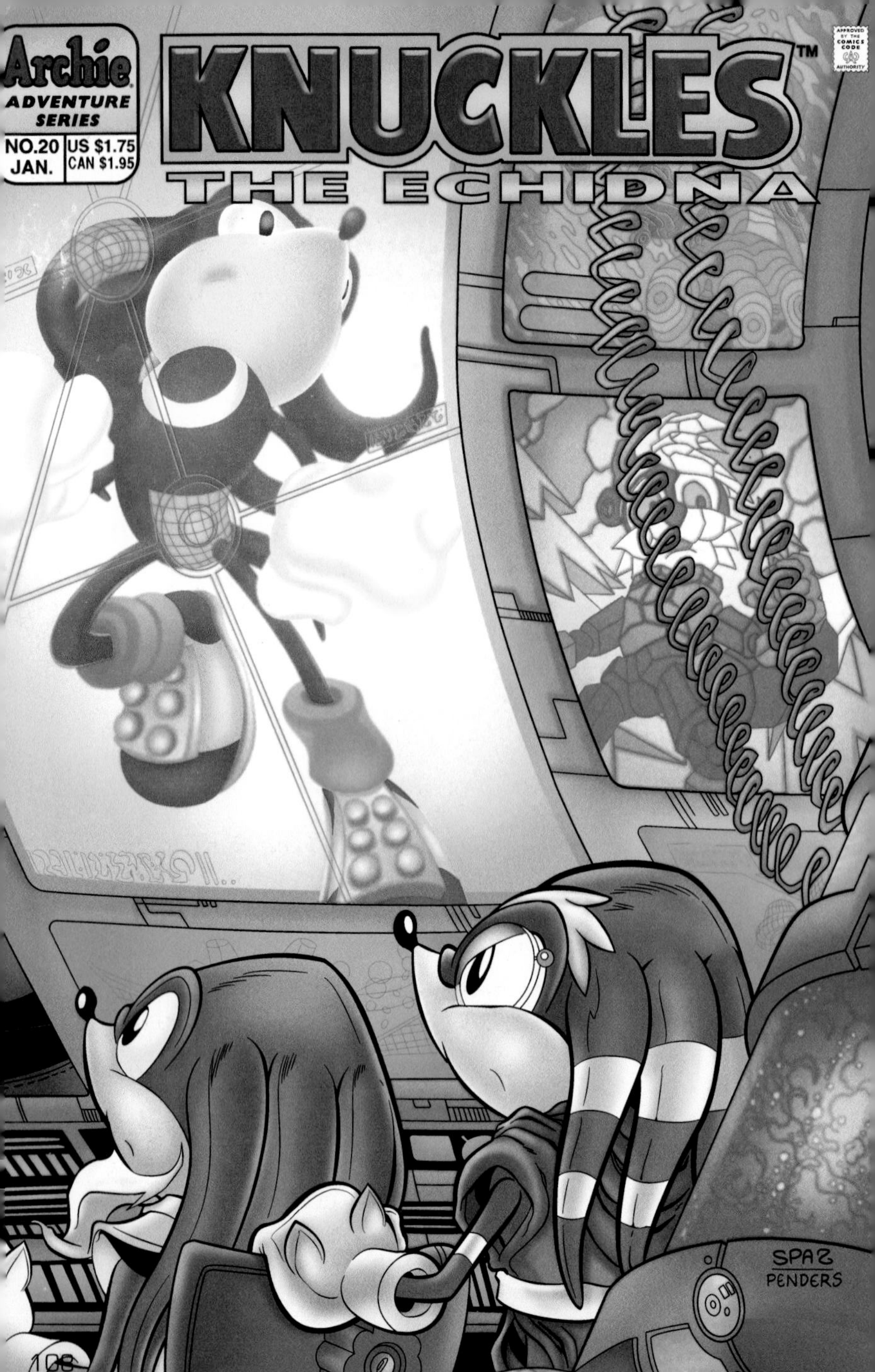
Archie ADVENTURE SERIES
NO.20 JAN.
US $1.75 CAN $1.95
KNUCKLES™ THE ECHIDNA
APPROVED BY THE COMICS CODE AUTHORITY
SPAZ PENDERS

KNUCKLES™
BOOK TWENTY

The Forbidden Zone
Part Two of Three

Ken Penders
Writer
Manny Galan
Penciler
Andrew Pepoy
Inker
Barry Grossman
Colorist
Vickie Williams
Letterer

Justin Gabrie
Editor

Victor Gorelick
Managing Editor

Richard Goldwater
Editor-in-Chief

Born to the most noble of Echidna houses,
the latest to continue the family heritage
and responsibility as
GUARDIAN OF THE FLOATING ISLAND,
defender of all the forces of evil from the world
beyond as well as those who would
threaten within, he is none other than...
KNUCKLES THE ECHIDNA!

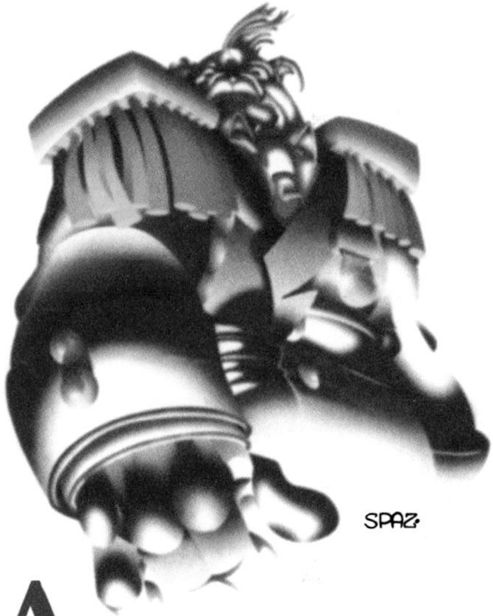
SPAZ

An uncommon force of nature has unleashed a **snowstorm** across the face of **The Floating Island**, wrecking havoc for all who dwell upon it. The **fury** that **nature** has created however, pales in significance to the events about to play out, with the participants on a collision course with **destiny**.

Somewhere in the snow-covered **Sandopolis Zone**, we find a downed shuttle containing **two** of the **key players...**

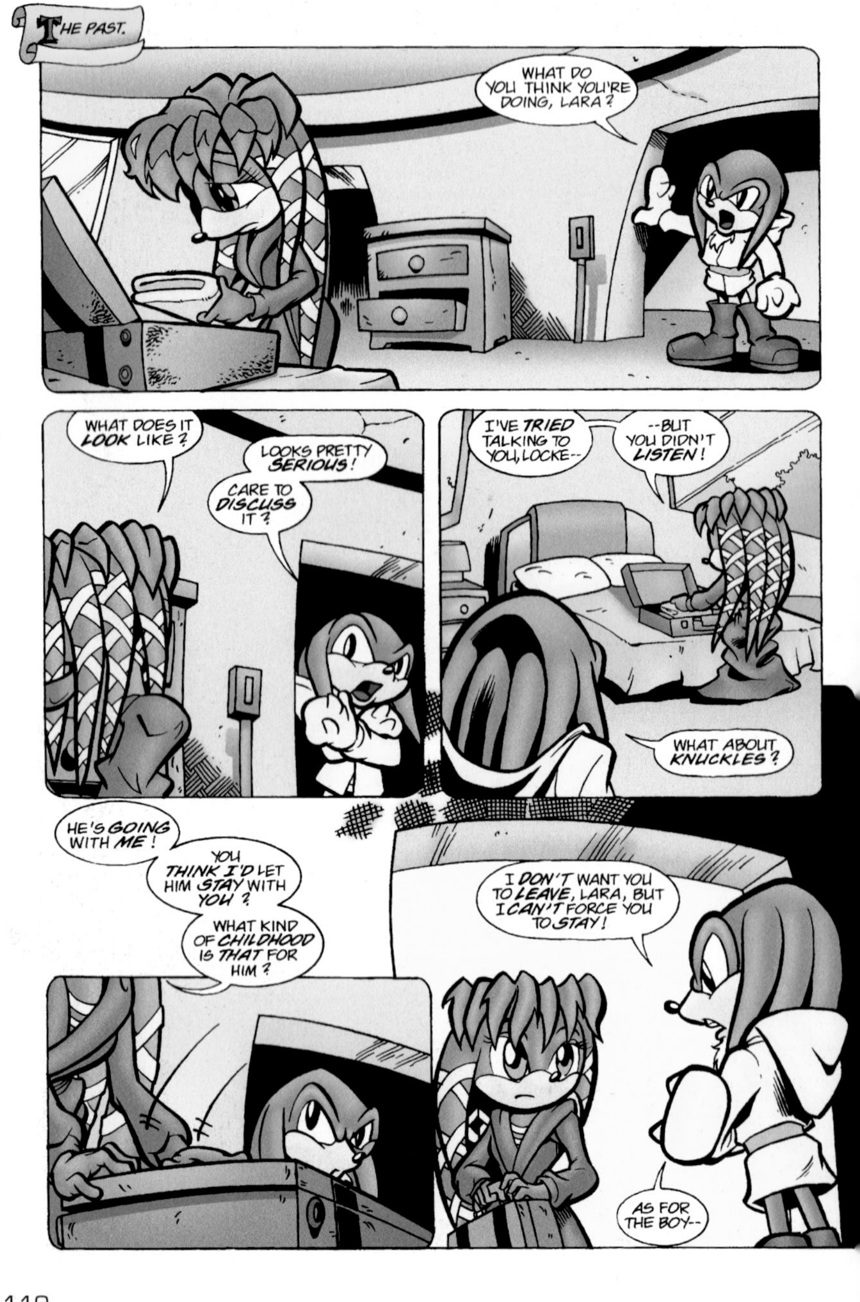
THE PAST.
WHAT DO YOU THINK YOU'RE DOING, LARA?
WHAT DOES IT LOOK LIKE?
LOOKS PRETTY SERIOUS!
CARE TO DISCUSS IT?
I'VE TRIED TALKING TO YOU, LOCKE--
--BUT YOU DIDN'T LISTEN!
WHAT ABOUT KNUCKLES?
HE'S GOING WITH ME!
YOU THINK I'D LET HIM STAY WITH YOU?
WHAT KIND OF CHILDHOOD IS THAT FOR HIM?
I DON'T WANT YOU TO LEAVE, LARA, BUT I CAN'T FORCE YOU TO STAY!
AS FOR THE BOY--

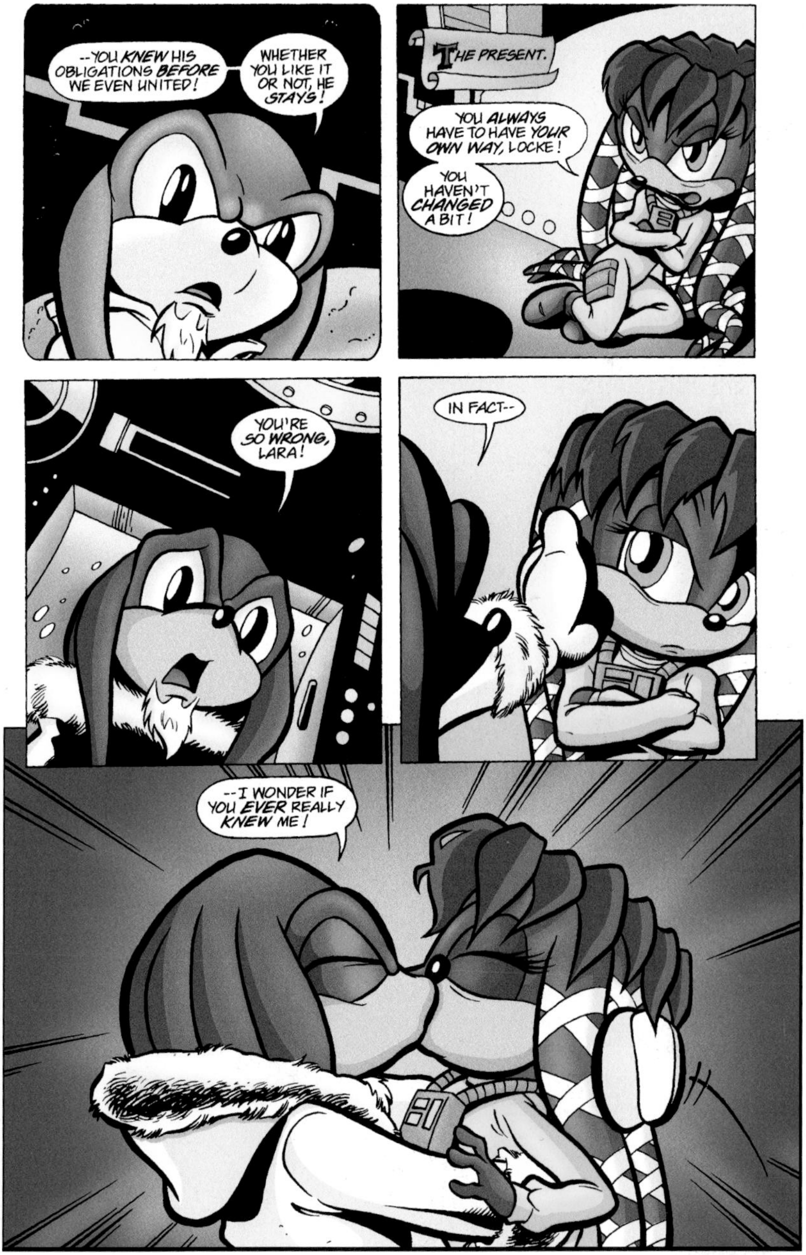
--YOU KNEW HIS OBLIGATIONS BEFORE WE EVEN UNITED!
WHETHER YOU LIKE IT OR NOT, HE STAYS!
THE PRESENT.
YOU ALWAYS HAVE TO HAVE YOUR OWN WAY, LOCKE!
YOU HAVEN'T CHANGED A BIT!
YOU'RE SO WRONG, LARA!
IN FACT--
--I WONDER IF YOU EVER REALLY KNEW ME!

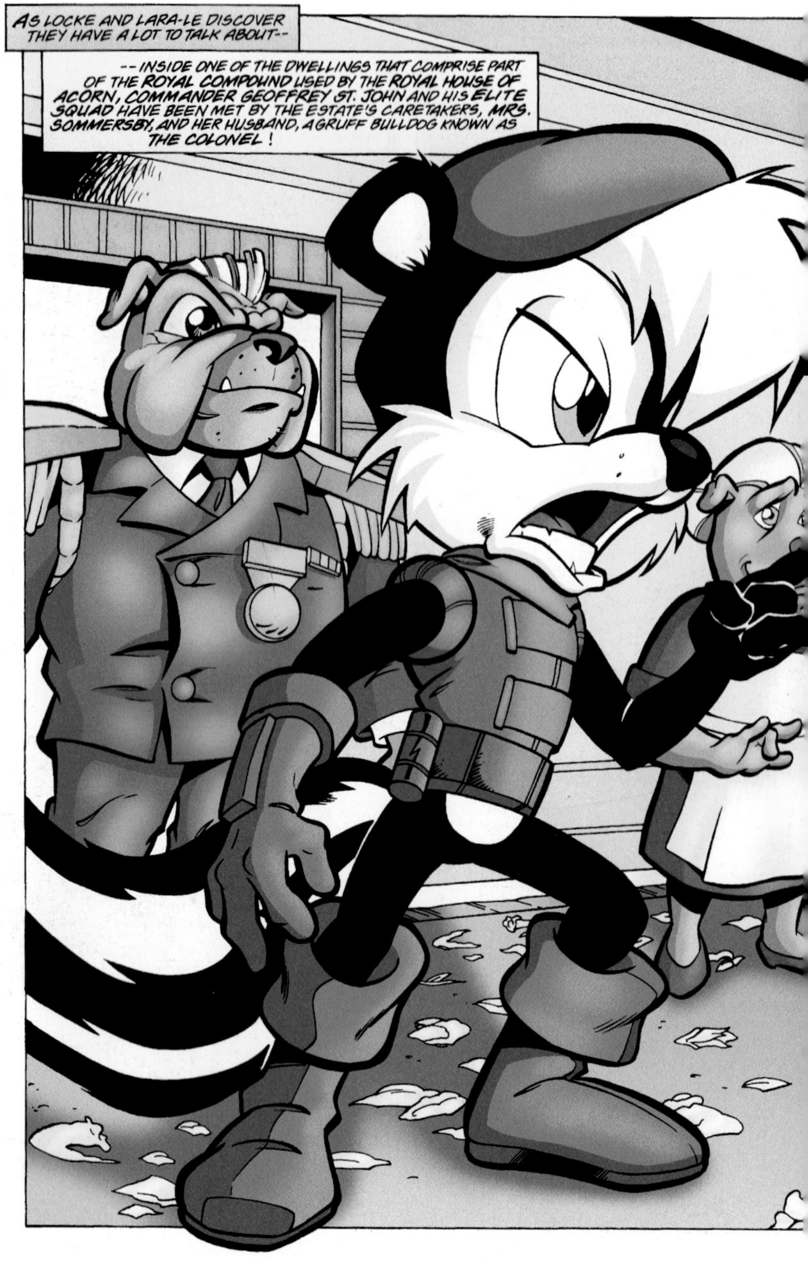
AS LOCKE AND LARA-LE DISCOVER THEY HAVE A LOT TO TALK ABOUT--
--INSIDE ONE OF THE DWELLINGS THAT COMPRISE PART OF THE ROYAL COMPOUND USED BY THE ROYAL HOUSE OF ACORN, COMMANDER GEOFFREY ST. JOHN AND HIS ELITE SQUAD HAVE BEEN MET BY THE ESTATE'S CARETAKERS, MRS. SOMMERSBY, AND HER HUSBAND, A GRUFF BULLDOG KNOWN AS THE COLONEL!

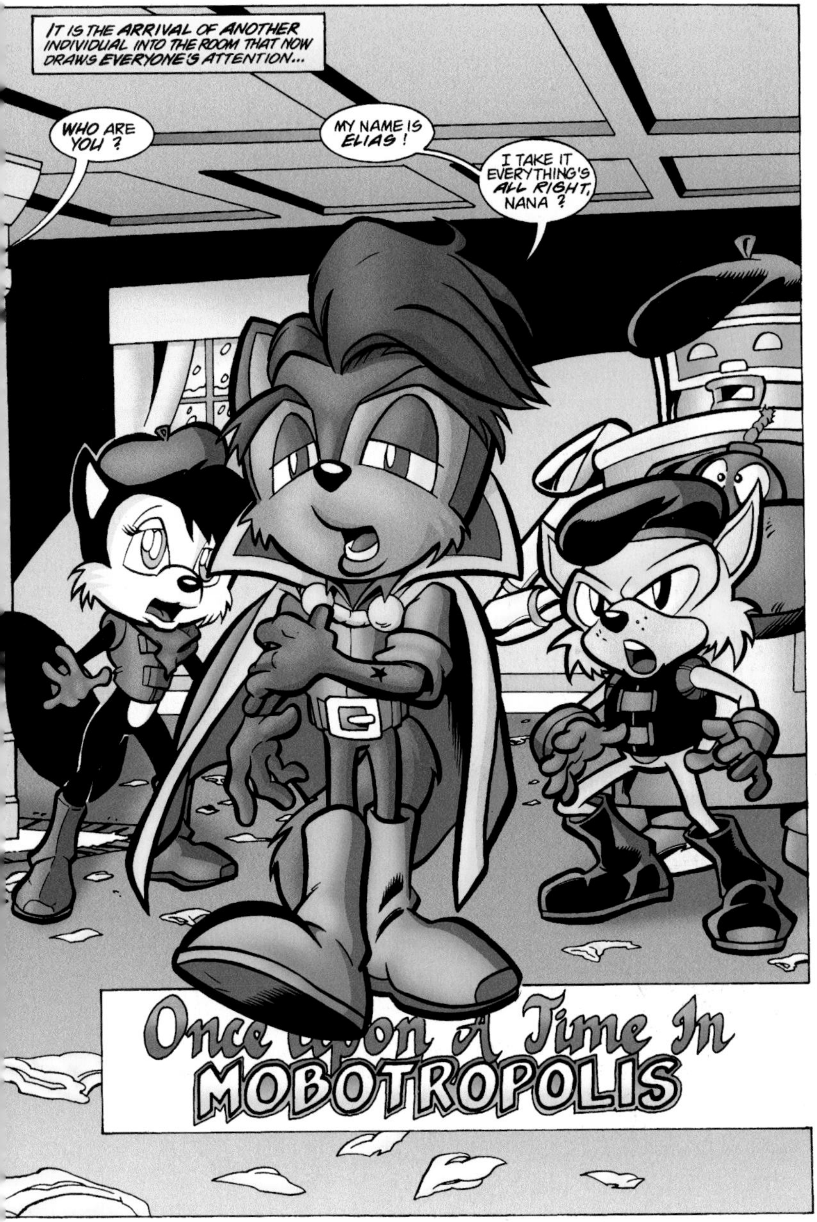
IT IS THE ARRIVAL OF ANOTHER INDIVIDUAL INTO THE ROOM THAT NOW DRAWS EVERYONE'S ATTENTION...
WHO ARE YOU ?
MY NAME IS ELIAS !
I TAKE IT EVERYTHING'S ALL RIGHT, NANA ?
Once Upon A Time In MOBOTROPOLIS

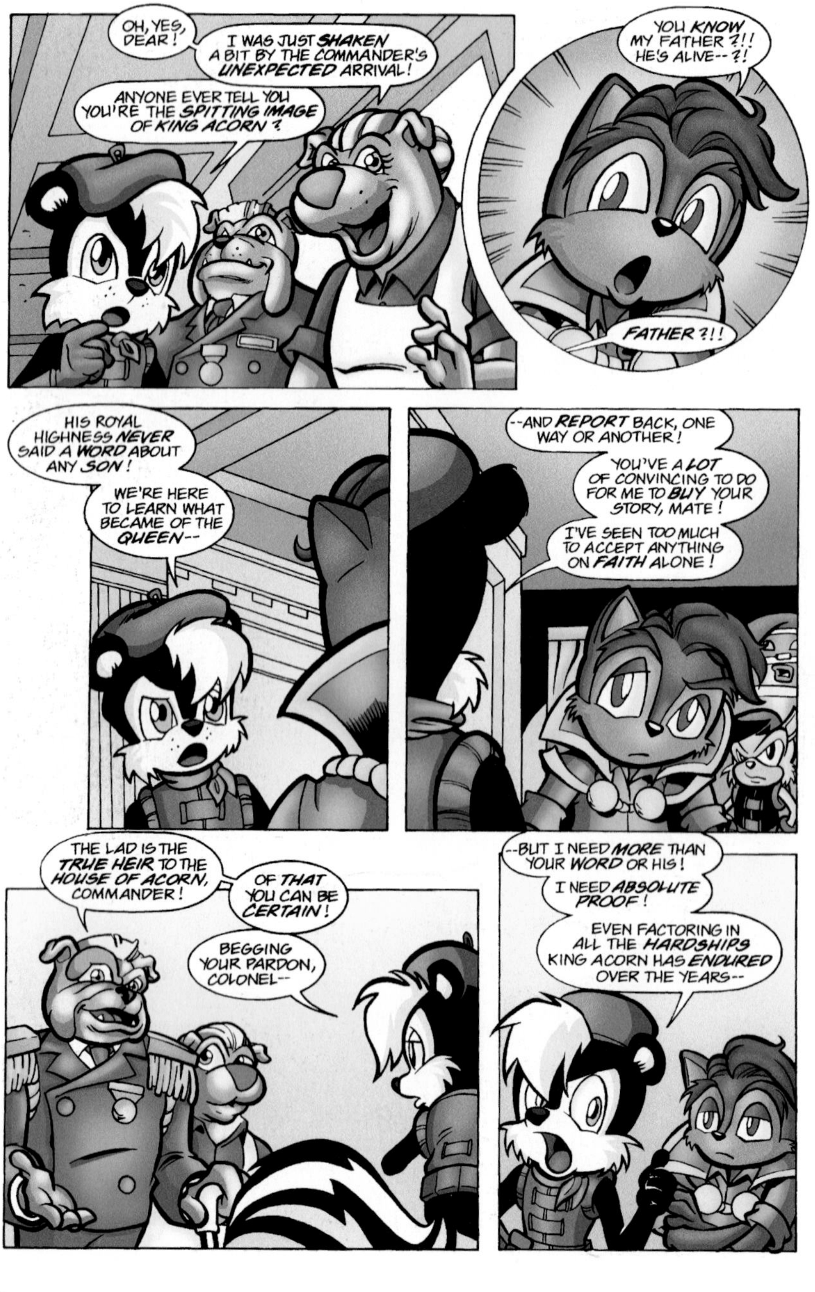
OH, YES, DEAR!
I WAS JUST SHAKEN A BIT BY THE COMMANDER'S UNEXPECTED ARRIVAL!
ANYONE EVER TELL YOU YOU'RE THE SPITTING IMAGE OF KING ACORN?
YOU KNOW MY FATHER?!! HE'S ALIVE--?!
FATHER?!!
HIS ROYAL HIGHNESS NEVER SAID A WORD ABOUT ANY SON!
WE'RE HERE TO LEARN WHAT BECAME OF THE QUEEN--
--AND REPORT BACK, ONE WAY OR ANOTHER!
YOU'VE A LOT OF CONVINCING TO DO FOR ME TO BUY YOUR STORY, MATE!
I'VE SEEN TOO MUCH TO ACCEPT ANYTHING ON FAITH ALONE!
THE LAD IS THE TRUE HEIR TO THE HOUSE OF ACORN, COMMANDER!
OF THAT YOU CAN BE CERTAIN!
BEGGING YOUR PARDON, COLONEL--
--BUT I NEED MORE THAN YOUR WORD OR HIS!
I NEED ABSOLUTE PROOF!
EVEN FACTORING IN ALL THE HARDSHIPS KING ACORN HAS ENDURED OVER THE YEARS--

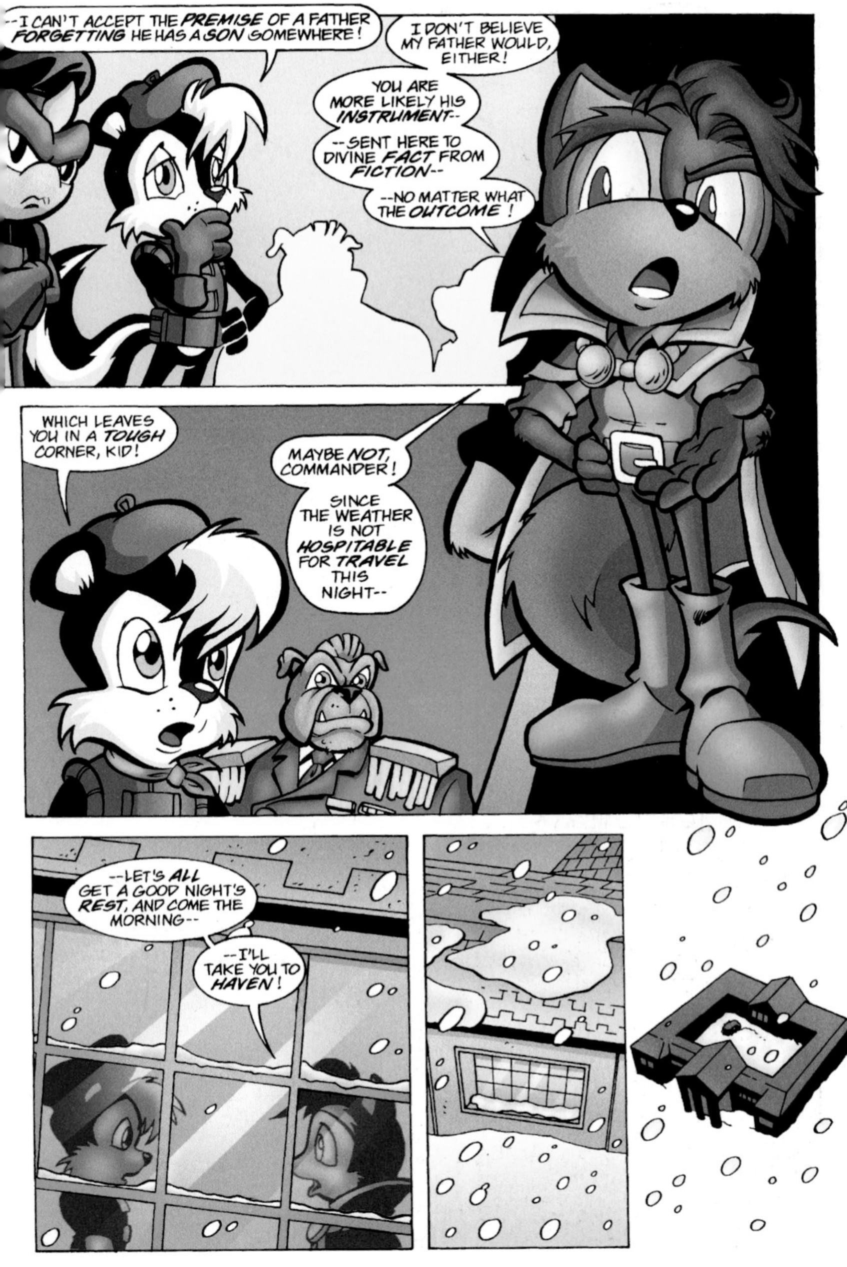
--I CAN'T ACCEPT THE PREMISE OF A FATHER FORGETTING HE HAS A SON SOMEWHERE!
I DON'T BELIEVE MY FATHER WOULD, EITHER!
YOU ARE MORE LIKELY HIS INSTRUMENT--
--SENT HERE TO DIVINE FACT FROM FICTION--
--NO MATTER WHAT THE OUTCOME!
WHICH LEAVES YOU IN A TOUGH CORNER, KID!
MAYBE NOT, COMMANDER!
SINCE THE WEATHER IS NOT HOSPITABLE FOR TRAVEL THIS NIGHT--
--LET'S ALL GET A GOOD NIGHT'S REST, AND COME THE MORNING--
--I'LL TAKE YOU TO HAVEN!

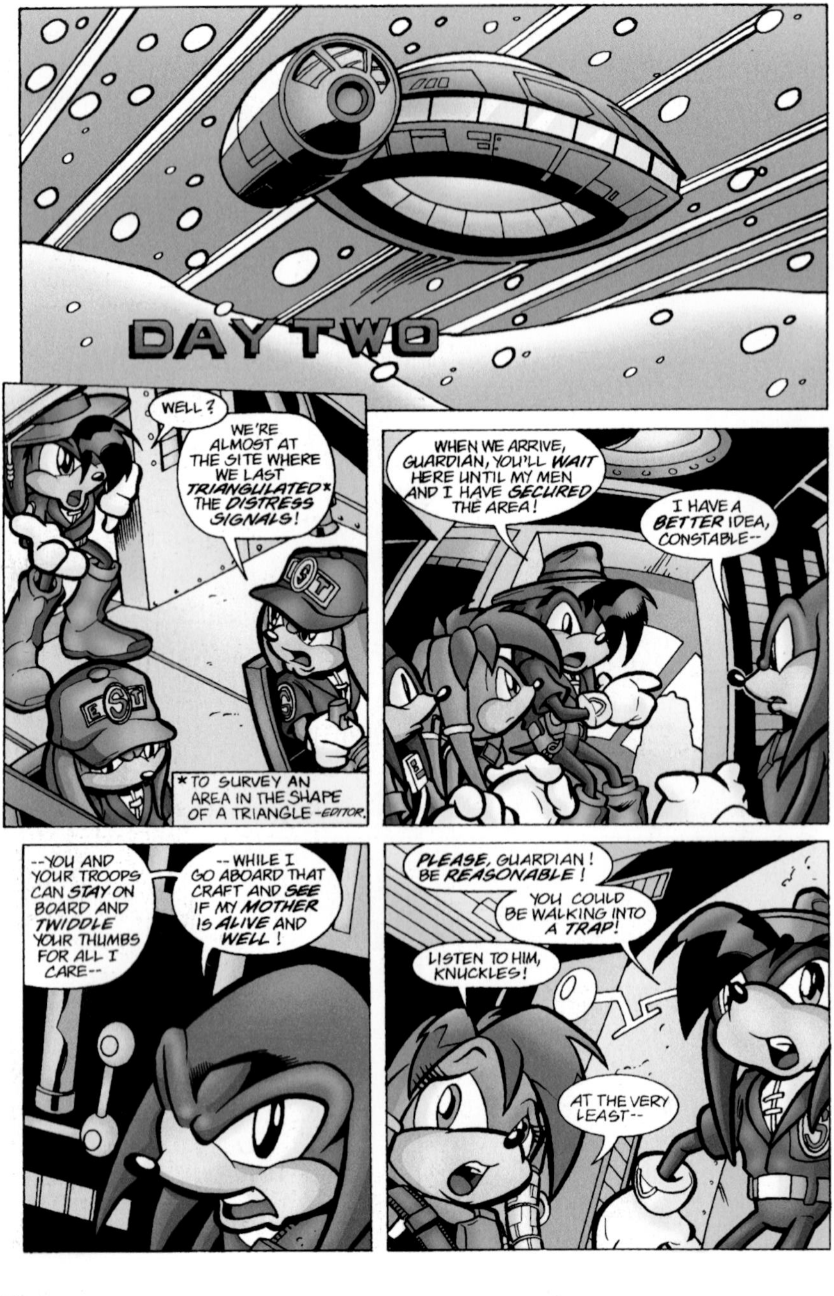
DAY TWO
WELL?
WE'RE ALMOST AT THE SITE WHERE WE LAST TRIANGULATED* THE DISTRESS SIGNALS!
*TO SURVEY AN AREA IN THE SHAPE OF A TRIANGLE -EDITOR.
WHEN WE ARRIVE, GUARDIAN, YOU'LL WAIT HERE UNTIL MY MEN AND I HAVE SECURED THE AREA!
I HAVE A BETTER IDEA, CONSTABLE--
--YOU AND YOUR TROOPS CAN STAY ON BOARD AND TWIDDLE YOUR THUMBS FOR ALL I CARE--
--WHILE I GO ABOARD THAT CRAFT AND SEE IF MY MOTHER IS ALIVE AND WELL!
PLEASE, GUARDIAN! BE REASONABLE!
YOU COULD BE WALKING INTO A TRAP!
LISTEN TO HIM, KNUCKLES!
AT THE VERY LEAST--

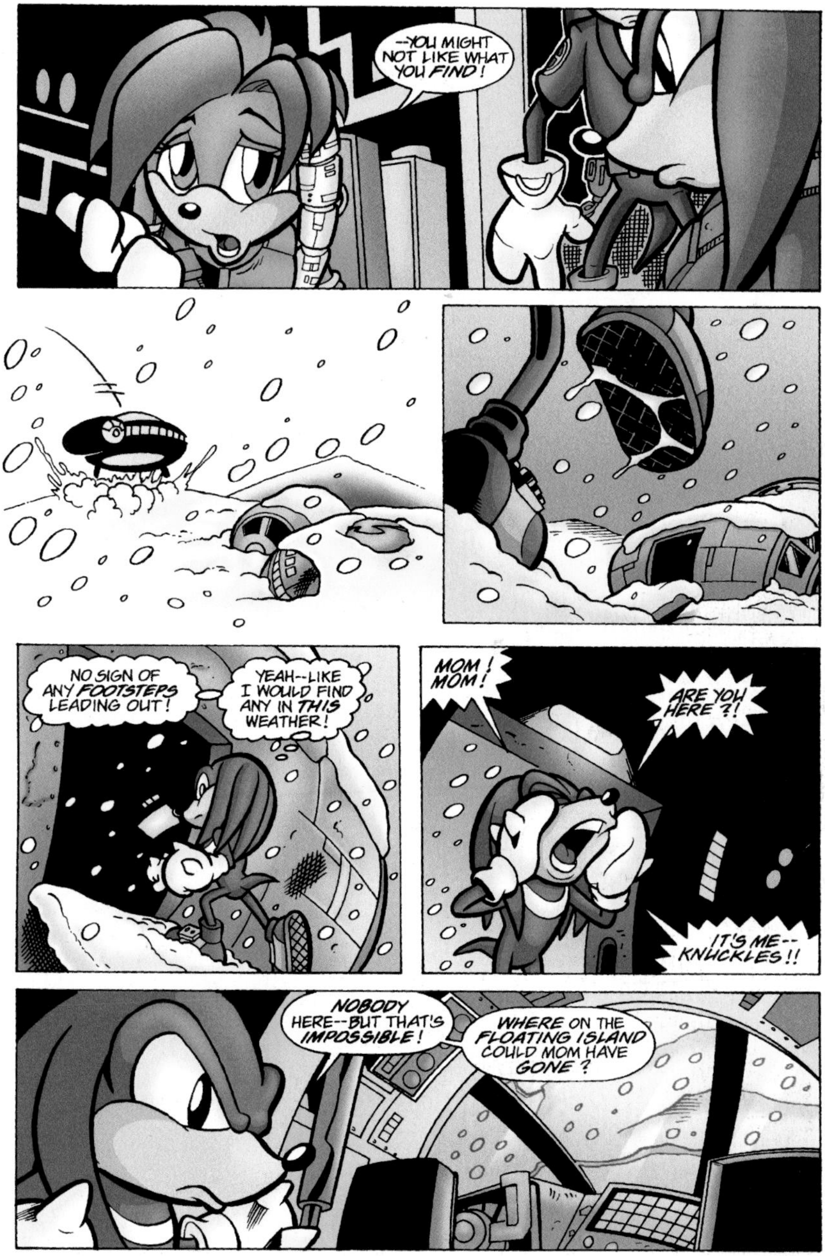
--YOU MIGHT NOT LIKE WHAT YOU FIND!
NO SIGN OF ANY FOOTSTEPS LEADING OUT!
YEAH--LIKE I WOULD FIND ANY IN THIS WEATHER!
MOM! MOM!
ARE YOU HERE?!
IT'S ME-- KNUCKLES!!
NOBODY HERE--BUT THAT'S IMPOSSIBLE!
WHERE ON THE FLOATING ISLAND COULD MOM HAVE GONE?

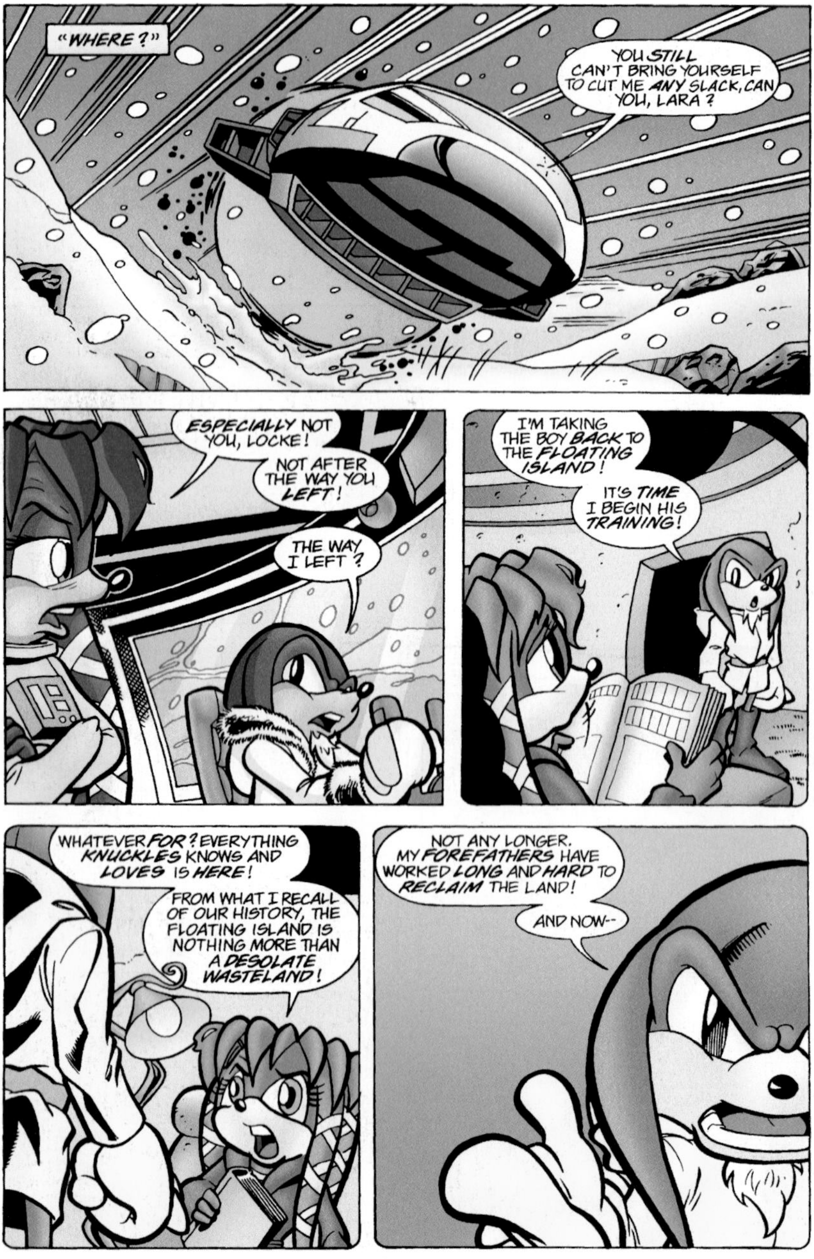
"WHERE?"
YOU STILL CAN'T BRING YOURSELF TO CUT ME ANY SLACK, CAN YOU, LARA?
ESPECIALLY NOT YOU, LOCKE!
NOT AFTER THE WAY YOU LEFT!
THE WAY I LEFT?
I'M TAKING THE BOY BACK TO THE FLOATING ISLAND!
IT'S TIME I BEGIN HIS TRAINING!
WHATEVER FOR? EVERYTHING KNUCKLES KNOWS AND LOVES IS HERE!
FROM WHAT I RECALL OF OUR HISTORY, THE FLOATING ISLAND IS NOTHING MORE THAN A DESOLATE WASTELAND!
NOT ANY LONGER. MY FOREFATHERS HAVE WORKED LONG AND HARD TO RECLAIM THE LAND!
AND NOW--

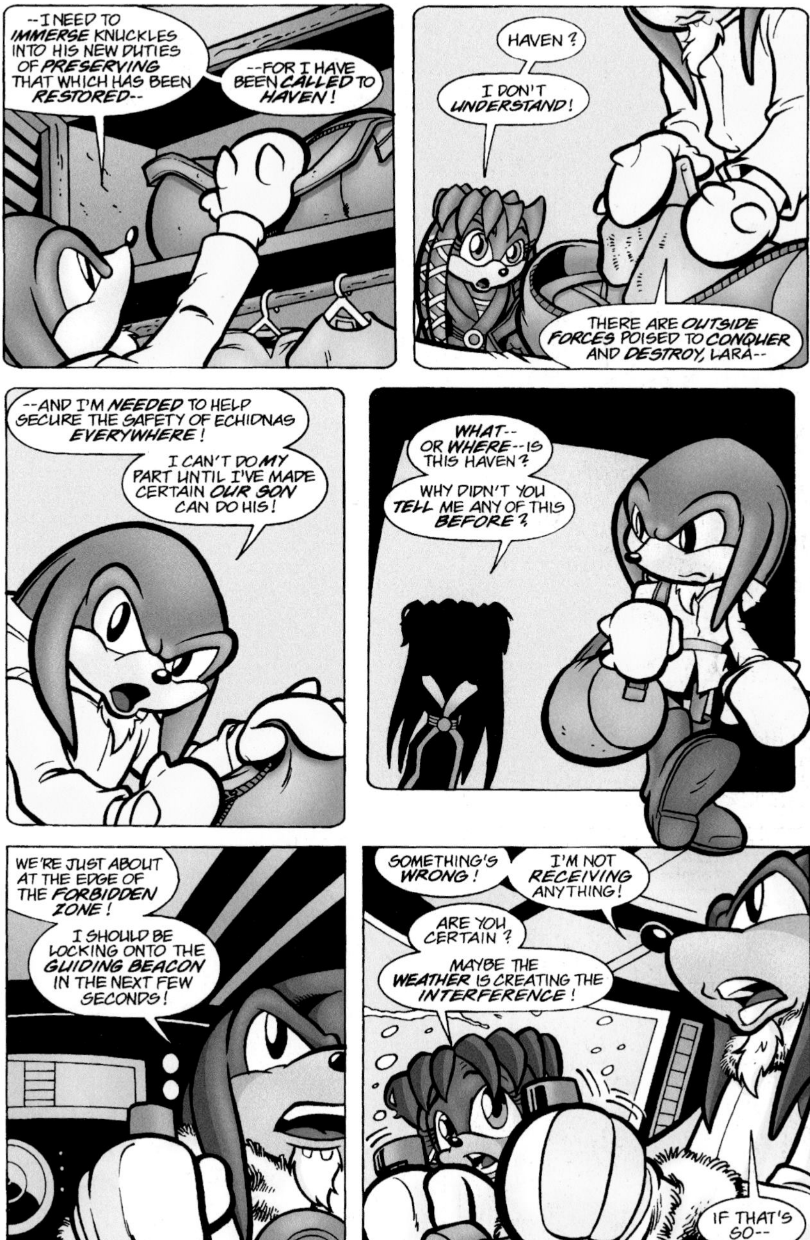
--I NEED TO IMMERSE KNUCKLES INTO HIS NEW DUTIES OF PRESERVING THAT WHICH HAS BEEN RESTORED--
--FOR I HAVE BEEN CALLED TO HAVEN!
HAVEN?
I DON'T UNDERSTAND!
THERE ARE OUTSIDE FORCES POISED TO CONQUER AND DESTROY, LARA--
--AND I'M NEEDED TO HELP SECURE THE SAFETY OF ECHIDNAS EVERYWHERE!
I CAN'T DO MY PART UNTIL I'VE MADE CERTAIN OUR SON CAN DO HIS!
WHAT-- OR WHERE--IS THIS HAVEN?
WHY DIDN'T YOU TELL ME ANY OF THIS BEFORE?
WE'RE JUST ABOUT AT THE EDGE OF THE FORBIDDEN ZONE!
I SHOULD BE LOCKING ONTO THE GUIDING BEACON IN THE NEXT FEW SECONDS!
SOMETHING'S WRONG!
I'M NOT RECEIVING ANYTHING!
ARE YOU CERTAIN?
MAYBE THE WEATHER IS CREATING THE INTERFERENCE!
IF THAT'S SO--

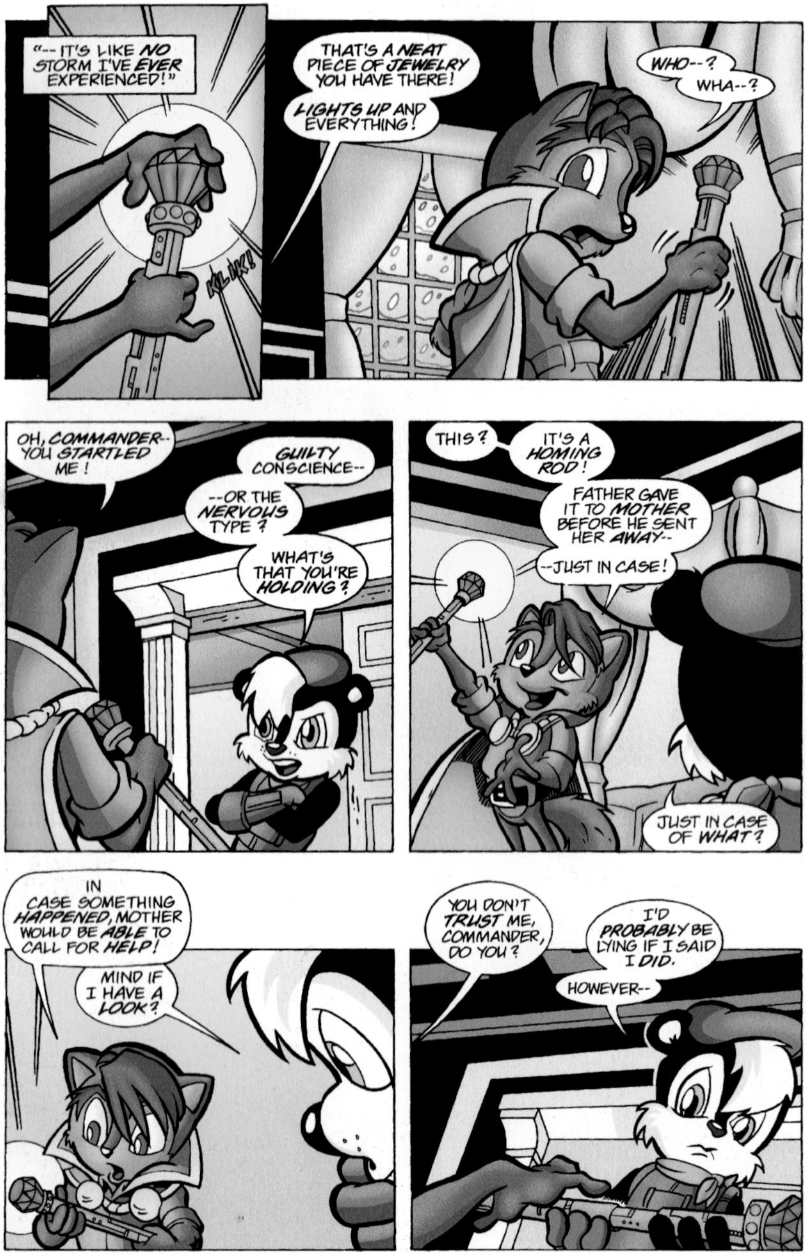
"-- IT'S LIKE NO STORM I'VE EVER EXPERIENCED!"
KLIK!
THAT'S A NEAT PIECE OF JEWELRY YOU HAVE THERE!
LIGHTS UP AND EVERYTHING!
WHO--?
WHA--?
OH, COMMANDER-- YOU STARTLED ME!
GUILTY CONSCIENCE--
--OR THE NERVOUS TYPE?
WHAT'S THAT YOU'RE HOLDING?
THIS?
IT'S A HOMING ROD!
FATHER GAVE IT TO MOTHER BEFORE HE SENT HER AWAY--
--JUST IN CASE!
JUST IN CASE OF WHAT?
IN CASE SOMETHING HAPPENED, MOTHER WOULD BE ABLE TO CALL FOR HELP!
MIND IF I HAVE A LOOK?
YOU DON'T TRUST ME, COMMANDER, DO YOU?
I'D PROBABLY BE LYING IF I SAID I DID.
HOWEVER--

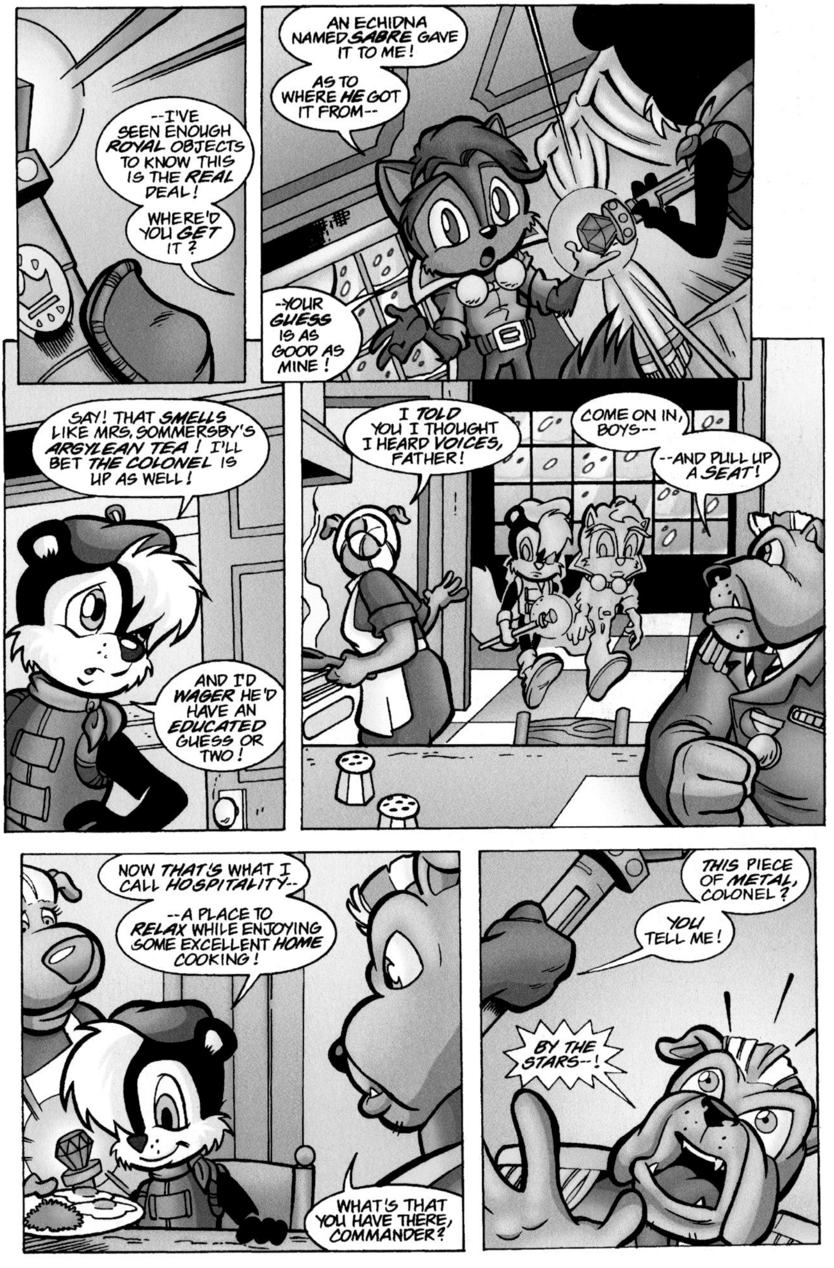
--I'VE SEEN ENOUGH ROYAL OBJECTS TO KNOW THIS IS THE REAL DEAL!
WHERE'D YOU GET IT?
AN ECHIDNA NAMED SABRE GAVE IT TO ME!
AS TO WHERE HE GOT IT FROM--
--YOUR GUESS IS AS GOOD AS MINE!
SAY! THAT SMELLS LIKE MRS. SOMMERSBY'S ARGYLEAN TEA! I'LL BET THE COLONEL IS UP AS WELL!
AND I'D WAGER HE'D HAVE AN EDUCATED GUESS OR TWO!
I TOLD YOU I THOUGHT I HEARD VOICES, FATHER!
COME ON IN, BOYS--
--AND PULL UP A SEAT!
NOW THAT'S WHAT I CALL HOSPITALITY--
--A PLACE TO RELAX WHILE ENJOYING SOME EXCELLENT HOME COOKING!
WHAT'S THAT YOU HAVE THERE, COMMANDER?
THIS PIECE OF METAL, COLONEL?
YOU TELL ME!
BY THE STARS--!

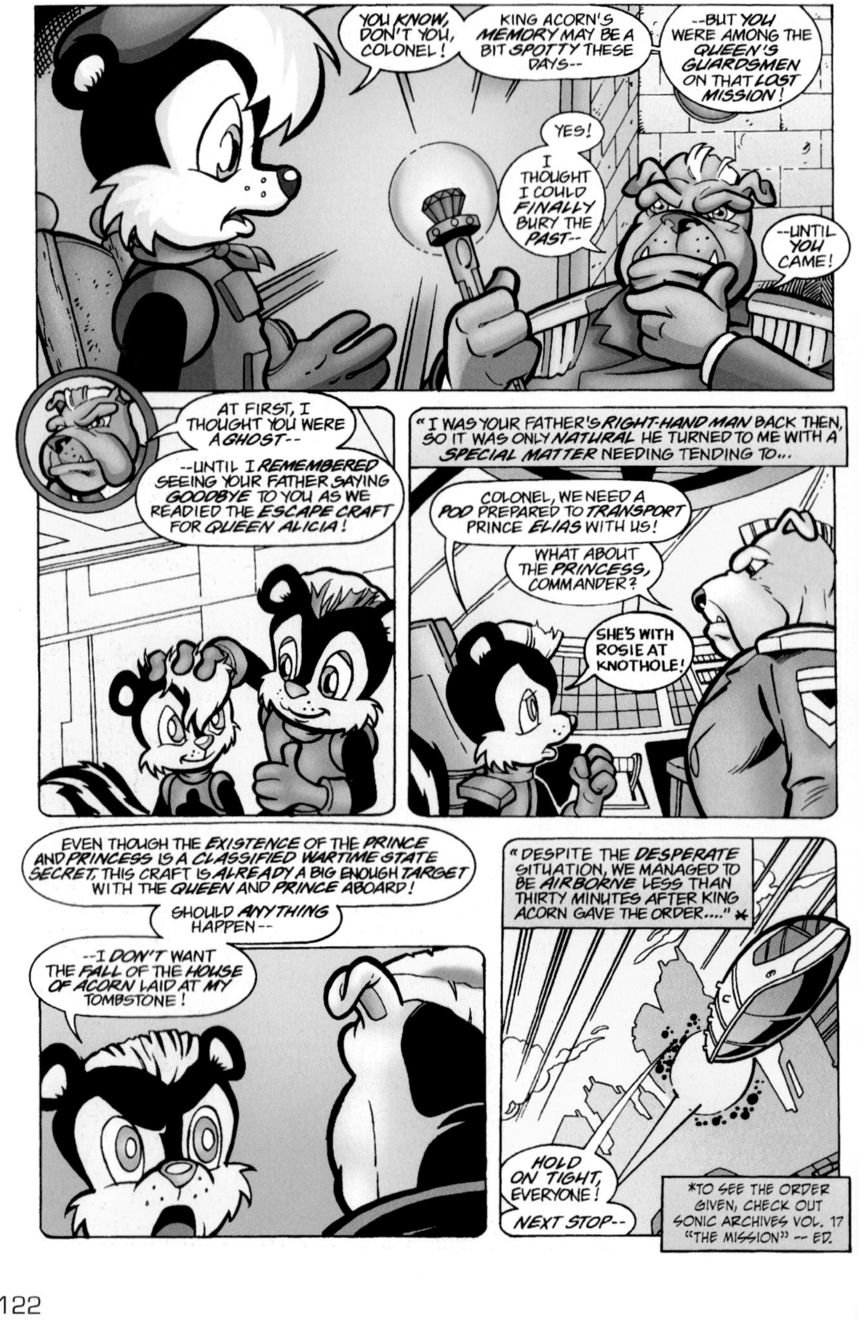
YOU KNOW, DON'T YOU, COLONEL!
KING ACORN'S MEMORY MAY BE A BIT SPOTTY THESE DAYS--
--BUT YOU WERE AMONG THE QUEEN'S GUARDSMEN ON THAT LOST MISSION!
YES!
I THOUGHT I COULD FINALLY BURY THE PAST--
--UNTIL YOU CAME!
AT FIRST, I THOUGHT YOU WERE A GHOST--
--UNTIL I REMEMBERED SEEING YOUR FATHER SAYING GOODBYE TO YOU AS WE READIED THE ESCAPE CRAFT FOR QUEEN ALICIA!
"I WAS YOUR FATHER'S RIGHT-HAND MAN BACK THEN, SO IT WAS ONLY NATURAL HE TURNED TO ME WITH A SPECIAL MATTER NEEDING TENDING TO...
COLONEL, WE NEED A POD PREPARED TO TRANSPORT PRINCE ELIAS WITH US!
WHAT ABOUT THE PRINCESS, COMMANDER?
SHE'S WITH ROSIE AT KNOTHOLE!
EVEN THOUGH THE EXISTENCE OF THE PRINCE AND PRINCESS IS A CLASSIFIED WARTIME STATE SECRET, THIS CRAFT IS ALREADY A BIG ENOUGH TARGET WITH THE QUEEN AND PRINCE ABOARD!
SHOULD ANYTHING HAPPEN--
--I DON'T WANT THE FALL OF THE HOUSE OF ACORN LAID AT MY TOMBSTONE!
"DESPITE THE DESPERATE SITUATION, WE MANAGED TO BE AIRBORNE LESS THAN THIRTY MINUTES AFTER KING ACORN GAVE THE ORDER...." *
HOLD ON TIGHT, EVERYONE!
NEXT STOP--
*TO SEE THE ORDER GIVEN, CHECK OUT SONIC ARCHIVES VOL. 17 "THE MISSION" -- ED.

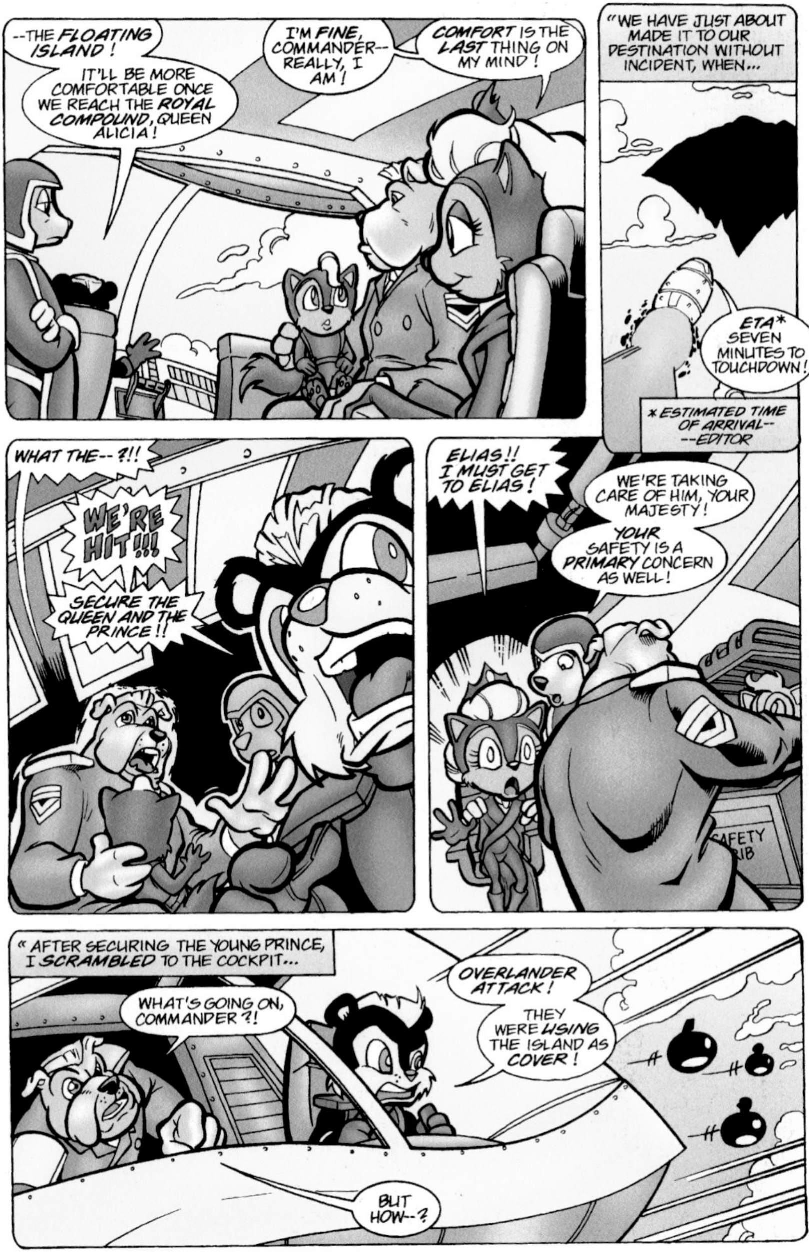
--THE FLOATING ISLAND!
IT'LL BE MORE COMFORTABLE ONCE WE REACH THE ROYAL COMPOUND, QUEEN ALICIA!
I'M FINE, COMMANDER-- REALLY, I AM!
COMFORT IS THE LAST THING ON MY MIND!
"WE HAVE JUST ABOUT MADE IT TO OUR DESTINATION WITHOUT INCIDENT, WHEN...
ETA* SEVEN MINUTES TO TOUCHDOWN!
*ESTIMATED TIME OF ARRIVAL-- --EDITOR
WHAT THE-- ?!!
WE'RE HIT!!!
SECURE THE QUEEN AND THE PRINCE!!
ELIAS!! I MUST GET TO ELIAS!
WE'RE TAKING CARE OF HIM, YOUR MAJESTY!
YOUR SAFETY IS A PRIMARY CONCERN AS WELL!
"AFTER SECURING THE YOUNG PRINCE, I SCRAMBLED TO THE COCKPIT...
WHAT'S GOING ON, COMMANDER?!
OVERLANDER ATTACK!
THEY WERE USING THE ISLAND AS COVER!
BUT HOW--?

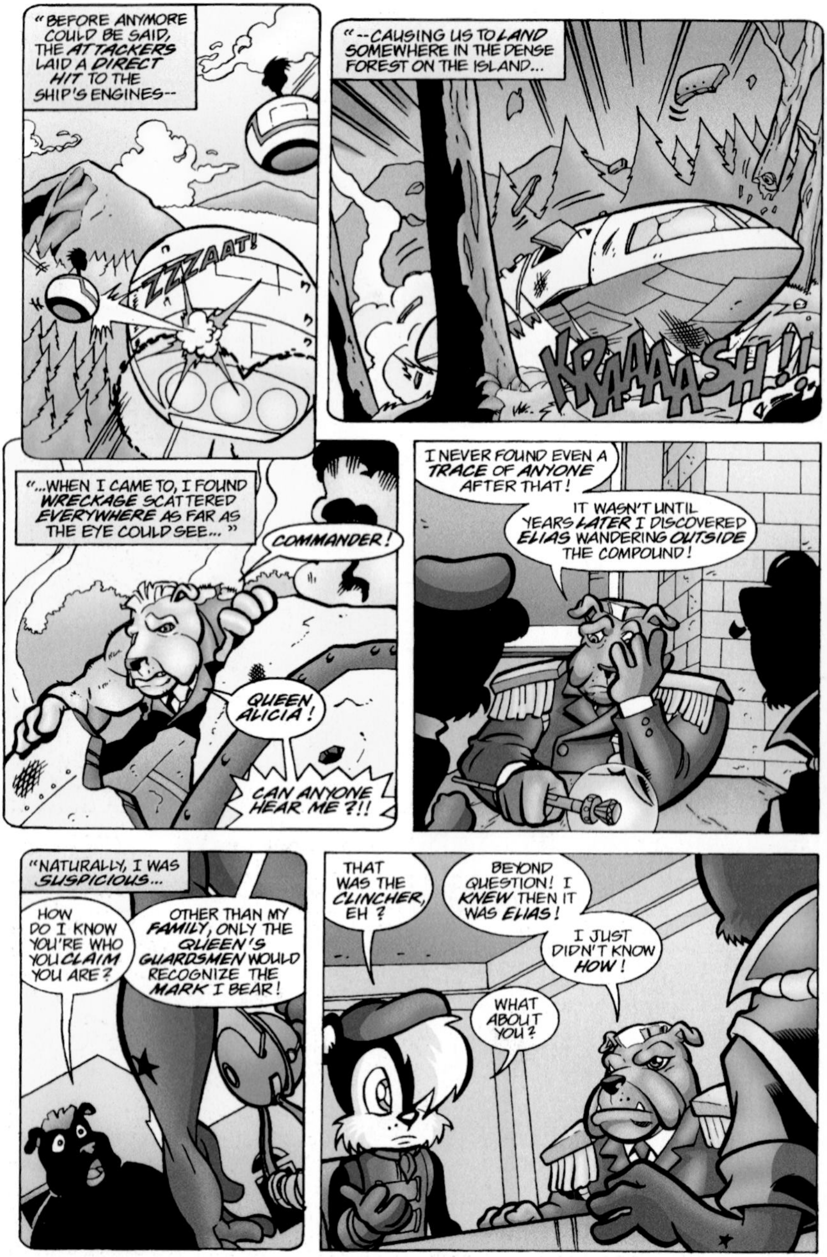
"BEFORE ANYMORE COULD BE SAID, THE ATTACKERS LAID A DIRECT HIT TO THE SHIP'S ENGINES--
ZZZZAAT!
"--CAUSING US TO LAND SOMEWHERE IN THE DENSE FOREST ON THE ISLAND...
KRAAAASH!!
"...WHEN I CAME TO, I FOUND WRECKAGE SCATTERED EVERYWHERE AS FAR AS THE EYE COULD SEE..."
COMMANDER!
QUEEN ALICIA!
CAN ANYONE HEAR ME?!!
I NEVER FOUND EVEN A TRACE OF ANYONE AFTER THAT!
IT WASN'T UNTIL YEARS LATER I DISCOVERED ELIAS WANDERING OUTSIDE THE COMPOUND!
"NATURALLY, I WAS SUSPICIOUS...
HOW DO I KNOW YOU'RE WHO YOU CLAIM YOU ARE?
OTHER THAN MY FAMILY, ONLY THE QUEEN'S GUARDSMEN WOULD RECOGNIZE THE MARK I BEAR!
THAT WAS THE CLINCHER, EH?
BEYOND QUESTION! I KNEW THEN IT WAS ELIAS!
I JUST DIDN'T KNOW HOW!
WHAT ABOUT YOU?

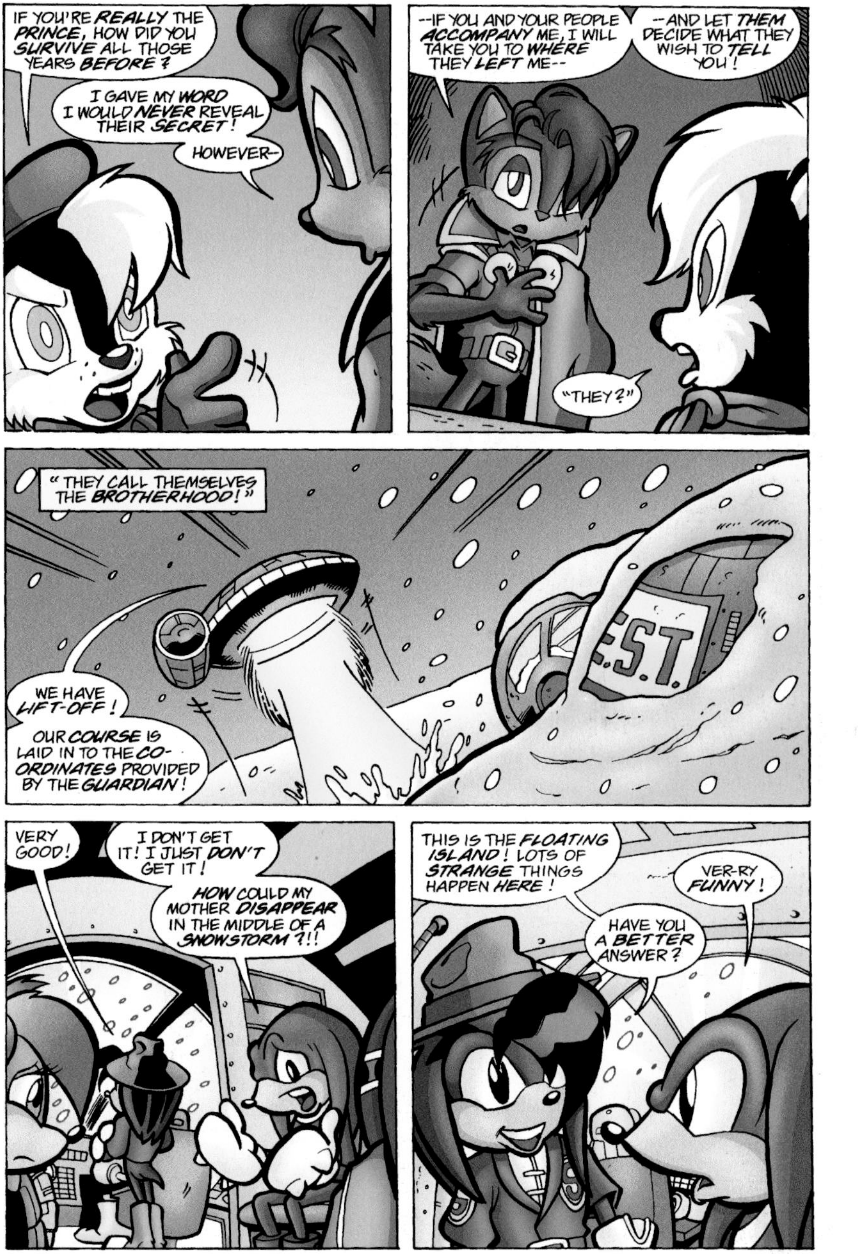
IF YOU'RE REALLY THE PRINCE, HOW DID YOU SURVIVE ALL THOSE YEARS BEFORE?
I GAVE MY WORD I WOULD NEVER REVEAL THEIR SECRET!
HOWEVER--
--IF YOU AND YOUR PEOPLE ACCOMPANY ME, I WILL TAKE YOU TO WHERE THEY LEFT ME--
--AND LET THEM DECIDE WHAT THEY WISH TO TELL YOU!
"THEY?"
"THEY CALL THEMSELVES THE BROTHERHOOD!"
E.S.T.
WE HAVE LIFT-OFF!
OUR COURSE IS LAID IN TO THE CO-ORDINATES PROVIDED BY THE GUARDIAN!
VERY GOOD!
I DON'T GET IT! I JUST DON'T GET IT!
HOW COULD MY MOTHER DISAPPEAR IN THE MIDDLE OF A SNOWSTORM?!!
THIS IS THE FLOATING ISLAND! LOTS OF STRANGE THINGS HAPPEN HERE!
VER-RY FUNNY!
HAVE YOU A BETTER ANSWER?

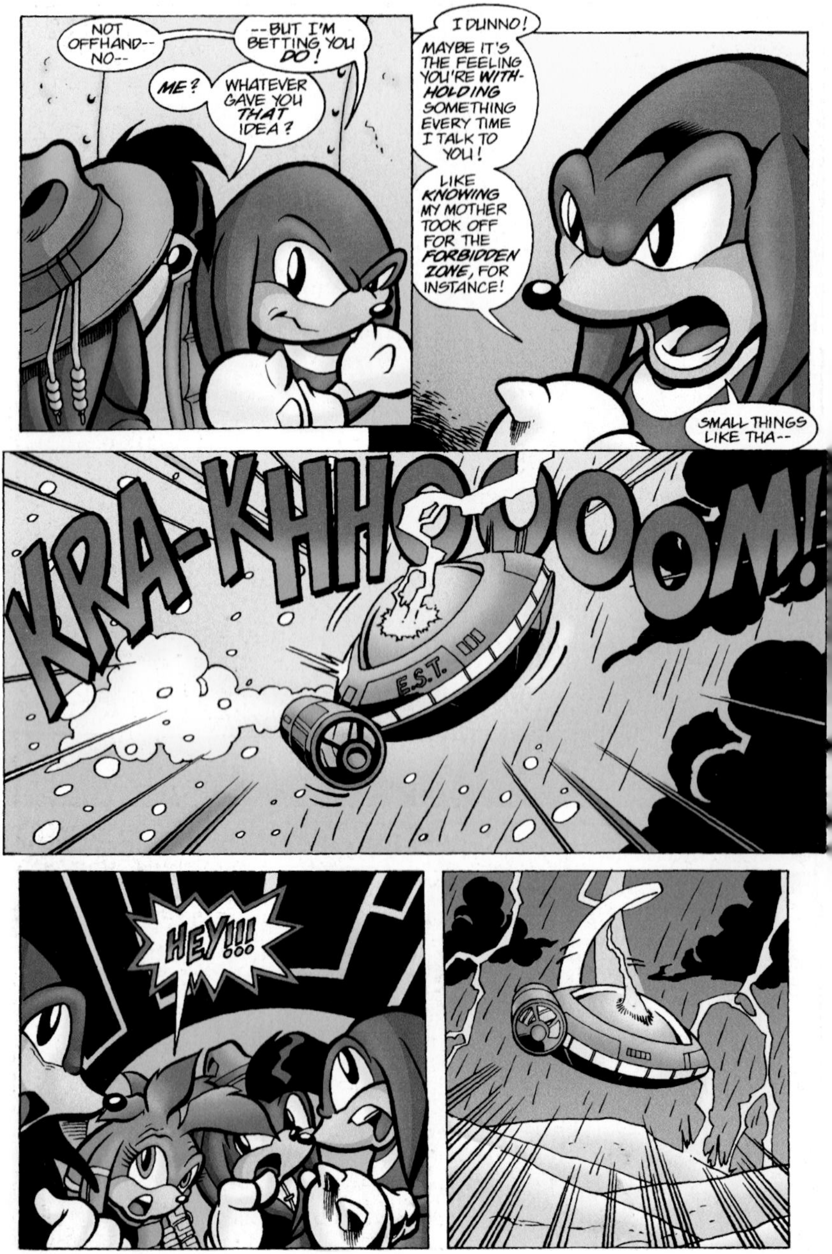
NOT OFFHAND-- NO--
--BUT I'M BETTING YOU DO!
ME?
WHATEVER GAVE YOU THAT IDEA?
I DUNNO!
MAYBE IT'S THE FEELING YOU'RE WITH-HOLDING SOMETHING EVERY TIME I TALK TO YOU!
LIKE KNOWING MY MOTHER TOOK OFF FOR THE FORBIDDEN ZONE, FOR INSTANCE!
SMALL THINGS LIKE THA--
KRA-KHHOOOOOM!!
E.S.T.
HEY!!!

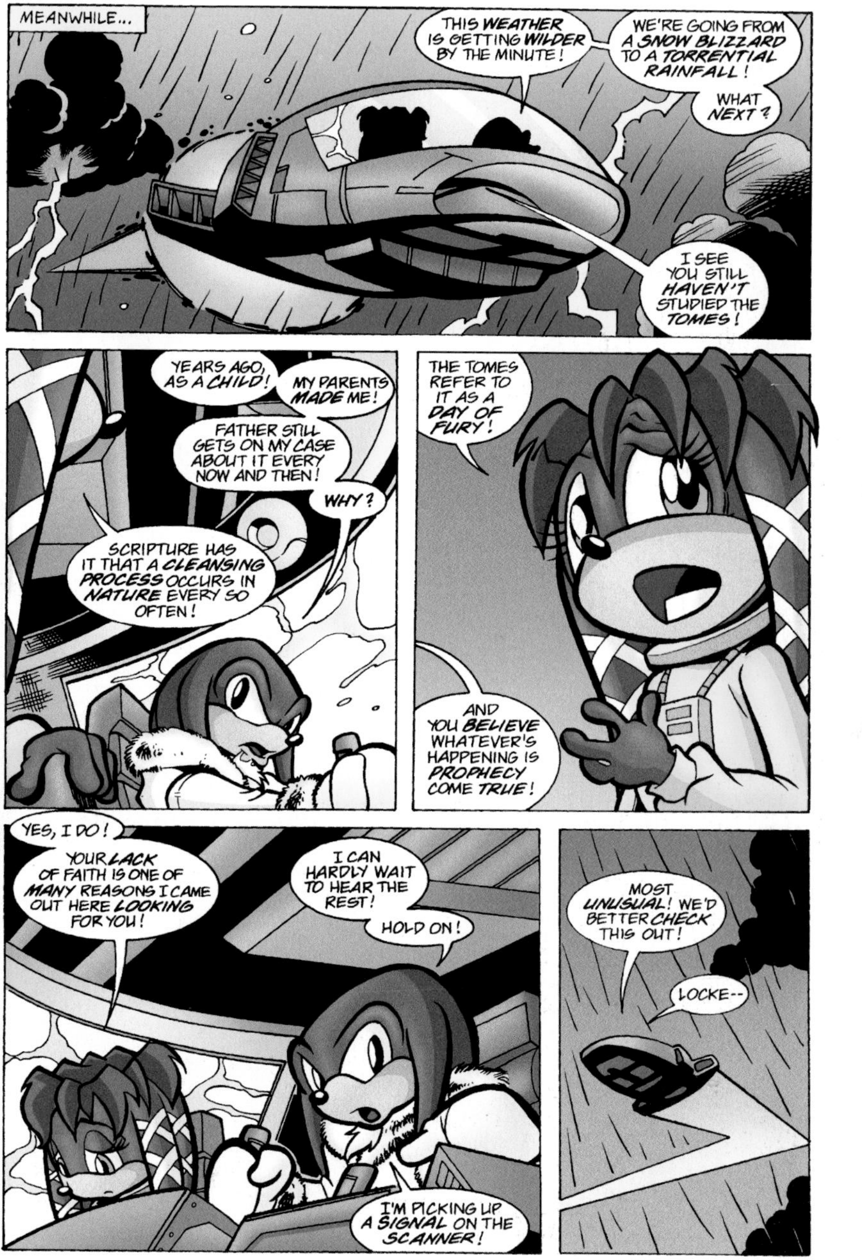
MEANWHILE...
THIS WEATHER IS GETTING WILDER BY THE MINUTE!
WE'RE GOING FROM A SNOW BLIZZARD TO A TORRENTIAL RAINFALL!
WHAT NEXT?
I SEE YOU STILL HAVEN'T STUDIED THE TOMES!
YEARS AGO, AS A CHILD!
MY PARENTS MADE ME!
FATHER STILL GETS ON MY CASE ABOUT IT EVERY NOW AND THEN!
WHY?
SCRIPTURE HAS IT THAT A CLEANSING PROCESS OCCURS IN NATURE EVERY SO OFTEN!
THE TOMES REFER TO IT AS A DAY OF FURY!
AND YOU BELIEVE WHATEVER'S HAPPENING IS PROPHECY COME TRUE!
YES, I DO!
YOUR LACK OF FAITH IS ONE OF MANY REASONS I CAME OUT HERE LOOKING FOR YOU!
I CAN HARDLY WAIT TO HEAR THE REST!
HOLD ON!
I'M PICKING UP A SIGNAL ON THE SCANNER!
MOST UNUSUAL! WE'D BETTER CHECK THIS OUT!
LOCKE--

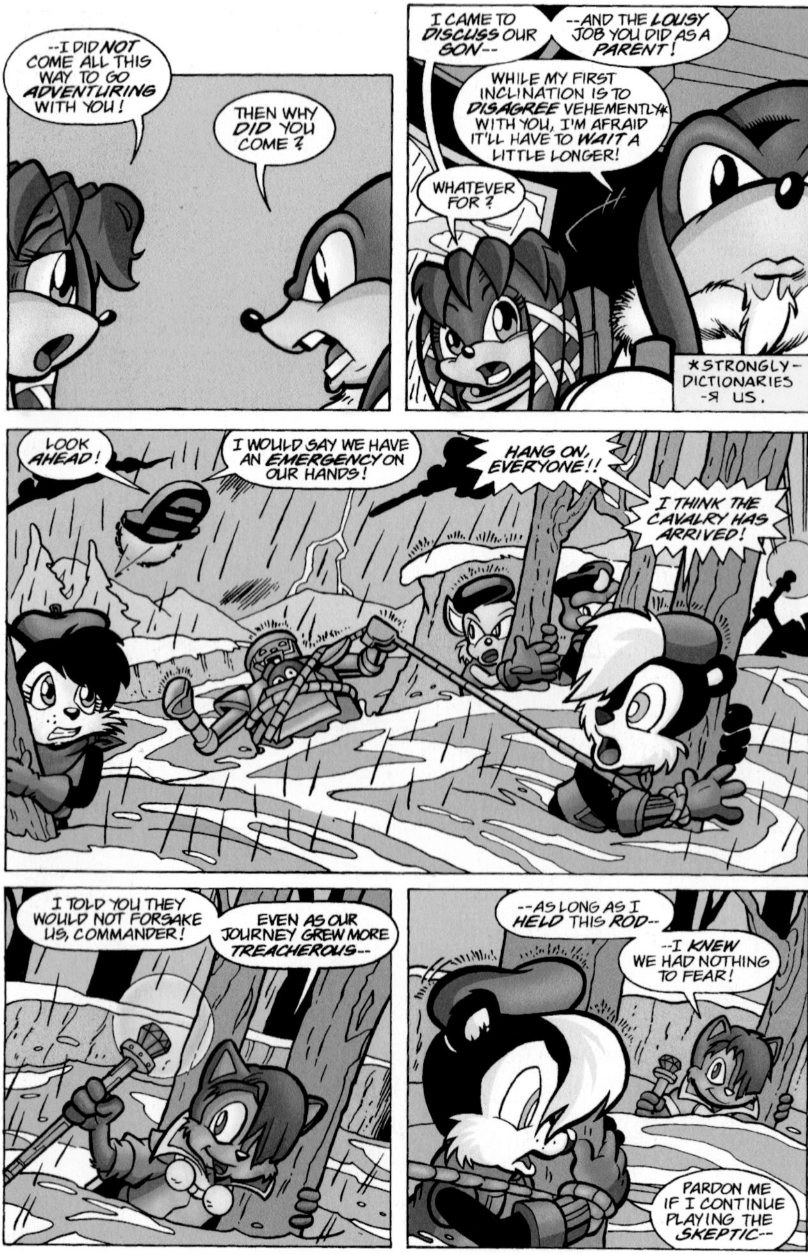
--I DID NOT COME ALL THIS WAY TO GO ADVENTURING WITH YOU!
THEN WHY DID YOU COME?
I CAME TO DISCUSS OUR SON--
--AND THE LOUSY JOB YOU DID AS A PARENT!
WHILE MY FIRST INCLINATION IS TO DISAGREE VEHEMENTLY* WITH YOU, I'M AFRAID IT'LL HAVE TO WAIT A LITTLE LONGER!
WHATEVER FOR?
*STRONGLY- DICTIONARIES -Я US.
LOOK AHEAD!
I WOULD SAY WE HAVE AN EMERGENCY ON OUR HANDS!
HANG ON, EVERYONE!!
I THINK THE CAVALRY HAS ARRIVED!
I TOLD YOU THEY WOULD NOT FORSAKE US, COMMANDER!
EVEN AS OUR JOURNEY GREW MORE TREACHEROUS--
--AS LONG AS I HELD THIS ROD--
--I KNEW WE HAD NOTHING TO FEAR!
PARDON ME IF I CONTINUE PLAYING THE SKEPTIC--

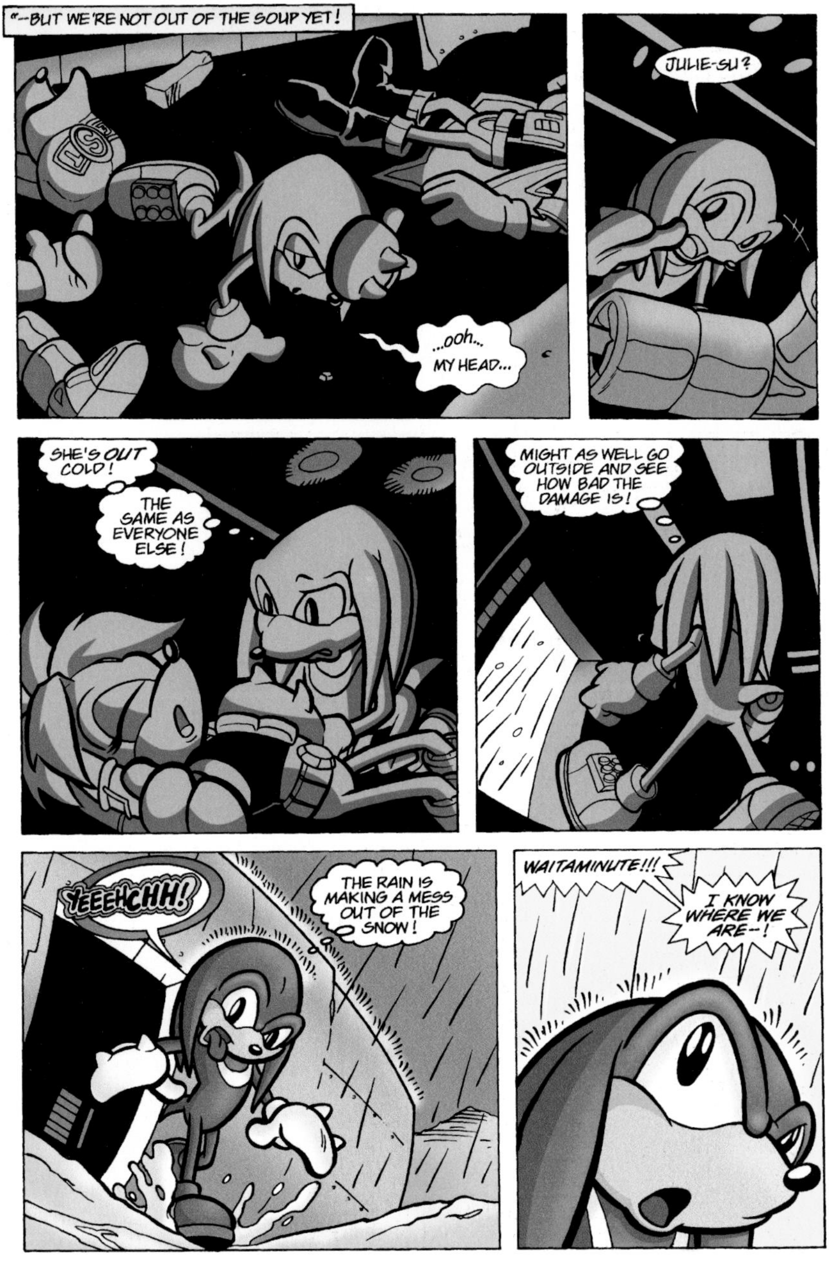
"--BUT WE'RE NOT OUT OF THE SOUP YET!
...ooh... MY HEAD...
JULIE-SU?
SHE'S OUT COLD!
THE SAME AS EVERYONE ELSE!
MIGHT AS WELL GO OUTSIDE AND SEE HOW BAD THE DAMAGE IS!
YEEEHCHH!
THE RAIN IS MAKING A MESS OUT OF THE SNOW!
WAITAMINUTE!!!
I KNOW WHERE WE ARE--!

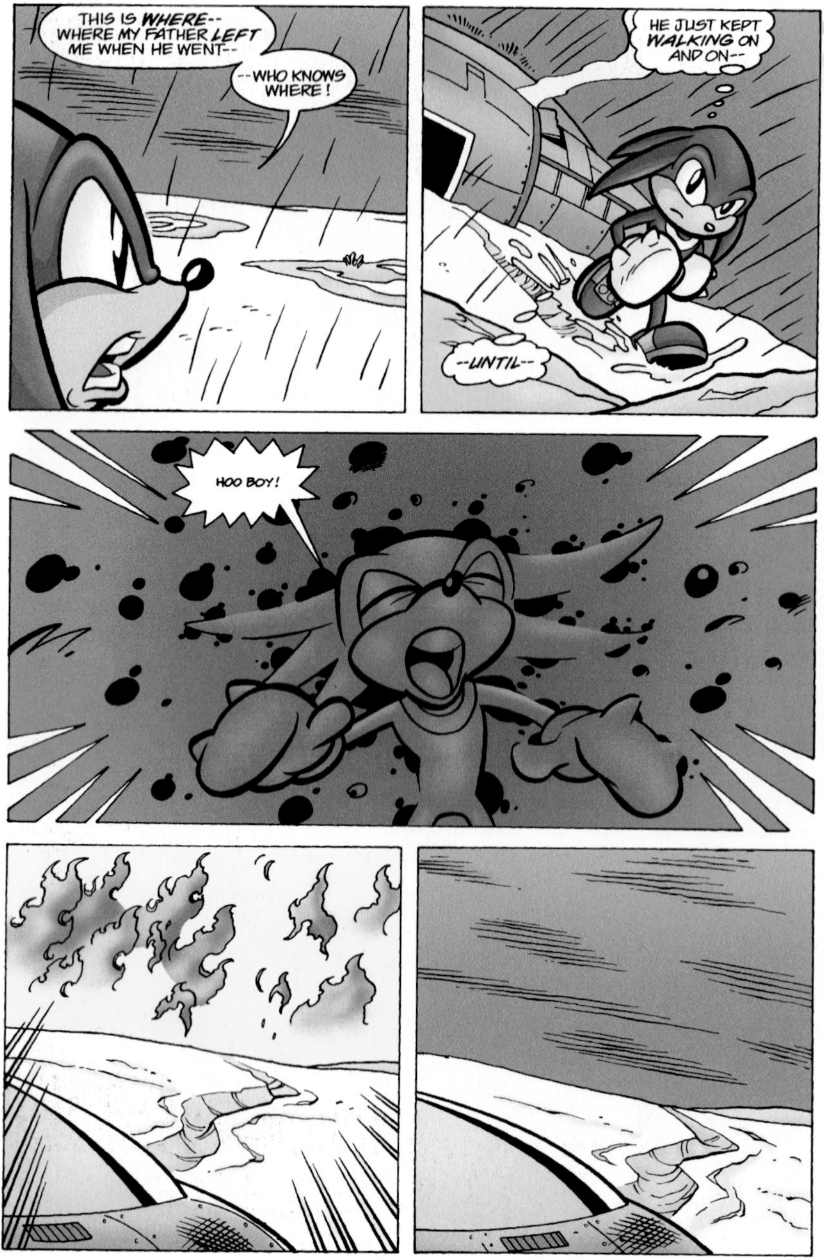
THIS IS WHERE--
WHERE MY FATHER LEFT
ME WHEN HE WENT--
--WHO KNOWS
WHERE!
HE JUST KEPT
WALKING ON
AND ON--
--UNTIL--
HOO BOY!

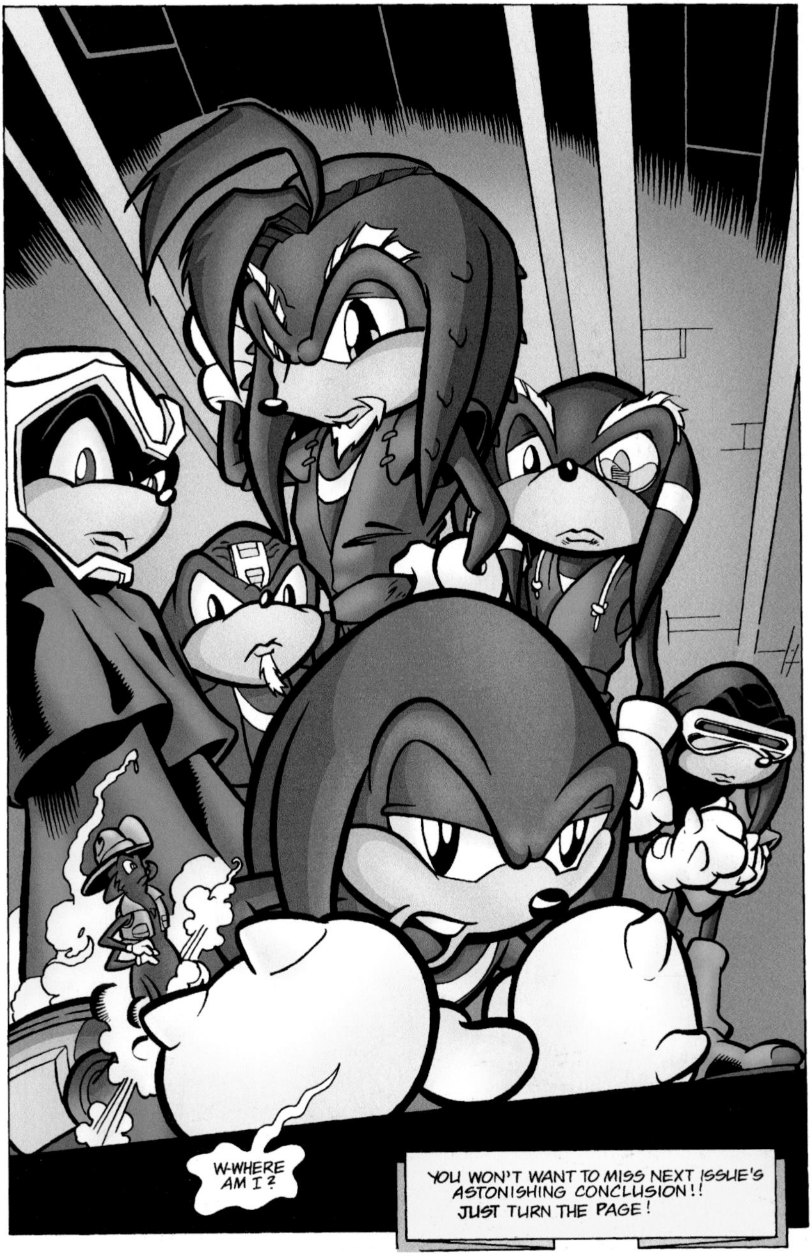
W-WHERE AM I?
YOU WON'T WANT TO MISS NEXT ISSUE'S ASTONISHING CONCLUSION!! JUST TURN THE PAGE!

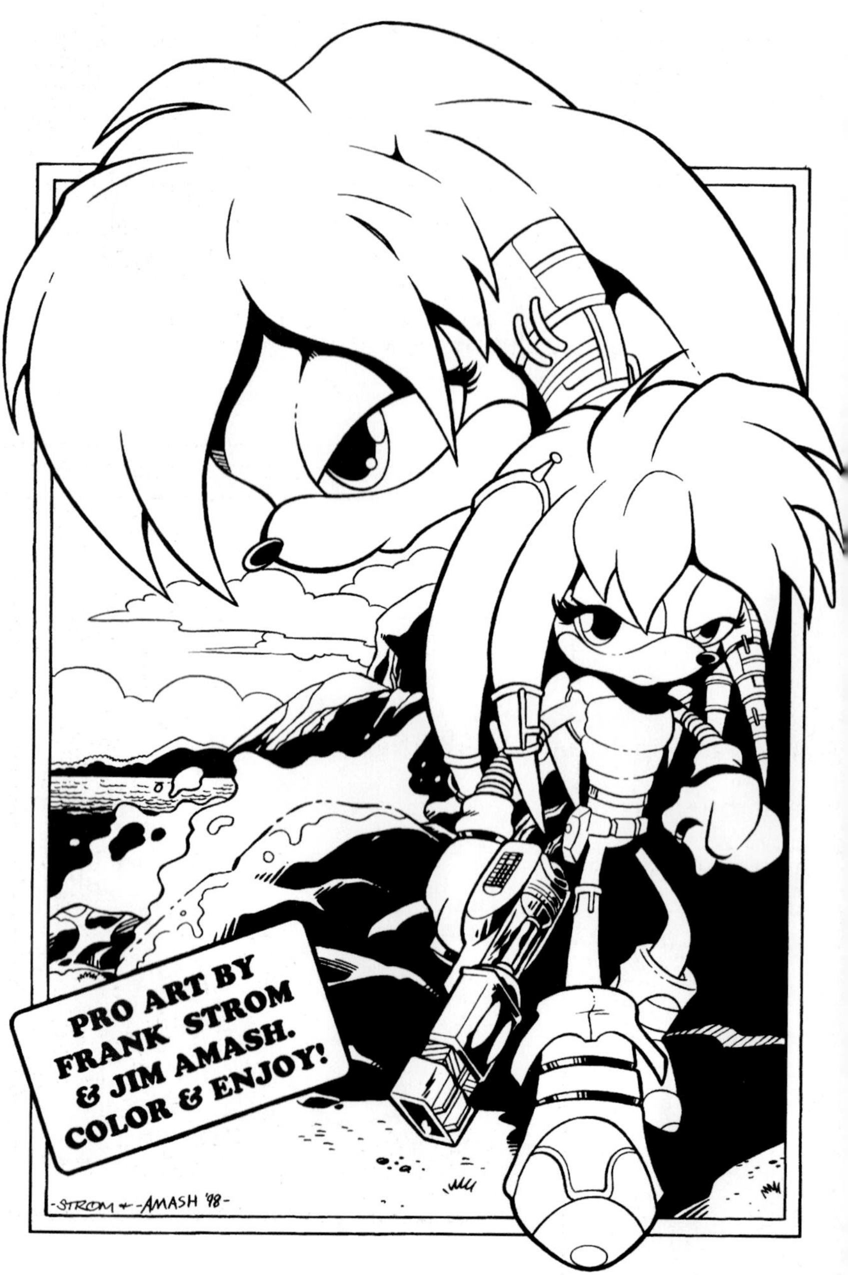
PRO ART BY FRANK STROM & JIM AMASH. COLOR & ENJOY!
-STROM + -AMASH '98-

KE AN EXCLUSIVE LOOK
HIND THE SCENES OF
UCKLES THE ECHIDNA,
S WE REVEAL...

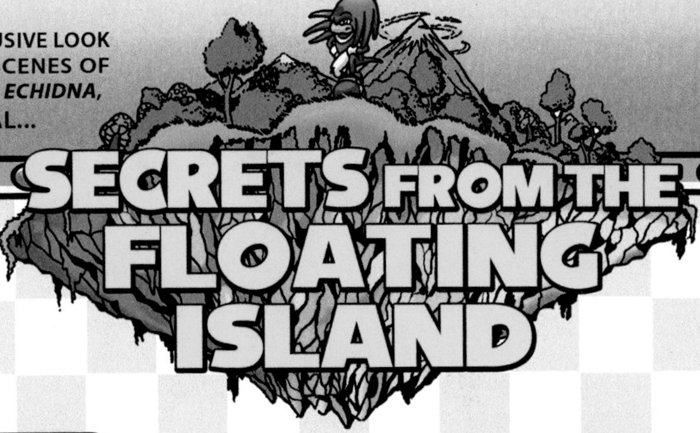

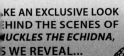

SECRETS FROM THE FLOATING ISLAND

KNUCKLES #20 COVER PENCILS

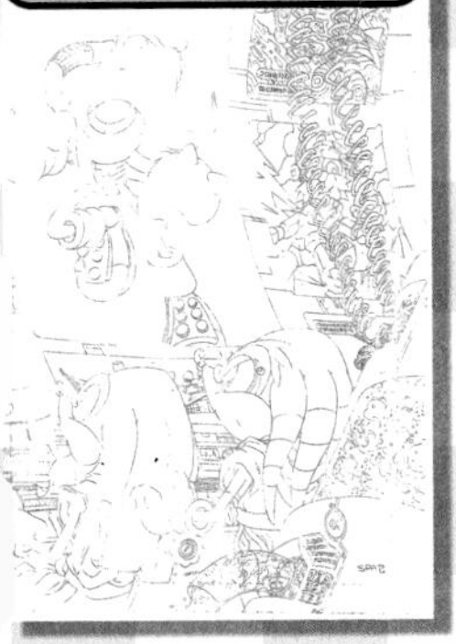

KNUCKLES #20 COVER FINAL INKS

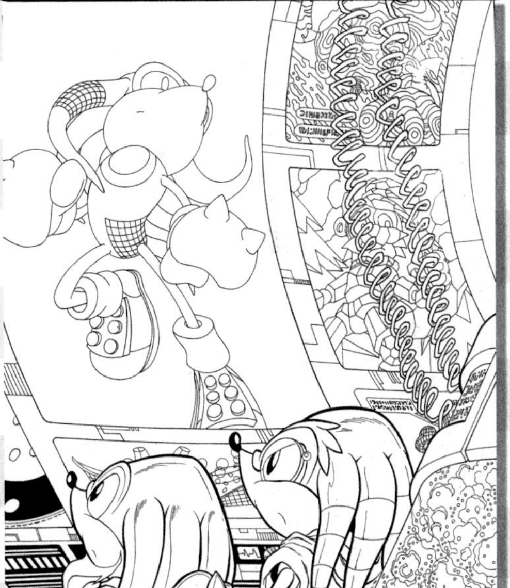
SPA2
PENDERS

KNUCKLES #20 COVER NEAR FINAL INKS

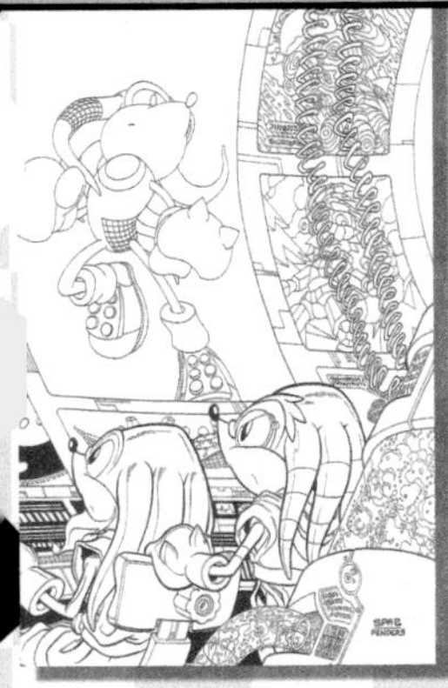

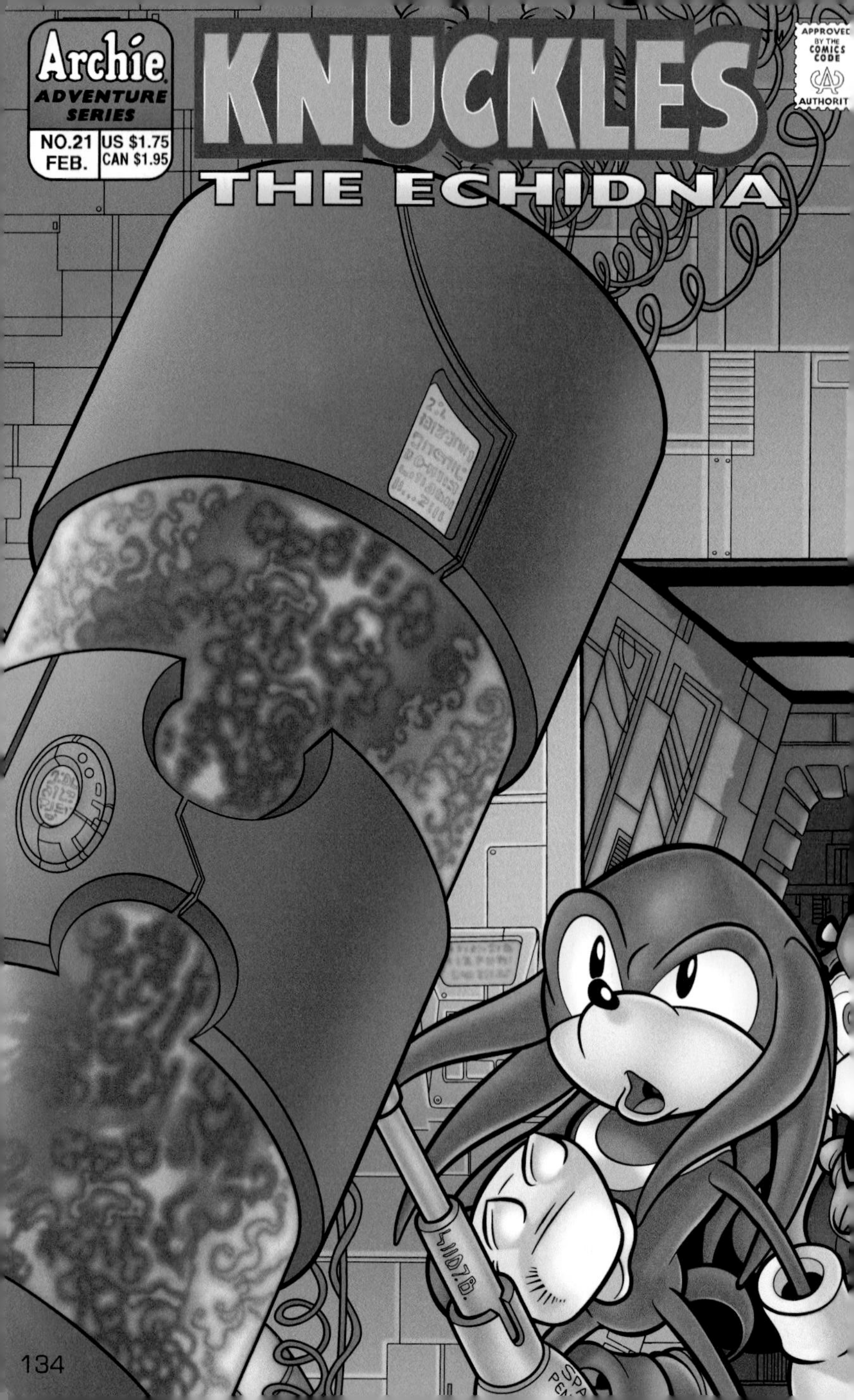
Archie
ADVENTURE SERIES
NO.21 FEB.
US $1.75
CAN $1.95
KNUCKLES
THE ECHIDNA
APPROVED BY THE COMICS CODE AUTHORITY

BOOK TWENTY-ONE

The Forbidden Zone

Part Three of Three

Ken Penders
Writer
Manny Galan
Penciler
Andrew Pepoy
Inker
Barry Grossman
Colorist
Vickie Williams
Letterer

Justin Gabrie
Editor

Victor Gorelick
Managing Editor

Richard Goldwater
Editor-in-Chief

Born to the most noble of Echidna houses, the latest to continue the family heritage and responsibility as **GUARDIAN OF THE FLOATING ISLAND,** defender of all the forces of evil from the world beyond as well as those who would threaten within, he is none other than... **KNUCKLES THE ECHIDNA!**

S P A Z

As the blizzard-like snows turn into torrential rainfall on **The Floating Island**, fate has conspired to set various individuals on a collision course with destiny, linking up **Locke** with his former wife **Lara-Le**, **Knuckles** with his ancestors gathered in **Haven**, and **Commander Geoffrey St. John** with **Elias**, who claims to be the son of **King Acorn**.

It is on the way to Haven that we find King Acorn's elite squad coping as best they can...

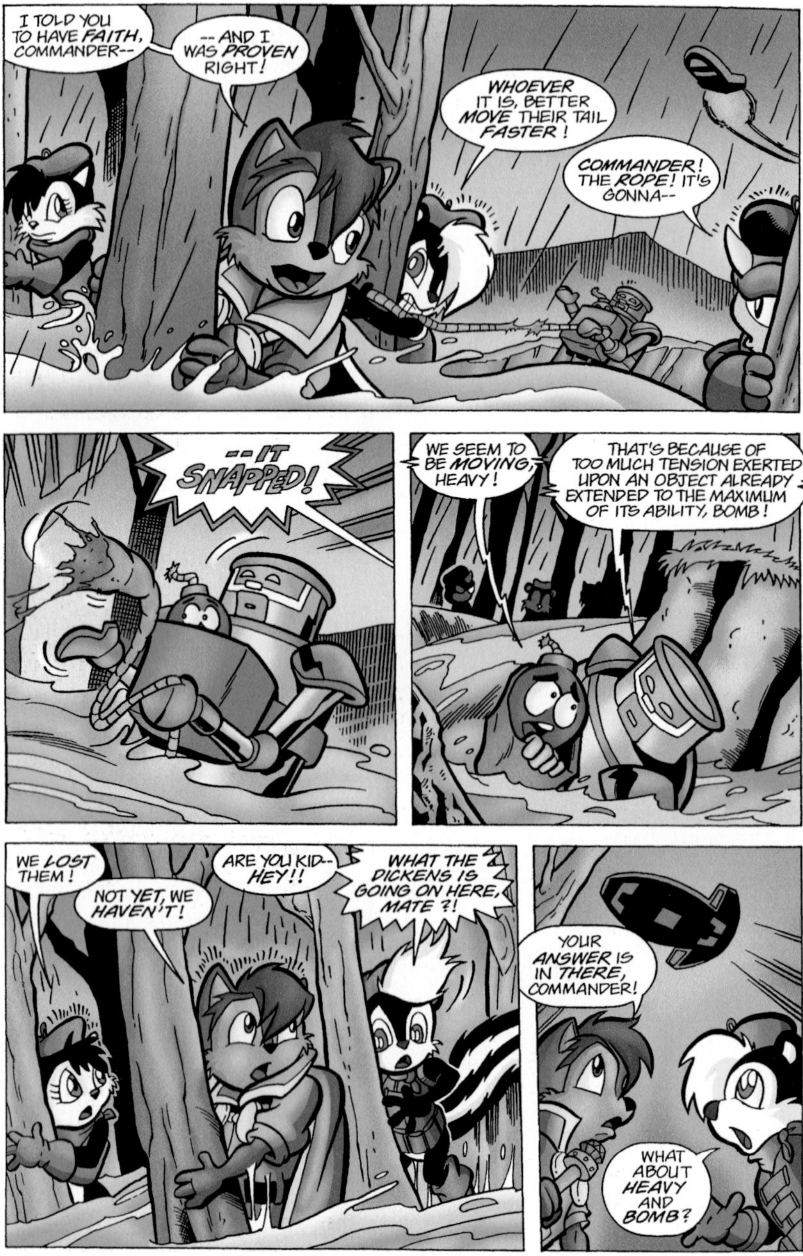
I TOLD YOU TO HAVE FAITH, COMMANDER--
-- AND I WAS PROVEN RIGHT!
WHOEVER IT IS, BETTER MOVE THEIR TAIL FASTER!
COMMANDER! THE ROPE! IT'S GONNA--
-- IT SNAPPED!
WE SEEM TO BE MOVING, HEAVY!
THAT'S BECAUSE OF TOO MUCH TENSION EXERTED UPON AN OBJECT ALREADY EXTENDED TO THE MAXIMUM OF ITS ABILITY, BOMB!
WE LOST THEM!
NOT YET, WE HAVEN'T!
ARE YOU KID-- HEY!!
WHAT THE DICKENS IS GOING ON HERE, MATE ?!
YOUR ANSWER IS IN THERE, COMMANDER!
WHAT ABOUT HEAVY AND BOMB?

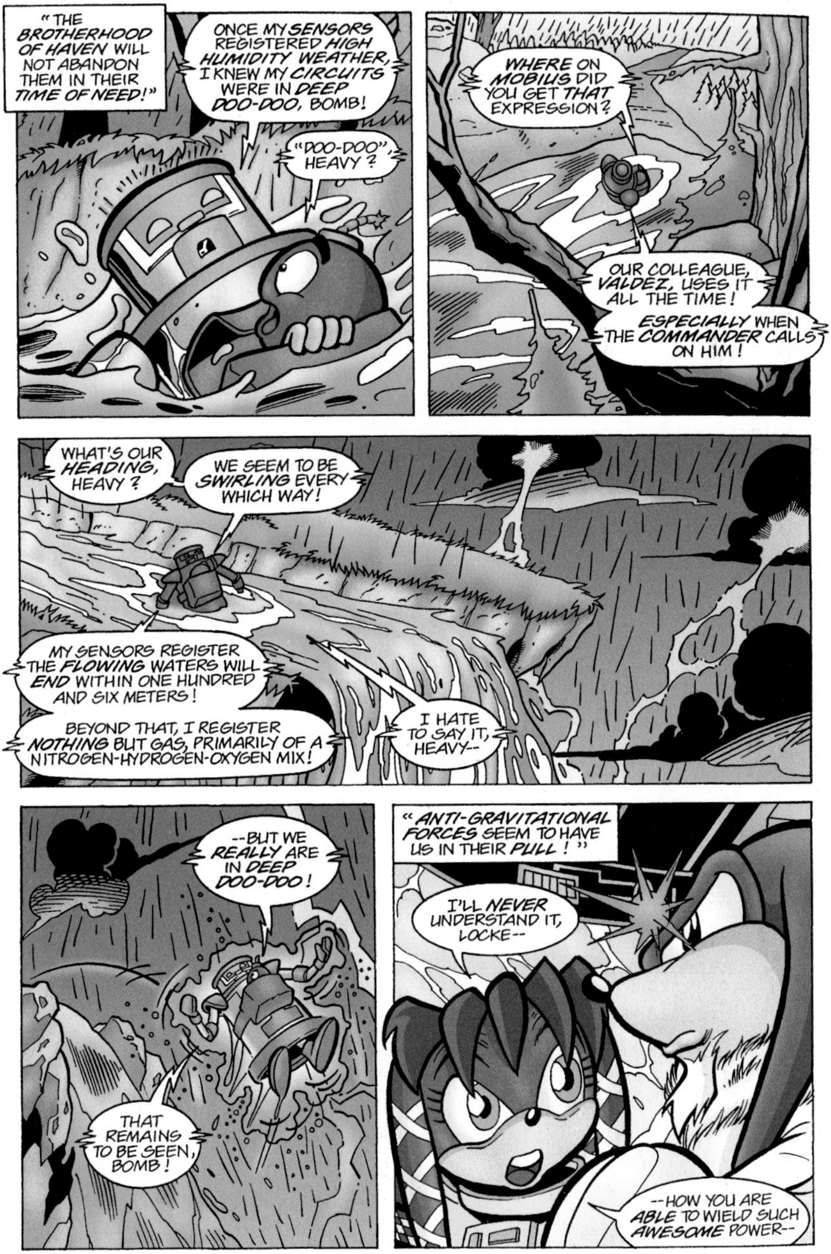
"THE BROTHERHOOD OF HAVEN WILL NOT ABANDON THEM IN THEIR TIME OF NEED!"
ONCE MY SENSORS REGISTERED HIGH HUMIDITY WEATHER, I KNEW MY CIRCUITS WERE IN DEEP DOO-DOO, BOMB!
"DOO-DOO", HEAVY?
WHERE ON MOBIUS DID YOU GET THAT EXPRESSION?
OUR COLLEAGUE, VALDEZ, USES IT ALL THE TIME!
ESPECIALLY WHEN THE COMMANDER CALLS ON HIM!
WHAT'S OUR HEADING, HEAVY?
WE SEEM TO BE SWIRLING EVERY WHICH WAY!
MY SENSORS REGISTER THE FLOWING WATERS WILL END WITHIN ONE HUNDRED AND SIX METERS!
BEYOND THAT, I REGISTER NOTHING BUT GAS, PRIMARILY OF A NITROGEN-HYDROGEN-OXYGEN MIX!
I HATE TO SAY IT, HEAVY--
--BUT WE REALLY ARE IN DEEP DOO-DOO!
THAT REMAINS TO BE SEEN, BOMB!
"ANTI-GRAVITATIONAL FORCES SEEM TO HAVE US IN THEIR PULL!"
I'LL NEVER UNDERSTAND IT, LOCKE--
--HOW YOU ARE ABLE TO WIELD SUCH AWESOME POWER--

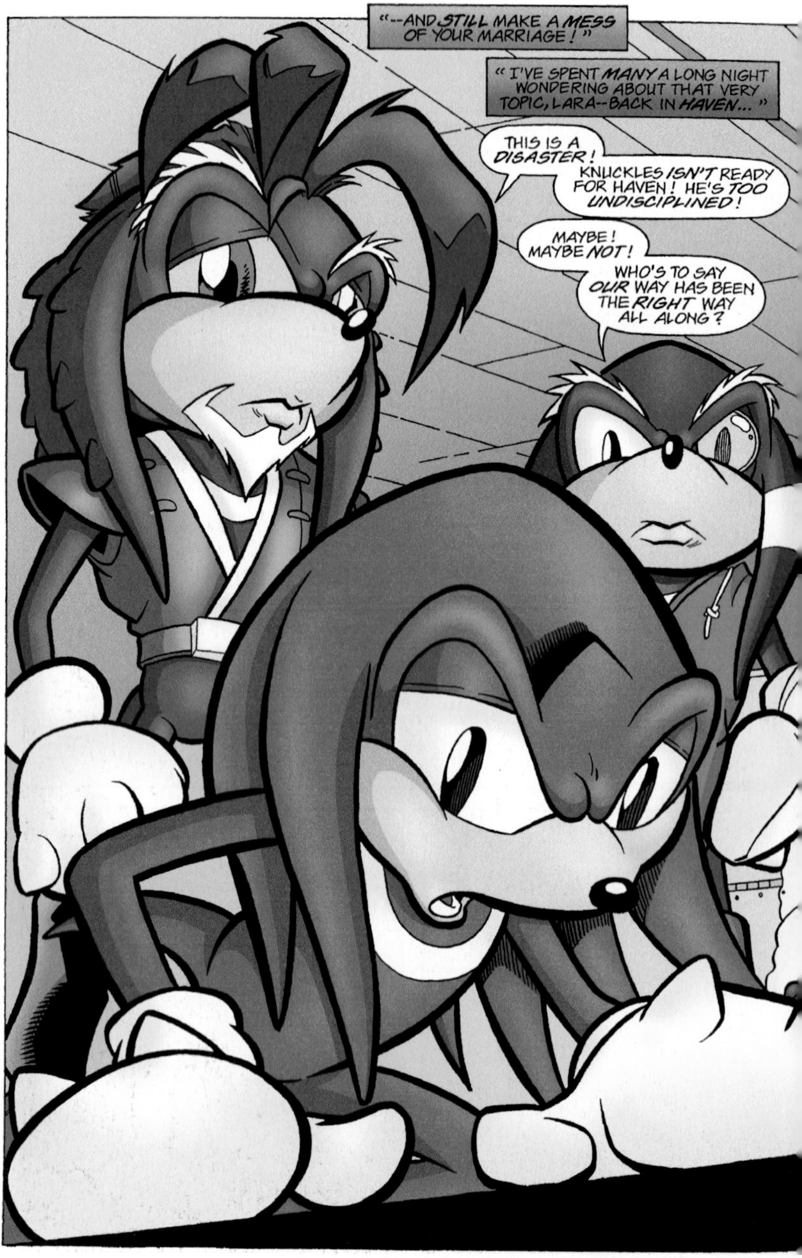
"--AND STILL MAKE A MESS OF YOUR MARRIAGE!"
"I'VE SPENT MANY A LONG NIGHT WONDERING ABOUT THAT VERY TOPIC, LARA--BACK IN HAVEN..."
THIS IS A DISASTER!
KNUCKLES ISN'T READY FOR HAVEN! HE'S TOO UNDISCIPLINED!
MAYBE! MAYBE NOT!
WHO'S TO SAY OUR WAY HAS BEEN THE RIGHT WAY ALL ALONG?

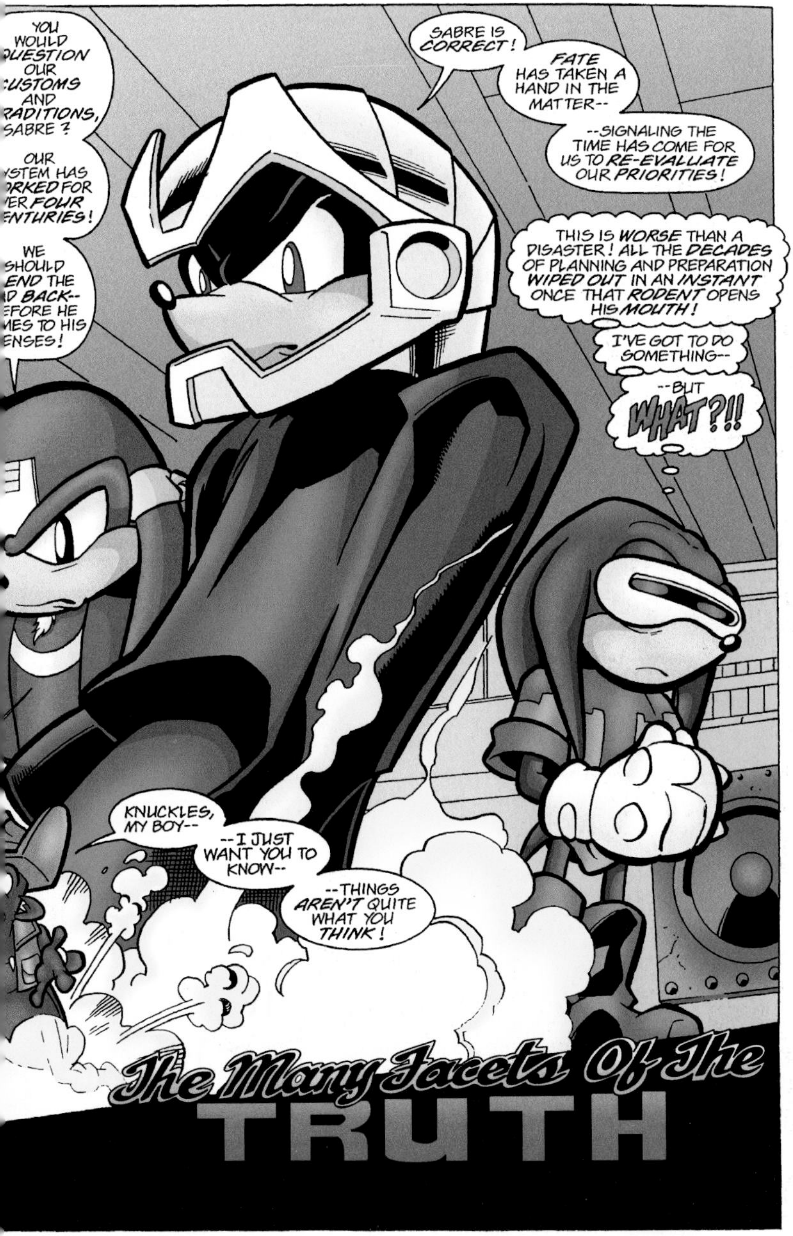

YOU WOULD ·UESTION OUR ·USTOMS AND ·ADITIONS, SABRE?
OUR ·STEM HAS ·RKED FOR ·ER FOUR ·NTURIES!
WE SHOULD ·END THE ·D BACK-- ·EFORE HE ·MES TO HIS ·ENSES!
SABRE IS CORRECT!
FATE HAS TAKEN A HAND IN THE MATTER--
--SIGNALING THE TIME HAS COME FOR US TO RE-EVALUATE OUR PRIORITIES!
THIS IS WORSE THAN A DISASTER! ALL THE DECADES OF PLANNING AND PREPARATION WIPED OUT IN AN INSTANT ONCE THAT RODENT OPENS HIS MOUTH!
I'VE GOT TO DO SOMETHING--
--BUT WHAT?!!
KNUCKLES, MY BOY--
--I JUST WANT YOU TO KNOW--
--THINGS AREN'T QUITE WHAT YOU THINK!
The Many Facets Of The
TRUTH

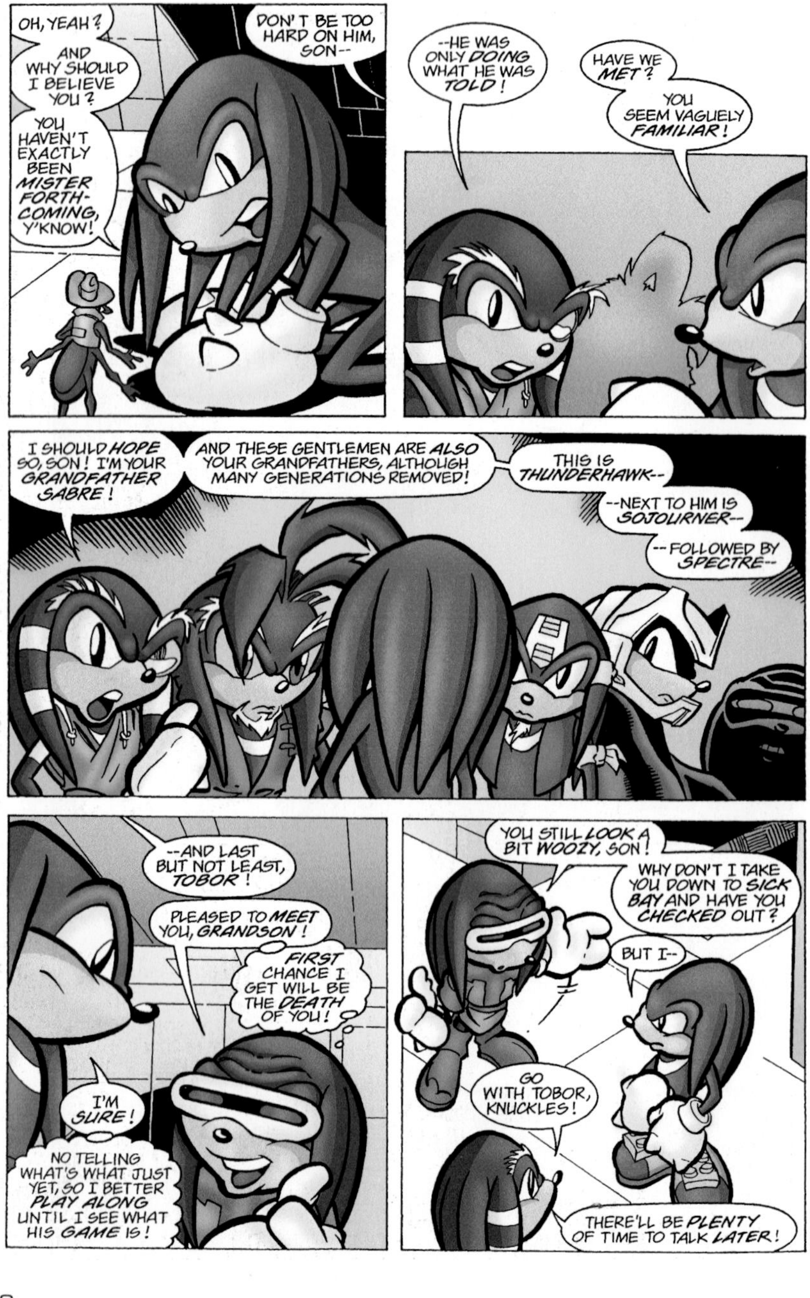

OH, YEAH? AND WHY SHOULD I BELIEVE YOU? YOU HAVEN'T EXACTLY BEEN MISTER FORTH-COMING, Y'KNOW!
DON'T BE TOO HARD ON HIM, SON--
--HE WAS ONLY DOING WHAT HE WAS TOLD!
HAVE WE MET? YOU SEEM VAGUELY FAMILIAR!
I SHOULD HOPE SO, SON! I'M YOUR GRANDFATHER SABRE!
AND THESE GENTLEMEN ARE ALSO YOUR GRANDFATHERS, ALTHOUGH MANY GENERATIONS REMOVED!
THIS IS THUNDERHAWK--
--NEXT TO HIM IS SOJOURNER--
--FOLLOWED BY SPECTRE--
--AND LAST BUT NOT LEAST, TOBOR!
PLEASED TO MEET YOU, GRANDSON!
FIRST CHANCE I GET WILL BE THE DEATH OF YOU!
I'M SURE!
NO TELLING WHAT'S WHAT JUST YET, SO I BETTER PLAY ALONG UNTIL I SEE WHAT HIS GAME IS!
YOU STILL LOOK A BIT WOOZY, SON!
WHY DON'T I TAKE YOU DOWN TO SICK BAY AND HAVE YOU CHECKED OUT?
BUT I--
GO WITH TOBOR, KNUCKLES!
THERE'LL BE PLENTY OF TIME TO TALK LATER!

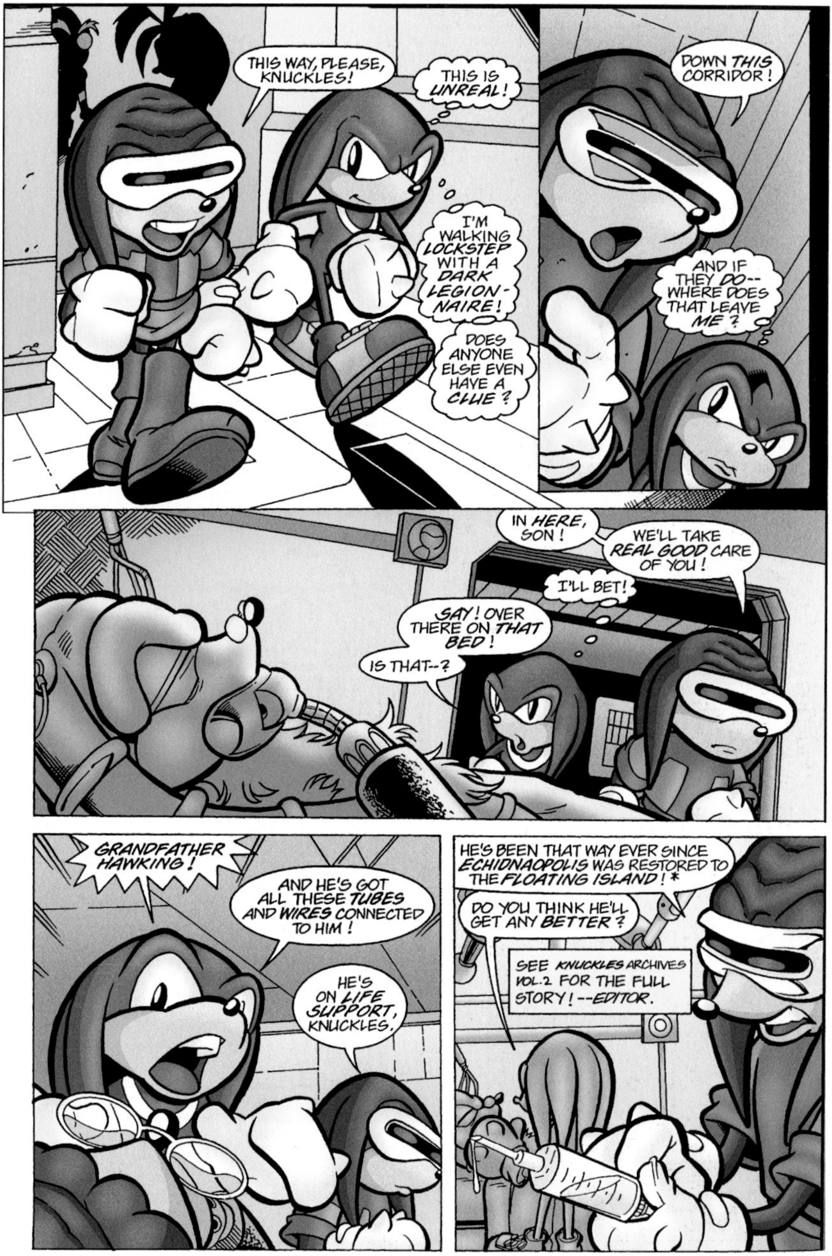
THIS WAY, PLEASE, KNUCKLES!
THIS IS UNREAL!
I'M WALKING LOCKSTEP WITH A DARK LEGION-NAIRE!
DOES ANYONE ELSE EVEN HAVE A CLUE?
DOWN THIS CORRIDOR!
AND IF THEY DO-- WHERE DOES THAT LEAVE ME?
IN HERE, SON!
WE'LL TAKE REAL GOOD CARE OF YOU!
I'LL BET!
SAY! OVER THERE ON THAT BED!
IS THAT--?
GRANDFATHER HAWKING!
AND HE'S GOT ALL THESE TUBES AND WIRES CONNECTED TO HIM!
HE'S ON LIFE SUPPORT, KNUCKLES.
HE'S BEEN THAT WAY EVER SINCE ECHIDNAOPOLIS WAS RESTORED TO THE FLOATING ISLAND! *
DO YOU THINK HE'LL GET ANY BETTER?
SEE KNUCKLES ARCHIVES VOL.2 FOR THE FULL STORY! --EDITOR.

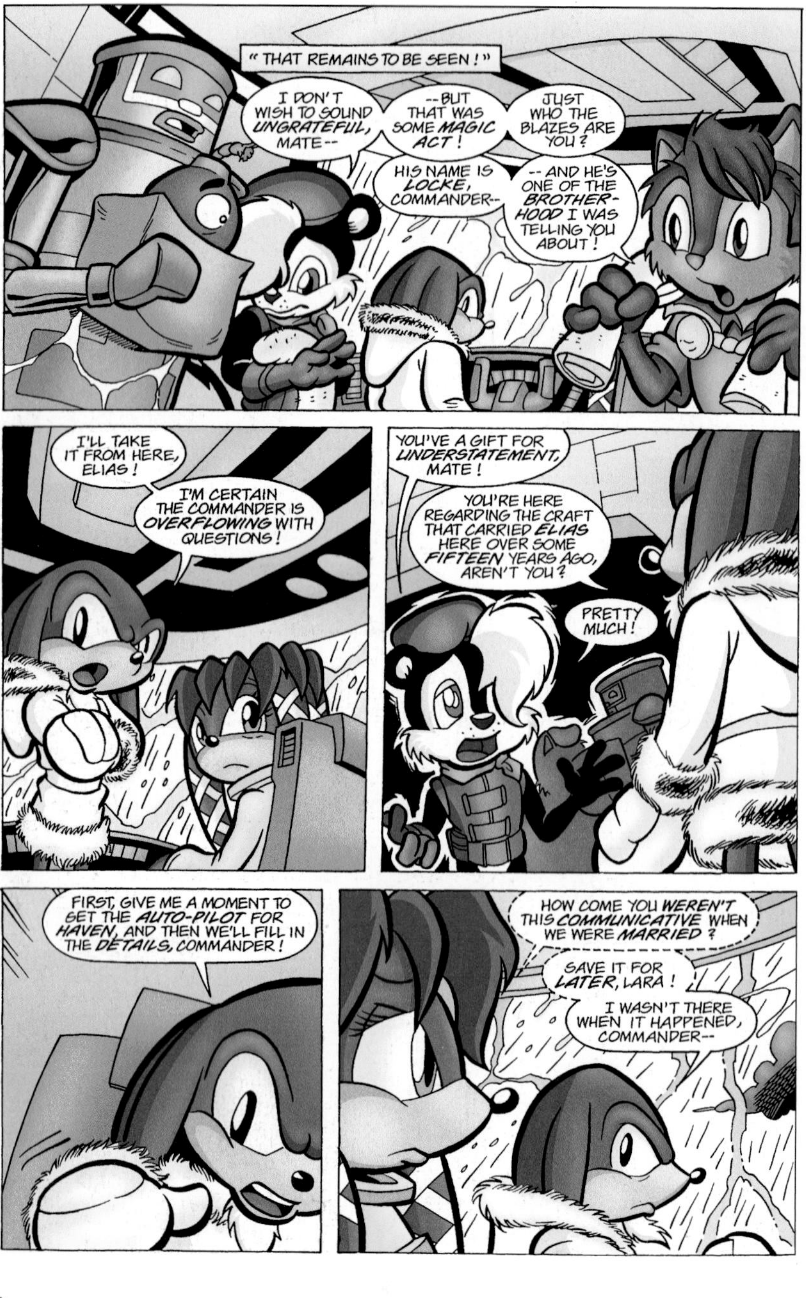
"THAT REMAINS TO BE SEEN!"
I DON'T WISH TO SOUND UNGRATEFUL, MATE--
--BUT THAT WAS SOME MAGIC ACT!
JUST WHO THE BLAZES ARE YOU?
HIS NAME IS LOCKE, COMMANDER--
--AND HE'S ONE OF THE BROTHER-HOOD I WAS TELLING YOU ABOUT!
I'LL TAKE IT FROM HERE, ELIAS!
I'M CERTAIN THE COMMANDER IS OVERFLOWING WITH QUESTIONS!
YOU'VE A GIFT FOR UNDERSTATEMENT, MATE!
YOU'RE HERE REGARDING THE CRAFT THAT CARRIED ELIAS HERE OVER SOME FIFTEEN YEARS AGO, AREN'T YOU?
PRETTY MUCH!
FIRST, GIVE ME A MOMENT TO SET THE AUTO-PILOT FOR HAVEN, AND THEN WE'LL FILL IN THE DETAILS, COMMANDER!
HOW COME YOU WEREN'T THIS COMMUNICATIVE WHEN WE WERE MARRIED?
SAVE IT FOR LATER, LARA!
I WASN'T THERE WHEN IT HAPPENED, COMMANDER--

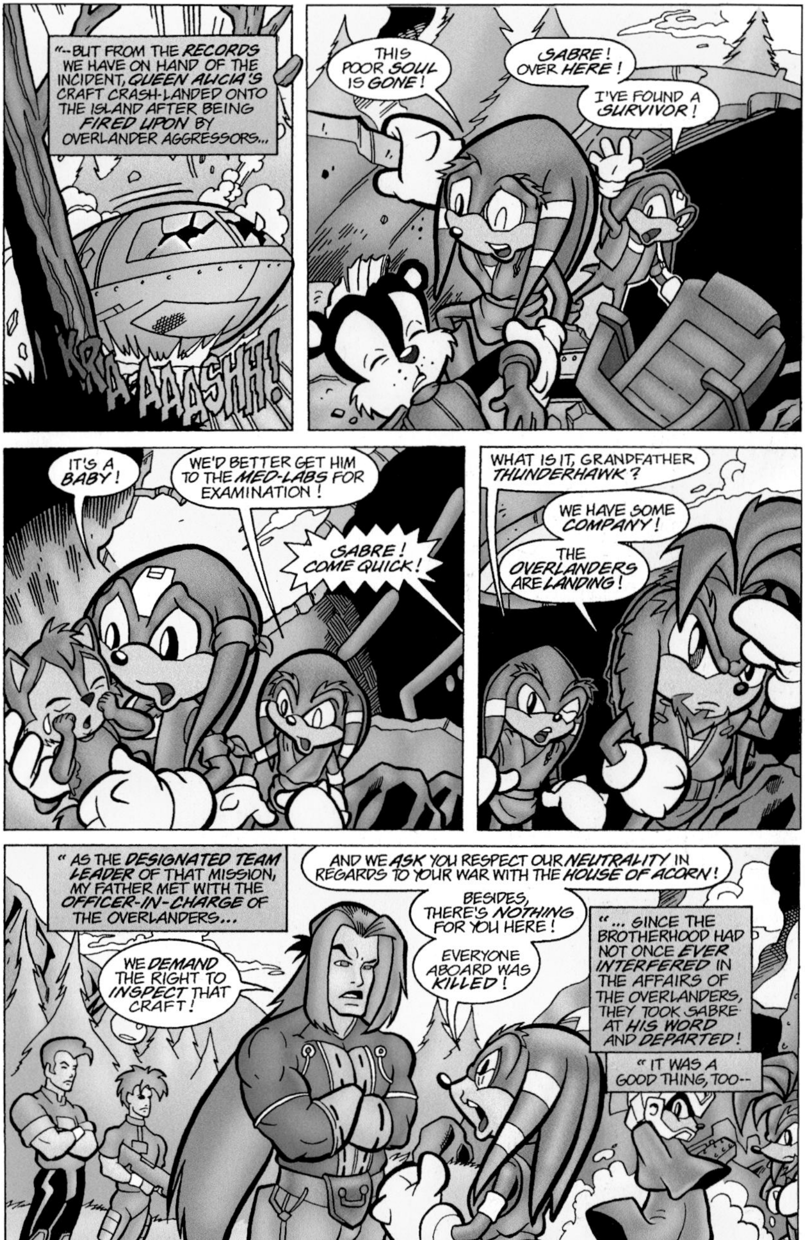
"--BUT FROM THE RECORDS WE HAVE ON HAND OF THE INCIDENT, QUEEN ALICIA'S CRAFT CRASH-LANDED ONTO THE ISLAND AFTER BEING FIRED UPON BY OVERLANDER AGGRESSORS...
KRA-AAASHH!
THIS POOR SOUL IS GONE!
SABRE! OVER HERE!
I'VE FOUND A SURVIVOR!
IT'S A BABY!
WE'D BETTER GET HIM TO THE MED-LABS FOR EXAMINATION!
SABRE! COME QUICK!
WHAT IS IT, GRANDFATHER THUNDERHAWK?
WE HAVE SOME COMPANY!
THE OVERLANDERS ARE LANDING!
" AS THE DESIGNATED TEAM LEADER OF THAT MISSION, MY FATHER MET WITH THE OFFICER-IN-CHARGE OF THE OVERLANDERS...
WE DEMAND THE RIGHT TO INSPECT THAT CRAFT!
AND WE ASK YOU RESPECT OUR NEUTRALITY IN REGARDS TO YOUR WAR WITH THE HOUSE OF ACORN!
BESIDES, THERE'S NOTHING FOR YOU HERE!
EVERYONE ABOARD WAS KILLED!
"... SINCE THE BROTHERHOOD HAD NOT ONCE EVER INTERFERED IN THE AFFAIRS OF THE OVERLANDERS, THEY TOOK SABRE AT HIS WORD AND DEPARTED!
" IT WAS A GOOD THING, TOO--

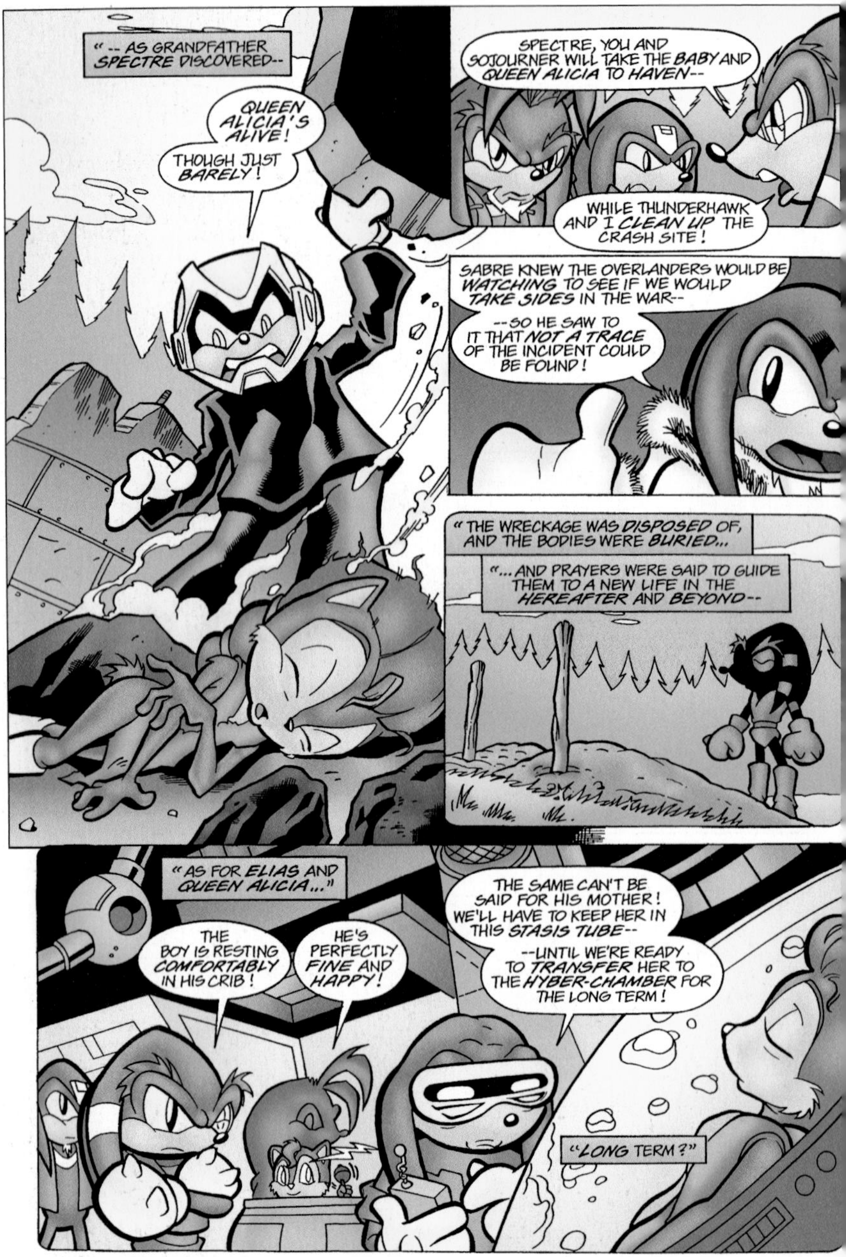
"-- AS GRANDFATHER SPECTRE DISCOVERED--
QUEEN ALICIA'S ALIVE!
THOUGH JUST BARELY!
SPECTRE, YOU AND SOJOURNER WILL TAKE THE BABY AND QUEEN ALICIA TO HAVEN--
WHILE THUNDERHAWK AND I CLEAN UP THE CRASH SITE!
SABRE KNEW THE OVERLANDERS WOULD BE WATCHING TO SEE IF WE WOULD TAKE SIDES IN THE WAR--
--SO HE SAW TO IT THAT NOT A TRACE OF THE INCIDENT COULD BE FOUND!
"THE WRECKAGE WAS DISPOSED OF, AND THE BODIES WERE BURIED...
"...AND PRAYERS WERE SAID TO GUIDE THEM TO A NEW LIFE IN THE HEREAFTER AND BEYOND--
"AS FOR ELIAS AND QUEEN ALICIA..."
THE BOY IS RESTING COMFORTABLY IN HIS CRIB!
HE'S PERFECTLY FINE AND HAPPY!
THE SAME CAN'T BE SAID FOR HIS MOTHER! WE'LL HAVE TO KEEP HER IN THIS STASIS TUBE--
--UNTIL WE'RE READY TO TRANSFER HER TO THE HYBER-CHAMBER FOR THE LONG TERM!
"LONG TERM?"

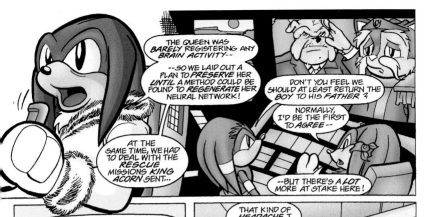

THE QUEEN WAS *BARELY* REGISTERING ANY *BRAIN ACTIVITY*--

--SO WE LAID OUT A PLAN TO *PRESERVE* HER *UNTIL* A METHOD COULD BE FOUND TO *REGENERATE* HER NEURAL NETWORK!

DON'T YOU FEEL WE SHOULD AT LEAST RETURN THE *BOY* TO HIS *FATHER* ?

NORMALLY, I'D BE THE FIRST TO *AGREE* --

AT THE SAME TIME, WE HAD TO DEAL WITH THE *RESCUE* MISSIONS *KING ACORN* SENT...

--BUT THERE'S A *LOT* MORE AT STAKE HERE!

IF THE OVERLANDERS DISCOVER WE *WITHHELD* THE FACTS *FROM* THEM, THAT WILL *FORCE* THEIR HAND INTO TAKING *ACTION*--

--UPON WHICH *WE* WOULD BE *FORCED* INTO TAKING ACTION, AND GETTING *DRAGGED* INTO A WAR WE HAVE NO INTEREST IN WHATSOEVER !

YOU WANT *THAT* ?

THAT KIND OF *HEADACHE* I DON'T NEED !

HOW'S THE BOY DOING, BY THE WAY ?

SEE FOR YOURSELF !

THAT'S SOME MODEL, ELIAS !

YOU REALLY THINK SO ?

I WISH I KNEW WHAT IT WAS !

YOUNG ELIAS TURNED OUT TO BE QUITE A *PRODIGY* !

UPON REACHING HIS *TENTH* YEAR, HE WAS ALLOWED TO VENTURE FORTH THROUGHOUT THE ISLAND !

SOMETHING JUST DOESN'T ADD UP HERE, MATE !

HOW D'YA ACCOUNT FOR *THE COLONEL* ?

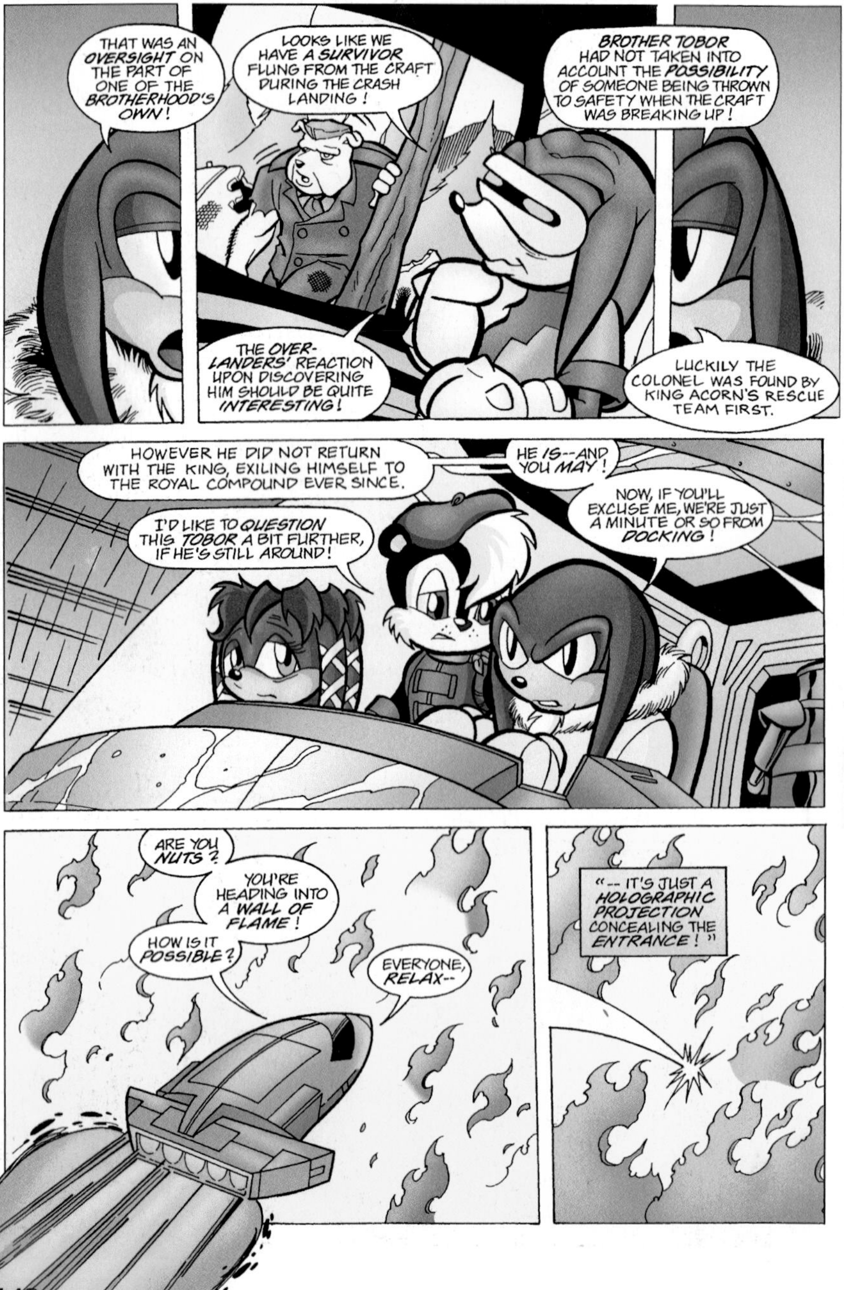
THAT WAS AN OVERSIGHT ON THE PART OF ONE OF THE BROTHERHOOD'S OWN!
LOOKS LIKE WE HAVE A SURVIVOR FLUNG FROM THE CRAFT DURING THE CRASH LANDING!
THE OVER-LANDERS' REACTION UPON DISCOVERING HIM SHOULD BE QUITE INTERESTING!
BROTHER TOBOR HAD NOT TAKEN INTO ACCOUNT THE POSSIBILITY OF SOMEONE BEING THROWN TO SAFETY WHEN THE CRAFT WAS BREAKING UP!
LUCKILY THE COLONEL WAS FOUND BY KING ACORN'S RESCUE TEAM FIRST.
HOWEVER HE DID NOT RETURN WITH THE KING, EXILING HIMSELF TO THE ROYAL COMPOUND EVER SINCE.
I'D LIKE TO QUESTION THIS TOBOR A BIT FURTHER, IF HE'S STILL AROUND!
HE IS--AND YOU MAY!
NOW, IF YOU'LL EXCUSE ME, WE'RE JUST A MINUTE OR SO FROM DOCKING!
ARE YOU NUTS?
YOU'RE HEADING INTO A WALL OF FLAME!
HOW IS IT POSSIBLE?
EVERYONE, RELAX--
"-- IT'S JUST A HOLOGRAPHIC PROJECTION CONCEALING THE ENTRANCE!"

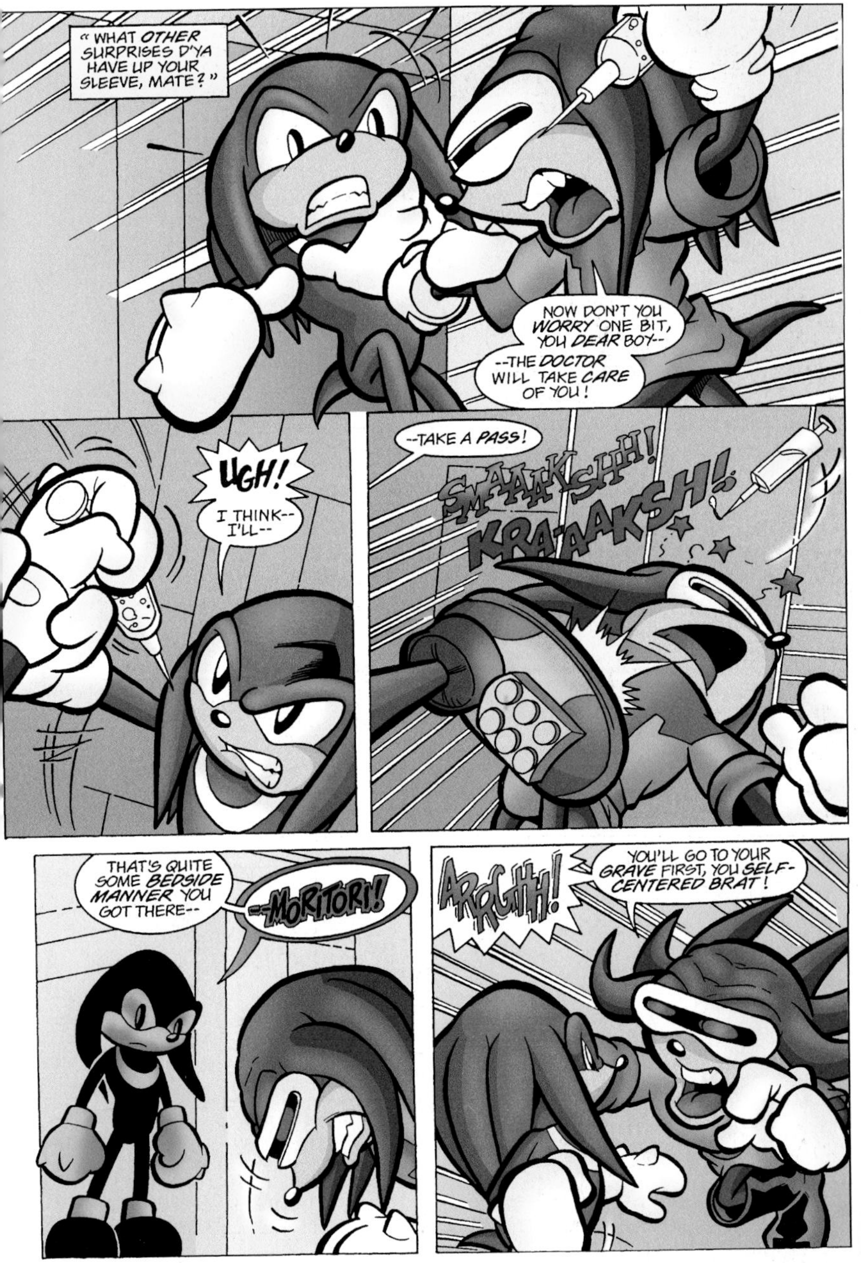
"WHAT OTHER SURPRISES D'YA HAVE UP YOUR SLEEVE, MATE?"
NOW DON'T YOU WORRY ONE BIT, YOU DEAR BOY--
--THE DOCTOR WILL TAKE CARE OF YOU!
UGH!
I THINK-- I'LL--
--TAKE A PASS!
SMAAAKSHH!
KRA-AAKSH!
THAT'S QUITE SOME BEDSIDE MANNER YOU GOT THERE--
--MORITORI!
ARRGHH!
YOU'LL GO TO YOUR GRAVE FIRST, YOU SELF-CENTERED BRAT!

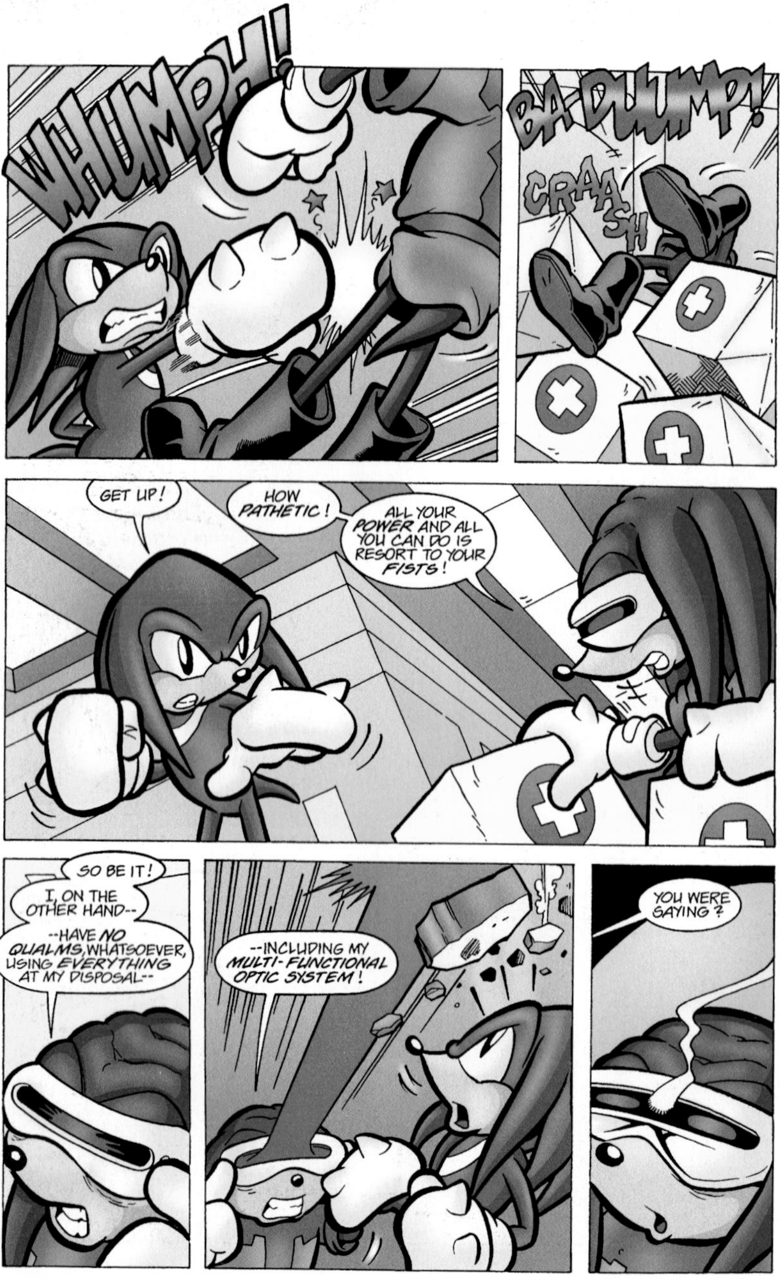
WHUMPH!
BA-DUUMP!
CRAASH
GET UP!
HOW PATHETIC!
ALL YOUR POWER AND ALL YOU CAN DO IS RESORT TO YOUR FISTS!
SO BE IT!
I, ON THE OTHER HAND--
--HAVE NO QUALMS, WHATSOEVER, USING EVERYTHING AT MY DISPOSAL--
--INCLUDING MY MULTI-FUNCTIONAL OPTIC SYSTEM!
YOU WERE SAYING?

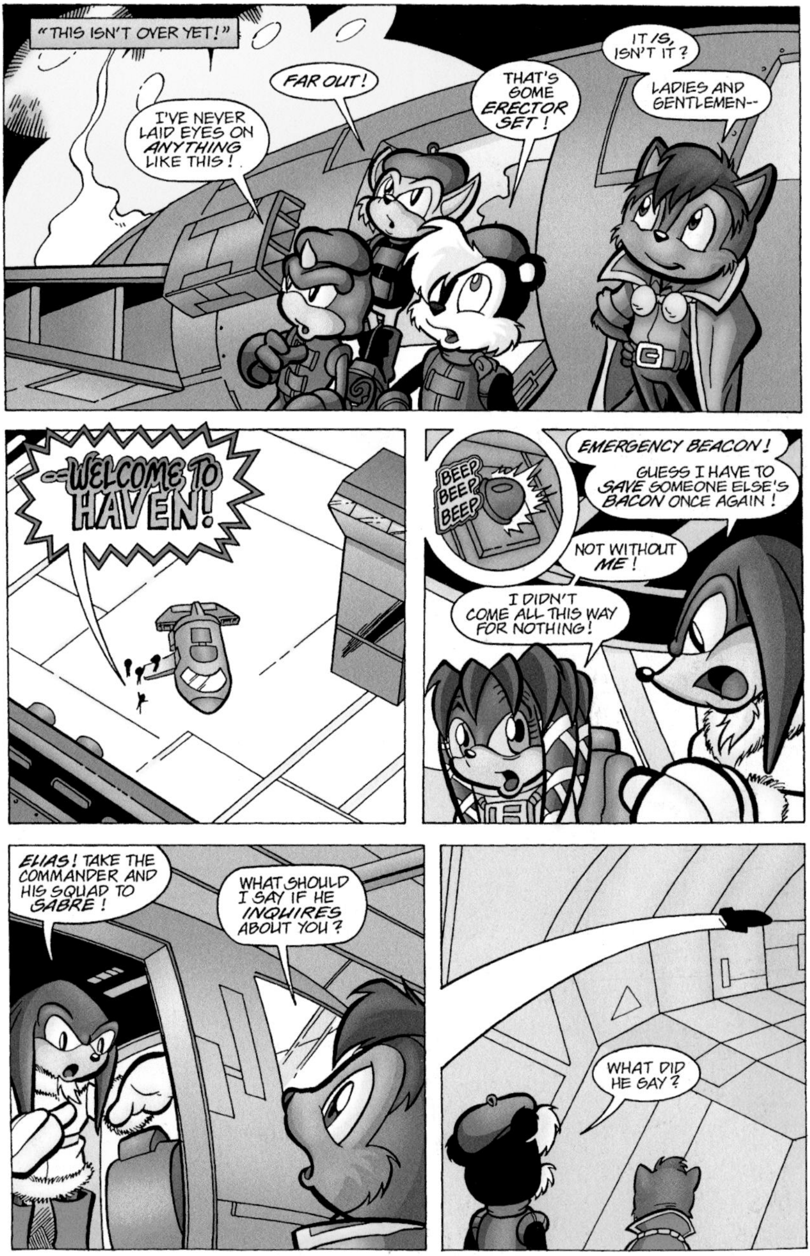
"THIS ISN'T OVER YET!"
I'VE NEVER LAID EYES ON ANYTHING LIKE THIS!
FAR OUT!
THAT'S SOME ERECTOR SET!
IT IS, ISN'T IT?
LADIES AND GENTLEMEN--
--WELCOME TO HAVEN!
BEEP BEEP BEEP
EMERGENCY BEACON!
GUESS I HAVE TO SAVE SOMEONE ELSE'S BACON ONCE AGAIN!
NOT WITHOUT ME!
I DIDN'T COME ALL THIS WAY FOR NOTHING!
ELIAS! TAKE THE COMMANDER AND HIS SQUAD TO SABRE!
WHAT SHOULD I SAY IF HE INQUIRES ABOUT YOU?
WHAT DID HE SAY?

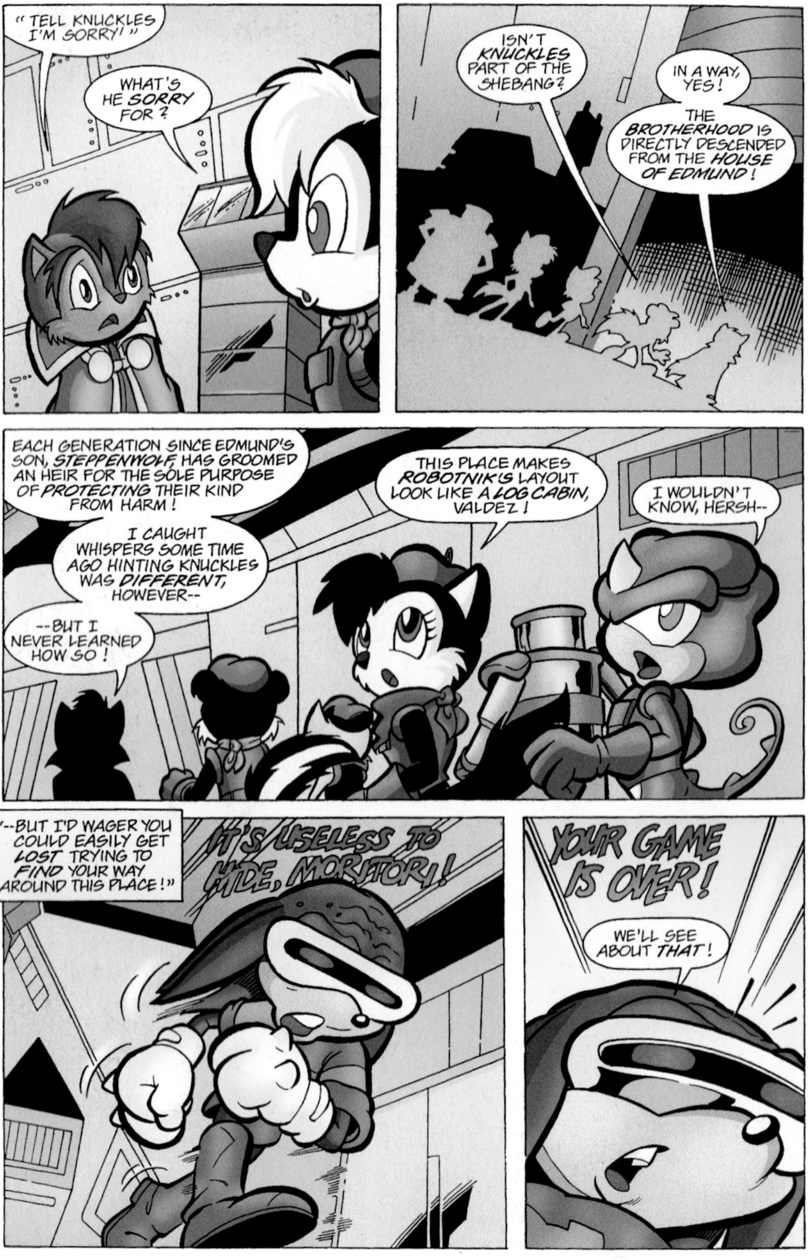
"TELL KNUCKLES I'M SORRY!"
WHAT'S HE SORRY FOR?
ISN'T KNUCKLES PART OF THE SHEBANG?
IN A WAY, YES!
THE BROTHERHOOD IS DIRECTLY DESCENDED FROM THE HOUSE OF EDMUND!
EACH GENERATION SINCE EDMUND'S SON, STEPPENWOLF, HAS GROOMED AN HEIR FOR THE SOLE PURPOSE OF PROTECTING THEIR KIND FROM HARM!
I CAUGHT WHISPERS SOME TIME AGO HINTING KNUCKLES WAS DIFFERENT, HOWEVER--
--BUT I NEVER LEARNED HOW SO!
THIS PLACE MAKES ROBOTNIK'S LAYOUT LOOK LIKE A LOG CABIN, VALDEZ!
I WOULDN'T KNOW, HERSH--
"--BUT I'D WAGER YOU COULD EASILY GET LOST TRYING TO FIND YOUR WAY AROUND THIS PLACE!"
IT'S USELESS TO HIDE, MORITORI!
YOUR GAME IS OVER!
WE'LL SEE ABOUT THAT!

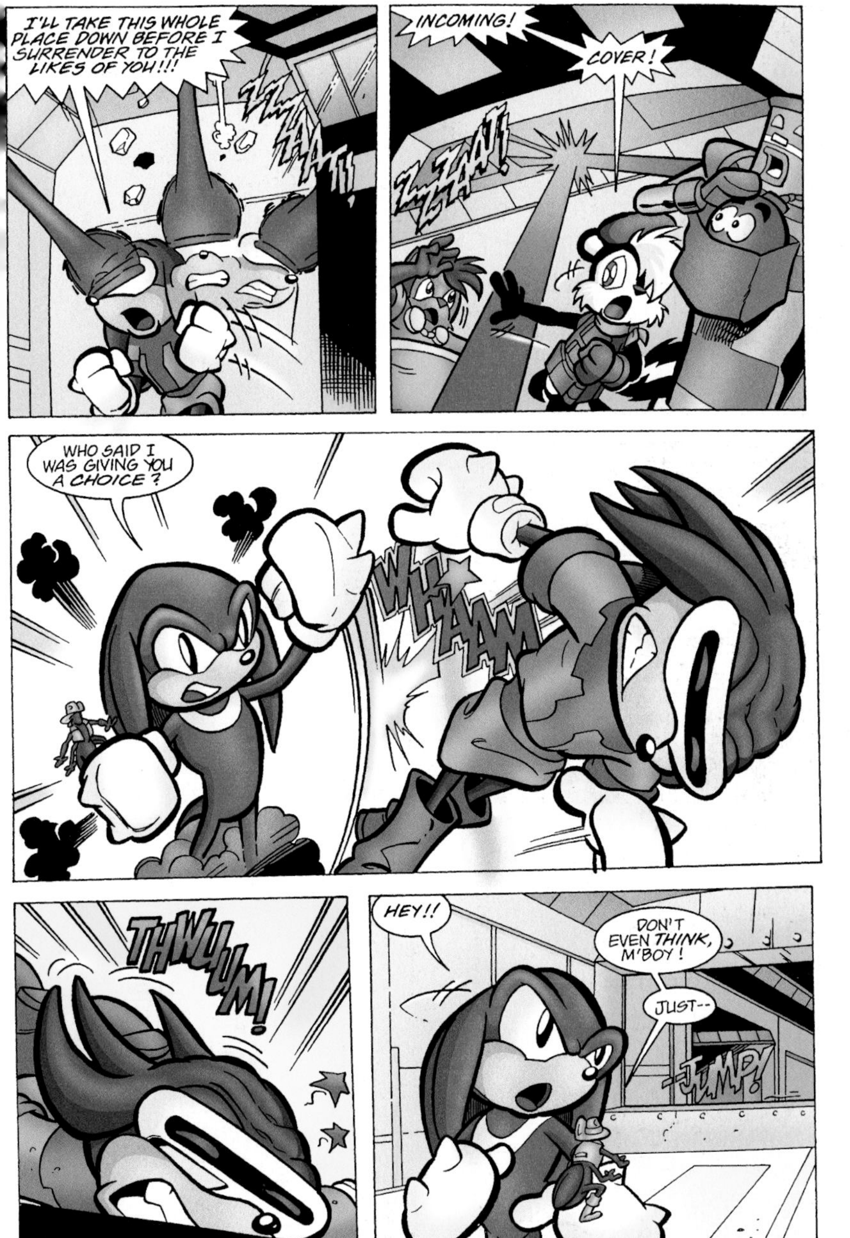
I'LL TAKE THIS WHOLE PLACE DOWN BEFORE I SURRENDER TO THE LIKES OF YOU!!!
INCOMING!
COVER!
ZZZAAT!
WHO SAID I WAS GIVING YOU A CHOICE?
WHAAM
THWUUM!
HEY!!
DON'T EVEN THINK, M'BOY!
JUST--
-JUMP!

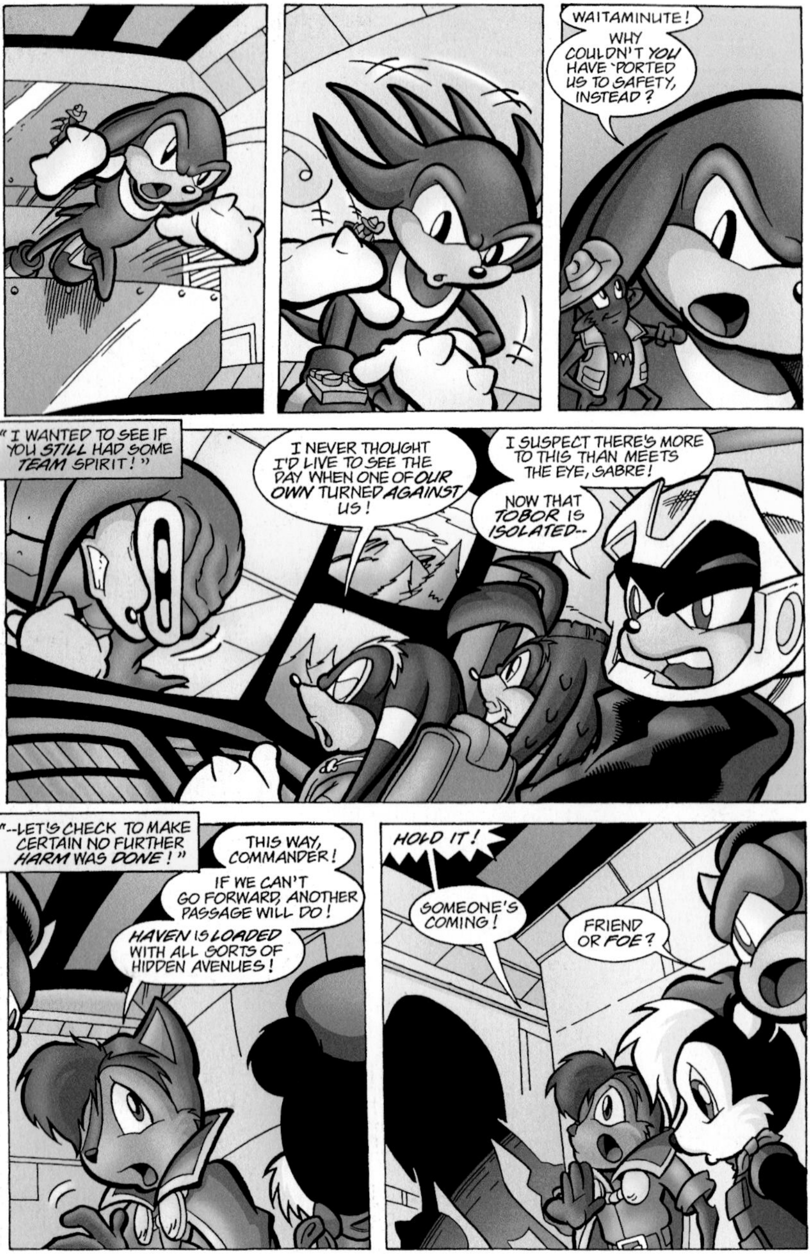
WAITAMINUTE!
WHY COULDN'T YOU HAVE 'PORTED US TO SAFETY, INSTEAD?
"I WANTED TO SEE IF YOU STILL HAD SOME TEAM SPIRIT!"
I NEVER THOUGHT I'D LIVE TO SEE THE DAY WHEN ONE OF OUR OWN TURNED AGAINST US!
I SUSPECT THERE'S MORE TO THIS THAN MEETS THE EYE, SABRE!
NOW THAT TOBOR IS ISOLATED--
"--LET'S CHECK TO MAKE CERTAIN NO FURTHER HARM WAS DONE!"
THIS WAY, COMMANDER!
IF WE CAN'T GO FORWARD, ANOTHER PASSAGE WILL DO!
HAVEN IS LOADED WITH ALL SORTS OF HIDDEN AVENUES!
HOLD IT!
SOMEONE'S COMING!
FRIEND OR FOE?

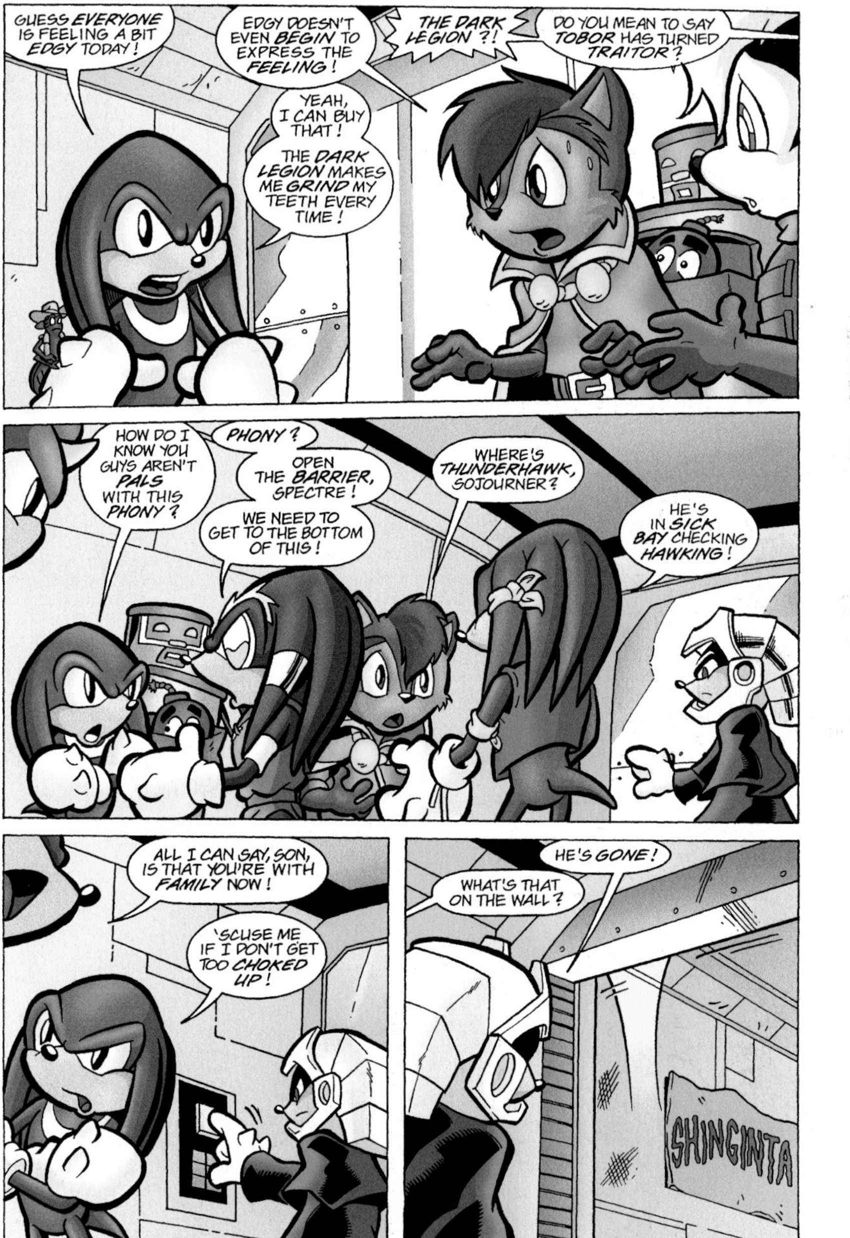
GUESS EVERYONE IS FEELING A BIT EDGY TODAY!
EDGY DOESN'T EVEN BEGIN TO EXPRESS THE FEELING!
YEAH, I CAN BUY THAT!
THE DARK LEGION MAKES ME GRIND MY TEETH EVERY TIME!
THE DARK LEGION?!
DO YOU MEAN TO SAY TOBOR HAS TURNED TRAITOR?
HOW DO I KNOW YOU GUYS AREN'T PALS WITH THIS PHONY?
PHONY?
OPEN THE BARRIER, SPECTRE!
WE NEED TO GET TO THE BOTTOM OF THIS!
WHERE'S THUNDERHAWK, SOJOURNER?
HE'S IN SICK BAY CHECKING HAWKING!
ALL I CAN SAY, SON, IS THAT YOU'RE WITH FAMILY NOW!
'SCUSE ME IF I DON'T GET TOO CHOKED UP!
HE'S GONE!
WHAT'S THAT ON THE WALL?
SHINGINTA

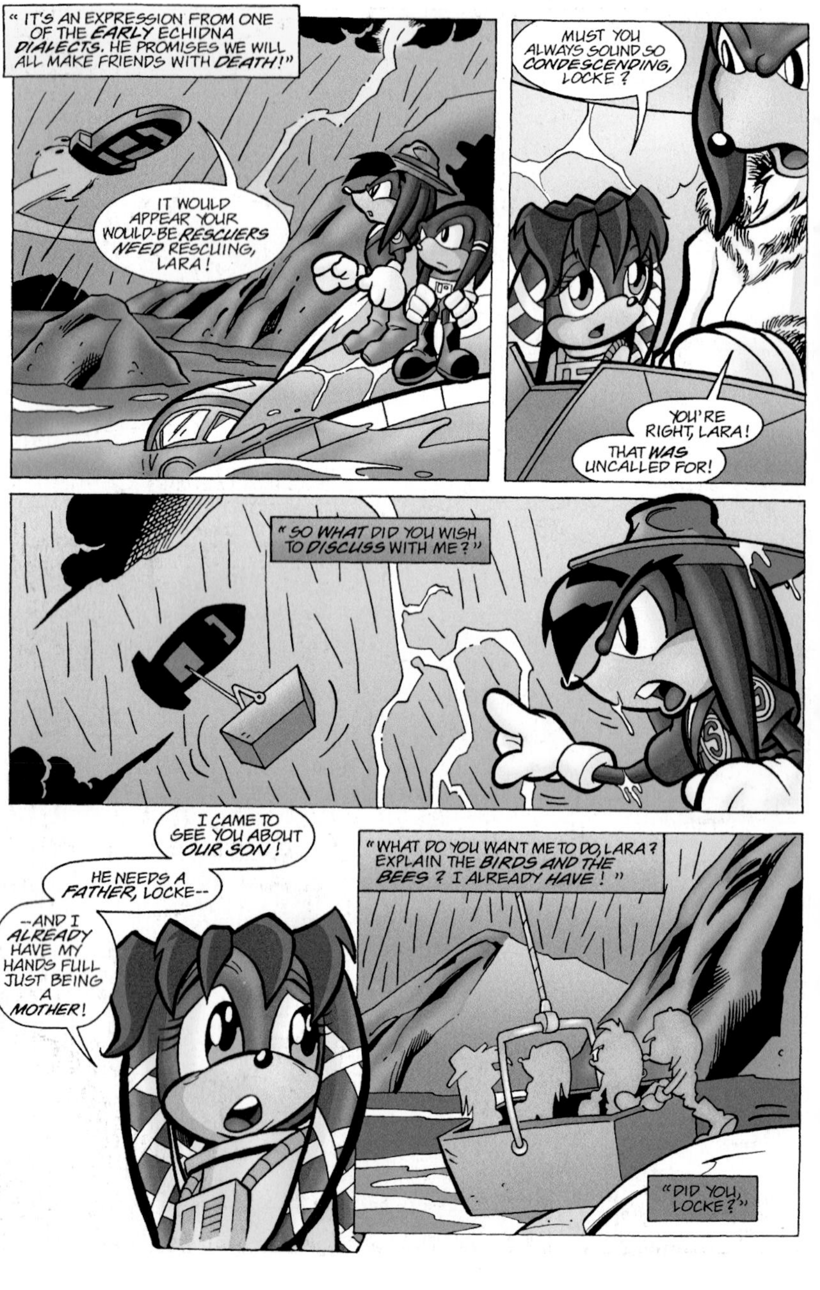
"IT'S AN EXPRESSION FROM ONE OF THE EARLY ECHIDNA DIALECTS. HE PROMISES WE WILL ALL MAKE FRIENDS WITH DEATH!"
IT WOULD APPEAR YOUR WOULD-BE RESCUERS NEED RESCUING, LARA!
MUST YOU ALWAYS SOUND SO CONDESCENDING, LOCKE?
YOU'RE RIGHT, LARA!
THAT WAS UNCALLED FOR!
"SO WHAT DID YOU WISH TO DISCUSS WITH ME?"
I CAME TO SEE YOU ABOUT OUR SON!
HE NEEDS A FATHER, LOCKE--
--AND I ALREADY HAVE MY HANDS FULL JUST BEING A MOTHER!
"WHAT DO YOU WANT ME TO DO, LARA? EXPLAIN THE BIRDS AND THE BEES? I ALREADY HAVE!"
"DID YOU, LOCKE?"

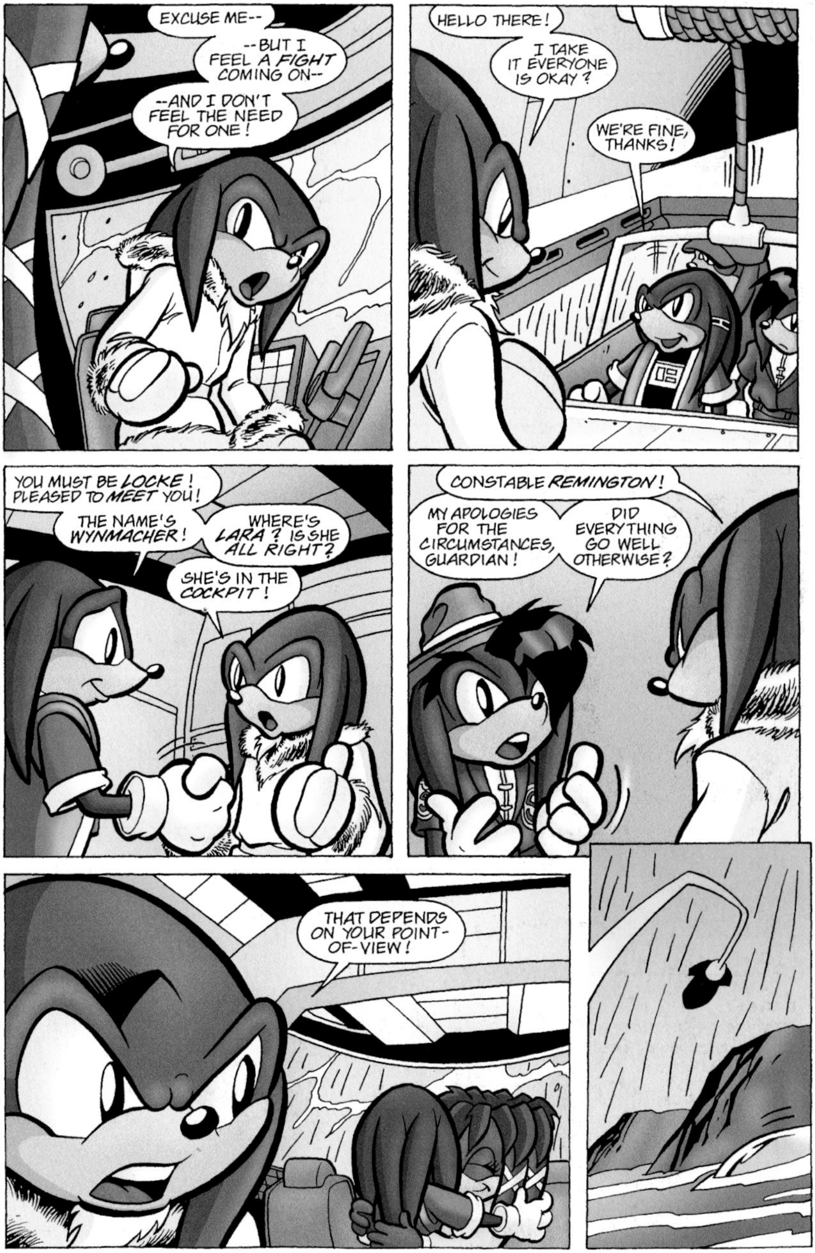
EXCUSE ME--
--BUT I FEEL A FIGHT COMING ON--
--AND I DON'T FEEL THE NEED FOR ONE!
HELLO THERE!
I TAKE IT EVERYONE IS OKAY?
WE'RE FINE, THANKS!
YOU MUST BE LOCKE! PLEASED TO MEET YOU!
THE NAME'S WYNMACHER!
WHERE'S LARA? IS SHE ALL RIGHT?
SHE'S IN THE COCKPIT!
CONSTABLE REMINGTON!
MY APOLOGIES FOR THE CIRCUMSTANCES, GUARDIAN!
DID EVERYTHING GO WELL OTHERWISE?
THAT DEPENDS ON YOUR POINT-OF-VIEW!

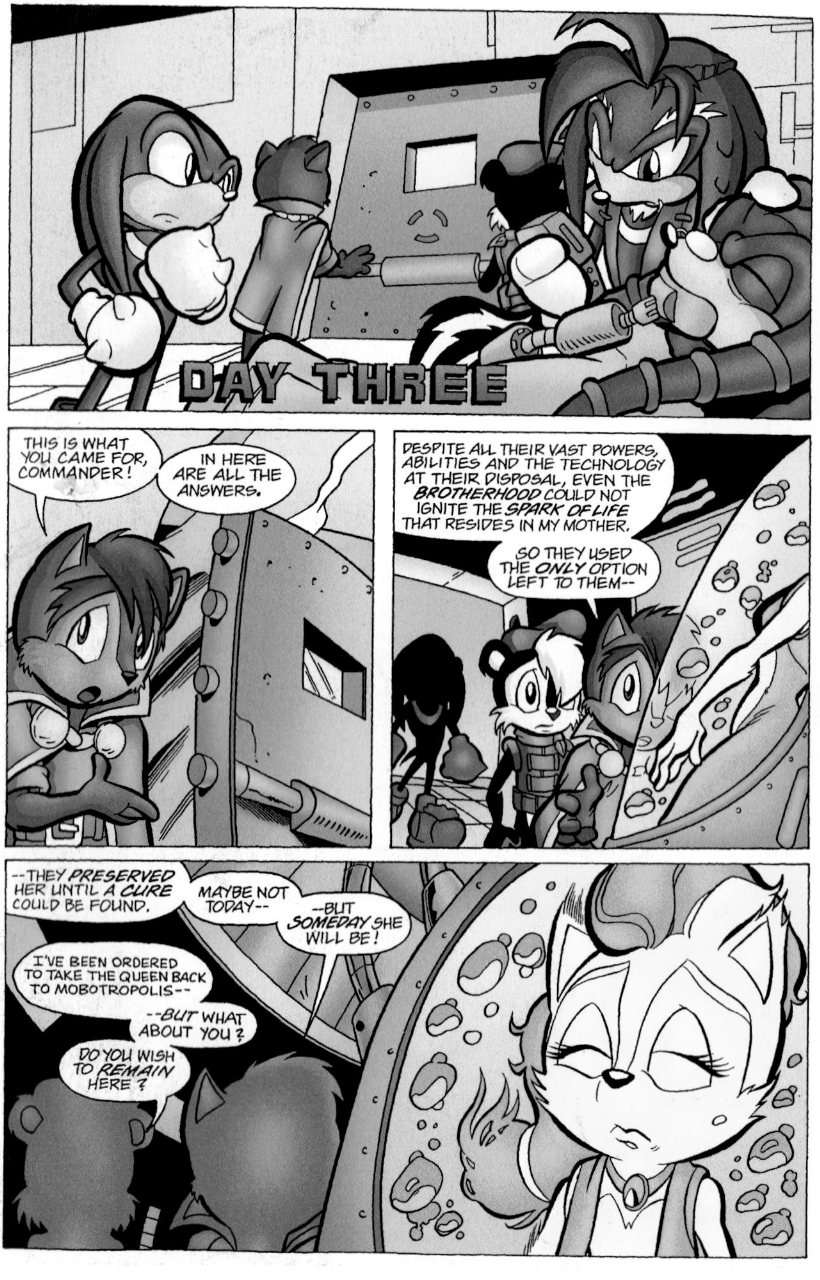
DAY THREE
THIS IS WHAT YOU CAME FOR, COMMANDER!
IN HERE ARE ALL THE ANSWERS.
DESPITE ALL THEIR VAST POWERS, ABILITIES AND THE TECHNOLOGY AT THEIR DISPOSAL, EVEN THE BROTHERHOOD COULD NOT IGNITE THE SPARK OF LIFE THAT RESIDES IN MY MOTHER.
SO THEY USED THE ONLY OPTION LEFT TO THEM--
--THEY PRESERVED HER UNTIL A CURE COULD BE FOUND.
MAYBE NOT TODAY--
--BUT SOMEDAY SHE WILL BE!
I'VE BEEN ORDERED TO TAKE THE QUEEN BACK TO MOBOTROPOLIS--
--BUT WHAT ABOUT YOU?
DO YOU WISH TO REMAIN HERE?

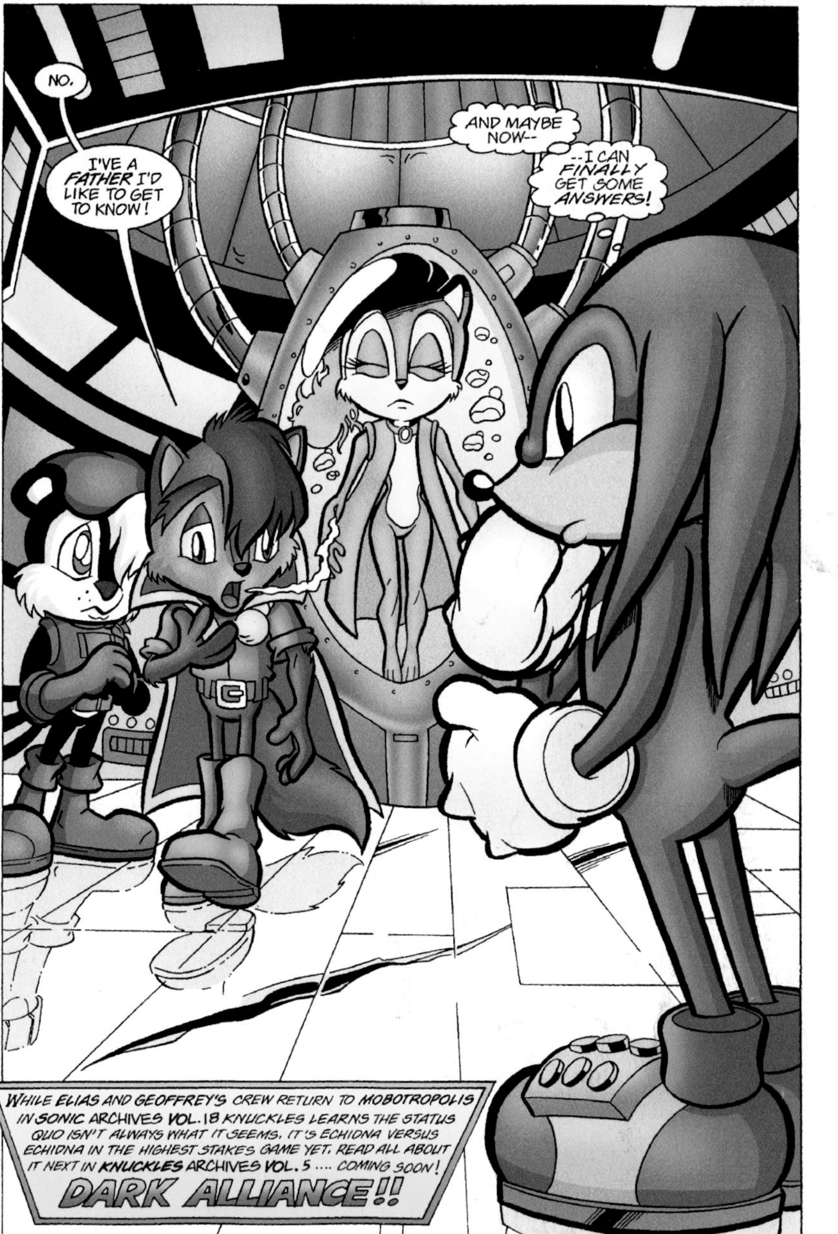
NO.
I'VE A FATHER I'D LIKE TO GET TO KNOW!
AND MAYBE NOW--
--I CAN FINALLY GET SOME ANSWERS!
WHILE ELIAS AND GEOFFREY'S CREW RETURN TO MOBOTROPOLIS IN SONIC ARCHIVES VOL. 18 KNUCKLES LEARNS THE STATUS QUO ISN'T ALWAYS WHAT IT SEEMS. IT'S ECHIDNA VERSUS ECHIDNA IN THE HIGHEST STAKES GAME YET. READ ALL ABOUT IT NEXT IN KNUCKLES ARCHIVES VOL. 5 .... COMING SOON!
DARK ALLIANCE!!

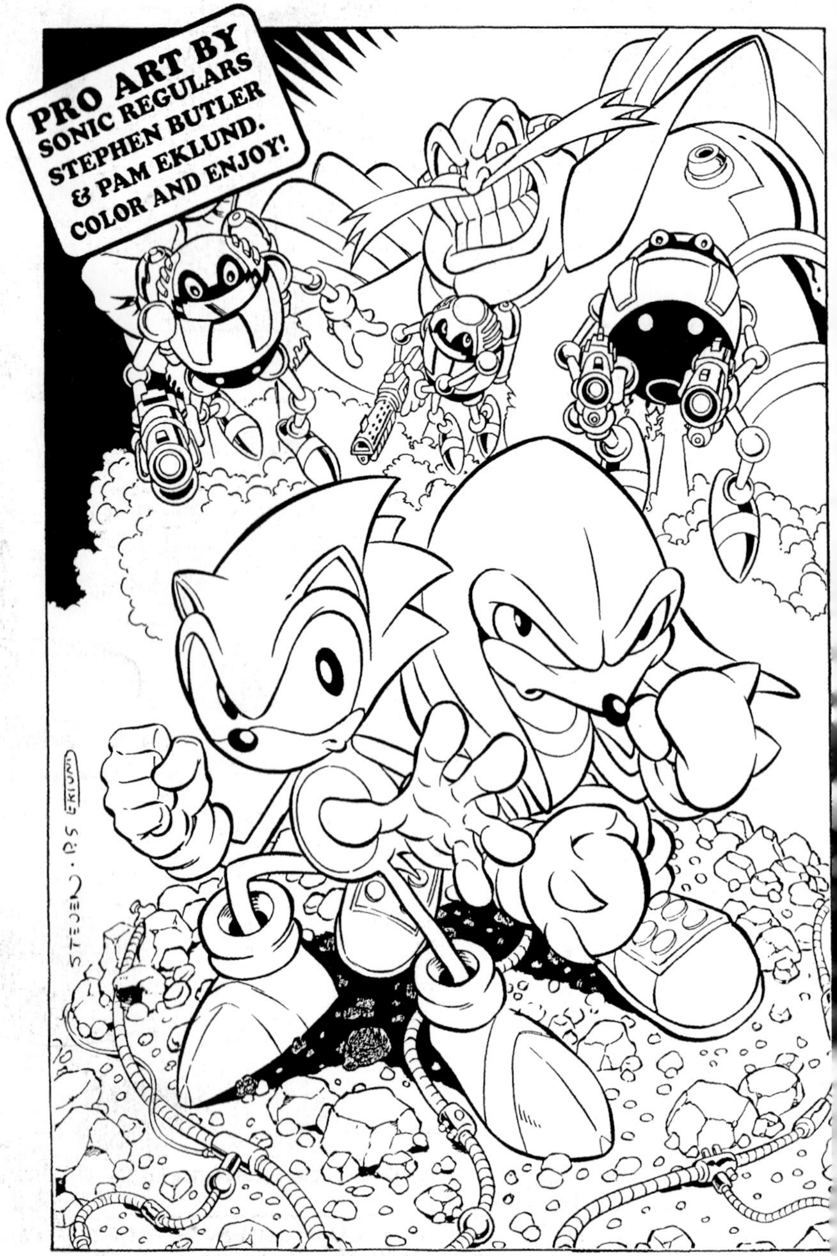
PRO ART BY SONIC REGULARS STEPHEN BUTLER & PAM EKLUND. COLOR AND ENJOY!

TAKE AN EXCLUSIVE LOOK BEHIND THE SCENES OF *KNUCKLES THE ECHIDNA*, AS WE REVEAL...

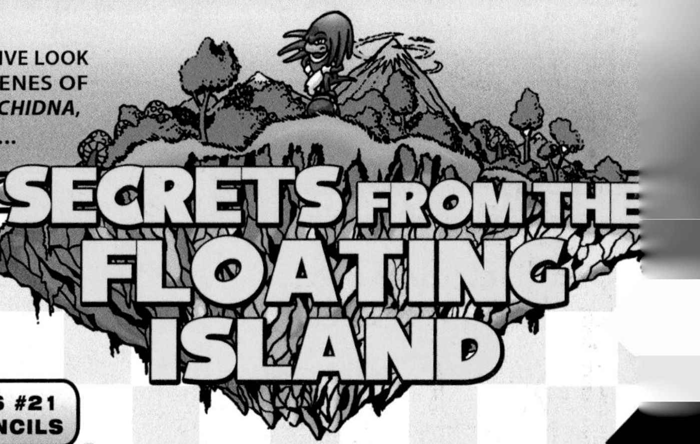

SECRETS FROM THE FLOATING ISLAND

KNUCKLES #21 COVER PENCILS

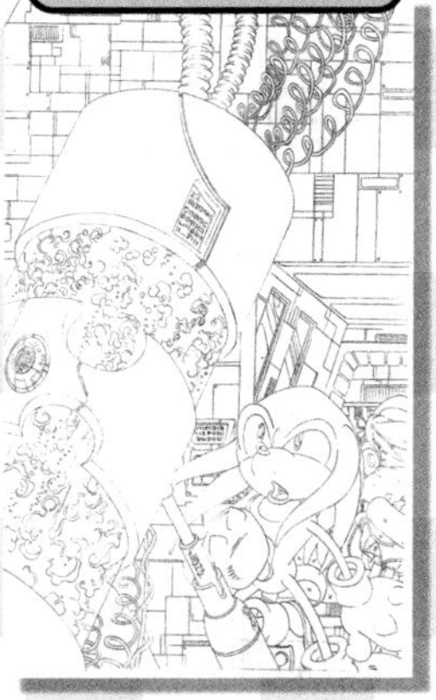

KNUCKLES #21 FINAL INKS

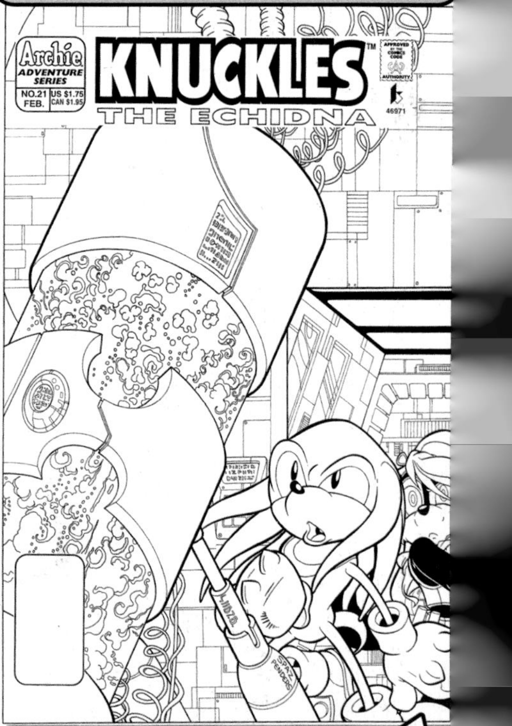

Archie
ADVENTURE SERIES
NO.21 FEB.
US $1.75
CAN $1.95
KNUCKLES
THE ECHIDNA

KNUCKLES #21 ALTERNATE COVER

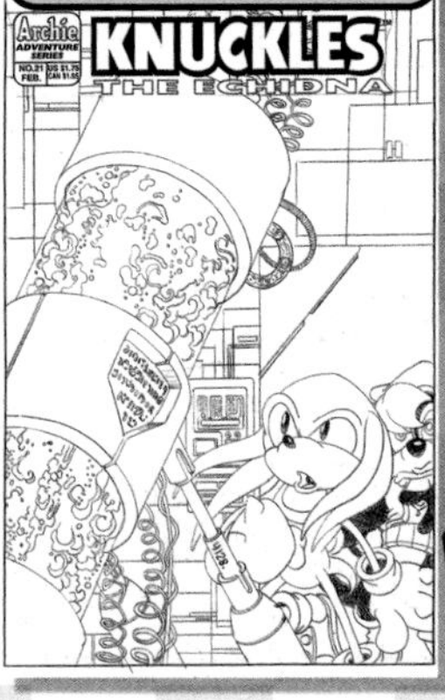

Archie
KNUCKLES
THE ECHIDNA

GEOFFREY ST. JOHN WAS ALTERED FOR THE FINAL VERSION OF THIS COVER

NEXT TIME, IN THE KNUCKLES ARCHIVES...

KNUCKLES™ THE ECHIDNA ARCHIVES VOLUME 5

SONIC THE HEDGEHOG™ PRESENTS
KNUCKLES™
THE ECHIDNA
ARCHIVES VOLUME 5

THE SAGA CONTINUES!

THE MYSTERIES SURROUNDING THE BROTHERHOOD OF GUARDIANS ARE FINALLY REVEALED! PLUS – FAMILIAR FACES, NEW FOES, AND MORE CHAOTIX ACTION NEXT TIME IN THE KNUCKLES ARCHIVES!

KNUCKLES ARCHIVES VOLUME 5
collects KNUCKLES THE ECHIDNA #22-27.

ISBN: 978-1-9369

MORE PULSE-POUNDING KNUCKLES ACTION AV

SONIC UNIVERSE™ KNUCKLES RETURNS

SONIC UNIVERSE
KNUCKLES RETURNS
FLYNN • YARDLEY • AMASH

ISBN: 978-1-936975-12-9

KNUCKLES™ THE ECHIDNA ARCHIVES VOLUME 1

SONIC THE HEDGEHOG PRESENTS
KNUCKLES
THE ECHIDNA

ISBN: 978-1-879794-81-8

KNUCKLES™ THE ECHIDNA ARCHIVES VOLUME 2

SONIC THE HEDGEHOG™ PRESENTS
KNUCKLES

ISBN: 978-1-879794-98-6

SONIC THE HEDGEHOG PRESENTS
KNUCKLES
THE ECHIDNA
ARCHIVES VOLUME 3

ISBN: 978-1-936975-17-

SEARCH THE GRAPHIC NOVEL SECTION OF

www.ARCHIECOMICS.com

FOR ART AND INFO ON ALL OF OUR SONIC COMICS!

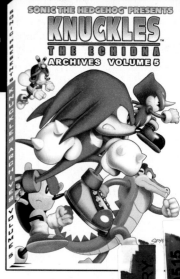